THE BRIDGE OF TIME

*" Through all the ages, thy soul and mine shall
be side by side. "*

THE
BRIDGE OF TIME

BY
WILLIAM HENRY WARNER
Author of "Mothers of Men," Etc.

NEW YORK
SCOTT & SELTZER
1919

TO
MY MOTHER

THE BRIDGE OF TIME

THE BRIDGE OF TIME

CHAPTER I

THE city lay shining under the hot rays of the February sun. Blue as a polished turquoise, the sky stretched above its gleaming palaces, gorgeous temples, and splendid avenues. It lay mirrored in the wide sweep of the Nile beyond the cool, deep shadows cast by the many boats moored along the busy quay, their painted sails sending reflections in long ribbons of brilliant colors quivering into the depths of the water.

Not far from the river's edge, on the East bank, lay the beautiful temple gardens. Above the delicate gray-green of the tamarisk showers and the waving feathery tops of the date palms just coming into bloom, towered the massive Pylons of the Temple of Amen-Ra. On either side, silent, vast and unchanging, sat the image of the god, the great hands, with sculptured fingers straight and close-set, held stiffly on the knees, the wide, stone eyes gazing into that impenetrable future whose secrets the gods alone may know.

Before them, two obelisks reared their tall heads skyward, catching on their summits the golden light of the great Ra, whose rays they symbolized. In the soft breeze that blew from the river gayly

colored pennants fluttered from tall poles. The
massive doors of the temple, fashioned of polished
electrum inlaid with gold, were wide swung, and
between them, one caught a glimpse of the stately
forecourt with its brilliantly painted walls and columns.

From the great gateway, a broad avenue ran
straight to the north where lay the mighty citadel
of the deity himself. Bordering its edges were
huge Ram-headed sphinxes set one next the other
in an unending row against a background of lux-
uriant gardens, whose deep, cool green was splashed
with the warm pink of apricot blossoms, purple
masses of bougainvillea, the scarlet of the pome-
granate, and here and there through the branches
could be seen the white gleam of stately villas.

On the other side of the river, familiarly called
the "House of Hathor," rose magnificent monuments guarded by huge figures of the gods; temples,
gardens, palaces, villas, and beyond, a soft golden-
pink against the deep blue of the sky, shimmered
the Libyan hills.

Majestic in her proud splendor, Weset, city of
Amen, the "Mysterious City," the "City of the
Hidden Name," known to the Greeks as Thebes,
through whose hundred gates many horses and
chariots could ride abreast, was always the wonder
of the world, but today the "Mistress of Temples"
shone with an added glory.

From the painted galleys floating on the river,
from every housetop and doorway, fluttered brilliant
pennants, waving streamers of gayly colored cloth,
strings of many-hued banners, some bearing the

figure of the Hawk, the emblem of the city, others, the disk and wings of the god.

It was the "beautiful festival of the Apt," the feast of Amen-Ra, and the "City of the Lord of Eternity," was celebrating the journey of the god from his mighty stronghold at the northern end of the capital, to his great temple in the south.

The streets were filled with joyous crowds, tossing flowers, laughing, shouting, jostling one another in gay abandon. Nubians, Jews, Greeks, slaves and nobles, rich and poor, high and low, all joined in the celebration.

In and out among the throngs, threaded the lean brown bodies of the water-sellers, their goatskins under their arms, cups of bright-colored pottery in their hands. At the corners of the streets acrobats tumbled and turned, punctuating their feats with boisterous shouts; jugglers tossed many-colored balls and caught them dexterously to the delight of the gaping crowds. Bands of buffoons, dressed in grotesque caps with long, brightly colored tassels which kept falling before their eyes and which they flung aside with all manner of ridiculous manœuvers, danced and contorted to the sound of a drum. As they whirled and pirouetted through the crowds, they shouted remarks, friendly or sarcastic, provoking shrieks of laughter.

Women, dressed in figured petticoats tied about the waist with brilliant sashes, their arms encased in wide linen sleeves, tossed plaited tresses and jangled great hooped earrings, as they turned narrow kohl-edged eyes on the men who ogled them. Slave girls, whose coarse black hair hung in a loop down

their backs, long tight robes showing the suppleness
of their figures, followed their mistresses with great
fans made of ostrich plumes which they waved
above them. Nobles walked disdainfully among the
crowds, picking their way carefully lest they should
soil their delicately wrought sandals. In their hands
they carried long walking-sticks, marked with their
names and tipped with ivory. Folded head-pieces
of striped linen, which fell over their shoulders in
straight, stiff lines, covered elaborately curled and
plaited wigs, the gold and jewels of their necklaces
and rings exciting the wonder of the rabble.

Flower venders ran here and there crying their
wares and tossing them into open casements from
which leaned elegantly dressed ladies. Fruit-sellers,
their baskets of woven rushes filled with dates,
apricots, pomegranates and figs, poised carefully on
their heads, went about among the crowds with
eyes alert for beckoning fingers.

In the bazaars, merchants tried to tempt the
people with rich displays of stuffs, bordered deep
with indigo and embroidered in blue, purple and
scarlet, or interwoven with gold and silver threads;
wonderfully wrought leather, gilded and embossed;
sandals painted and richly decorated, and costly
ornaments inlaid with precious stones.

Purchasers and idlers, bargaining or watching the
passing throngs, lounged on the little benches before the shops. Children, brown-skinned and naked,
with their round heads shaven of all except the
side lock, ran gleefully shouting in and out among
the merrymakers, while occasionally some patrician
child passed, dressed sedately like his elders, his

hand clinging to that of a guardian. Stately soft-footed camels swayed through the narrow streets, their trappings brilliant with scarlet tassels and little jingling silver bells. Tiny gray asses laden with rushes, or panniers filled with flowers and fruit, patiently followed their guides. Slaves led to the sacrifice large prize bulls with gold-tipped horns, hoofs grown slightly upward from lack of exercise, huge gold earrings clanking in their ears and wreaths of flowers strung about the great necks.

Everywhere was the sound of laughter, spontaneous, carefree. It seemed that all Weset danced and sang on this great feast day. But a keen observer would have noticed that the happiness on the faces of the common people was not reflected on those of the nobles, nor the priests who hurried toward the temple.

Among these, one might have heard whisperings of evil tidings that had come from the north; rumors, still unconfirmed and not to be told of lightly, that the Assyrian was hammering at the gates of Memphis! Were this ancient stronghold against the invader to fall, might it not be possible for his marauding hosts to reach Weset, where was stored the treasure and art of the world?

It seemed incredible that Kampt, which had withstood the ravages of Time and the hand of man for thousands of years, should now, at the apex of her glory, succumb to these uncouth barbarians.

And yet, through all the merry-making and abandon of the people, the vague fears of those who

knew, ran in an undercurrent of unrest and apprehension.

Presently, from somewhere in the distance, came
the sound of music, the beating of drums, the clashing of cymbals, the loud blare of trumpets.

The crowds paused a moment to listen, then
helter-skelter, they rushed toward the quay, pushing and jostling, laughing, shouting, craning their
heads over each others' shoulders in order to see
the better. Mothers lifted eager children; youths
made space with insistent elbows for maidens at
their sides, as in the distance, the richly embroidered
and colored sails of the fleet came slowly into
view.

The god was approaching!

The people grew wild with enthusiasm, shouting,
cheering, throwing flowers into the air and on the
water, where they floated delicately, making a fragrant carpet for the sacred barge.

The great galleys drew nearer and the emblems
on the sails could be clearly seen, the phoenix, the
sacred ram, the disk and wings of Amen-Ra.
Painted and decked with flowers, they sailed majestically toward the Temple, their prows and
sterns decorated with carved figures of Hermachis
and Isis, the cow heads of Hathor, the sacred
ibex, and from tall standards fluttered gay streamers. In the prow of each, straight and tall, his
bare skin like polished porphyry, stood the pilot, a
long pole in his hands with which, from time to
time, he sounded the depths of the water. Each
galley was rowed by twenty slaves and the long
wooden shafts of the brilliantly colored oars moved

rhythmically backward and forward as the over-
seer, his whip across his knees, clapped his hands to
mark the time. The huge rudders were painted in
blue and scarlet and decorated with the lotus
flower, and in their wake, floated the sacred
barge, its sides glittering and resplendent in the
sunlight. On the rich purple sails was cunningly
wrought with threads of gold and silver, the emblem of the god, and behind the gigantic ram's
head of bronze which surmounted the bow, erect
and impassive as a carven figure, stood Hotep, High
Priest of Amen-Ra.

Into the midst of the crowd along the river bank,
now ran soldiers bearing long rods, which they swung
right and left among the throng, making a pathway
for the procession which was approaching from
Karnak.

Reverently, the people fell back, with awe rather
than love, for it was more than man who was to
pass, it was almost the equal of the god himself;
the Pharaoh, ruler of Upper and Lower Egypt,
son of Amen-Ra, who in going to the Temple to
make offering, paid homage also unto himself.

The sound of the drums grew deafening, the
blare of trumpets ascended in resounding waves of
ecstasy, the crowds swayed to and fro, fluttering
their gay banners as the procession came in sight
along the avenue between the long lines of ram-
headed sphinxes.

Now the sun was caught and flashed back from
the shields and spears of the soldiers. Rhythmically,
they advanced, their short folded aprons swinging
in unison as they marched. On either flank walked

standard bearers, their long gilded staffs crowned
with images of the sacred barque, rams' heads and
other emblems, beneath which bright-colored pennants rippled in the sunlight.   Then came grooms
leading two of the Pharaoh's gilded war chariots,
the horses prancing and champing at their bits.
Following them came drummers, huge Ethiopians,
whose skins shone like polished ebony. Great clus-
ters of colored ostrich plumes nodded in their hair,
their short white skirts contrasting sharply with their
black bodies.   They beat the skin-covered drums
with a sharp rhythmic insistence that marked time to
the thud of the many marching feet.   Women in long
blue robes, their round arms and bosoms bare and
decked with golden ornaments, carried silver sistra
which were shaken in accompaniment to the hymn
they sang in praise of Mut, the patron goddess of
the city.

Behind them the sun gleamed and sparkled again
on armour and swaying standards, and the air was
once more filled with the clash of castanets, the thun-
der of drums and the brazen voices of trumpets.

The crowd cheered and shouted as they passed,
waving their banners, throwing flowers, struggling,
eager that no detail of the glittering pageant should
be lost.

Now through the clouds of incense that rose from
'censors swung by white-robed acolytes, advanced the
scribes, their heads bound about by feathers. Following, came a group of priests with shaven crowns,
long full aprons reaching to the ankles, their fine
smooth skin bare to the hot rays of the sun.   On
their shoulders they carried poles supporting the

litter on which rested the sacred barque where was enshrined the image of the deity. The rich ornaments, gold, and precious stones which adorned its sides flashed and shimmered as one massive jewel.

The people raised their voices shouting praise to Amen-Ra, king of gods, while their eyes turned toward the approaching Pharaoh, his son and representative on earth.

The royal litter was borne on the shoulders of giant slaves from Nubia, to whom the King's weight was but a feather. The chair in which he sat was fashioned of ebony, ivory, and precious stones, its gilded feet carved to resemble those of a lion. A long robe of finest linen clung closely to his figure from neck to ankles, its great loose sleeves falling away from the powerful arm that held the golden sceptre aloft. Over his knees was spread an apron of colored leather ornamented with lions' heads and bordered with a row of asps, emblem of royalty. Upon his head, he wore the *pshent*, the red and white double crown of Egypt, and about his neck were many strands of gold and gems that flashed back the sun in rainbow prisms. On his feet, set close together and stiffly straight before him, were fine sandals of gilded leather, the points turned sharply up, and over the back of the chair was thrown a magnificent leopard skin which he would assume later when offering to Amen-Ra in the Temple.

The clear pallor of his skin shone almost deathlike; the firm fold of his lips, the strong chin, and prominent features, all spoke of an indomitable will and the arrogance of power.

To the marvelling people, he seemed the very in-
carnation of a god, but among them were those
of keener vision who read on the royal countenance
an expression of vague alarm. The inscrutable
calm in which his finely moulded features were set,
seemed stirred by a faint ripple of wonder, of in-
definable apprehension. Was there a possibility that
the throne, upon which he and his ancestors had sat
for so many centuries, was trembling on the edge of
a bottomless pit, into which himself and his gods
might be hurled forever?

On the air rose the praise, the cheers, and adula-
tion of a loyal people that hushed the unvoiced
foreboding in his heart. Egypt was set upon a
rock against which the storms of ages had beat in
vain; as enduring as the river that divided her
palm-bordered shores, would she continue to be mistress of nations!

The procession wound its glittering length toward
the temple. At the gateway it met and merged into
the one from the river. Louder, more frenzied
grew the music; wilder and more ecstatic the shouting populace, and silent, stony, emotionless as his
own colossal image, sat the Pharaoh.

In through the massive gates they swung, the
people crowding after, across the forecourt, through
the vast dim stretches of the great Hypostyle Hall,
the trumpets blaring louder, the drums beating
deafeningly, the sistra and cymbals clashing and
jingling. Faster and faster whirled the dancing
women, their voices rising in shrill song, the people
joining in the chant. Clouds of incense floated about
the sacred barque as it swayed on its way, the thud

of thousands of feet marked time on the silver inlaid pavement, the hymns of praise from the thousands of throats echoing against the lofty ceiling.

The procession came to a halt before a magnificent curtain of deepest purple wrought with gold and silver, scarlet and turquoise, which hung across the recess where dwelt the god There was ·a pause, definite, breathless, as though that vast throng had been frozen into stone.

Suddenly the heavy curtains parted, the people fell on their knees bowing their heads to the floor. The women's voices rose in exultant praise, the drums beat wildly, the trumpets blared forth a deafening blast of sound, and tall and straight even in the presence of the sacred shrine, the Pharaoh raised a golden ewer in his mighty arms, and poured a libation to the god.

Before the wondering, awe-struck eyes of the multitude, in the niche their forefathers had built for him, stood the image of Ámen-Ra the king of gods, the rays of the noonday sun falling cunningly through an aperture, planned for the purpose, full on the golden wings, the sacred disk, and the glittering crowned asps that were his symbols.

To the people, the still, calm face of their Pharaoh had seemed almost godlike in its serenity, the vague unrest that lay deep in the long dark eyes meant to them merely the inscrutability of a being beyond their understanding.

But there was one who observed the King, to whom the royal mind was as a written scroll. This was Hotep, High Priest of Amen-Ra, he, who had stood alone and majestic in the prow of the sacred barge as it was towed up from Karnak. It was his office to meet the Pharaoh at the temple gates and lead the way into the Holy of Holies. He had assisted when the Royal One had burnt incense and poured libations. His hand had given the signal which had caused the heavy curtains of the sanctuary to be drawn apart.

Above the hymns of praise, through the clouds of incense and amid the rich gifts of gold and silver, of ivory and precious stones that the Pharaoh had brought as offerings to the god, the High Priest seemed to hear a faint murmur of impending disaster. As in a vision, he saw beyond the temple walls, to the far edge of the northern horizon, where, blotting out the sunlight, a menacing pall of devastating blackness crept nearer and nearer.

Hotep, the High Priest of Amen-Ra, was the descendant of High Priests. In himself was embodied all the lore of a hundred generations of his craft, and through the Pharaoh, he ruled all Egypt. Was it possible that the accumulated knowledge of the ages was to be cut down root and branch? That he, the flower of finest culture on this mighty plant, was to wither and be blown away like dust in the desert thus bringing to naught all the labors of his predecessors and himself?

Full of these thoughts, he followed in the wake of the King's litter as, the ceremonies over, the Pharaoh and his escort left the great temple.

The throng, their offerings made, turned and crowded after the Royal procession, eager for another glimpse of the King of Kings. The day would be devoted to joy and merriment. Generous feasts would be given the people, and in gayly decorated booths along the way, stood slaves preparing meats, fruit and wine which they dispensed to the eager crowds.

The Pharaoh's cortège went majestically on its way to the Royal Palace amid the cheers and waving banners of his adoring subjects and the High Priest stood at the temple's entrance watching ·the splendor and glitter of the monarch's train as it swung along the broad avenue of Sphinxes.

His tall, lean figure seemed little more than a pigmy's in the shadow of the mighty statue by which he stood. He was an old man, yet with the lean, fine vigor of perfect health. The tall dome of his head was clean shaven. His heavy brows overhung a pair of keen eyes, whose vision saw not only to-day, but yesterday and tomorrow. His mouth was firmly set, but the slight fullness of the well-formed lips, and certain indefinite lines about the corners, gave a hint of kindness, a touch of the human, to a face which austere asceticism and passionate devotion to a cause, would otherwise have made appear hard as the great stone visage towering above him. About his thin loins was wrapped a short apron, and over this hung a long loose robe of sheer linen fastened by a richly embroidered girdle whose ends fell to his knees. His feet were bare of the sandals he had slipped off while performing his religious duties in the temple.

Tall and straight, he stood in the shadow of the great stone figures at his side, as silent as they, and as inscrutable:

The worshippers had all thronged out through the massive Pylons, and the temple gardens were deserted. Beyond the gates, the sun lay hot and sparkling. The colors of fluttering pennants and the gay raiment of the people contrasted pleasantly with the cool green of the tamarisk and sycamore, and into 'the eyes of Hotep came a look of almost passionate longing that all this beauty, this splendor, and gayety might last forever.

"If man could but pierce the veil that hangs between each day's birth!" he murmured. "But with the experience of ten thousand yesterdays, he still stumbles blindly over the threshold of every tomorrow!"

A new day was dawning for Egypt. Would it bring added glory, or had the gods decreed otherwise?

With a sigh, his head bent low, his strong, lean hands clasped behind him, he turned and paced slowly along the cool paths. Musing, lost in the vision of his country's future, his silent steps carried him far into the recesses of the temple gardens. Presently his far-roaming thoughts were brought back by the sound of young voices, soft spoken, full of a vibrant thrill that reached even the ascetic heart of the High Priest.

Lifting his head, he saw through the branches of a feathery tamarisk by the side of the path, a secluded nook, cool, translucently green, and perfumed with the delicate fragrance of the pale lotus blossoms that floated on the surface of a tiny pool nearby.

A smile played about his lips. For a moment,

some of the fear and apprehension that had been disturbing him was forgotten. For here in the cool of the temple gardens, Nature, with a craft and lure so much older than the ancient knowledge that was his, was weaving again the wonderful fabric that held the promise of life's eternal renewal.

On an ebony bench inlaid with ivory, which the priests had caused to be set in this lovely spot as a resting-place for meditation, sat a youth and a maiden so engrossed in one another that even the passing of the Pharaoh had not disturbed the tranquility of their enchanted world.

The man, a little above what is called medium height, wore the princely badge at the side of his head, its golden fringe falling to his shoulder, the jeweled band that held it in place, bound about his temples. The slight breeze stirring among the leaves, fluttered the edge of the soft white robe that hung full and loose about his straight figure with its delicate, though strongly moulded lines. His eyes, soft and velvet-black, looked tenderly into those of the girl at his side, the long narrow brows that arched them, showing dark as midnight against the clear olive of his skin.

The girl who answered his look with tender adoration, was as slender and graceful as the reeds growing in the tiny pool at their side. Her dark hair fell over her shoulders in many plaits, each fastened with a tip of gold. It was bound with a golden fillet whose enameled clasp was fashioned in the form of an acacia blossom, its ivory tints matching the clearness of her own fair skin. As she turned her head shyly, the softened sunlight falling through the green canopy of leaves, touched her hair with lights like burnished bronze, elusive, shifting, that made one wonder if they were real or fancied. Her eyes were baffling, iridescent, filled with a glow that dazzled one, so that it was difficult to determine their color. Heavy black lashes rimmed them and the dark, finely penciled brows were like a delicately poised pair of wings.

Hotep knew those eyes well. He had known them almost from the time of their opening, for the girl was Teta, his ward, the child of a sister who had died and left her in his keeping. He had watched with pleasure and approval the ripening of love between this perfect pair whom the gods must have chosen to mate.

The young Prince Rames was his pupil, fitted both by birth and intellect to delve deep into that hidden lore which the priest knew so well. He eagerly forsook the pleasures and recreations so alluring to youth and would sit for hours drinking in the wisdom of his master, and Hotep dreamed of the heights his favorite might reach with his aid and guidance.

He had watched the girl's character unfold day by day. Her sweetness, her devout observances of the tenets of their faith, her charity to the poor and tender compassion for those who suffered, had endeared her to the strong old heart that in spite of the austere hiding of its emotions, still was capable of deep and earnest affection.

They turned as the priest came into view and rose to greet him, the girl's slender figure outlined elusively by the long narrow robe she wore, its jeweled girdle clasped about her delicate waist.

"Art come to tell me," began the young Prince eagerly, "that the evil tidings from the North are but the conjuring of those who, through malice, would disturb the peace of the Pharaoh?"

The girl caught her guardian's hand and drew him to the bench.

"Sit here, my father," she said, "the day has been a long and hard one for thee, come rest with us, thy children."

Hotep sank wearily between them on the seat, and the apprehension of impending evil which the sight of their young faces had for the moment dispelled, returned.

"My son," he said sadly, "I fear that peril indeed threatens. May Amen-Ra and Mut, the Mother, guard us!"

Teta leaned her soft cheek against his shoulder and Rames, his eyes alight with the optimism of youth, and youth in love, smiled confidently.

"These tidings be mere vapors, venerable father," he said, "they must fly before the first breath of our invincible armies. Egypt always has been! Egypt always shall be! Is she not beloved among nations by Amen-Ra himself?"

The priest turned to caress the bronze tresses.

"Dear children of my soul," he said tenderly, "I have watched you both grow from childhood into the fulfillment of your youth. May Isis, and Holy Hathor have you in their keeping and may Amen-Ra, in whose name come blessings, grant that Rames prove a true prophet indeed, and the glory and wisdom of Egypt be perpetuated!" And with a sigh, he rose, his head bent in meditation.

They watched him as he threaded his way through the mazes of the temple gardens, till at last his tall, spare figure, dwarfed by the giant images standing guard at the great gates, passed in through the shadows and out of their sight, then they turned again to one another.

What though Hotep, the High Priest, knew all that yesterday had to teach, was troubled with forebodings of the morrow, for these two looking deep into each other's eyes, there was only the glory and the happiness of today.

CHAPTER II

BEYOND the quiet of the temple gardens, the shouts and laughter of the populace rose joyously. •Voices lifted in song, passed and died away in the distance. The "Beautiful Festival" was at its height, the momentary awe of the Pharaoh and the gods had passed, and the people gave themselves up wholly to enjoyment. Later in the day, the sacred barge would float back to Karnak and their brief playtime would be over.

But to the girl and the man sitting by the little lotus pool in the cool shadow of the tamarisk showers, this day was the beginning of all things.

Rames held her close against his shoulder and lifted her face to his. How sweet she was, how pure and delicate. The wonder of the iridescent eyes! In their magic depths burned a flame, that sent the blood singing through his veins.

"Teta," he murmured, "as long as Egypt herself shall endure; yea, even after she has passed away, I shall love thee!"

The girl turned restlessly in his arms.

"Tell me, my beloved," she said, "what are the evil tidings of which thou didst question my venerable uncle?"

He wound his fingers in the glory of her hair.

"My sweet," he said, "today is ours! Come, forget the whisperings that have disturbed thine ears.

Love fills our world! It encompasses all our desires, beyond, all else is naught!"

But the girl refused to be satisfied.

"No," she said, "what troubles thee and Hotep,
who is more than father to me, must needs touch
me. Tell me, beloved!"

And holding her close to still her trembling, he
told her how the invader had set his foot on the
soil that had been theirs and their ancestors for
countless ages; how he was already beating at the
gates of Memphis and that men, here in Thebes,
dreaded lest he might reach even thus far.

"But have no fear, my lotus blossom, Thebes is
mighty! She bids defiance to her enemies! Has
she not been called the Victorious City? When
have her armies failed to return triumphant, and
laden with spoils? Hast forgotten the deeds of
Aahmes, destroyer of the Hyksos? Of Thothmes
the conqueror, and the great Rameses of whose
glorious house I come?"

"But those were the men of yesterday," she replied,
"will their great deeds preserve us today?"

"Hast not faith in the sons of such fathers?" he
asked, the assurance of youth ringing in his voice.
"Kampt is chosen of the gods to endure forever!"

Rames' words quieted her fears.

With a little sigh she leaned back in the hollow
of his arm, her eyes once more clear and untroubled.

"Let us speak of thee, my beloved," she said,
"thee and thy ambitions!"

Rames had been left an orphan very young. In
his veins ran the blood of Rameses himself. The

deeds of his forefathers were sculptured deep on many a temple wall and obelisk. The desire, which is inherent in all men, for the glory of the battle-field, the triumph of the conqueror, clamored for expression. He was already skilled in the use of the bow, the sword and the battle-axe. Teta had often watched him with pride as he drove past her in his two-wheeled chariot, as guard to the Pharaoh, the reins of the spirited horses knotted about his waist, his finely moulded arms holding the long spear or the bow.

The blood of his ancestors called loudly for a career that should be like theirs. But the gentle girl at his side saw only in these sculptured records of her lover's family, the pitiful strings of weeping captives, the piles of severed hands and heads which counted vanquished slain, saw only the horror and bloodshed of it all, heard only the unrelenting cry, "Woe to the conquered!" and so urged him to the allurements of the mart.

They talked long and earnestly of the wonders of the foreign lands into which his merchant caravans would take him. Judea, where his stores of finest linen, gold, wrought leather, gems, and incense could be bartered for their precious woods, their spices and balsam; Babylon, whose wonders made the girl's eyes widen as he told her of them; Tyre, where the merchants were all princes, the traders, the greatest nobles, where they would exchange their rich dyes for stores of corn, the medicinal herbs for which his country was far-famed, the carved ivory and fleece of trees which could be woven into beautiful fabrics. He would sail to the island of Cyprus in one of the Phoenician galleys and bring back stores of timber, copper, iron, and even that wonder which was puzzling men, Cyprian adamant, to make armor through which no arrow could pierce.

"I shall deck thee, oh my beloved, with rich feathers from Ethiopia, with gold and silver and precious gems from the Mountains of the Moon, with fine stuffs from Babylon and Tyre and ivory from beyond the Red Sea. I shall sail away as far as Mauretania, where lies the world's edge, from whence I shall bring thee loops of pearls as large as dove's eggs, whose lustre thy cheek alone can equal, and ear-rings set with flawless emeralds, green as sunlight through the tamarisks. These slender fingers shall be ringed with ruddy gold and carven gems, and round the white pillar of this throat I love to kiss, I shall hang strand upon strand of rubies, in whose glowing hearts thou shalt see the fire of my adoration! I shall seek to discover thy every wish so that I may grant it thee!"

She smiled at him tenderly as she pressed his hand against her soft cheek.

"But Rames," she said, "how far this journeying will take thee from my side! How can I bear thy absence even for a day?"

"Sometime," he assured her, "thou shalt sail with me. Thou, too, shalt see the wonders of strange countries, of different peoples, shalt see those lands where dwells the griffin, and look with me from the edge of the world across the primeval waters!"

His eyes grew dreamy with a vision of the future.

"Who knows," he said softly, almost to himself, "thou and I standing by those far shores, perhaps shall see the shadows of a coming age, which may surpass even the wonders of mighty Kampt!"

The girl looked at him in amazement.

"Rames," she said, "what art thou saying? Hast thou not, even now, assured me that Egypt shall endure forever?"

He held her close.

"Nay, be not troubled," he said tenderly, "but there are moments when I long to know all the wisdom the world can offer."

"Art thou yearning to be a scribe, my Rames, a man who sits forever bent over his roll of papyrus and but records the deeds and thoughts of others?"

To Teta, raised as she had been in the shadow of the priesthood, knowledge meant the suppression of all the human emotions, the curbing of the young fierce blood that sang aloud for expression. It meant the fading of the bloom of youth in the chilly cloisters of the temples, the shutting away of the sunlight and life of today into the dusty tomes and mouldy archives of the past.

"Knowledge brings so little worldly gain," she said almost piteously. "It is appreciated by so few in comparison with those other attainments which make men splendid to their fellows. Thou hast spoken of my sailing with thee in thy great galleys to those distant lands of which we have been dreaming There, my beloved, I can follow thee, but think, can thy Teta, with her woman's brain, who knows no other lesson save her love for thee, can she follow thee into those vast, mystic regions of wisdom where so few have penetrated?"

The shadows that lay on the pathway were lengthening and as she spoke, the girl rose to her feet. Their love had been so wonderful, their comradeship so perfect, the thought that he might grow beyond her and leave her striving to attain his heights, touched her with a sense of loneliness.

"My princess," he said tenderly, "where I go, shalt thou go also. This life and all my others, I consecrate to thee!"

Teta knelt by the side of the pool. Between the delicate green of the lotus stalks, her lovely face was mirrored in the water.

"Look," she said, "there is my *Ka,* my soul! Bend low and let me see thine beside it!"

Rames knelt, his arm about her shoulders.

"Through all the ages, my beloved," whispered the girl, "thy soul and mine shall be side by side, even as they are mirrored here in the pool of Isis. Kiss my lips so that our souls, too, may make the vow," and half as an indulgence to her whim, half seriously, he bent his head and touched her lips reverently with his.

"Now I must return," said the girl, "thou hast thy duty to perform on this, the feast day of the Apt, I must not cause thee to tarry always at my side. Come!"

And hand in hand, with lingering steps, they passed through the quiet of the perfumed gardens, out into the sunlight of the crowded street.

As they threaded their way through the jostling

throngs, the girl spoke happily of their future journeys into distant countries, of the time when his caravans should come back to Thebes laden with the riches of foreign lands. She planned and dreamed, and as he listened, Rames was almost persuaded that the course of his ambition, was to become a great merchant prince.

But when he had left her at her own gate and she had kissed her slender fingers to him as he turned away, in his heart still lingered the desire to know, to pierce the veil of Time, to see what lay beyond.

CHAPTER III

THE day of the "Beautiful Festival" had joined the waiting yesterdays. The sacred barge of Amen-Ra and its escorting galleys had floated down the Nile to Karnak, mighty among temples. The brief twilight of the East had come and gone and night, a wonderful, star-filled, purple night, wrapped close the city that slept like a peaceful child after its happy day. The streets were silent and deserted, save where the footsteps of the watch or the half-finished measure of some late reveler's song echoed against the close-set walls, or when, far off in the desert, a jackal howled.

In the house of Rames, its master was still astir. The wonderful calm of the Egyptian nights held a lure for the young scholar that he could scarcely ever resist. Here in his garden under the stars, he loved to review the fascinating subjects he had studied during those charmed hours when Hotep could spare him leisure.

But now as he paced the narrow path, his thoughts were neither of the High Priest, nor of the wonders he had revealed to him, but of the fair face of a girl, whose delicate hands were to lead him into Paradise.

Presently, a knocking at the barred gates broke his meditation and he paused, as the shuffling step of a slave went sleepily down the walk. A figure, wrapped close in a woolen cloak, slipped through the door which the porter opened, and brushing past the sleepy servant fell on its knees before the master.

"Speak! What is thine errand?" asked Rames. The figure threw back the covering from a face that showed a network of wrinkled lines and blackened hollows in the moonlight.

"Bagoas! What brings thee here?" cried the prince in astonishment. "Thy mistress,—the Lady Teta,— is all well with her?"

The man rose to his feet and took from his sleeve a small roll of papyrus.

"My lady bade me bring the noble Rames, this," he said, and withdrew into the shadows to await the answer.

"Amrou, a light," called Rames, and the slave hurried into the house as his master unrolled the little script and pressed it to his lips.

Presently the man returned with a horn lantern, which he held above the scroll.

"Teta to Rames," it read, "Greeting! Since that happy hour by the Pool of Isis, I have dreamed much of those days which we shall spend together. And to speed their coming, I go tomorrow to the tomb of my mother in the Libyan hills. There I shall pray her beg the gods to hasten our joy. But did I not tell thee that even one day seems death without thee? So come, my beloved, and bid me farewell. I await thee at my casement at the hour of the moon's full, for with the sunrise I must be on my way!"

Rames rolled the little note and placed it carefully in his bosom.

"Amrou," he said, "my cloak and staff!"

The slave set his lantern on the path at his master's feet and bending his supple body in a quick obeisance, turned and disappeared into the shadows.

Rames' brow was troubled. Teta going alone into the Libyan hills was no thought to take lightly. But his training as well as hers had taught him that respect must be paid to those departed ancestors who might plead one's cause in the hall of the gods. He well knew that she could not be persuaded to forego this journey, but now, when the tidings of the invaders' approach were whispered on all sides, it made him uneasy. True, it was but a day's travel, but the vast wastes of the desert that stretched beyond the range of hills where lay the City of the Dead, were so silent, mysterious, so much peril lurked in their yellow reaches. His heart misgave him.

Tomorrow the Pharaoh himself had bidden his presence at the Palace, and the Pharaoh's word was law. But how could he bear that Teta should go alone?

While he stood thinking, the slave ran swiftly from the house, a long, ivory-tipped staff in his hand, a woolen cloak over his arm. As he wrapped his master close in its scarlet and blue-bordered folds, Rames looked deep into the faithful eyes.

"Amrou," he said, "wilt thou guard well what is dearer than life to me?"

"Yea, Lord," whispered the slave eagerly.

"Then do thou go and arm thyself and meet

me quickly by the House of the Acacia where dwells the Lady Teta!" and turning, he followed the steps of the bent figure who had brought the message.

They threaded their way through the narrow streets, the lantern in the old man's hand trembling and sending flickering yellow lights through the black shadows of the houses.

Presently, they came to a halt before a gateway set deep in the recess of a wall. The slave rapped softly and it was opened from within. They slipped through into a small garden, fragrant with the scent of acacia blossoms and cool with the drip of water into a hidden pool. Bagoas led the way along a narrow path, black in the shadows of the bordering trees, to the side of the house where, bowing low, he left him.

The young man stepped close under a latticed window and called softly.

"Teta, it is I, thy Rames! Hasten. The hour is late!"

After a moment there was a slight sound, the shutters were quietly opened and the girl leaned out, her face like carved ivory in the moonlight, framed by the dark masses of her hair.

"My beloved," she said tenderly, "hast thou thought me mad to send for thee at this hour and in this secret way?" Her round arms, bare of ornament, were held out to him. Rames took her hands in his and pressed the pink-tipped fingers against his lips.

"What thou dost, I question not," he said, "save this journey into the Libyan hills!"

"I shall take my women," she replied, "old

Bagoas, also, besides my litter-bearers. We shall be safe and oh, my beloved, I long so for those days when we are to be one, that I go to pray my mother to implore the gods there be no more parting!"

"Teta." Rames held her hands against his heart, "thou art so dear, so precious to me that if harm should come to thee, I——"

She laughed happily.

"What harm can come, my Rames? I go as I have gone before, to pour libations on my mother's tomb, to take sweet cakes for her *Ka*. Thou wouldst not grudge the love I give her memory when I still have so much to give to thee!"

"But must thou go tomorrow? Canst thou not go another day when the Pharaoh shall have no need of me?"

She shook her head

"Nay," she said earnestly, "when the sun rises over the Libyan hills, I must start forth! Listen,—yesterday when thou hadst left me, I and one of my women stole out to the house of Schalmanazu, the soothsayer, he who reads the future in the desert sands.—Nay, do not frown, I want happiness so much!—He told me I must make this journey on the morrow, for only so could I fulfill my destiny."

"Teta," his voice was stern, "thou shouldst not have gone alone to the house of any soothsayer. I beg thee put aside this journey until another time, my heart misgives me, I fear,—I know not what!"

She bent her dark head down to his and wound her arms about his neck.

"Be not wroth with me," she whispered. "I feel that I must go. It is but the journey of a day. We shall rest in the shadow of my mother's tomb. There Holy Hathor will protect me! And when the golden barque of Ra shall sail into the darkening west, I shall again be with thee!"

He drew her lips to his.

"My sweet," he murmured, "if thou wilt go, I cannot stay thee, but Amrou, my faithful slave, goes with thee. When thy caravan starts forth at sunrise, Amrou will be at the gate."

Teta let her eyes rest tenderly on his.

"Guardian of my happiness," she said at last, "thou speakest as though I go on a long journey, indeed. 'Tis but to the edge of the Libyan waste. But if the going of thy slave will satisfy thee, Amrou shall join my caravan. And now, oh my beloved, I must make me ready for the dawn. Kiss me and know that until my lips shall rest again on thine, until mine arms shall once more hold thee, I shall know neither happiness nor peace!"

Rames drew her close, too filled with a vague unrest to trust himself to speak. At last she slipped from his arms and as he turned from her window with a sigh, the lean, bent figure of old Bagoas glided from the darkness and with meek obeisance, led the way through the scented shadows.

As Rames passed through the gate and heard its bolts fastened behind him, he turned his troubled eyes toward the west.

Far away on the other side of the Nile, rose the masses of the Libyan suburb, silvered by the splendor of the moon and beyond, above the dim outline of the hills, sparkling and splendid, hung a single star like a promise.

With a sigh he drew his cloak about him, when from the shadows, stepped a figure and knelt at his feet.

"Thy slave is here, my lord," said a low voice.

"Good, Amrou," answered Rames, "listen, this thou must do. At sunrise the Lady Teta journeys to her mother's tomb. Join thou her caravan and on the sacred bones of thine ancestors, never leave her side till she returns here safe, to me!"

"I hear, my lord," answered the slave, "thy will is mine!"

"So be it!" and turning, Rames bent his steps thoughtfully toward his own house.

His heart was heavy with a strange foreboding. A wordless voice seemed crying despair. He tried to shake off the feeling that gripped him, but the waning moonlight wove strange phantasies of shadowy white arms held out to him, and deep, translucent eyes that looked yearningly across a gulf he could not cross. The wind, whispering through the palm trees, seemed to cry his name in tones of silver sweetness. Tomorrow and its tomorrow seemed so endlessly far away. He must busy himself with other thoughts, to shut away this nameless fear. But restlessly, he wandered through the narrow streets, across the wide empty squares and along the deserted quays where the sleeping galleys rocked on the Nile's bosom, and it was not until the golden boat of Ra, fresh from its journey through the underworld, had sent the first blaze of its coming glory over the eastern sky, that he stood once more before his own gate.

"Father of Gods," he prayed, "Mut, the Holy Mother and Khonsu thy son, carry my beloved safely to her journey's end. Let not Sekhmet, the fierce lion goddess, consume her with her flaming breath; let not Mert Segar, the serpent, lover of silence, claim her for her own; O, overcomers of evil, guardians of the earth and skies, bring her safely back to me!"

In the courtyard of the House of the Acacia preparations were going on for the journey of the Lady Teta. Three great camels from Nubia, their ungainly forms vague in the dim light, grunted ill-naturedly as the slaves made them kneel, the little silver bells of their trappings, jingling musically. Several grey asses stood patiently while the hampers of provisions, jars of water and linen tents were loaded on their backs. Ostanes, the giant steward, whose deep bass voice rolled out in solemn orders to the hurrying slave boys, stood majestically in the doorway superintending the preparations.

In her chamber, their young mistress was burning incense before a small shrine in which, under a richly gilded and carved cornice, stood a statue of the young Horus made of delicate blue porcelain, whose polished surface flashed in the wavering flame of the rush-light burning before it.

Teta's women had arrayed her in a narrow robe of blue tissue, richly embroidered, and covered the bronze masses of her hair with a long gauze veil of azure edged with silver. About her throat, she slipped a golden chain hung round with amulets of precious stones, the sacred eye, the disk and wings of Ra, and scarabae of amethyst and emerald.

As the clouds of incense waved in long filmy wreaths about the little shrine, a noisy shout arose in the courtyard, followed by the sound of grunts and the flicking of a whip. She went to the window and leaning out, drank in the mysterious beauty of the early dawn.

The air was heavy with the scent of jasmine, of acacia blooms and the elusive perfume of the lotus. Over everything lay an opalescent blue light, in which all the accustomed objects on which the girl gazed, seemed different, unfamiliar. She stretched her round, white arms toward the sleeping city.

"My beloved," she whispered, "the god of slumber still holds thee, while thy Teta goes forth that she may fulfill the destiny that is foretold us both. Isis guard thee safe till I return."

When she came down into the courtyard later, a small cart stood waiting for her, the brilliant colors decorating its painted sides and broad six-spoked wheels, already faintly seen in the growing light. A large canopy of striped linen rose above it and two black and white spotted oxen stood patiently in the shafts.

Ostanes bowed low before her, his hands on his knees, and two of her women who were to accompany her, helped her into the vehicle. Old Bagoas was to ride ahead on one of the stately camels that now rose with his slight weight, grunting and snarling. The other two were to carry Teta's women and ride beside her cart, and in the rear, the slave boys drove the asses laden with necessities for the journey.

As the man, leading the spotted oxen, swung them into the roadway, a figure rose from the shadow of the wall and prostrated itself in the dust.

Teta rapped sharply with a small ivory stick on the side of her cart and the little cavalcade came to a halt.

"Who art thou?" she asked and the man answered softly:

"Amrou comes from his lord Rames, star of the morning, to watch and guard thee on thy journey."

"Ah, slave of my beloved," answered the girl, "walk thou beside the one who leads my oxen," and as the man leaped to his feet, she rapped sharply again with her ivory staff and the little train moved on.

The streets were silent, save for the jingle of the silver bells on the harness of the camels. A faint primrose began to show above the housetops, brightening into pink, and as they crossed the Nile, the sky was suddenly gold, splendid and glittering with the glory of the sun! Along the river path through the fields, the *fellaheen* were already trudging behind their slow-moving buffaloes, and clouds of tiny larks rose from the grain, settling again beyond them.

The great temples shone greyish-rose in the early light, touched with a wonderful gold, and deep, warm lavender shadows.

Women passed going to the wells with water jars on their shoulders, long blue cotton veils wrapped about them, their anklets jingling as they walked.

As the caravan wound its slow way along the wide sphinx-bordered ·avenue, clear on the morning air, like the snapping of a harp-string, came the faint tones of the giant image of Amenophis, as he sang his praises to the rising sun, and for awhile the little train stopped in the shadow of the great walls to which the huge stone figures led. Then on again, past temples and gardens, monuments and tombs, until the villas and palaces of the Libyan suburb were left behind, and before them lay vast stretches of fine, heavy sand, sparkling and golden under their feet.

Wilder, more barren and rugged, grew the country about them, hot, desolate, twisting itself into grotesque mounds, startling hummocks, and crumbling cliffs. All traces of habitation had been left behind, and beyond lay the City of the Dead.

The silence of the desert enfolded them, broken only by the voices of the women in occasional chatter or the plaintive minor of a love song softly chanted by one of the slaves, but Teta sat motionless, filled with her own thoughts and memories.

The heat of the sun was growing almost intolerable. She had drawn the thin tissue of her veil across her face to protect it from Sekhmet's fierceness. Her head rested against the pole that supported the canopy, her eyes closed against the pitiless glare, when she became aware of a sudden cessation of the murmured sounds of the caravan, a breathless hush that spoke of fear.

She roused herself, and opening her eyes wide, stared into the set face of Amrou, whose hand gripped the side of her cart.

In the distance a cloud of dust was whirling toward them, out of the midst of which came faintly a long thin cry that struck terror to the girl's soul and made her women cower, whimpering on their camels.

"Bagoas," called Teta, "Bagoas, what is it? Why do we stop in the full glare of the sun?"

The old man had dismounted from his camel and knelt in the sand at her feet.

"O light of the universe," he quavered, "deadly danger approacheth. What protection can an old man and a few slave boys give thee and thy women?"

Teta turned to Amrou, who stood tense and watching by the side of her cart, his eyes on the ever-nearing dust cloud in the midst of which could now be seen glimpses of galloping horses, brandished weapons, flying draperies, and ever louder and more blood-curdling, came the long, fierce yell.

"On! On!" she cried imperiously. "Are we to stand here without effort to escape a fate that is worse than death?"

"Lady," answered the slave in a low voice, "of what use are thy slow-moving oxen and great camels, against the fleet horses of the desert men? Of what aid is Bagoas shaking with age, or thy few slave boys, young and trembling with fear?"

"Ah woe, is this my destiny?" cried the girl, for well she knew that once carried away into the Libyan waste, no power on earth could bring her back to Thebes and Rames.

The women wailed and beat their breasts and the slave boys grovelled in the sand. Old Bagoas made a brave effort to straighten his bent back and lift the spear he held.

Nearer and nearer came the fierce band whose keen eyes had discerned the little caravan and scented gain in gold and women.

Across Teta's mind flashed the thought that perhaps Schalmanazu, the soothsayer, who was of the same race as these desert people, had laid this trap for her, and advised this visit to her mother's tomb so that he might have a share in the spoils. It was cruel, but if the gods so willed it, she must bow. The gods were all wise.

"Listen, Amrou," she said hurriedly, "if thou escapest, make thy way to Rames, thy master, if it be thy last breath that takes thee. Tell him that Teta will come to him again. He must watch and wait, for she cannot tell the hour of her coming. Tell him her heart will live only for him, and though it wait for ages, still will it wait! Tell him to be true as she will be true."

As she finished speaking, the women raised their voices in a shrieking wail that rose above the shouts of the desert men who, grinning and wild-eyed, pulled their foam-flecked horses back on their haunches, and surrounded the little caravan.

Bagoas' lifted arm was felled with a cruel blow and without a sound, the old man rolled quivering on the sand and then lay still, his eyes wide to the sun. The slave boys, trembling and begging for mercy, were bound and strapped on the backs of their own beasts of burden. The women were dragged from the camels and thrown across the saddles of their captors.

But before the little cart where Teta stood alone, Amrou held the robbers at bay. His sword flashed swiftly in a circle of fire, his eyes glared hate and defiance on these marauders who were seeking to deprive his master of that which was more than life.

But what was one blade, however keen and sure, against so many?

A crashing blow, a great blackness, and Amrou lay still and motionless on the yellow sand that deepened crimson beneath his head.

When at last he came again to consciousness, the sun was low in the west and not a trace remained of the little caravan that had journeyed forth with the sunrise, save the dead body of old Bagoas, stripped and naked, lying staring at the sky.

* * * * * *

The shadows of the late afternoon were long and purple in the temple garden when Rames and the High Priest paced its paths. The heart of the young man was turned longingly toward the Libyan hills from whence Teta would soon be coming, but he listened respectfully to the low voice of Hotep, propounding wisdom at his side.

Presently they reached the little grove where he and Teta loved to come, and the priest motioned him to sit beside him on the ebony bench.

"My son," said the old man after an interval of silence, "thy thoughts are far away to-day. Canst thou not gird thy soul with patience? I, too, am anxious for the return of my beloved niece, but thou dost dream of nothing else!"

Rames bowed his head in his hands.

"Venerable father," he said, "thou canst not know how dear she is to me, how empty is even one short day that echoes not the music of her voice!"

As he spoke, a step sounded on the gravel, a tottering, dragging step that yet seemed to hasten toward them feebly. Rames leaped to his feet as a gaunt, bedraggled figure threw itself prone on the ground before them.

"Gods of my fathers!" he cried, "what is this!"

"Lord, lord," wailed the creature at his feet, "Amen-Ra give thee patience to hear my tale! Isis give thee strength to bear it!"

Rames staggered and caught at the back of the ebony bench, his voice choked in his throat. Hotep, stern, impassive, his face as emotionless as a sphinx, raised his lean hands that did not tremble, though from the depths of his piercing eyes the dread at his heart peered through.

"Speak, slave!" he said steadily.

The broken figure tore at the grass with his trembling hands.

"May I never know peace again!" he groaned. "That I should be the bearer of such evil tidings!"

Rames bent swiftly, his eyes burning and fierce in his white face.

"Amrou," he said, "an thou speakest not quickly, by Anubis, thou shalt never speak again!"

Hotep put a hand on his shoulder.

"Stay, my son," he said, "the man has come through some sore trial. Be patient!—speak slave!" and trembling, shaken with his own suffering and bitter sorrow for his master, Amrou told the story of Teta's abduction.

He had scarcely finished, when Rames' hands were clutched about his throat. Ruthlessly, he jerked the poor creature to his feet and shook him fiercely as a terrier does a rat.

"Wretch, thou sworest by the bones of thine ancestors to guard her with thy life!" he panted. "Thou darest come back alive to tell me she is lost by worse than death?" But the High Priest's lean arm dragged him away from the fainting slave.

"Rames," he said, "Stay thy hand! Hear all!"

"Yea—lord—a message—," whispered Amrou. "The Lady Teta bade me come to thee and say that she will return again despite the fact that no one has recrossed the mysterious sands whose boundaries are beyond the knowledge of man. She bade me tell thee to be true to her, even as she would ever be true to thee! Oh master, master, when I awoke from the swoon in which these wounds had sent me, the sands had blown across their footprints. She was gone, I know not whither."

The desert men!

Even the priest's austere face grew dark at the thought. But to Rames, it seemed as though he must go mad. He was crushed, hopeless. Teta was lost to him forever! No man could pierce the hidden fastnesses of the desert, no army find her in its trackless wastes. Life for him was empty, desolate! Teta knew the impossibility of ever coming back, her message must have meant their meeting in that underworld where dwelt the gods. He would journey thence to find her.

With a swift turn he drew the jewelled dagger from his girdle and was about to plunge it into his heart, when again the strong hand of the High Priest stayed him.

"Stop!" he cried imperiously, and the slave, still grovelling on the ground, beat the dust and wept aloud. "The life thou wouldst take so lightly can never be recalled. Dost thou not know these tidings cut deep into my soul as into thine? But life is not given to idly throw away. Thou must live now, not for thyself, nor for the woman thou hast loved who awaits thee somewhere along thy way, but for mankind. It is time to choose whether thou shalt do what no man has ever done before,—Be a pioneer along a path of human experience where no footstep has ever trod, or go down into dust and ashes where thy future is but to feed the filthy worms."

Rames, torn by anguish though he was, paused, awed in spite of himself.

"Venerable father," he said brokenly, "I know thy grief is equal to mine own, but in thy great strength and wisdom thou canst master it. Read me the meaning of thy words. My life is nothing more to me, do thou what thou wilt with it." And bowing his head on his folded arms, he crouched, silent and miserable, on the little ebony bench.

Hotep motioned the trembling slave to be gone and paced back and forth on the pathway, fighting his own sorrow and giving Rames time to master his.

At last he stopped before the bowed figure.

"Listen, my son," he said. "Teta's message says she will return to thee, some way, somehow. Dost thou not wish to prepare thyself for her coming, oh doubting bridegroom? Come thou to me tonight at the hour of the moon's full, in the little chapel of Khonsu. There I shall await thee!" and with a sigh, he went slowly down the path and disappeared through the trees. Overhead, the leaves whispered Teta's name, a hoopoo swung slowly on a tamerisk branch nearby, his brown crest rising and falling.

Rames knelt by the little pool of Isis where he and Teta had watched their mirrored lips kiss. He seemed to hear again the sweet voice.

"Through all the ages, thy soul and mine shall be side by side even as they are mirrored here" and those other words that Amrou had brought, "Tell him that Teta will come again!"

He threw himself prone by the edge of the water, his hands clutching the stems of the pale lotus blossoms, emblems of her sweetness, and lying so, wept out his bitterness, his misery, till the temple garden lay dim and mysterious in the deepening twilight and Nut, goddess of night, shook over him her starry robe.

CHAPTER IV

IN the great Temple of Karnak, before the shrine of Khonsu, the moon god, stood Hotep, the High Priest.

The red glow from two tall braziers, on which burned the sacred fire, mingled with the moonlight streaming on the stone face of the god, staring inscrutably out over the heads of his worshippers. Two young priests, their linen upper robes laid aside, exposing their powerful torsos, walked noiselessly back and forth on bare feet, with offerings of oil and honey. Clouds of perfumed incense swirled in wraith-like spirals toward the dim recesses of the great roof where no light penetrated. Four women in long, silver-embroidered blue robes, sown with stars like the mantle of Nut, shook sweet-toned sistra, accenting the rhythm of the hymn of praise they sang. The minor cadence echoed and reechoed among the lofty columns of the great Hypostile Hall beyond, across whose shadows the moonlight cut a wide path, faintly revealing the figures of the Pharaoh, which were cut deep, and inlaid with bronze and gold on the jambs of the mighty doors.

The resonant voice of the High Priest rang out above the singing of the women.

"Khonsu, beloved of Ra,

"Lord of the Fields of Night,
"Whose youth is ever renewed with the waxing moon,
"Who saileth across the sky in a silver boat,
"Exalted art thou among the gods!
"To thee, thy father Ra has entrusted the guarding of the skies while he traverses the underworld!
"Hail to thee, oh radiant One!
"Praise to thee, beautiful among the gods!"

The women danced about the shrine, their draperies whirling wide about their slender limbs, the sistra tinkling sweetly. The young priests drew the heavy curtains across the impassive face of the god, and swinging their silver censers, walked slowly out of the chapel into the shadows of the great hall beyond, the women following. The sound of their chanting and the music of the sistra grew fainter and fainter, and at last died away in the deep silence of the vast temple, but still Hotep stood in an attitude of supplication before the curtained shrine, the moonlight painting his tall, lean figure with a silver brush, a faint glow from the dying embers in the great braziers touching the strong lines of his face.

To know all that Khonsu, the moon god, with his eternally renewed youth, had ever looked on! To know all that he would look upon when these, his people, should have crumbled into dust, and their mighty temples be no more! This was the prayer in Hotep's heart.

His grief for Teta, the niece whom he so loved, had been crushed and silenced. No earthly ties must hinder him who would penetrate into the heart of

Truth, no human sentiments must stir the depths of his soul. He who would know all that the gods knew, must be even as the gods, calm, impassive, unchanging!

As he stood so, a figure detached itself from the shadows and stepped out into the moonlight.

"Behold, oh venerable father, thy son has come!"

Hotep turned his keen eyes on the bent form whose every line expressed the terrible despair that was devouring it.

"My son," he said, laying his hand on the young man's shoulder, "dost thou still wish to cut the thread of thy life and go out into unknown darkness, or art thou willing to dare an adventure that will require all thy fortitude and courage?"

"Oh opener of mine eyes," answered Rames, "thou hast made clear to me the selfishness of mine own grief. Say but thy bidding and I will obey!"

"Come, then!" and Hotep led the way out of the little chapel and among the mighty pillars of the great hall.

Rames followed him across the wide spaces into a narrow corridor roofed and walled with alabaster and flagged with silver, on whose surface lay patches of moonlight which came through the narrow, high-set windows. Down this they hurried, turning as it turned right, then left, then· right again. At last they stopped before a small door of bronze that clanged echoingly as the priest opened its secret lock.

When he had closed and secured it again, the young man found himself in a vast chamber stored with many rolls of papyrus and great stones carved deep with mystic letters. The chamber was lighted by nine lamps of precious metal which swung on long chains from the lofty ceiling where, faint and mysterious in their flickering light, shone the signs of the Zodiac. Across the far wall glittered the winged disk of Amen-Ra, and on another, the figure of the goddess Nut arched above the earth.

Hotep drew forth two chairs of ebony inlaid with ivory, and motioned Rames to be seated.

"My son," he said in his low, deep voice, "here in this chamber of which but few have the secret, are accumulated the spoils of many centuries. Beneath our feet are gathered the treasures of the earth, vast stores of gold and jewels and precious things. These are the means to all the pomp and worldly splendor men covet, although their total sum may not purchase one moment's happiness!"

Rames looked at him. Was this the compensation he was to be offered for the loss of Teta? But Hotep, divining what was passing through his mind, raised his hand solemnly and continued,

"My son, the most priceless thing the world can yield is knowledge. It will open the doors of all our desires. It needs to be coupled with but one thing, the Sword of Faith!"

The heart of Rames that had seemed to die with the loss of Teta, stirred again into life at the priest's words. Knowledge was everything! Perhaps here, hidden among these vast treasures and mighty secrets, lay the pathway back to love and happiness.

Hotep watched the young face which, in the light of the rich lamps showed plainly the deep lines of its suffering. Here was the man who, through great sorrow and a willingness to renounce the world, should be able to make the experiment of which the priest had dreamed.

"Ages ago," he said, "when the first stones of mighty Kampt were laid, a foundation upon which the accumulated wisdom of the world will always rest, there was begun a college of priests, earnest seekers, who were willing to sacrifice everything to the one end, that Truth might be known. They learned to control, and bend to their will, those potent forces of nature which men worshipped as gods. In their efforts to understand the evolution of all organic things,. they traveled the long, long road that led back to the shadowy beginnings of life itself.

"All the knowledge thus gained was carefully stored away, not only on these dusty rolls of papyrus that could be destroyed, not on these blocks of carven stone, but in the minds of men where it would be forever safe from the prying eyes of the inquisitive vulgar by whom such things would never be appreciated, nor understood."

Rames looked about the vast chamber.

"What are these?" he asked.

"The nine lamps which hang above our heads," answered Hotep, "typify in their sacred number, the ocean and the horizon. All numbers are comprehended in their number, all numbers revolve within it. The great vault of the ceiling stretching above us, pictures the wonders of the heavens, these sculptured stones and many rolls of papyrus record the root and branch of that great tree of knowledge, but its flower has never been entrusted to scribe or sculptor. It lies safe hidden within the minds of those highest in our order."

"But has it been just," questioned the young man, "so to safeguard this wonderful store that the world at large may know nothing of it?"

The High Priest shrugged his shoulders.

"Who knows?" he said. "But this has been ·the custom for many centuries and the ways of Egypt are unchanging. From generation to .generation, this knowledge has been handed down. It is almost as though one man has lived for five thousand years, so unbroken has been the chain. In me, behold the last link, the possessor of those mightiest of secrets of which I am left sole guardian. The enemy is beating at our gates, the barbarian foe threatens to engulf our land in ruin. Shall all this wisdom, this quintessence of the· labor of centuries, be lost to posterity? Will the glory of Egypt be buried in the desert sand that may cover deep our splendid temples, our colossal works? Is the sacrifice of ages to be for naught?"

His keen eyes stared through the dim shadows of the vast chamber as though they would pierce the veil that hung between them and the coming years.

"To know what destiny the gods have decreed for mighty Kampt," he continued solemnly, "this must be the crowning act of Hotep, High Priest of Amen-Ra, to whom has been entrusted the flower of Egypt's wisdom!"

Rames stared at the exalted face opposite him. The high dome of the shaven brow shone like polished ivory, the eyes burned with a fire almost supernatural.

"To know what lies in ages yet unborn even as thou knowest the past?" he asked in an awed voice, "Can this be done?"

.The priest nodded.

"It can, my son, and furthermore it shall be! The door of the future must be opened! Some one of those who live today must pass through and see the world·as it will be when Egypt's span of years shall have been doubled, even as thou and I can see these lamps which hang above our heads."

"The way," panted Rames, his face ablaze with eagerness, "point thou the way and let me be thy messenger!"

The priest raised a warning hand.

"Stay, my son," he said. "He, who would cross the long, long span that bridges Today and that far away Tomorrow, will have need of unparalleled courage, unusual intellect and untiring strength!"

"Courage is mine, and strength!"

"Yea, and intellect!" said Hotep.

"My feet have trod but a little way along the path of learning," answered Rames humbly.

The High Priest looked· at him fondly.

"Wisdom is not·measured by knowledge, my son, but by understanding! If youth were mine as it is thine, I myself would make this journey, but youth, for me, lies buried in the yesterdays. Listen, thou hast said thy life is worthless to thee, wouldst thou lay thy young manhood, thy intellect, and strength at the feet of Egypt and· civilization?"

"Thou knowest well," said Rames, "that my days mean nothing to me now that the light of them is gone. I had determined that Ra should shine no more upon my living face, that when I went forth from thy presence, venerable father, I should go to meet Anubis, lord of the dead!"

The priest's voice was stern.

"An thou destroyest thy life, the thread may never more be united through all the ages to come, for Ra who gave it thee, has decreed that thou shalt not by violence take it! Remember, I have told thee that it is not by that path that thou shalt meet thy lost love!" His voice softened, the exalted light deepened in his eyes. "Take rather the course I offer thee, follow this great adventure and thou canst live through all posterity. Thou wilt come to understand the subtle force men call life which like an ever-renewed torch is handed on from father to son, making its existence possible to the latter because of its having been the heritage of the former. This life, then, that thou deemest worthless, wilt thou give it for Egypt's sake?"

"How can this thing be done that seems so beyond my human understanding?" asked Rames.

"Wilt thou nobly, fearlessly, with a clear mind, tread this long path and being sworn to observe all thou mayest see along the way, return again after one year with the burden of thy knowledge?"

Rames stared into the keen eyes so near his own. Was this thing possible that Hotep was urging upon him?

In the weird light of the nine lamps and the odor of the musty papyrus rolls, he felt his brain whirl with the wonder of it. But Hotep was the High Priest, the keeper of all wisdom. His mind was as the sun that penetrated the deepest shadows.

However this journey was to be made, he was ready to take it. One way of oblivion was as good as another—anything that would still the bitter anguish in his heart that cried for Teta.

"Knower-of-all-things," he said at last, "thy disciple is ready!"

"Patience, my son! There is much that must be prepared before thou goest into those distant to-morrows. When I send for thee, be thou ready!" and opening wide the bronze door, he bade the young man go forth.

At the first turning of the alabaster corridor, Rames paused and looked back.

Silhouetted against the weird light of the vast chamber, stood the tall figure of the High Priest, the wisdom of the buried ages piled about him.

CHAPTER V

THROUGH all the next day and the next, Rames waited for word from Hotep, but no sign came. He went up to the great Temple of Amen, but a stranger priest stood in the sanctuary, and at Karnak it was the same. Disconsolate, broken-hearted, he wandered through the temple gardens, by the little pool of Isis that held such sweet memories of his lost love. Here his longing for Teta became so great that he was tempted to break his promise to Hotep and end it all. But the thought, that perhaps the priest's plan would make it possible for him to find her, stayed his hand, and so at last he went back to his own house, resolving to leave it no more until summoned.

And then the message came.

He was sitting by the side of the pool in his garden long after the sunset hour and the perfume of the sleeping lotus flowers was heavy on the cooling air. As he leaned over the marble edge, his heart aching to see again reflected in the purple waters, the delicate oval of Teta's face, there came a step on the path, and startled, he leaped to his feet to find himself facing the High Priest.

"Art thou ready, my son?" asked Hotep quietly, as though there had not been those empty days since that hour in the temple. Rames drew the folds of his long cloak about his shoulders.

"Ready and anxious, oh my father," he said, "it has been bitter waiting!"

"Come then," he said, "ask no questions, but follow close!" and turning, he led the way out of the garden.

They hurried through the mazes of the city and crossed the river into the Libyan suburb. The priest walked with the firm, sure step of a man who, like the oak, grows stronger with the years and Rames, lithe and young though he was, found his pace no easy task to follow. But despite their rapid progress, it was nearing midnight when at last, the city far behind, they found themselves in a sort of sandy valley, with crumbling limestone cliffs on either side.

The moon, now sailing low, outlined the hills sharply and cast deep shadows where their edges showed rugged.

Presently the priest turned from the open rocky space and picked his way up the side of the cliff. Stumbling over the loose stones, sinking into the shifting sand, they climbed until they came at last to a deep fissure in the rock, that made an irregular black line down the face of the moonlit hillside.

Here Hotep paused.

"Mark well the path, my son," he said, "and mark, too, this spot, for thou wilt have need to come again this way when thy year's pilgrimage is ended."

Rames turned and looked back over the valley which lay gaunt and desolate under the pallid rays of the moon. In the distance, the towers and temples of Thebes, the city that was to endure through all the ages, lay calm and beautiful, its white palaces among the palm groves gleaming in the silver light and beyond, sweeping away in shimmering curves to the edge of the horizon, wound the Nile. No living thing was in sight, no sound broke the stillness save the long-drawn howl of a prowling jackal, and once a hyena laughed. In all that waste of black shadows, theirs were the only ones that stirred.

"I shall not forget the way," he said quietly.

"This too, mark well," said Hotep, and Rames bent close as the priest pointed out to him a crude mark on the rough surface of the rock, a circle and under it a cross.

"The *Anch*," he whispered as he recognized the symbol, "the sacred Key of Life!"

Hotep nodded and raising his staff pressed heavily just in the center where the cross and circle touched. Slowly the huge slab of stone that had seemed a part of the hillside, swung inward on a bronze pivot and before them lay a narrow opening blacker than the deepest shadows about them.

"Here lies our path," said the priest, "no man now living, save us two, knows the way. The slaves who built it, were led here blindfold and put to death when their work was finished so that the secret might be kept. Come!" He stepped into the darkness and Rames, with one last look at the stars, followed.

Just inside, Hotep paused to light a small agate lamp, and having instructed Rames in the method of opening the door which had swung to after them, proceeded down the long, narrow passage. No breath of air stirred in the hot, fetid atmosphere and the young man groped his way after the patter of the priest's feet which went along quickly as though the path were a familiar one. Presently the passage widened and ended abruptly in a wall.

Hotep lifted the lamp and carefully indicated a rough knob or inequality on the surface of the stone. Placing his hand on this, he pressed heavily. An irregular section, whose edges had seemed to be but the natural fissures in the rock, gave slowly, and taking Rames' arm, the priest guided him through the narrow opening.

"Wait here," he said. From an ivory box, he poured some fine dark powder into a tall metal brazier which stood in the center of the room. Holding his lamp to it, a faint, perfumed smoke arose, and a clear blue light penetrated all the corners of the chamber, which proved to be quite spacious and cut exactly four square.

The low roof was supported by four huge pillars of limestone, placed so as to form an inner square that enclosed about one-half the area of the room. Two of them were capped with heads of the god Min, the male principle, roughly hewn and crude of feature, their giant faces terrible to look upon where the weird light brought them into relief. The other two bore the serene cow heads of Hathor, the female principle, and in the center of the rocky ceiling, deeply carved and inlaid with gold, was the circle and cross of the Key of Life.

From one corner stared the lion face of the goddess Sekhmet, she who typified the fierceness of the sun's rays. In another, brooded the great hawk-winged Mentu, god of war; from a third, peered the jackal head of Anubis, leader of the dead, and in the last was the tall Ibis-headed Thoth, recorder of the deeds of men. On one wall glittered the disk and wings of Ra, and on another, the sacred eye of Horus. Against the walls, on tables of porphyry, stood painted coffers bound about with metal, ancient rolls of papyrus, and steles of alabaster covered with mystic inscriptions.

Hotep made a wide gesture with his staff.

"Behold," he said, his voice echoing against the rocky walls, "the cradle and treasure trove of Egypt's wisdom! Here are the All-seeing Eye, the Life Principle, the forces of Death and Destruction, the Knowledge that is eternal!

"Through thee, I hope to add the crowning gift to these priceless stores. If the gods so will it, thou shalt journey as far into the future as these things have come down through the past. But know, my son, with all my wisdom, I cannot assure thee that the experiment will not cost thee thy life, or compel thee to lie in a perpetual state of suspended animation, a living mummy, whose bonds no man may loose!"

"Lord of wisdom," said Rames, "I hear. Thou knowest that my life is naught to me, I have no fear, nor care. But if I awaken in that distant future of which thou speakest, I shall have no friends, no worldly goods with which to buy food and obtain shelter. What are thy instructions then?"

Hotep went to one of the painted coffers and raised the lid.

It was filled with golden coins of an ancient date.

He opened another and the light danced on the heaps of jewels it contained.

"These," he said, "shall fill thy need. The lack of material things must not hinder the success of the great experiment toward which the wisdom of ages has been tending!"

Rames gazed with wonder on the glittering treasure that would buy a kingdom.

"What if these people, among whom I may find myself, prove to be barbarians, who have overcome and vanquished the ancient civilization of Egypt? I shall not be one of them. May they not hold me as a slave, or perhaps take my life before my task is finished?"

"I have told thee, my son, that the way is beset with dangers which I can neither foresee nor prevent. The gods will have thee in their care, but thou wilt be mortal, even as thou art now! Thou wilt have one year in which to examine, to study, to absorb the knowledge of that period of the world's evolution in which thou shalt find thyself. Then if thy life is still thine, thou must return here to this secret place and take again the potion I shall give thee, which eons of time will not have destroyed. So wilt thou recross the mystic bridge that spans that far off Tomorrow with Today."

Rames stood erect, his chin set firmly.

"Thy messenger is ready," he said.

But the priest raised his hand.

"First, must thou swear by the gods thou holdest sacred, by the wings of Ra, and the eye of Horus, by the mummy of thy mother, and the soul of thy father, that nothing is to turn thee from thy task!

That thou wilt put aside all worldly things! That
whatever the riches and glamor which that new
world may hold, they will not attract thee save
only as a student to examine and to study. And
above all, there must be no woman!"

Rames laughed bitterly.

"Needst thou say that, oh my father, to me
whose heart is in the underworld with her it loves?"

The priest waved aside the interruption impatiently.

"There must be no woman!" he repeated. "Remember thou wilt be in the world, yet not of it.
If thou shouldst yield to the fascination of woman,
then would all our endeavors come to naught! Art
thou strong enough to swear the oaths I ask of
thee?"

And standing tall and straight between the gigantic images of his country's gods, beneath the shadow
of the wings of Amen, Rames swore.

"May the mummies of my ancestors be torn
apart by jackals, may mine own *Ka* seek in vain
for sustenance or peace, and may my heart be never
more reunited to her I love, if I fail thee, oh Hotep,
High Priest of Amen-Ra! I have sworn!"

For a long moment the two men stood looking
into each other's eyes. When at last the echo of
Rames' oath had died away, the priest lifted his
lamp and walked slowly toward the figure of Thoth,
whose long-billed Ibis head peered from its shadowy
corner. On a small stand nearby lay a scroll, an
ink horn and some reed pens.

"Here we shall record the day and hour," he
said as he unrolled the papyrus, "even as each step

in the pursuit of knowledge has been recorded," and he nodded toward the other documents and steles in their dim niches.

"Thy name and mine shall be written here before Thoth who chronicles all deeds both of gods and men!" and picking up one of the reed pens he proceeded to cover the creamy white surface of the papyrus with inscriptions. This done, he re-rolled it carefully and placed it on the little stand at the feet of the god. Then he drew from the folds of his robe a curious ring set with a marvelous gem whose like Rames had never seen before. It's color was a strange, vibrant gold; across the polished surface the light played in filmy, palpitating waves, half-imagined colors appeared in its depths, and flecks of fire as of smouldering embers. His shadow fell across it and a sheen of blue veiled the surface like a cloudless twilight sky.

The stone was encircled by a row of tiny figures of the gods whose hands held it in place as though it were a mighty globe. They were of a workmanship so cunningly perfect that in spite of their small size there was wrought in each the strain of every muscle, the graceful curve of every limb.

"Look into its depth, my son," said Hotep, "behold how radiance throbs from its heart like crystal water from a spring. Other gems but reflect light, this alone bears it in its bosom. Ra himself bestowed it upon that great Pharaoh who laid the foundation stones of mighty Kampt. It is the symbol of the Universe surrounded by the gods whose straining hands reach up to grasp and yet support it.

"I shall place it here where its glow shall remind thee of thy oath! Never let it be parted from thee!" and lifting Rames' right hand, he slipped the ring upon the little finger. Then holding the lamp before him, he turned to the grinning, jackal-headed figure of Anubis, leader of the dead.

Presently he called, "My son, come hither," and Rames following, found him before a curious recess in the breast of the image.

"Here," he said, "is stored that which shall make thy journey possible, if possible it be. Here again wilt thou find it when thy year shall be finished. In all the world there is no more than what thou seest. It is the quintessence of that great knowledge of which I told thee and I alone possess the formula!"

From the depths of the recess, came two points of light, one scintillating like the heart of a ruby, the other, white and glowing steadily with a strange intensity that seemed to grow as they gazed.

Hotep drew forth two small phials of rock crystal, hermetically sealed, whose contents sparkled dazzlingly in the lamp-light. His eyes shone with exultant pride as he looked at them lying in the hollow of his hand.

"Behold," he said, "the medium by which thou shalt cross the bridge of Time!" Obscuring the lamp, he held them in the shadow.

Rames gazed with awe at the tiny phials surrounded by a nimbus of their own light, one gleaming radiant and silver as an imprisoned moonbeam, the other, glowing and ardent as the clearest ruby, as though the precious stone itself had been melted and poured into it.

He set them carefully aside and lifted a slender jar of alabaster, carved and painted like the mummied figure of Osiris that was shown at feasts, to remind men how fleeting is life. As he turned back the lid, a strong pungent odor assailed the nostrils.

"Now doff thy robes," he said, "and anoint thy body with this oil!"

Rames let his cloak and linen robe slip from his shoulders and untied the girdle from about his waist. As the priest stood before the lithe figure outlined in the lamp light, his eyes widened.

"Beauty thou hast, too, my son," he said, "and with that also as a gift mayest thou conquer!" and pouring some of the oil from the alabaster jar into his hands, he proceeded to rub and knead the firm, beautifully moulded muscles that rippled under the satin skin.

Rames was conscious of a feeling of utter relaxation as though he possessed no bony structure whatever, only supple, smooth flesh. A delicious lightness filled his being He felt that he could have stepped over mountains and ridden upon the air.

The oil thoroughly rubbed in, his body left glowing and almost but not quite dry, the priest took up a golden goblet, cunningly wrought like the half-open bud of a lotus flower. He then proceeded to unseal the little phial of crystal liquid.

"This," he said, "I will pour into the goblet. Thou must drink instantly. The other I will place here to await thy coming! Now seat thyself."

Rames sank on the ebony couch the priest had designated. It was richly carved and inlaid with ivory, with a pillow of close woven cloth-of-gold, stuffed tightly with sweet smelling herbs.

"Take thou thy cup in thy left hand," said Hotep. "Now give me thy right. The gods of our fathers and the blessings of ten thousand ancestors speed thee on thy journey, oh son, beloved of my heart!" and lifting the phial, he poured the sparkling fluid' quickly into the golden goblet.

Instantly the heart of the lotus bud became a lambent flame, weird, pulsing, restless, as with life.

The young man's muscles tightened, his heart leaped wildly against the prison bars of his chest. He heard one word as though coming from a great distance.

"Drink!" and almost without volition, he raised the goblet to his lips and drained its contents.

Instantly a frightful, grinding agony convulsed him. Every atom of his being seemed torn asunder. Horrible, dreadful emotions clutched his soul, tortured his body, and peering at him, as though from the heart of a thick cloud which blotted out all else, he saw the face of the High Priest watching him.

Then this, too, disappeared. He reeled and seemed to whirl in a wild vortex, a mighty circle, as though a giant arm swung him round and round in loops thousands of miles in diameter. There was a last terrific sweep, the grip that held him was loosed, and he was sent whirling, hurtling, spinning into space!

      *   *   *   *   *   *

As from a great height, he seemed to see his body

lying upon the couch in the secret chamber, with the figure of the priest bending over it.

The soul, or whatever he now was, that had inhabited that still form, poised above it motionless, without thought or will.

Gradually, the chamber with its impassive figures of the gods, Hotep, the High Priest, bending over the body on the couch and even that body, the beautiful lines of its slim suppleness, pitifully inert, faded slowly away.

He seemed to be falling, falling into a bottomless abyss, dark, meaningless at first, then lit by dazzling vistas of light through which gleamed curious scenes, vast stretches of forest and plain, glittering palaces, multitudes of strange peoples. Once he caught a glimpse of a cross raised on a barren hillside, on which hung a pathetic figure, which seemed mocked at and despised. Again, he whirled past a great city over which that same cross was raised on its most splendid buildings and throngs were worshipping before it. Mighty armies flashed across his dizzy path, triumphant, glorious. Nations seemed to grow, develop, alter, melt and pass away into oblivion! Strange forms rose up along the way, and dropped behind, unfamiliar sounds beat upon his straining senses, and through it all, sweetly smiling as he had seen it last, the elusive, haunting face of Teta beckoned across a measureless gulf. Then darkness, black, impenetrable, void of thought or emotion, wrapped him close and he knew no more!

CHAPTER VI

IN the silence of the rock-hewn chamber, shut away beneath the Theban hills, reigned a darkness so dense that it seemed to have weight, substance, tangibility. All things were enveloped in its velvet, suffocating folds, lost in its mist, obliterated.

But if eyes could have penetrated the blackness, they would have seen the nude form of a man lying stretched on an ebony couch, still, motionless, not with the languor of sleep nor the rigidity of death, but of something even more intensely still. It was as though all the vital forces had been arrested by some mighty enchantment which had been pronounced above the sleeping body and the drawn breath were waiting to be expelled.

The head lay slightly raised against the cloth-of-gold cushion, the palms against the graceful thighs. The finely formed chest was rounded and full, the flat lean stomach, deflated, the narrow feet lay straight and close-set.

About him nothing stirred, no insect, no smallest living thing. If it had been possible to see within the chamber, it would have been observed to be wholly free from dust, curiously dry, yet not with the emptiness of death. A strange sense of vitality would have been felt, much as one is conscious of life in the kernel of wheat, which can slumber for centuries and yet awaken green and fertile.

Time was not in the blackness of the secret chamber, neither yesterday, today, nor tomorrow, but in the outside world came the morning of the second of February, nineteen hundred and fourteen.

And if eyes could have watched beside the ebony couch with its golden pillow, its carved and inlaid tracery, they would have observed a faint, almost imperceptible tremor pass over the silent form lying there. An undulation as delicate, as one that ruffles the bosom of a little pool when the gentlest of zephyrs breathes upon it.

After a moment, came a more apparent trembling and then a long shudder that rippled the muscles under the smooth skin. The lips parted and a long-drawn sigh issued from between them. The rigidity left the limbs, although they still remained motionless. It was as though the Angel of Life were breathing into a human form and bidding it awake.

Slowly the eyes opened, covered with a mist that gradually cleared before the light of dawning intelligence. Painfully, stiffly, the man rose to a sitting position, panting in the suffocating darkness that beat against his straining eyeballs.

"Hotep!" he whispered hoarsely, "Hotep!" but the echo of his voice was all that broke the silence.

With a groan, he stumbled to his feet and groped his way through the impenetrable blackness to where the priest had hung the lamp. His fluttering hands found it at last with the two fire sticks lying near and presently a soft, yellow flame dispelled the darkness. The huge stone gods stared impassively above his head as they had done upon his entrance. The gilded wings of Ra glittered in the flickering lamp light. Everything seemed exactly as it had been when he had sunk into oblivion.

He seated himself on the couch, his clearing mind going over the events of yesterday. The priest's wild story of a visit into unborn centuries! The strange potion he had swallowed! The frightful convulsions that had seemed to rend his very soul!

He stretched his arms and body. The muscles were stiff, their usual suppleness was absent, but otherwise he felt no pain, no sense of illness. He smiled. Hotep, the High Priest, had but dreamed dreams as do so many, who delve into the hidden mysteries. The fiery potion had failed in what it had been meant to do, but his strength and natural vigor had survived its deadliness.

What keen disappointment this would bring to Hotep who had given his life to the study and development of that which had but ended in failure.

He let his eyes wander about the chamber. On the little stand before the statue of Thoth lay the roll of papyrus on which the priest had made the record of their experiment. He rose and carrying the lamp, examined it by its yellow flame.

The smooth surface seemed somehow to have altered. The creamy white that had contrasted so sharply with the deep black of the written characters, now looked dingy and gray. He held it nearer his eyes to scan it more closely and as he did so, it broke beneath his touch, bits of it falling to the ground in tiny flakes.

In astonishment, he laid the remains of it on the little stand. Papyrus rolls were carefully prepared. He had never known one to break. He wondered what change had occurred in so brief a time, as to render this one so fragile and brittle to the touch.

Perhaps there had been a destroying substance in the draught he had taken, an effervescing quality that had dissipated fumes, injurious to such substances. He had heard Hotep himself tell of strange changes that could be wrought in material things by the releasing of noxious gases.

Even now there seemed to hang on the still air, the faint, elusive odor of the elixir he had drunk.

He was suddenly conscious of a feeling of suffocation. His tongue was dry, his eyeballs ached. His parched throat and panting lungs longed for air.

His cloak and linen robes lay in a heap on the floor where he had let them fall when the priest had anointed his body. He gathered them hastily and threw them about his shoulders, when lo, long rents gaped in them and as he tried to adjust them, his garments fell in dust about his feet.

A strange sense, almost of fear, came over him. Stumbling, choking, he ran to the side of the room where hung the great stone door and threw his weight against it as Hotep had taught him. As it slowly swung on its massive pivot, his composure returned and, ashamed of his momentary terror, he picked up the lamp and stepped out into the blackness of the long passage, carefully swinging shut the great door after him.

But here the desire for freedom, for sunshine and all the familiar things of life, returned. He almost ran along the narrow way. Its heavy, fetid air was even more suffocating than yesterday. His lungs seemed bursting, his heart pounded against his ribs as he flung himself against the great slab of stone at the end of the corridor.

But here, cutting sharply across the longing for the light of day, came the memory of Teta. Teta whom he would never see again. Of what use were the sunshine, the flowers, the beautiful gardens of Kampt, without her, their fairest blossom?

He sank on his knees in despair. Even the oblivion he had hoped for in the mystic elixir was denied him. But he realized that he must find Hotep and tell him of the failure of the experiment. After that, he would be free to seek peace in the underworld.

He rose and pressing against the carving in the stone, the great door gave slowly.

A dazzling light blinded his eyes, a hot breath of air smote him in the face. For a moment, his pupils, dilated by the darkness of the hidden chamber, were blinded by the brilliant sunshine, but when gradually, sight came back to him, his heart ceased beating, his breath stopped in his throat.

For Thebes, the glorious, the beautiful, had disappeared, and instead of the mighty pylons of its temples, the glittering terraces of its palaces, he beheld in the distance a few ragged, broken stones that stared desolately at the silent Nile, a few strange buildings of a form never dreamed of nor seen by mortal eyes before.

CHAPTER VII

HE stared at the river winding peacefully away
in the distance. Surely that had not been
its course yesterday. And this great ocean
of sand that spread above what or was Thebes,
how desolate and barren it looked, how pitiless. His
eyes widened unbelievingly. This must all be a
dream, a delirium brought about by the powerful
draught he had swallowed. He would awaken
presently and see again Thebes as she was in all
her glory, instead of the few ragged teeth of stone
where had been her splendor.

On the other side of the Nile, he could see glim-
mering among the palm trees, the wide façade of
a great building, the very form of which was unlike anything he had ever seen before, and here and
there along the banks rose tall slender towers tapering upward into the clear sunlight with smoke pouring from their summits. What new temples were
these, he wondered? And where were the painted
galleys, the scarlet sails that had rocked beside the
city's quays? The small dingy craft, that drifted
by, did not belong here, and that monstrous flat-
roofed white box pierced by many windows which lay
moored beside the wharf, could it be a ship? There
was no sign of sails nor oars, no long painted
rudder, not even a mast, nothing except a huge
wheel fastened to the end. Surely he must soon
awaken from this dream or else go mad!

The sun was blistering and he crouched in the shadow of the rocks, from where he could look out over the plain that had once been Thebes.

Slowly, as he gazed, it was borne in upon him that this was no dream, no fevered picture of delirium, but reality. The figures he could see moving about in the distance, were real people, the slender towers, from whose summits gushed black clouds of smoke, were actual buildings, not the fancies of a disordered mind. The desolation about him was the ruins of Thebes that lay buried beneath this cruel yellow sand!

With a breathless pang he realized that the High Priest's experiment had succeeded. Some mighty change had taken place since yesterday, some terrific upheaval of gods and men had visited Egypt, the mighty. In human consciousness, how long a period of time had elapsed, he wondered, since he had swallowed the magic fluid? Was it a year, was it twenty years, or was it twenty centuries?

His heart sank. He felt horribly, frightfully alone. The people who had built those strange temples, would they prove friends or foes?

He looked down at his naked limbs glistening in the sunlight, and smiled ruefully. Save for the ring that Hotep had given him, he had come into the world as a babe, naked, portionless, possessing only one thing, knowledge.

The sun's heat was pitiless, it beat upon his unprotected skin like a searing flame. The first problem was to procure clothing to cover his nakedness. In the distance the river wound cool and inviting. If he could make his way there unobserved he would not only refresh himself, but offer the excuse that his clothes had been stolen while bathing, perhaps some one would supply him with others.

Cautiously, he made his way across the barren waste. A train of laden camels passed him, their bells ringing musically, their great padded feet noiseless in the soft sand. The men accompanying them were so wrapped in great white cloaks he could not see their faces. He hid behind a friendly rock until they had passed and then plodded on, the hot sand burning and blistering his feet.

Toward the noon hour he came to the narrow strip of rich green that lay near the river. Here had stretched the magnificent avenue leading to the Pharaoh's palace and now as he hurried along under the sweltering, burning sun, his wondering eyes saw nothing save deep ruts cut in the grass by heavy carts and two huge broken figures which had once been the statues of Amenophis the mighty, staring desolately on the emptiness that had been the splendor of his kingdom.

At last he came to the river bank and although the water was muddy and uninviting, he slaked his thirst and plunged in gratefully. A group of children were splashing about in the shallow ripples. Dirty, unkempt little urchins in long, tight blue robes, the lids of their dark eyes and their shaven heads covered with flies whose presence did not seem to disturb them in the least.

They stared as Rames waded ashore and beckoned them to come near.

"My garments have been stolen," he cried, "can

you get me others, so that I may enter yonder town?"

But his words were either unintelligible or unheeded, for the children huddled together and continued staring.

He came closer and tried with motions to explain his plight. Suddenly the oldest of the children turned and ran up the bank, followed by the smaller ones who screamed words he could not understand.

He swam back into the cool water, grateful for its refreshing touch. Presently he observed a group of men coming toward him, and he splashed back to the shore.

They were tall and brown and unlike the men of Thebes, but in a curious, yet definite way, resembled them. One or two were naked as himself, excepting for the narrow breech cloth, familiar to him as the garment of the peasants of Thebes. The others wore long, loose, white linen robes, their heads wound in a strip of the same material.

He repeated his request for clothing, but they looked at one another in perplexity, and from their actions he judged they thought him a little mad. Finally, an old man with a long gray beard, stepped forward and addressed him in a curious jargon that he could not understand.

Here was a contingency that had not been thought of. Even the language of mighty Kampt had passed away. He was indeed like a new-born infant, and must be taught to speak. This knowledge accentuated the feeling of utter loneliness that oppressed him, the sense of isolation. Hotep's words rang again in his ears.

"Remember, thou wilt be in the world, but not of it." Verily, he was indeed a thing apart.

He sank down on the river bank, his head in his hands, and when he looked up again the men had disappeared. His plan had failed, he must think of some other way to obtain covering for his nakedness.

At last, late in the afternoon, he saw the ancient gray beard coming toward. him alone and he rose quickly to meet him. The man stopped and raised his staff threateningly, but Rames assuring him by signs of his friendliness, he finally drew near.

After a great effort and many gestures, the young man managed to explain his needs and shaking his head vigorously, the ancient one slipped out of the dirty white cloak he wore and wrapped it about the stranger's shoulders, leaving his own shrunken frame dressed in a tight blue robe almost like the one the children had worn.

Rames thanked him gratefully and, in response to his gestures, followed him to a small boat which quickly bore them across the river. As he stepped ashore, the old man immediately turned his small craft about and put off again. The look of satisfaction in the wrinkled face that so simple a ruse could take a mad man from their midst, amused Rames, and smiling, he started into the town which lay before him.

An almost overpowering sense of being in a dream possessed him. Yesterday his feet had trod the streets of a city that was the mistress of the world, a city whose glories were unsurpassed. But it had vanished, and in its place was a dirty, evil-smelling town. Its narrow streets were filled with unfamiliar white-robed figures, Nubian women with clanking bracelets and straight blue robes, ragged boys running after small gray donkeys, men about whose arms were strung ropes of colored beads which they were offering for sale.

Everywhere he heard shouting, calling, chattering, and not a syllable which he could understand.

With great difficulty he made his way to the place where had stood his house. But no vestige of it remained. In its stead was a row of filthy hovels filled with dirty children and staring women. Sick and disgusted, he turned to seek the house of the Acacia, under whose window he had bade that last farewell to Teta. Here, too, all was changed, no slightest trace of its charming elegance was left, and, grief tearing at his heart, he turned his face toward the great temple of Amen-Ra. Could this, too, have passed away?

As he wandered out along what had been the magnificent avenue, the devastation that met his gaze awed him. Gone were the stately villas which had gleamed from between the palm groves, broken and defaced were the few remaining Ram-headed sphinxes which had bordered it, and as he came in sight of the temple itself, the awfulness of its ruin filled him with an emotion beyond expression. He needed all the courage he could command to bear up under the crushing knowledge that the sleep or oblivion, into which the High Priest's draught had sent him, must have lasted centuries, for only centuries could bring so mighty an edifice to such complete destruction.

Where were the gods since their temples had fallen into decay? To whom could he cry his need, his anguish, if Ra himself no longer sat upon his throne? He shook with the terror of his thoughts as with an ague; this was indeed a stupendous task Hotep had imposed upon him.

He was roused from the profound revery into which these thoughts had plunged him, by an experience so strange that it turned his thoughts in an entirely new direction. Coming toward him, were a number of people, two small, white clad boys running ahead and a dignified elderly man seated astride a gray mule, following. The man wore a loose black robe and tight cap on his head and kept turning his dark face toward the other members of the party as they rode along.

These last were so fantastic, so different from anything Rames had ever seen, that he stopped and stared open-eyed and mouthed as they passed.

In a small, four wheeled carriage drawn by a lean little horse, sat two women. The younger one had a wonderful white skin, her hair, where it could be seen under the broad head-dress, a head-dress decked with flowers and floating ribbons, shone a glittering golden. Her hands were covered with white cases which followed the outlines of each finger. On her feet were curious sandals which hid them entirely. Her dress, also of white, tightly enclosed her figure at the waist, from where it hung loosely about her. The other woman at her side was much older and rather fat. She, too, wore a great head-dress with a floating veil and carried a shade for the sun not unlike the one that sheltered Teta's ox cart.

The appearance and costume of these women was passing strange, but more amazing still was the man, who, mounted on a small donkey, rode beside them.

On his head, he wore a helmet, though quite unlike those of the Pharaoh's warriors. It was mound shaped, rising in several tiers, and was the color of the desert sands. About it, was wound a green veil, the ends of which fell between his shoulders. Beneath this curious head dress, his face shone a brilliant red. His limbs were encased in dark cloth tubes, his feet covered with ugly brown sandals which laced above his ankles, closely encircling his thin neck was a band of some glossy white material and on his nose were perched two queer round bits of glass through which he gazed at the landscape. But most wonderful of all, at intervals he blew puffs of smoke from his lips and nostrils which he drew from a small white tube at whose end smouldered a spark of fire.

The little cavalcade passed and left the wondering derelict of a forgotten age staring after it.

What manner of people were these whose men could encase their bodies in such garments and yet withstand the fierce heat of the sun? Was there some magic in the smoke they caused to gush from their mouths and nostrils which defied Sekhmet's fierce rays? He tried to imagine Teta dressed as this girl, her slim loveliness covered by ugly, enveloping folds, her beautiful hands enclosed in cases, her slender, delicate feet bound in queerly shaped sandals and above all, the bronze glory of her hair, hidden by an ugly head-dress nodding with the fruits and flowers of the fields.

He turned and made his way back to the town, and

when he again threaded his way through the narrow streets, a young crescent moon had risen in the purple sky and along the quay the river washed in silver ripples. Presently he came in sight of the great building that he had observed from a distance when first his eyes had looked on the new world.

Its broad front was checkered with many windows and doors from which dazzling light poured forth in golden streams.

As he turned into the avenue that led to its entrance, other lights suddenly flashed among the trees as though by magic, for no one was near. He looked to see the torches or the swinging lanterns that he knew so well, but they were nowhere visible. Near him stood a tall bronze staff from which hung a cluster of transparent balls that suddenly burst into brilliance as he watched and when he looked closer he saw no flame, only a tiny glowing thread of quivering fire in their center. Here indeed was magic of which even Hotep had never dreamed!

Behind the radiant squares in the face of this great temple, (for temple it must be, not even a Pharaoh could have so splendid a palace), figures moved to and fro. As he watched, the stillness was cut by a medley of sound that thrilled him with awe, wonder and amazement.

A soft blending of harmonies, the sweetest, most alluring, he had ever heard. His senses reeled with delight. Silver tones hung sustained on the listening air; intervals of swelling cadence, vibrant with passion, ripples of melody that fell like cascading waters and died away in an enchanting whisper!

As he listened, scarcely breathing, there floated out

into the night, a voice, a woman's voice, singing as Rames had never dreamed a human voice could sing.

How long he stood in the shadow of the tamarisk trees he did not know, but at last the moving forms against the squares of light drifted away, the music came no more, and one by one the magic lights sank back into darkness.

With a sigh, he turned and wandered out through the garden and along the silent river, his soul still thrilling to the golden notes he had heard. The wonder of music had waked in his heart new emotions that in his other life he had never known.

When at last he came to what had been the Temple of Ra, he crouched among the broken pillars, which in their splendor had but yesterday witnessed the mighty pageant of the Pharoah.

Musing on the fleeting glory of man and his works, weary and faint with hunger, the scion of a hundred kings wrapped his tattered cloak about him and sank into an uneasy slumber amid the ruins of the temple of his gods.

CHAPTER VIII

THE early morning shone on the heap of rags beneath which Rames lay. He lifted his heavy lids and stared about him stupidly. When at last full consciousness returned, he rose to a sitting position and drew his tattered cloak about him, shivering, despite the warmth that was already in the air.

Hunger gnawed at his vitals, and the filthy garment about his shoulders filled him with a sense of loathing. He remembered what little notice he had attracted in his walks about the town the day before, and most of that had been disgust for his rags, disdain for his apparent poverty. How little the world had changed. Today, as in that far-off age that was his own, man's status among his fellows was determined by worldly possessions.

Food and clothing he must have without delay, but how?

Across his mind flashed a picture of faint lamplight on glittering heaps of gems and gold in painted coffers. Here was the source which would supply him in abundance. Hotep had builded wisely against the day when he could send forth a messenger into unborn ages.

The sun was already high in the heavens as he crossed the sandy waste that had been Thebes and made his way back to the hill in whose breast lay the secret chamber.

Once he passed a group of men, ragged and unkempt like himself. They paid no heed to him. To them he was merely a beggar seeking some shade where he might sleep through the heat of the day.

When he reached the entrance, he paused and looked about carefully to be sure that he was unobserved, then plunged once more into the blackness of the hidden passage-way. He had left the lamp just inside and lighting it, made his way along the narrow tunnel.

Inside the rock hewn chamber, the lamp-light struggled pitifully with the darkness. It touched the weird features of its grim guardians, making their eyes seem to live.

Were they not mocking him for daring to match their own immortality?

For how many centuries had they looked down on his inert form?

What dreadful vengeance had they planned during that long vigil to punish his presumption?

A cold fear touched his heart. Dared he lay hands on the treasure they guarded?

With a shudder, he approached the painted coffers which rested on stands of porphyry and onyx. He went from one to another and as he gazed on their contents, his fears vanished and he was filled with wonder and amazement.

There were chests of sycamore bound with copper bands, filled with golden coins of an ancient date; alabaster jars, heaped with dazzling emeralds fashioned into scarabs and amulets; golden vessels of incomparable beauty, laden with pearls whose delicate sheen was like sunlight on the falling spray of a fountain, and cups of ivory, carved, and inlaid with dull gold, piled with rubies, glowing, scintillating, melting into masses of vibrant flame as the lamp light fell upon them.

Here indeed was a treasure that would satisfy the desires of a Pharaoh!

Rames tore a strip from his ragged garment and filled it with gems; rubies, emeralds, pearls. In all, many times a king's ransom, and still the treasure from which he had taken them, seemed almost untouched.

He selected an emerald, one of the smaller stones, but of a beautiful deep color. This, with ten of the gold coins, he laid aside. Then rolling the others carefully in the long strip of linen, he fastened the improvised treasure-belt securely about his naked body.

This done, he stood a moment thinking. Hotep had given him a task more difficult than he had dreamed. A year utterly alone in a world in which he would have no fellow! Had he the courage, the strength to go on?

Slowly he walked to the statue of Anubis grinning in the shadow and from the recess in its breast, took the crystal phial in which flashes of ruby flame burned and glowed.

He weighed it in the palm of his hand. Here was the key that would unlock the door leading back into that other age, that other life wherein he had a place.

Outside, beyond these walls, was a world of wonder. Yet a world that for him was filled with mystery, inhabited by a people of whom he knew nothing, whose tongue and manners were strange to him. A world in which he must always be a creature different and apart. But he could not break the oath he had uttered here in the presence of his gods, mighty, even though their temples had fallen in ruins, their priests and worshipers scattered as the desert sands.

Resolutely, he replaced the tiny phial in the recess and with a last look into the shadows about him, retraced his steps. Just inside the great stone slab that guarded the entrance to the passage, he carefully extinguished the lamp and placed it where it could readily be found.

Once more in the sunlight, he paused for a moment. What was to be his next step in this wonderful adventure?

During his exploration of the town the day before, he had observed shops displaying food and articles of wearing apparel. He would appease his hunger, doff these filthy rags and clothe himself as were these other people.

As quickly as possible, he made his way to the market-place and entered the most pretentious shop.

A tall lean merchant with a white beard and crafty eyes, came forward smiling and rubbing his hands as the shop-keepers of Thebes had done even in the days of its splendor.

Rames tried to make his wants known, but the man shook his head blankly and answered in a jargon which he could not understand. But gold speaks a universal language and without further delay the young man displayed two of the coins he had brought with him.

The merchant's shrewd eyes widened. A look of avarice, of cunning curiosity, swept over his wrinkled face as he bent over the coins and carefully examined them.

His words were unintelligible to Rames, but his expression and the vehement gestures that accompanied them, said plainly:—

"Where did you get these?" For the practiced eye of the old dealer had recognized the great value of the ancient pieces of gold.

Rames smiled and shook his head. Their source must be as profound a secret as his own origin. But food and clothing he must have, so he indicated by signs that if the exchange were not agreeable, he would go elsewhere to make his purchases. This the shop-keeper was not willing to allow.

"Tell me, illustrious stranger," he said, his eyes on the filthy rags that hung from the other's shoulders, "only tell me how you came by these and then we can conclude our bargain!"

The insinuating craft in his eyes made his meaning clear to Rames, who with a shrug turned to go. But the dealer laid his lean, claw-like hand on his arm and signed his readiness to sell him all the shop contained if such were his will.

With the aid of many more expressive gestures, he managed to convey the amount of clothing and the number of queer-looking white metal coins he was willing to give in exchange for the two pieces of gold.

The garments included a long flowing blue cloth robe richly embroidered in its own color, a handsome underdress of silk striped in red and yellow, and a round cap of red cloth with a gay scarf to twist about it. There was also a silk girdle and a pair of red leather slippers.

All these things carefully wrapped and secure under his arm, the white metal pieces clasped in his hand, Rames handed the eager merchant the two gold pieces and made his way to a lonely spot on the river bank.

Here, free from prying eyes, he bathed, and having fastened the strip of linen containing the gems, more securely about his body, carefully dressed himself in his new garments, adjusting them according to the merchant's directions.

This done, he stooped above the water and gazed long and curiously at his image.

The striped scarf which he had twisted about his cap set off the clear olive of his skin. The heavy folds of the rich blue robe hung gracefully from his fine shoulders and the long slim lines of his figure showed to beautiful advantage under the clinging folds of the tight underdress.

The smooth, lean lines of his face, sharpened by hunger and the ordeal through which he had passed, the inscrutable depths of his velvet-black eyes, the firm set of his mouth that told of a bitter sorrow, an unquenchable longing, made him look like a bronze figure, a symbol of the desert itself.

He rose to his feet satisfied with his scrutiny and with the confidence proper apparel always brings, made his way back to the town and into the market-place.

At one corner was a small shop where trays of fruit and vegetables were displayed. There were figs and dates and baskets of some large gold colored fruit which he did not know. Inside, a huge Nubian, in a dingy white garment, his black face shining with perspiration, was pouring some steaming dark fluid from a curious spouted vessel into tiny cups set before a number of men seated about the room.

The place was dirty and uninviting but the smell of cooking food accentuated the cravings of hunger and entering the shop, Rames tried to make his wants known, but the black only shook his head and grinned. Whereupon, the starving man displayed a handful of the little coins the merchant had given him and pointed expressively from the food to his mouth. The man nodded vigorously and hurried away.

Rames' strange language and the gestures by which he had conveyed his meaning, attracted the attention of the men sitting about the room. They stared curiously and evidently discussed him among themselves.

Presently the Nubian returned with food and the spouted pot, out of which he poured some of the steaming black liquid. It was acrid and bitter and Rames pushed the cup aside, but there were dates and bread not unlike that which he had known. There was also a kind of stew which to his starved palate was excellent.

He dipped into the dish with his fingers in imitation of those about him and ate ravenously. When he had finished, the Nubian brought him some of the unknown golden fruit. Its juicy pulp proved delicious and slaked his thirst.

At last he pushed his stool back with a sigh of satisfaction and allowing the black to take what pay he would from the handful of coins he held out to him, went again into the sunlight of the crowded little street.

In the windows of many of the small shops were hung strange pictures of the temple ruins, some in colors, others in black and white. He paused before them in wonder. What marvelous artists these people were to so exactly reproduce what the eye beheld.

A number of times some of the better dressed men in the street spoke to him, but he only smiled and, shaking his head, passed on.

At last in his rambles, he found himself once more before the great edifice from which had issued, the night before, that divine music. Could he venture to enter here, he wondered? What was the custom, the manner of worship that prevailed. To what god was it dedicated?

As he stood gazing at it, a group of people, evidently of the same strange caste as the three he had seen yesterday, came down the steps and stared at him as they passed.

One of the women stopped and said something to a fat elderly man with tufts of white hair on the sides of his very red face. He turned and addressed Rames. The words, he could not understand, but the tone was one that he himself would have used to 'Amrou, had his slave suddenly appeared.

He shook his head and turned away.

These people then, with their white skin, their curious clothes, were the kings, the rulers. The others, dressed as he, were inferiors, perhaps their slaves for all he knew.

Plainly, these people who wore such strange headdresses, who hid their feet with such curious sandals, were of a vastly superior caste.

There were groups of them all about; on the terraces of the great building; strolling through the gardens; starting out on the backs of tiny gray donkeys led by small black boys in white slips and caps.

Perhaps they were priests and priestesses of the new cult that had made Egypt forget her ancient gods.

Their arrogant manners plainly proclaimed them the over-lords. But how inferior most of them were physically, with their covered bodies, their red faces, their lean young women, their fat old ones, to the stately dignity of his own people.

Filled with wonder and interest in all about him, he wandered along scarcely knowing where his footsteps led, when suddenly his musings were interrupted by coming into violent contact with a man who had just stepped from the shadow of a doorway.

He was young and dark-skinned, although his clothes, except for a red cap similar to his own, which he wore rather jauntily on the side of his head, were the same as those of the people of that higher caste.

He smiled pleasantly, showing a row of very white, even teeth and said something which was quite unintelligible. But seeing the other's blank look, he repeated what was evidently the same thing in another tongue.

To Rames' ears the two languages spoke their difference without their meaning and he shrugged helplessly as he shook his head.

The young man looked at him curiously. His interest was aroused in this stranger who wore the clothes which he knew to be those of a Bedouin chief and yet could not understand either Arabic or English.

"You do not speak our language and yet you wear our dress. What are you?" he asked, punctuating his words with smiling gestures so as to make their meaning clear.

And Rames, although the expressive face, the animated hands had made themselves understood, shook his head and, imitating the other's manner asked the same question.

"Thou—who art thou?"

The youth puckered his brows in bewilderment.

"I, who know all the languages of all the tourists, cannot understand yours," he said, and then he tapped himself on his narrow chest. "Egyptian? *musree— Badawiy—Kempf?*" At the sound of the last word, a light came into Rames' eyes. There was a vague familiarity in the tone, a something that, though changed by usage and many ages, still held the sound of his own tongue.

This man, then, who stood before him, was a descendant of the people who had walked these very streets as Rames knew them.

He looked at the thin shoulders, the insignificant form, the weak chin, the simpering little smile, the subservient manner. He spoke many languages, therefore he was learned, perhaps a scribe.

How different was this small, narrow-shouldered smiling man in his queer dark clothes and red cap, to those ancestors of his with their tall, finely formed, straight bodies, their brooding, inscrutable eyes, their cleanly cut aquiline features.

But the smile on the young Egyptian's face was so

friendly, he seemed so anxious to please, that Rames
felt here might be a means of learning something of
these strange people and their customs.

As they stood facing one another in the narrow,
sunny street a party of the people from the great
edifice on the river bank rode by on little donkeys,
laughing and talking. Rames watched them pass
then turning to his new-found friend, asked by signs:
"Who are these?"

The man came close and repeated a word slowly
several times as one does when trying to impress
something on the mind of a child, the sharp sibilant
sound of the "s" striking unpleasantly on the ear.

"English!"

Rames followed the disappearing group with his
eyes, repeating the word, "English," half aloud, then
turned and swept his arm in a wide, comprehensive
gesture toward the town.

"What do men call this?" he asked.

Studying him incredulously, the little man answered his question and added his willingness to go
with the inexperienced stranger and be his guide.

"I am free, illustrious one," he said in Arabic.
"May I not accompany you about the streets of Luxor
and show you the places and things of interest?" and,
his meaning becoming clear to Rames, it was decided
that they continue their walk together.

They strolled through the town and over the
ruined temples until late in the afternoon, the young
Egyptian repeating carefully in English and Arabic
the name of each object that his companion pointed
out. Rames' mind was so alert and eager to drink in
the knowledge that would leave him less lonely, that

he was soon able to understand and· repeat many words in the language of his guide.

This meeting had been fortunate. It would assist him in acquiring the wisdom of which he had come in search. He must keep this mentor by his side.

Pausing in the shadow of one of the ruined columns in the great temple at Luxor, Rames, after a great effort, managed to convey to the young Egyptian his desire for his services and his willingness to reward him for them.

The little man smiled rather dubiously. Had this mysterious stranger the means with which to pay, he wondered, and Rames, remembering the look of greed and evident surprise that the clothes merchant had displayed over his golden coins, slipped his hand into a fold of his robe and brought out one of the eight that still remained.

"This shall be thine," he said, "if thou wilt be my guide and teacher!"

The young Egyptian looked at the coin closely.

"Illustrious one," he said in astonishment, "where have you come upon this? What tomb has opened up its treasures for you? What mummy have you found and robbed?"

But the words meant nothing to Rames. His eyes on the eager face, he waited for his answer.

After some difficulty, it was arranged that for the possession of the coin, the young Egyptian was to give the stranger his exclusive time between the rising of the young moon, through its full and decline and ending with its wane—a month, as he explained carefully and painstakingly to his ambitious pupil.

"My name," he said, resorting again to the familiar gesture of tapping his narrow chest, "my name is Abdullah, and yours, illustrious stranger?"

"Rames," was the answer and so the compact was made.

In Abdullah's oriental mind cupidity and curiosity were roused. Who was this man who could give away ancient gold pieces for which the English would pay a sum equal to many times their weight, who spoke a language he had never heard, and who knew no more about the world than the babe unborn? However, it was more than the glitter of the rare coin that made him decide to cling to Rames. Back in his mind was forming a plan to discover if possible the source of his wealth, the secret of his origin.

That night Abdullah conducted him to one of the native caravansaries. As they crossed the noisy courtyard filled with Arabs, camels, donkeys and piles of rubbish, Rames managed to make his guide understand that he wanted a place to himself for the night, a room which he could lock and bar, and Abdullah, only too willing to keep his find for himself, promised that he should have his wish.

Once safely away from prying eyes, Rames bade his teacher be seated on the rough mat at the foot of the pallet where he was to sleep and patiently they went over the words learned during the day helping each other to understand by means of pantomime.

"Tell me what temple is that great one by the river?" he asked. "The temple where the English worship?"

And when Abdullah understood, he answered, smiling,

"No temple, only a caravansary such as this!"
Rames looked out into the crowded courtyard.

"Why go we not there?" he asked.

Abdullah laughed.

"People of our class are not received as guests within those hospitable walls," he sneered, "that is meant for the English lords, not Arabs."

The sneer conveyed its meaning and Rames drew himself up proudly at the insult in the other's words.

"My place is with the best!" he said with dignity.

And Abdullah, looking into the deep eyes, saw the spirit of a caste that was above even those who called themselves the highest.

"One has need, my lord," he said, "of clothes such as the English wear, even as those upon my humble limbs, before one can be a guest in an English caravansary. If the illustrious stranger has more coins such as this, I will sell them for him and they will prove the means to open many doors."

His gestures and the gold he held in the palm of his hand, explained his meaning.

Rames thought quickly. His remaining seven coins must be carefully guarded.

"I have no more," he said, "but I have this," and he held up to the light that was burning in a small lantern hung against the rough wall, the emerald he had laid aside from the treasure store.

Abdullah gasped.

"Allah," he cried, "the Sheik is indeed rich! I will sell this for him and we can buy many wonderful things!"

Rames nodded.

"When the sun rises again, come thou for me here. We will go forth and find a purchaser!"

And suavely, although Abdullah would rather have stayed and questioned the source of the stranger's riches, Rames bowed him from the door, which he then securely locked and barred and throwing himself on his narrow pallet, fell into a sound, dreamless sleep.

Abdullah knocked at his door early, and together they picked their way carefully through the groups of huddled natives who squatted about the courtyard which looked dirtier than ever in the hot morning sunlight.

The dealer, to whom Abdullah had been the night before, promising a rare gem, looked at the emerald Rames laid before him, with little squinting eyes that were half hidden under shaggy brows.

"Not very much," he shrugged, pursing his thick lips, "I have a hundred such."

Rames picked up the stone and turned away.

"Wait!" called the merchant, "I can give something for it, because of my brother who is your friend," and he began counting piastres onto the worm-eaten counter.

"Hah, son of a thief," shrieked Abdullah in Arabic, "dost think my illustrious lord will sell his precious emerald for so filthy a sum as that? Never!" and seizing Rames by the arm, he started to leave.

"Stay, protector of the poor," coaxed the old man, "for thee I will pay twice what it is worth!"

Rames smiled, here was something he could understand. Even so had the merchants of Thebes bargained and haggled.

Abdullah held up the fingers of both hands——

"Twice this many English pounds," he cried, "no less!"

"By the prophet!" wailed the merchant, "wilt thou rob me? I will give ten, though it will ruin me!" But Abdullah was firm, and finally, after more words, more gestures, the old·man counted out twenty English pounds and well content with his bargain, took the emerald and bade them good day. As they walked away from the bazaar, Abdullah handed Rames the gold. He looked at the coins curiously. So this was the money of the new world. It seemed to differ only in the stamp on its face.

His companion watched him closely.

"Great sheik," he said, "to the northward is a beautiful city where you will see wonders Luxor cannot boast of. Shall we journey there?"

His expressive gestures made his meaning clear.

"How far?" asked Rames.

"Four hundred miles," answered Abdullah, "nearly at the river's mouth."

A great city to the northward! There lay Memphis!

He seemed to hear again the vague rumors whispered on the day of the Beautiful Festival, that the barbarian was hammering at its gates.

Had Memphis, then, by some miracle survived, while the glory of Thebes had passed away?

This must he ascertain for Hotep, who had so often recounted to him the marvels of the great city where dwelt the sacred Apis. But it was a journey of many days and required powerful galleys and a retinue of slaves.

His eyes followed the shimmering river to where it journeyed to the sea.

"Lead me thither," he said at last, the movements of his slender hands interpreting his words, "when the moon shall have waxed and waned we should be there."

"We can be there before the setting of tomorrow's sun!" answered Abdullah, pointing to the two horizons to make his meaning clear.

Rames looked at him in astonishment.

"Art talking magic?" he said, "a journey to the mouth of the Nile in less than one short day?"

Abdullah stared at him with increasing astonishment. Was this man mad or was it possible that there could exist someone who knew nothing of the modern world and its inventions?

"Come with me," he said, "and I will show you that which will seem magic indeed!"

Some hours later, when Abdullah had gathered his few belongings and they stood on the platform of the railway station, Rames' eyes widened with amazement.

For what purpose was this ponderous black thing which gave forth flame and jets of hissing white vapor? Surely, it could be in no way connected with Abdullah's wild tale of a journey to Memphis within the compass of one day! Its mighty wheels proclaimed it a vehicle of some sort, but its vast weight precluded all possibility of men or oxen dragging it any distance. And what was the little car astride its huge round back from whose window peered a dark face?

As he stared, a grimy figure clambered nimbly

about it. In one hand, he held a long-spouted vessel from which he poured something on certain polished spots.

In an even row behind it, stood large roofed carts with many square openings out of which leaned a number of people.

"Behold the magic which will carry us on our journey," said Abdullah, his hands waving toward the smoking monster.

Rames stared incredulously.

The Priests of Kampt had been all wise, but even they in their wisdom could not have sent a thing of such ponderous weight across the shifting sands of the desert.

He followed Abdullah as he climbed into one of the roofed-in carts and, as they took their places, there came a shrill, piercing sound, thrice repeated, and a terrific jolt accompanied by a grinding of metal. To his utter amazement, the landscape began to glide past, slowly at first, but with increasing momentum, until at last trees, houses, fields and villages flew by in a mad race.

He grasped the arms of his seat almost in terror, as the cart in which they were, rocked and swayed. But a glimpse at Abdullah's complacent smile reassured him, and the occupants of the opposite seat seemed to pay no slightest heed to this surpassing magic.

At last the wonder of it erased from his mind all sense of fear, leaving only a feeling of marvelling awe.

Even though the mighty edifices of his own era

had crumbled into dust, the torch of Progress had been handed on!

After a while, his composure returned. The fields through which they flew, were the same fields he had known. The *fellaheen,* trudging behind their plodding buffaloes on whose horned heads birds perched, were like those who had ploughed the fields when Thebes was in her glory. Now and then they passed mud villages built much as those with which he was familiar, shaded by the unchanging palm trees. The feeling of strangeness wore away and he turned to Abdullah again with a request for the English names of the objects flying past the windows, for his observations had told him that the English language would be more useful than any other.

All through the journey the lesson continued and by the time the light had died and they were approaching the city, his plastic mind had stored away many words which he would never forget and which were to form the foundation of his mastery of the language of that strange race who seemed to dominate this new world.

When the train pulled in at last at the great railroad station and came to a panting stop, his excitement returned.

Here indeed was something he could never describe adequately to Hotep awaiting his emissary.

Streets filled with shouting Arabs, huge Sudanese, Nubians and Turks, slippered and *tarbushed, burnoosed* and in straight white Egyptian robes; little grey donkeys and stately camels with scarlet tassels, the tinkling of their silver bells mingling with the noises of the streets. All these were much like

Thebes, but the brilliant lamps that turned night into day, the strange chariots that rolled by without horses or visible means of power, the marvelous clanging vehicles blazing with lights that were propelled by means of a tall stick attached to a vine, made Rames stare about him in ever-increasing wonder.

"Memphis!" he said, half to himself, "can this be Memphis?"

Abdullah, at his elbow, looked at him sharply.

"Memphis lies buried in the sands, *effendi,* we will go one day to see its site. This is Cairo!"

Rames looked about him.

So ancient Kampt was dead and her winding-sheet was the desert sands!

Abdullah hailed a passing *arabîyeh* and directed the man to one of the native *khans.*

"We will rest now," he said; "tomorrow you shall see more wonders and we will purchase the clothes that will make you like the English."

They rolled through the fascinating streets to the inn, where, exhausted by the excitement of the day, Rames fell into a troubled sleep, wherein he wandered amid clanging iron monsters spouting fire, and magic lights blazing out of darkness. Crowds of the conquering host of white-skinned strangers in tube-like clothes and round stiff head-dresses bound and pinioned him and tore from him the secret of the hidden chamber, where lay the key back to his own world.

CHAPTER IX

THE crowded courtyard was blazing with sunlight when Rames at last awoke from the deep sleep into which his restlessness had lapsed. For a moment, he thought he had awakened again in Thebes, all his strange experiences only the figment of a dream. But a quick glance about his room and out of the small barred window, dispelled the illusion.

Shouting camel boys and stately merchants, donkeys laden with fruit and vegetables, huge Nubians and long-bearded Jews crowded past his window.

Thebes was buried in those many centuries that to him were only yesterday!

Not knowing the method of summoning assistance in this strange world, he decided to use the manner of his own times, and walking to the door, clapped his hands loudly twice. Instantly, a tall black creature, dressed in a long white robe and red slippers, came running across the courtyard.

"The Sheik calls?" he said in Arabic and Rames answered his question without understanding his words.

"Abdullah—to me!" The man nodded vigorously and disappeared.

Rames stood looking out over the crowded courtyard. It was bordered by a sort of colonnade of slender pillars with a small well in the center. About this, hundreds of turbaned heads were grouped. Some swaying backward and forward as they read aloud in a sing-song voice from written pages spread upon their knees, others, silent and inscrutable, sat staring into space. Some squatted close together, flashing quick-moving fingers before each other's eyes, bargaining, planning, working out the day's routine. Here and there a green turban stood out among the red *tarbûsh,* the white head-dresses, the close brown caps.

Nearly all of them were engaged in that mysterious occupation which seemed prevalent among all the men of this new world.

On the air floated bluish rings and spirals which issued from their lips as they puffed at the tiny white rolls which Abdullah had called "cigarettes," or the amber stems of long tubes attached to ornamental bottles in which bubbled water.

Presently, he saw the red *tarbûsh* of Abdullah as its owner threaded his way among the chattering groups, and folding his *burnoose* about his shoulders, he went to meet him. He was so eager to see the life of this strange city that he resented each moment of delay.

"Clothes," he said when the little Egyptian was once more at his side, "English clothes—I buy!" and Abdullah smiled and nodded rapidly to show that he understood.

They hurried through the crowded native quarter on foot, but once outside the *Muski,* Abdullah hailed a carriage and they drove through streets whose marvels were even more astounding in the brilliant sunshine than they had been the night before.

They stopped before an imposing looking building and Rames gazed with wonder on the great sheets of glass that enclosed the front of the shop. He paused to study the figures which stood motionless behind the crystal windows. They seemed to be Englishmen with ruddy skins and staring, glassy eyes, dressed in a variety of costumes.

"Men?" he asked in wonder, and Abdullah laughed heartily.

"Wax," he told him, and pointed, by way of making his meaning clear, to the marble statue in the square.

The shopkeeper was an Englishman and came forward to greet his statuesque customer with a rather disdainful air, but when Abdullah explained that his master wished to order a complete European outfit, his manner changed to one of respectful interest, all of which Rames noticed and put down correctly to the power of gold.

He listened attentively to the tailor's explanations of what was to be worn and when, but the phrases, except one or two which stood out as those he had already learned, were a meaningless jumble. His quick ear told him, however, that this man and Abdullah pronounced their words alike and from this he reasoned that Abdullah's English must be correct.

Painstakingly, patiently, the tailor and the little Egyptian explained to this man for whom there was no interpreter in the world, clothes to be worn in the morning, the afternoon, the evening, and, having selected a supply of the best, Rames, with an air of finality, announced that he must have them at once.

"Now," was a word he had learned early and

this he repeated several times, but the tailor shook his head vigorously and assured him that at least one week was required to finish them.

Having been fully measured and all their selections made, the tailor requested something in a suave, though insistent tone, which resulted in Abdullah reluctantly parting with most of their remaining gold pieces.

Once more in the streets, Rames signed that he wished to walk among the bewildering wonders of this fascinating city. Here, as in Luxor, he noticed the lofty disdain with which the English threaded their way among the natives, and regretted the seven days that must elapse before he could take his place among this superior caste, to the accession of which, apparently only good clothes and money were needed.

As they passed Shepheard's Hotel, the military band was playing, and the clashing cymbals, the throb of the drum, the blaring French horns held Rames spell-bound.

In Thebes the music had been either the soft strumming of strings, the silver tinkle of the sistra or the toneless blast of the war trumpets, but this held the sweetness of the one accented by the strength of the other. His ear caught melodies that his memory could hold and repeat, unlike the minor chants of his own people.

At last he turned away and followed Abdullah across the crowded street, stopping to stare at the tram cars and the many motors whirling past. These last were a never ceasing marvel to him. What spirit drove them, what force was hidden in their wheels?

"Where do you come from, my master," asked Abdullah, "that all these things are so wonderful to you?"

And Rames, understanding only the one word "where" shook his head and smiled.

In the *Muski* the noise and chatter of the native life brought his own world nearer to him again and, feeling less lonely and strange, he followed Abdullah through the maze of narrow lanes. The shrieks of the carriage drivers, the clinking cups of the sellers of drinks, the braying of the small donkeys, the shouts of their drivers calling loudly, "Oa," as they hurried along, the blind beggars with their pitiful cries, were all familiar to his ears, but his eyes drank in the strange costumes with interest.

There were the more prosperous Arabs, dressed as he was, moving along with dignity, the red *tarbûsh*, like spots of blood everywhere, the occasional green turban of the pilgrim from Mecca, the women in their black silk cloaks and gay stockings, with the cruel gold bars on their noses, their great eyes gleaming over the black *yashmak,* and here and there the stiff, uncomfortable clothes of the English. His mind was like a canvas on which these new impressions were laid with an indelible brush, pictures for Hotep the High Priest of Thebes to gaze upon and wonder at.

Here and there, the bright red and yellow of the many pairs of slippers hung in the shops caught his eye; the curtains and tent coverings displayed for sale, splashed color against the dingy walls; here were stuffs whose names he did not know, weaves he had never seen, gold and silver, amber and precious gems, bowls and vases of copper and brass, and shops of incense and perfumes.

Once they passed an open window through which came the droning sound of young voices reciting in chorus.

He could hear the word "Allah" repeated over and over, and Abdullah explained that this was a school, a place to learn to read the Koran.

"Koran—sacred book," he said, "Allah—Arab's god!"

And Rames understood. Amen-Ra had been forgotten. Another reigned here in his stead whose name was Allah. He bowed at the name. All the gods were mighty, homage must be paid them.

Presently they turned into a street so narrow that the great carved wooden windows nearly touched.

Here Abdullah paused before a doorway and rapped loudly on the panel.

"A friend lives here," he said, explaining his meaning, "we will rest and refresh ourselves."

The gate was opened by a slender, dark-skinned girl of about fourteen, who stepped aside as they entered the wide courtyard. Her fingers were stained with henna and in her ears were great metal rings.

She bowed humbly before them and led the way across the courtyard to where a dignified Arab in a long white robe sat on a cushion in the sunlight, smoking a long pipe, the water in its crystal bowl bubbling musically.

He rose graciously as they approached.

"Welcome, Abdullah," he said in Arabic, "my house is thine and thy friend's."

"My friend speaks not our language, Hassan,"

said Abdullah, "he comes from a far country, we speak to one another by signs."

The old man eyed Rames curiously.

"Will you both honor me by breaking bread in my humble house?" he asked, and Abdullah accepted with alacrity.

"We stay to eat," he explained to Rames in English, "eat—food, drink!" and his master following the motion of his brown hands as they illustrated his words, smiled understandingly.

They followed their host through the clean courtyard into the house. As they entered the great banquet hall, he clapped his hands and two Nubians appeared, their bare feet making no sound on the marble floor. They brought scarlet silk cushions and spread rugs under the beautiful stained glass windows, and at a motion from their host, Rames and Abdullah seated themselves cross-legged beside him.

Rames' eyes wandered about the handsomely carved walls, the rich ceiling with its delicate stalactites painted in blues and golds, the intricate fretwork of the carved *mashrabiyeh*.

"*Harim*," explained Abdullah, "women live there," and Rames saw through the delicate wooden meshes, dark eyes peering at him curiously.

Presently the blacks returned with trays of sweetmeats and fruit which they set down before the guests and Rames ate gratefully. The mutton of the caravansary had revolted him. In Thebes sheep were sacred and had never been slaughtered, but here their flesh was eaten. While he ate the figs and dates which he knew so well, the old man and Abdullah carried on a voluble conversation in Arabic, glancing frequently at Rames sitting silent but interested.

He realized that they must be speculating about him for Abdullah's thin shoulders shrugged, his expressive hands waved negatively in the air, as their host's voice rose in interrogation. At last the little Egyptian rose to take his leave and Rames followed. As they bowed before their host, he repeated as nearly as his unaccustomed tongue would permit, Abdullah's words of gratitude.

The young girl who opened the gate for them smiled sweetly as a coin was dropped into her hand and they went out again into the sunshine of the noisy street.

As the days passed, Rames realized that to accomplish most successfully the purpose for which he had come, he must be prepared to associate with this ruling caste, he must be as one of them, and in order to do this he must be able to speak their language and read its written signs.

Abdullah's curiosity about this strange man had developed into admiration. His mysterious beauty awed him a little. Despite his ignorance of the world, there was something in his manner and appearance that classed him as superior to the stately Arabs and the arrogant English.

Patiently, he repeated words, phrases and idioms. Rapidly the quick mind of his pupil that was receiving its impressions as a child does, grasped his lessons, and before long Rames could carry on a sort of conversation, stilted but gaining in ease and fluency.

Abdullah used the signs over the English shops

and the names on the tram cars as a spelling-book, and little by little the alphabet ceased to be merely cryptic marks and took form and meaning.

Rames signified his desire to fill the days while waiting for his English clothes, with explorations about the city, its native life, the wonders of its ruins. He had determined that once his limbs were clothed in the fashion of this important caste, he would take his place among them. Until then, he must learn everything he could of their ways and manners and of what had occurred during that period of transition from his world into this.

Thebes had rung with the glories of Memphis, its only rival. Rames had never seen the wonders of the great pyramids nor the Sphinx who guarded, like a faithful watch dog, the beautiful temple between its paws.

Were these mighty works of man in ruins too, he wondered? Would he see only the sadly shattered remnants of their grandeur as at Thebes?

Abdullah wished to drive out to the plains of Gizah, but Rames decided in favor of a tram. This new form of chariot must be tried also.

They climbed into the seats reserved for the natives and gazing about at the sharp line of demarkation, he smiled ironically at a civilization where the cut rather than the quality of the coat made the man.

The beauty of the road along the river under the shade of the *lebbekh* trees was lost upon Rames in his interest in the rocking little tram, with its clanging bell and guiding charioteer whom Abdullah called "the motorman."

As they waited for their donkeys at the Mena

House, Rames wondered at the number of hotels there were. These English, had they no homes, no palaces of their own, that they must always live in caravansaries? For here, as at every other one Abdullah had pointed out, were swarms of them covering the terraces, drinking a curious amber-colored liquid which he had learned was called "tea." Some of them were paying off donkey boys who shouted angrily at the amount of money given them, or ran shrieking after them as they started over the sand.

The two castes seemed to be in constant altercation and the words "too much!" soon became familiar to him.

As they drew near the mighty pyramid of Cheops, Rames sighed bitterly. How cruel, how pitiless was the hand of Time.

Hotep had often described the wonders of the polished surface with its marvelous carved records. He had told of the Mysteries performed in its secret recesses, the readings of the stars that had been made from its lofty summit.

But here it stood, defaced, ragged, lonely in a sea of sand, the polished sides gone, the huge rough blocks, that were its skeleton, bare to the sun.

"What for?" he asked Abdullah, wondering what explanation these people gave as to the purpose of this huge mass of stone.

"Tomb," answered the little Egyptian, "tomb of great king."

Rames smiled. Everything these people had forgotten or did not understand of these ancient ruins, they had labeled either a temple or a tomb. What a store of knowledge he could lay before them if he so willed.

He watched the staid English make the ascent of the great pyramid. How ridiculous they looked, how lost was their dignity between the none-too-gentle hands of two natives, while a third, no respecter of their persons, pushed from behind.

The Arabs at first regarded him curiously, his costume creating some confusion in their minds, but when they discovered he was not one of them, he became subject to their importunities.

However, he scorned their offers of assistance. Their lithe agility was nothing to his own suppleness and energy. He would climb this mighty edifice unaided and, from the summit, look upon the city which had risen above the ruins of buried Memphis!

Even for his strength and vigor, the huge blocks of stone were a trial. He climbed up the widely set steps with difficulty, but once at the top, he lifted his head, his fine shoulders squared.

"Amen-Ra," he said aloud in his own tongue, the tongue that had echoed from these stones when they were first laid upon each other, "thou whom these people have forgotten, thy son pays thee homage, here from the summit of the symbol of thy enduring flame!"

The breeze caught the folds of his long blue robe and swung them about him, the brilliant light touched his skin and turned it to living bronze. As he stood, there were those of the phlegmatic English who looked in wondering admiration at his beauty, which although they knew it not, was the beauty of Egypt in her glory.

He turned slowly, drinking in the panorama at his feet.

Westward lay vast stretches of tawny sand, track-less, desolate, that had swallowed the splendors of Memphis and would cover as relentlessly this later civilization when its time was run. In the distance rose the shadowy forms of other pyramids. In his imagination he could see the beacon flames that had sprung from their summits to remind the world that Ra would return again. To the eastward, the silver ribbon of the Nile wound its way through the lush green of the fields, the waving groves of palms. Against the sky rose the slender minarets of Cairo, and below him, silent, inscrutable, brooded the Sphinx, gazing with the same calm on the scenes surrounding it, as it had on the vanished glories of a forgotten age.

Before it stood the ruined gateway through whose entrance the mummies of the great ones of his race had been carried to their last resting-place.

Hotep had pictured to him many times the marvels of this vast city of the dead, built and planned by his own ancestor, the High Priest of the first great Pharaoh.

The magnificent causeway, that had led up from the plain, was covered and almost forgotten under the sea of yellow sand, and all that remained of the beautiful temple where the priests of Khufu had sung hymns for the rest of his soul, were some blocks of porphyry, which had been its pavement.

Far below him, a small speck against the sand

he could see Abdullah waving his hand, and with a sigh he began the difficult descent.

Hotep had described to him the sacred rites which had been celebrated within the huge pile, and·in spite of the fact that Abdullah suggested. returning to Cairo, Rames insisted on a visit into the interior of the Pyramid.   .

But gone was the splendor of which the High Priest had spoken. The narrow, dark passage with its close, evil-smelling atmosphere, reminded him of the entrance into the secret chamber in the heart of the Theban hills.

The Arab guide led them into what Abdullah called the Queen's Chamber, and as he stood in the small, wonderfully constructed room, Rames' eyes saw it as it must have been before its despoliation.

How bare were the cunningly fitted blocks of stone, how empty and forlorn this hidden room that must have held vast treasures!

They had followed the guide into the principal chamber, the chamber of the king.

Here had taken place those beautiful ceremonies of which Hotep had told him. Here the princes of the blood had been brought by the priests for their initiation into the mysteries of their faith. Here had been drunk that strange potion which had sent them into a deathlike sleep for three days, out. of which they had awakened Kings, supermen, filled with a divine understanding of this life and the next.

Had they, too, wandered into the fields of the future as he was doing, and was it because of the knowledge thus gained that they had built these marvels of masonry to defy the ruin they had foreseen?

He stood wrapped in thought beside the lidless sarcophagus, broken, yawning empty in the far corner of the chamber.

Hotep had spoken of this huge red granite receptacle and its great antiquity. Here had Khufu, the mighty, thought to lie through all eternity, and now Rames stood at its mutilated side and mused.

Ancient even when he had been born, what races and nations had sprung into being and passed away since then. How its yawning emptiness mocked the vanity of man!

He came out into the sunlight with a heavy heart.

As they made their way over the clinging sand to the Sphinx, Abdullah quarrelled loudly with the Arab guides who as usual were dissatisfied with their fees, and silent, wrapped in thought, Rames walked alone.

During those years of oblivion in the quiet of the Theban hills, and for as many years before, the great stone face had stared at the horizon where rose the god whose image he was.

"Ra-Harmakhis," murmured Rames to himself, "mighty Horus, lord of the dawning, art thou sad as is thy son and worshipper? Art thou also filled with pity for thy people who thought their works eternal? Now does thy son understand the strange, inscrutable look in thine eyes. They saw for Egypt what now is, they see for this new age what will be!"

They drove back to Cairo in one of the magic chariots which never ceased to fill Rames with wonder. He made Abdullah repeat its name over and over to him, until the word "automobile" fell as glibly from his tongue as from his teacher's.

That evening Abdullah suggested that they go to see some native dancing, and Rames complied with alacrity.

In Thebes the spirit of the dance was one that held all the people in thrall. The gods loved it and every temple had its dancing girls. Even the Pharaoh himself sometimes danced before the altar in thanks for special favors.

They made their way down a narrow, dirty street, dimly lit by one or two lanterns which hung from iron arms projecting above closed doorways.

At one of these they paused and following several other turbaned men, they climbed a dark, unclean stairway into a large, bare room. Sitting about a cleared space, cross-legged on ragged cushions, were silent men smoking the eternal *narghile*. Some wore the long blue robe and striped *Kaftan* Rames himself was wearing, others were in great turbans and loose, dingy white gowns, and one or two in English clothes and the red *tarbûsh* like Abdullah.

They took their places in the circle.

A dwarf, a repulsive though pathetic looking figure, placed coffee and cigarettes before them and picking up the coins Abdullah threw him, shuffled away.

Rames stared at the misshapen form curiously. In his world such creatures had been treated with the most kindly reverence as the bearers of the soul, or second self, of the noble in whose household they were. Here, however, they seemed to be reduced to the most menial positions.

A dirty Arab in a corner was beating on a small drum with the palms of his hands and a boy squatting next him whistled a weird, long-drawn minor melody on what resembled a thin metal pipe. Presently two women came out of a door and crossed to the center of the cleared space.

They wore their heavy, brownish hair loose over their shoulders and bound about the forehead with strings of coins. Long, transparent skirts fell from the hips, and about their necks and round arms were beads and bands of silver.

As the music rose and fell, they twisted slowly from side to side and rippled the muscles of their arms and bodies.

After watching them for a time Abdullah leaned toward his master with a smirk.

"Do you like this?" he asked, and Rames, remembering the dance and its beautiful background at Thebes, shook his head disdainfully.

What could these people know of graceful, sensuous rhythm, who had forgotten the culture and splendors of glorious Kampt?

These women with their fat, over-developed bodies were grotesque, nauseating. He thought of the lovely slenderness of the temple girls swaying amid the painted pillars, the wreaths of fragrant incense, the jingle of the silver sistra.

How crude this was, the bare, ugly walls, the fetid odor of human bodies and tobacco smoke, the ring of evil-eyed men, the women rippling their muscles, jerking, swaying.

He rose in disgust.

"Come," he said imperiously, and led the way into the dark street.

"*Effendi,*" said Abdullah, "tell me who are you, and where you come from, that even the dancing of women is new to you?"

Rames paused in the yellow ring of light cast by a street lantern. His knowledge and understanding of English were growing rapidly and this one phrase of Abdullah's, "Who are you and where do you come from?" had been repeated so often that it was quite intelligible to him. He must make it clear that for questions such as these there was no answer.

"Abdullah," he said sternly, "ask no more, who, where!" and turning on his heel, he hurried down the street followed by the little Egyptian, to whom the look in the deep, black eyes had carried more weight than the words in their halting English.

The look had said, "never shalt thou question me again on subjects which must remain unknown to thee, else must thou go out of my life forever!" and as the affection for his master grew, he resolved to put aside his curiosity and ask no more.

One day still remained before the English clothes would be ready and this Abdullah decided to spend in the great museum.

"You will see what Egypt once was," he said proudly.

"What Egypt once was!" The phrase rang in Rames' ears insistently. The irony of showing him what had been the glories of Kampt, the wonders of Thebes and Memphis!

When they entered the massive building, his first emotion was one of horrified amazement which soon gave place to rage, that the tombs of his fathers should have been violated to make a show for these people whose hearts held no reverence for the sacred houses of the dead.

He stared at the images of his gods, broken and defaced. Why had they not smitten the sacriligeous hand that had dared to tear them from their sanctuaries?

The corroded metals, which he had seen flashing in the sun, seemed tawdry and insignificant. The funerary barques, which he remembered afloat on the sacred lakes, resplendent with painted colors and gorgeous sails, were worm-eaten, ragged and forlorn, but many of the gems and ornaments of gold and silver still shone with the same lustre as when they had adorned smooth round arms and slender delicate throats now mingled with the desert sands.

There were cases of amulets torn from the unresisting dead, the Key of Life, the sacred Eye of Horus, scarabae of emerald, cornelian and lapis lazuli and the little instrument with which the traveler in the nether world could loosen the habiliments of the tomb.

As he looked down on the rows of silent mummies wrapped in their yellow swathings, he almost cried aloud his horror at the desecration that had taken place. These forms, bound so reverently in spices and fine linen and laid carefully away to await the day when the *Ka* should need again his human form, had been ruthlessly torn from their quiet resting-places, and exposed to the vulgar eye of the curious. No offerings made them of funeral cakes! No libations of sacred wines! No pictured scenes about them of their daily lives! How restlessly their souls must wander in the nether world!

"All that ye do, oh priests, all that ye plan and strive for, is vain!" he thought. "Not even the gods are eternal!"

What a messenger of evil tidings he would be when he returned to Thebes!

Slowly, sorrowfully he followed Abdullah from one gilded sarcophagus to another, wondering only at the brightness of their painted colors. These had lasted as well as the stone upon which they were laid, he mused, while the brain that had created them was borne away on the air like a pinch of desert sand.

Abdullah stopped before a case in which lay a blackened and shriveled mummy, whose right hand was raised in a gesture of command.

"Rameses the second," said Abdullah, "very great Pharaoh!"

Rames looked at the shrunken, though still powerful face with its high arched nose and shriveled lips drawn back from the strong teeth.

Rameses the great, who had written upon his colossal statue: "Look upon my works ye mighty, and despair!" Whose glory was the glory of Thebes as Rames knew it! Whose blood beat in the heart that looked upon him!

"Look upon my works ye mighty and despair!"

"Ay, of a truth, despair," mused Rames, "for all your works, ye who were the great ones of the earth, are brought low and covered with the desert sands and ye yourselves are carried here to be gazed upon by eyes which hold no reverence, only curiosity!"

Sadly he turned away and wandered further among the great corridors.

"Abdullah," he said in his stilted phrases, "can men read these priestly writings?" and he pointed to the inscriptions on the sarcophagi and steles.

Abdullah shook his head.

"Some wise men can a little," he said, "but no one is sure!"

Rames smiled bitterly.

Of what use are records of great deeds and lofty ideals carefully inscribed on enduring papyri, or deeply carved on temple walls, if the language in which they are written has passed from the memory of man?

He paused before a beautiful sarcophagus almost entirely covered with gold leaf and incrusted with precious stones and enamel. On one end was painted the jackal-headed Anubis, lord of the dead, on the other Horus the resurrection, and about its sides the judgment of the soul before the throne of Osiris.

What king or great noble was this, he wondered, as he bent over the inscriptions.

Then his face whitened, his eyes filled with terror, his heart seemed to stop its beating, for what he read was:

"Hotep, High Priest of Amen-Ra, the glorious! May his *Ka* make its journey safely through the realms of the dead. May he be judged according to his good works! May his wisdom never perish!

"I am he who closeth and who openeth and am but One.

"Mine eye is as the sacred eye of Horus bound upon the forehead of his father, Ra."

"I am all things, yesterday, today and tomorrow, for I am born again and again.

"I am the powerful soul. Let way be made for me to the place where is Ra and Hathor.

"I am Osiris-Hotep, High Priest of Amen-Ra, lord of the world and the universe, now and forever!"

As Rames stared at the ancient sarcophagus and its meaning became clear to him, he bowed his head in his hands and wept like a child.

Abdullah was frightened.

"Master," he whispered, "what is wrong? Come, people will believe that you are mad!"

"Mad," echoed Rames. "Would that I were mad, and that what I gaze on here lived only in my disordered mind."

And lifting his head he gazed long and earnestly at the withered form lying in its rich receptacle.

The skin was blackened and tightly shrunk over the bones of the skull, the eyes that Rames remembered so full of fire and intelligence, were sunken deep beneath the shriveled lids, and the lips were drawn away from the strong yellowed teeth as though the High Priest smiled at the littleness of the knowledge he had thought so vast.

"Alas," he groaned, "the vanished glories of my country but tell of days when that which now surrounds me shall also pass away, and yet, will Hotep believe, when I return with the burden of my knowledge? Would the people of this new world believe were I to be a prophet here?"

He shuddered. He must leave this horrible place at once.

What if these despoilers of graves, whose ferret eyes had discovered the most secret hiding-places of the mummies of his people, had found Teta where she may have lain in some remote spot within the hidden reaches of the desert? What if he should find himself gazing on the shriveled form that had been her loveliness?

Gods of his fathers! The very thought was unbearable. He felt as though he would suffocate in the musty air of this vast charnel house.

He must get away! Anywhere, but away from this tomb of his country's glory.

And Abdullah, looking at the troubled beauty of the dark face, drew his slender brows together.

Was this man indeed mad? Was he one of those beloved of Allah, who in his majesty and might took away men's senses when he loved them well? Or was he perhaps from some country of which even the colleges of England had not taught him!

Inshallah, he would stay close. Gold and jewels must not be left in the care of a mad man. Abdullah, the faithful, would watch over him.

CHAPTER X

THE money they had brought with them from Luxor was almost gone. Abdullah was beginning to jingle the few remaining coins anxiously in his pockets, remembering the fashionable and expensive wardrobe his master had ordered. This would be ready by now, and he wondered if there would be money to pay for it. Perhaps the tailor would hold him responsible.

He walked into the small room in the noisy caravansary the next morning with a worried look on his brown face.

Rames was busily bent over some sheets of paper on which he was practicing to write. He looked up from the large, irregular characters he was making, and smiled.

"Good morning," he said, with only the faintest trace of an elusive accent. "What for today?"

Abdullah drew his hand from his pocket, the few remaining coins in his outspread palm.

"There is no more than this," he said ruefully, "and today the English tailor finishes your clothes."

Rames smiled.

"There will be more," he said. "Come to me again!" and he bent once more above his writing lesson.

When Abdullah entered the little room some hours later, his eyes were caught by scintillating points of light flashing from a glittering heap that lay on his master's outspread cloak. Rames had chosen no more than a twentieth part of the jewels about his waist, and of those the smallest and least valuable, and yet what the little Egyptian saw lying upon the cloak represented a fortune.

There were five pearls, eight rubies, and fourteen emeralds which in the faint light of the dingy little room flashed and glowed with deep prismatic colors.

His eyes sparkled with wonder and cupidity. To him, the display of these rich gems suggested the possibility of some hidden treasure chamber of ancient Egypt of which the Arabs were always dreaming and for which many of them spent their lives in vain search.

"Where have these come from?" he asked eagerly. "So great and rich a sheik need never want for anything."

Rames puckered his brows as he tried to catch the rapid flow of words.

"More slowly, my Abdullah," he said, "your pupil understands not all your difficult English!"

The secretary bit his lips. He must indeed go more slowly if he would learn the secret of this treasure store.

"May not your servant know the source of so much wealth?" he pleaded.

Rames looked into the small Oriental eyes where cupidity battled with a certain dog-like devotion.

"Some one dies, these are mine," he said in his stilted English, "now I will sell!"

"I understand," said Abdullah, "they have come to you as a legacy!"

The new word caught Rames' ear. He repeated it over and over until he could say it almost as his teacher did and at last, satisfied with his pronunciation, he gathered the gems and rose to his feet.

"Now to the best dealer in the city," he said, "perhaps two—three—so that we may receive much for these!"

Abdullah bent over his master's hands, in which lay the sparkling jewels. He knew precious stones and their value, and so as he examined these, his eyes glittered. This would be a day of golden memory to him.

They turned from the noisy, crowded *Mùski* into the wide, sedate *Shari'a Kamel* and Abdullah led the way into one of the largest shops whose windows blazed with costly ornaments, many of which Rames observed were fashioned after the manner of his own world.

An attendant came forward bowing courteously and, in response to Abdullah's request that they might see the proprietor on some important business, ushered them into a small office at the rear of the shop, where a stout, elderly Frenchman sat at a table adjusting a delicate pair of scales.

He greeted them politely and motioned them to be seated.

His business had trained him to conceal his emotions when engaged in negotiating a bargain, and as he bent over the gems which Rames spread before him, his face betrayed none of the astonishment he felt at the sight of this magnificent collection of ancient stones. He carefully examined each gem under a powerful magnifying glass, and a spot of dull color appeared in his cheeks. He looked at his visitors curiously.

"Where did these come from?" he asked in his own language, and Abdullah answered for his master.

"Perhaps you will not mind speaking English," he said, "my friend knows very little French."

"Certainly," and the dealer turned to Rames, "these are yours?"

"A legacy," he said, repeating the newly learned word. "I wish to sell!"

The man held the stones up to the light.

"They are very unusual gems," he said at last, "the cut and polish is especially interesting. Have they been in your possession long?"

Rames wondered what the man would have said could he have known, but he only smiled and pretended not to fully understand, and after some bargaining, in which the efficient Abdullah proved a fair match for the shrewdness of the merchant, the stones were finally sold for five thousand English pounds.

"Has Monsieur any others which he wishes to dispose of?" he asked.

Rames looked suspiciously at the crisp notes he handed him, but a quick word from Abdullah reassured him, and he bowed as the merchant continued.

"If so, may I beg you to come to me first, either here or at our place in Paris?" He presented his card with both addresses on it, and having concluded a splendid bargain, bade them a smiling good day.

As they left the shop, Rames turned to Abdullah dubiously.

"What are these?" he asked, indicating the bank notes.

"Money," was the cheerful answer.

"But it is papyrus, a thing of no value. In Luxor the merchant paid gold!"

Abdullah laughed.

"This represents gold, any bank will exchange it!" and he carefully explained the system by which paper replaced the precious metal held in reserve by banks and governments.

The full significance of a bank was carefully gone into and Rames admired the wisdom of a people who had circumvented the power of thieves by doing away with the individual strong-box. He thought of the temple riches and the vast treasure chambers of the Pharaohs, with their massive walls and secret doors. But these were only for the few. Here in this new world, each man could· have his wealth guarded even as the king.

At the English tailor's, they found his clothes ready and awaiting him, and with the assistance of one of the attendants, he tried them on. The frock coat, the evening clothes, the dinner jacket, the light suits for the morning, all the various articles of his new wardrobe, were carefully adjusted. The tailor had been commissioned to buy him all the most correct accessories, and the ties, shirts and collars, sleeve links and studs, even the various pairs of shoes and socks were carefully looked over and tried on, and Abdullah, looking on the beautiful lines of the lithe figure which the modern clothes set off, knew that even among the tall athletic Englishmen his master would attract attention.

The well cut clothes showed off to advantage the fine back, the long slender limbs, the narrow waist and hips, and the whiteness of his linen brought into relief the dark face with its sad mouth and inscrutable eyes.

He had decided to be all European and lay aside even the *tarbûsh*, and when at last he was ready for the street in one of the light morning suits, Abdullah paid the bill to the bowing, smiling tailor.

"Where shall I send the gentleman's clothes?" he asked, and Abdullah answered quickly.

"I am his secretary," he said, "I shall return later, and let you know."

As they left the shop, he explained the need of traveling bags and trunks.

"Where are we going now?" he asked.

"Out of the filthy caravansary where herd the filthier natives," said Rames with emphasis, "we go to the best! It is my place!"

Abdullah looked sidewise at the proud lift of the shoulders under the unaccustomed blue serge, the dominant raising of the chin.

"I understand," he said. "It will be as you wish," and having purchased bags and a trunk, they drove back with them to the tailor shop, where he superintended the packing of the precious wardrobe.

"Shepheard's," was his instruction to the driver,

as the packed and strapped cases having been put in place, they stepped into the carriage.

When they crossed the terrace of the great hotel, more than one of the women seated at the little tables turned from her companion to stare at the handsome stranger, more than one feminine mind made a mental resolve to learn his identity and if possible meet him, but Rames' eyes held no particular vision. To him, this first view of European life at close range was all-absorbing.

The graceful women in their charming costumes, the laughter, the gayety, the splashes of color made by the English and French uniforms, the clicking of china and glass as the native waiters set down their trays on the many little tables, the sound of music mingling with the cries of the Arab venders jostling each other on the pavement below! It was like a wonderful kaleidoscope of changing scene and color and Rames stood entranced, looking about him while Abdullah superintended the porters who were taking in their luggage.

"Will you sign your name?" asked the little Egyptian, as they made their way into the hotel, "or shall I?"

"Sign my name?" asked Rames. "Why? what is the custom?"

"One writes one's name in a great book in European caravansaries—hotels, you must learn to say. Records are kept each day."

"Ah," Rames saw the wisdom of that. Were not the scribes of Thebes for this very purpose?

He wrote, in the large flowing hand which practice had given him, "Prince Rames," and upon Abdullah selecting one of the most expensive suites available, they were shown to the lift with much bowing and scraping.

As the elevator rose with them, Rames uttered a sharp exclamation, but Abdullah touched his arm with a reassuring smile. So here was another wonder, a room that was lifted skyward by unseen forces! He must be ready for any strange experience that might present itself.

When they were installed in the beautiful apartment, and the attendant had left them, he stared about him in wonder. The handsome bed with its damask curtains, the chairs and mirrors, the elaborately appointed bath, the long, curtained windows, were objects of much interest. But most wonderful of all was the small gilt object from which came an incessant ticking sound.

This, Abdullah explained, measured the time and indicated each hour by the musical ringing of a tiny bell.

In the native hotels where they had lived, the furnishings suggested the poorer houses of Thebes, but this was different, unlike anything he had ever seen.

The rich tapestries and gilded carvings of his own house were more splendid, the alabaster and rock crystal jars and vessels, the ebony and ivory furniture, the glazed plaques and copper mirrors that adorned it were richer, and these curtained windows were very unlike his own many-latticed ones with their gaily colored hangings that shut out the fierce sunlight.

As he went about from one thing to another while

Abdullah unpacked the bags, he was startled by the insistent ringing of a bell, and to his surprise, the little Egyptian stepped to what looked like a small vase standing on a table and taking up part of it, began talking to it as though it were a human being.

"Yes, thank you," he said, "everything is satisfactory, we have all we need. No—very well, goodbye!" and replacing the ornament, he went back to his unpacking.

Rames stood for a moment in amazement. Had Abdullah gone suddenly mad?

He went quietly to the table and picking up the object as he had seen Abdullah do, set it to his ear.

Suddenly it spoke to him in a clear, small voice.

"Are you there?" it said, and frowning at the rapid beating of his heart, he set the ornament hastily back on the table.

Abdullah turned and saw the consternation in his face.

"What is it?" he asked startled.

"It speaks," said Rames.

Abdullah laughed.

"That is a telephone!" he said.

"Telephone!" A new word, another wonder, and after Abdullah had explained its use, he would not be satisfied until he had spoken through it again and heard the answering voice from the office.

So many and so wonderful were the new impressions, that his mind, in order to record them all, must submerge the old ones, and Rames found himself thinking less of Hotop and Thebes, and even

Teta came to be a cherished, beautiful dream to be indulged in only in those rare moments when he could be alone with his thoughts.

That night, faultlessly attired in his new evening clothes, in the wearing of which Abdullah had carefully schooled him, they sauntered through the crowded corridors and into the great dining-room.

How beautiful and strange everything was. The unfamiliar dishes served him by a silent slave, who in the curious fashion of this age was dressed in a costume similar to his own; the many instruments of silver with which food was eaten, even the manner of eating which Abdullah explained was very important; the lights, the wine, the music of the great room, thrilled him.

If Hotep, the High Priest, could have read his pupil's thoughts, he would have been filled with a sense of misgiving, for Rames was comparing Thebes in all its glory with this, and vague doubts filled his mind.

About him rose the sweet voices of women, the gay laughter of men. White shoulders gleamed in the soft light, colors flashed and intermingled in gorgeous blending, uniforms and shimmering satins, laces, silks, and everywhere the sparkle and glitter of jewels. They were wound in strings about graceful throats, trembled in delicate ears, circled arms and fingers. Here in this new world everyone seemed to possess fabulous riches. In Thebes only those in the highest places could so adorn themselves. Were all these English, Pharaohs, and all their women, queens, he wondered?

For a time, he and Abdullah sat together on the

terrace watching the crowds as they came and went. Presently music floated out to them and Rames rose.

"Let us hear," he said, for this new blending of harmonies, that his ear had never known in Thebes, was an unceasing joy to him.

At the doors of the great ballroom they paused, and Rames stared in wonder at the scene before him.

Whirling couples flew past him in an ecstasy of color and motion. The white shoulders and lustrous gowns of the women enhanced by the sombre clothes or brilliant uniforms of the men. Gliding, bending, swirling, locked in each other's arms, close against each other's breasts. This was wilder than any orgy he had ever seen in Thebes. Young and old, lean and fat, puffing, panting; swaying full of grace, or hopping along without it; the great ballroom was a blur against his bewildered eyes.

"These people dance, *effendi,*" explained Abdullah. "It is a ball,—a festival,—a fête!"

"Hah!" Rames understood, "for some god, some religious feast?"

"No," laughed Abdullah, "it is for their own amusement."

The slow, stately dance of the temple girls flashed across Rames' memory, the ecstasy of the victorious Pharaoh before Amen-Ra, the sensuous undulations in the Palace of the King. But these all danced alone! He had never seen two people hold each other close and whirl about to music in this manner before. It seemed so lacking in dignity, so beneath the grandeur of these stately women, these domineering men.

But this was their world, not his!

His dark, interested face, his handsome eyes with their hint of mystery, attracted much attention.

Abdullah, close at his elbow, saw many pairs of feminine eyes cast languishing glances at him, saw more than one beautiful mouth curve into a half smile, more than one deliberately made opportunity for his handsome master, but Rames was blind to these advances. Women held no charm for him. His heart was too full of the memory of a pair of deep, soft eyes, of bronze glints on dark masses of hair, of a slender graceful form and a voice like water falling in a quiet pool. There was no other woman in Eternity save only Teta.

As the days passed, Rames insisted that Abdullah use much of the time in teaching him new phrases, new words and idioms. They spoke English altogether now and his progress was very rapid. There was still the faint, unplaceable accent in his pronunciation, and the phrases were disjointed, hesitating, but his ear was becoming accustomed to the sibilant, hissing sounds of the language.

Shepheard's gave ample opportunity for the study and comparison of the ruling caste of this new world. How different they were from his own people and yet how many traits of character were alike in both. There was the same arrogance of power and position, the superciliousness for what was beneath them, the intolerance for things they could not or would not understand. The same bowing and scraping to material things, jewels, money, worldly possessions, the spurning with the foot, the pulling aside of garments from the beggar and the outcast.

The difference seemed to exist only outwardly. People were people. In Cairo, as in that far distant age from whence he had come, human nature was the same.

As he studied them and observed their manners and customs, he came to know that there were grades even in this caste, divisions of it, each part having little in common with the other.

The military, in their brilliant uniforms, seemed to take precedence, although here and there a dignified man in clothes similar to his own, was greeted by a high-sounding title, and among the women, it was not always the most beautiful or richly gowned who commanded the most respect.

One division he was quite unable to place. This was represented by little groups of dowdily dressed men and women who wandered in and out among the gay throngs of the huge hotel merely as onlookers, who seemed to be out of place in all this splendor.

In his explorations about the city with Abdullah, he encountered them everywhere. Many of them carried a small red book which they studied with the most engrossing interest. They were usually in charge of an officious, worried-looking man whose duty appeared to be to point out objects of interest, which he did in a monotonous, sing-song manner clearly indicating frequent repetitions.

"Who are these?" he asked the omniscient Abdullah, who laughed and said:

"Cookies!"

"Cookies?" repeated Rames, and Abdullah explained.

"Tourists, people who try to see the greatest number of things in the fewest number of days!"

Rames learned that it was not only monuments and museums, but individuals as well, who were objects of interest to these strange people. He himself had had the unpleasant experience of being singled out for attention.

As he sat on the terrace of the hotel one morning, he heard the word, "prince," in a loud whisper, and turning, saw a little group of this peculiar sect scrutinizing him curiously. He rose and walked away, equally divided between amusement and wrath.

His rapid progress in English was now fast obliterating the stilted phrases and isolated words, and even the faint, elusive accent was disappearing. Gradually, he allowed himself to be drawn into conversation and listened with interest to the different topics that were discussed. Politics, art, literature, music, all came to have a meaning for him.

His mind received new impressions like a child, and as readily as a child assimilated them, till he came to know the great names of the modern world.

One day as he sat watching with never-tiring interest the merging of the life of the East and West as it flowed past the great hotel, an elderly gentleman came and took the chair beside him.

They had spoken before on one or two occasions, and he greeted him courteously.

"Cairo is the gateway between the old and the

new, don't you think, Prince?" he said as he sat down.

"Cairo is very beautiful," was the guarded answer.

"But wonderful as those old chaps were who built the pyramids," went on the other, "what pygmies they were compared to the ancient Greeks who were still barbarians when their culture was at its height!"

Rames was interested.

So there had been a great civilization which had superseded that of Kampt, a civilization which had budded, bloomed and fallen into decay during that long period of oblivion in the Theban hills!

The few straggling Greeks whom he remembered in Thebes had come as slaves in the Phoenician galleys. Could it be that these wretched people had built an empire that had overshadowed his own?

"The ancient Greeks?" he asked, "mankind owes much to them?"

"All the art and literature of our Western culture is patterned after theirs," said the other.

"And their chief city was——?"

"Athens, the city of Minerva, the goddess of wisdom. You have not been there, sir? Even its ruins are among the most beautiful sights in the world!"

They talked a little longer of other things and finally the courteous stranger departed.

Rames watched the tall, well-preserved figure disappear down the terrace.

"Abdullah," he said, as his secretary came toward him, "make ready our luggage. We go to Athens!"

CHAPTER XI

THEY left Cairo early the next morning, the flat, lovely country of the Delta, with its brilliant green fields, waving palm trees and mud villages, flew by the train windows, but Rames' vision was turned inwards.

Egypt and her glory, vanished and forgotten but for the speculations of the curious! Another civilization come into being and fallen into decay!

Before him rose the half-forgotten memory of those swiftly flying scenes that had flashed by after he had swallowed the mysterious elixir—those visions of strange peoples and unknown countries.

Had he beheld something of the history of the ages in his flight through Time, as a falling star might glimpse vistas of each world it passed?

So lost was he in meditation that he was unconscious of Abdullah's scrutiny.

The little Egyptian had ceased to covet the knowledge of the secret horde from which he was certain his master drew his wealth. But for the hundredth time he asked himself, who was this mysterious man who came from he knew not where, whose object in life he could not understand, whose very thoughts were cryptic. The month originally planned for had slipped away, but a genuine affection, a sympathy with the loneliness he only vaguely understood, made him resolve that if Rames so willed it, henceforth their ways should lie together.

As the train pulled into the station at Alexandria, Rames awoke from his reverie.

"How is our journey made?" he asked. "This land we visit lies across the waters. Are there galleys that will take us?"

Abdullah smiled as he directed the Arab porter to collect their luggage.

"There is a ship in port today," he said, "we shall go aboard at once!"

When they came in sight of the crowded harbor, Rames' wonder grew again. The dock was crowded with Arabs, Turks, Nubians, Europeans, a medley of nations and tongues, pushing, jostling, hurrying between the heaps of luggage, the bales of cotton and freight stacked in huge piles.

Abdullah led the way toward the end of the dock where loomed a most curious structure. Its sides were pierced with little round holes, and from its roof rose huge black towers that belched forth clouds of smoke.

"*The Morning Star*," said Abdullah pointing.

"What is it?" asked Rames.

"Our ship, *effendi!*"

He followed the secretary up the gangplank, marveling, and as they stepped aboard, he looked about him in amazement. Surely Abdullah was mistaken. This was no ship, but another one of the hotels in which these people lived.

The hurrying sailors in their white uniforms, the officers standing by with so much dignity, these were perhaps the attendants like those at Shepheard's.

As they went into the suite Abdullah had engaged, he stared about him curiously. "These hotels differ in plan, it seems," he said.

"We are on board a ship," reminded Abdullah.

Rames sank into one of the comfortable chairs.

"A ship?" he repeated, "surely you jest with me. I saw no sails, nor do I believe there could be sails so huge as to carry a palace such as this!"

"You wondered at the railway train," smiled Abdullah, "the same power drives this great vessel, also. This is an age of steam, of wonderful mechanical contrivances. Has your country been asleep that it has not even heard what the world was doing?"

Rames sighed.

His country was indeed wrapped in a slumber from which no magic known to these wise people could ever awaken her, and how much knowledge of all their wonderful creations could he carry back with him across that mystic bridge which lay between?

Suddenly he was conscious of a curious motion, a quivering of the huge bulk, a gentle, almost imperceptible pulsing, and as he looked up startled, Abdullah handed him a cap which he had unpacked from one of the bags.

"We are leaving," he said, "shall we go on deck?"

They leaned over the rail and watched the city drift away.

The low hills with their windmills and the great forts at the harbor's entrance faded from sight

until the only point against the sky was the tall
shaft of that granite pillar which stands a solitary
reminder of the greatness that once was here, a
splendor that was as yet unborn when Rames and
Teta had walked together in the temple gardens.
At last even Pompey's pillar dipped below the horizon, and the broad blue expanse of the Mediterranean lay about them, sparkling and beautiful.

He glanced at the rows of chairs ranged along the
deck. Almost every one was occupied, a plaid shawl
and a cap designating the men, a plaid shawl and a
floating veil, the women.

The sea was smooth and calm and the motion of
the ship was barely perceptible. Rames watched the
billowing folds of grey smoke as they spread in a
long trail after the steamer. He recalled the painted
sails and long wooden bodies of the giant galleys that
had carried Pharaoh's hosts. How insignificant they
seemed beside this stately ship plowing her way
through the blue waters, and Abdullah had told him
there were others far larger, more elegant than even
this!

His mind could scarcely grasp the fact that the
long ribbon of smoke, unfurling against the sky,
was the successor of those countless slaves whose backs
had bent in tireless unison over the heavy oars.
How could they chain and make captive this mighty
power as his own people had enslaved the men of
the land of Cush?

"Abdullah," he asked, "is it possible to see the
magic that pours forth such smoke, the power that
can send a palace such as this across the waves?"

"Certainly." Abdullah was like Alladin's genie;

nothing that was asked him seemed impossible, and Rames, Oriental like himself, thanked the god of chance that had sent the efficient little Egyptian across his path.

They spent several hours going over the great ship. The mighty engines, the boilers with their roaring fires, the grimy, sweat-covered, naked bodies of the stokers feeding them; the shining, oil-dripping pistons that shot so noiselessly back and forth; the whole intricate system of a mighty steamship held this scion of a forgotten age spellbound.

Here was magic unknown to the priests of whose accumulated knowledge Hotep had been the guardian. He remembered the High Priest had told him that those mighty forces of Nature, which had terrified man so that he worshipped them as gods, would one day be understood and harnessed, and as slaves, do man's will, but had Hotep even dreamed of things like this?

In the little room of the wireless operator, he sat for hours.

The priests of Thebes had sent messages to distant temples, mysteriously, without the aid of man. But the priests were all wise. Here in this new world he had as yet seen no priests, but every one was wise. Were the gods pleased with this, he wondered? Would they not some day turn their wrath against man who had torn away the veil and was making himself their equal?

When at last he grew weary of watching the little machine and pondering over its magic, the motion of the ship had increased considerably. The sun was still clear and brilliant but the long, oily waves that had slipped so smoothly from under the keel of the great ship, now danced choppy and white-crested.

Rames heard a curious sound at his elbow and turning, was startled at seeing Abdullah's face, a greenish pallor spreading over it, a sickly smile on his pale lips.

"Abdullah! What is it?" he cried. "You are dying! You are poisoned!"

Abdullah waved him away with a feeble gesture.

"No cause for alarm," he said thickly. "I'll— I'll be all right soon—I——"

"Let me help you!" but Abdullah, with a groan, staggered toward the railing, to which he clung weakly. Rames stared at him in consternation. Fate had sent this descendant of his own people to guide him on this strange pilgrimage. What a calamity if he were to lose him! Abdullah must not die!

He hurried to one of the officers pacing the deck and explained his anxiety.

"He is very ill," he said, pointing to the limp figure. "What shall I do?"

The man smiled.

"Don't worry, my dear sir," he said, "look about you. Two-thirds of the ship's company are down. There are very few who are seasoned sailors like you and I. Sea-sickness is a very uncomfortable malady, but it is never serious, only damned disagreeable!" and he resumed his pacing.

Rames looked up and down the long line of steamer chairs. The officer had been right. Under nearly every cap or floating veil, above every plaid rug, was a greenish-yellow face, hollow-eyed and gaunt; as livid as those in Thebes when the plague had ridden through the city.

"Sea-sickness!" Another new word—but the officer had assured him it was not serious, so he could look about and wonder at his own immunity. He could even administer to the suffering Abdullah without the fear that his faithful secretary was passing away.

The ship was pitching and rolling heavily now and it was with difficulty that he kept his feet. He looked with awe at the tossing masses of water. How unconquerable they seemed. Huge as was this mighty vessel, it was but a reed in their embrace. How marvelous, that man was able to pit his ingenuity against so resistless a force!

The next day dawned on a smooth, calm sea, and hearing the laughter and gay voices of those whom yesterday he had thought dying, he agreed with the officer.

"Sea-sickness is not serious, only damned disagreeable!"

Abdullah was once more on deck, his own cheerful self again, and the lessons, of which Rames never tired, were resumed.

At breakfast the little Egyptian unfolded a wide sheet of paper covered close with long, uniform rows of black marks.

"This is a newspaper," he said. "A sheet like this is printed daily in all the cities in the world, and tells everything that is happening."

Rames held the paper before him and gazed at the long, even columns, the large letters of the head lines, which were slowly becoming intelligible words to him.

"Does every one know what all the world is doing?" he asked curiously, "even the common people?"

Abdullah laughed.

"Newspapers are for every one and they tell every thing!" he said. "Even the most intimate personal affairs are discussed openly in spite of the wrath of those concerned. Philosophers and prize-fighters, statesmen and actresses use its pages to exploit themselves, and merchants extol the merits of their wares in its columns!"

As they sailed up Phalaron Bay and anchored off Pireaus, Abdullah's lively Oriental imagination painted vivid pictures of the conquering galleys that had floated here, of the glorious deeds of the Grecian heroes and the achievements of those master minds that had left their influence on all posterity.

The capable little Egyptian superintended the unloading of their luggage and engaged a carriage to take them to Athens.

"You will hear the language that was spoken when Greece was young," said Abdullah, "changed by time and colloquialism, but still the language of Homer, whom some day you will read."

After they had arranged for their stay at the hotel, they walked toward where, bold and sharply outlined against the sky, rose the Acropolis Hill, with its crown of ruined glory, which, battered and despoiled though it is, still stands unrivaled among the works of man.

At the Theseum they stopped, so that Abdullah might explain to his eager pupil the meaning of what lay before them.

Rames stared at the warm, creamy pillars against the cloudless sky. How different were these fluted columns with their simple capitals and rich, creamy coloring, to those massive ones of his own temples, lotus-topped, their painted shafts, rich with gold and carving. How different was the frieze, with its sculptured record of the hero's triumphs, to those massive walls of imperishable granite covered over with inscriptions of the Pharaohs' conquests.

"Here stood the ancient market-place," said Abdullah pointing, "and there the city gates. Here the court met in the dark of night and judged their prisoners, because they believed the visible emotions biased their justice; against these stones have echoed the voices of Pericles, Socrates, Demosthenes, and those others whose names have echoed down the centuries."

Abdullah waved his hand toward the Acropolis.

"How many armies have hurled themselves in vain against that citadel," he said. "But it was the harpies of other nations, and not the soldiers, who carried away most of its ornaments to grace their own cities, which have copied, though never equaled, its grandeur."

As they climbed the ruined Propylae, Rames mused on the circular course of human progress. A birth, blossoming, fruitage, and dissolution. Out of its ashes, the tree of life springing once more into sturdy growth, and then the inevitable decay. Was

there any end to it all, would it ever reach that perfection in which there was no death?

Standing on the summit, they looked at the panorama spread at their feet.

"There lies modern Athens," said Abdullah.
"Looks like the Greek flag, doesn't it?" and indeed
the white of its marble buildings and the cloudless
blue of the sky reflected the colors of the flag that
was flying over the Palace.

He swung his hand toward the western horizon.

"There lie the Peloponnesian hills. There is
Phalaron Bay on whose shore Demosthenes argued
above the sound of the waves. There lies the Bay
of Salamis, where Xerxes, from an ivory throne,
saw his fleet beaten and scattered. There is the
plain of Attica. Can you see the thin white line of
a road winding along? That is the Sacred Way that
led to Eleusis, the City of Mysteries."

To the north rose the glistening sides of Pen-
telicon, that inexhaustible mountain of marble, hard
as granite.

"All these temples are built of that," said Abdullah, "its pure white turns with age to the mellow
gold you see in these ruins. Look, can you see the
pass to Marathon? And over there lies the Ægean
sea. Theseus came sailing over it bringing good
tidings, but he forgot to change his sails from
black to white and his father, Ægeaus, thinking him
dead, threw himself into its waters, and so the
Greeks gave it his name! They were marvelous,
those old Greeks, so full of poetry, so full of everything that was wonderful!"

Those old Greeks! Rames smiled as he listened. What would this youth at his side think if he should tell him that before these things were, he had been?

Abdullah touched his arm, his voice low and vibrant.

"Turn slowly," he said, and threw out his arms eloquently.

"Behold! The Parthenon!"

To this man, whose living eyes had gazed on the stupendous magnificence of ancient Thebes, the shattered loveliness of this most glorious of the world's architecture looked delicate, fragile, a thing almost like a dream, its marble columns mellowed by time, a dull gold against the deep blue of the sky.

Rames seated himself on a fallen shaft, his eyes filled with a bitterness he might tell no one.

Egypt and her wisdom was forgotten! Greece and her beauty was a memory! Even the springtime youth of this new world in which he had awakened must pass away! Of what good the striving, the building toward perfection, when dust and ashes were the ultimate end?

He sighed as he rose.

"Come," he said at last, "let us go, I am sad when I look on what has once been so surpassingly beautiful!"

At the top of the ruined Propylae, Abdullah stopped him.

"Look!" he said. "In this lovely little temple, the Greeks placed the statue of the wingless Victory. They said she laid aside her wings when

she came to make her home in Athens. Clever
conceit, wasn't it?"

Rames smiled and pointed to a vast amphitheatre
below them.

"What was that?" he asked.

"That is the first theatre that ever was in the
world," was the answer.

"Theatre?" Rames puzzled over the word.

"Theatre," repeated Abdullah, "the place where
Euripides, Aristophanes and Sophocles saw their
plays acted. Here is where the drama was born."

"I see there is much that you have still to teach
me," smiled Rames, "and I have so little time in
which to learn!"

Abdullah laughed.

"Youth is yours," he said, "and the world lies
before you. If it so pleases you, I will accompany
you everywhere, and my small store of knowledge
shall be yours!"

Rames looked at his secretary quickly.

"But yes!" he said, "where I go, you shall go!
I wish it!"

Abdullah hid a smile at the imperious words and
pointed to some ruined arches below them.

"Those," he said, "are what the Romans have
left."

"The Romans? Who were they?"

"The conquerers of the world!" answered Abdullah as they started the descent.

"Where was their country?"

"Italy! Their city was Rome. Shall we go
there next?" Abdullah loved to plan a journey;
this traveling companion to whom expense meant

nothing, who listened eagerly and attentively to all he said, was the joy of his life.

"Shall we go to Rome?"

The torch of civilization led away from Egypt where it had first been lighted. Rames knew that Hotep's advice would have been to follow it.

"Yes," he said, "when we have seen everything here, we will go to Rome!"

As they walked toward their hotel, a man passed wearing a short blue tunic covered with brilliant brass buttons, his legs were encased in white tights, the long upturned points of his shoes were decorated with red pompoms. On his head was a soft red cap with a black tassel hanging down on the shoulder.

"A noble?" asked Rames.

"A policeman, a man who guards the city," was Abdullah's answer.

"And those others, are they slaves?" he nodded toward a group of men in short, white, stiffly starched petticoats and round red caps, their richly embroidered jackets and slippers contrasting with the white of their skirts and hose.

"Slaves?" Abdullah looked puzzled. "There are no slaves today. These men are wearing their country's national costume."

"But," said Rames, "everywhere I find that men dressed as you and I, are of the ruling class. I thought these others, both here and in Cairo, wore different clothes as a badge of servitude."

Abdullah reflected. There was much truth in Rames' statement. In all the countries into which the European had gone, no matter how incongruous his clothes were to the climate, he clung to their use in the unshaken belief that his apparel was the proper one, and it was the native's which was grotesque. And because of this, those who would not depart from the traditions of their fathers came to be regarded as inferiors.

"It is not yet two months since our first meeting in Luxor," he said, as they sat over their dinner at the hotel some days later, "then your language was one that even I with all my gift of tongues, could not comprehend, and there was no word of mine that conveyed any meaning to you. Yet here tonight we sit and converse with perfect understanding. It is marvelous! I myself am quick to learn. We Orientals have the gift of imitation highly developed, but you, my pupil, have surpassed me!"

Rames smiled.

"The human mind is a machine, my Abdullah," he said, "it can be made to bow to the will. Concentration overcomes all obstacles."

The next day they left Athens.

CHAPTER XII

THE progress of man was leading them westward. Abdullah had told him the Romans were the conquerors of the world. What would their civilization be like, he wondered? What elements were needed in a nation to become the conqueror of the world?

Was it toleration for the affairs of other peoples? Was it by the cultivation of those arts which lifted man above the barbarian?

Did the road to glory lie beneath the wheels of the war chariot, or in the mind of the philosopher, the mallet of the sculptor and the creation of splendid edifices erected to gods and posterity?

Abdullah said the Greeks had developed to the highest degree those attributes which grace civilization, yet they had not conquered the world!

Must the throne of the conquerer, then, be elevated on the bodies of the vanquished?

This was the way of the Pharaohs, yet mighty Kampt lay buried in the desert sands!

It was as though this new world, into which he had awakened that February morning, were a huge book, the pages of which he could turn but one at a time.

On their journey toward Rome, Abdullah endeavored to speak of other lands beyond, but Rames stopped him.

"No," he said, "let me learn each thing as it comes. Tell me more of Rome."

The ship was to stay over night at Corfu. They found the city gay with flags and decorations, its many streets filled with people.

Abdullah questioned a passer-by, and turned to Rames eagerly. "The German emperor arrives today," he said, "he has a palace here and comes to rest in the sunshine!"

"The emperor of the Germans?" asked Rames. "Are they greater than the English?"

"They believe their culture to be superior to anything on earth," smiled Abdullah, "their ruler is called the Cæsar, and in his vanity he thinks himself the peer of the greatest Romans!"

As he spoke, the imperial escort came in sight, and the people crowded curiously to the edges of the sidewalk.

In Rames' mind was a clear picture of the retinue of the Pharaoh as he entered his city, the splendor of the countless chariots and soldiers, the priests and attendants in their rich costumes. With what magnificence would an emperor of this new world appear?

But instead of the pomp and display he anticipated, there came a handful of mounted men in trim, well-fitting uniforms, who preceded a handsome, dark blue motor car.

Seated in it was a very erect man of about fifty-four with a strong, sharply marked face, a proud lift to the firm jaw. The ends of an aggressive mustache turned up sharply toward a pair of very keen gray eyes. The left arm, which seemed in some way different from the other, was held across his breast, and with the other hand he touched the rim of his cap in answer to the cheers of the people. At his side sat a simply dressed, rather stout woman with grayish hair.

When the carriage had passed, Rames turned to Abdullah, disappointed.

"This emperor of a great country travels simply," he said.

"Of all the modern rulers he loves display the most," replied Abdullah. "I suppose he considers Corfu too insignificant for a demonstration of his pomp."

"Is he indeed a great warrior," asked Rames. "He does not seem possessed of unusual strength."

"He is not great in any sense," replied Abdullah, "but he is the most dangerous man in Europe."

"You mean as a fighter?"

"No, as a politician! He is regarded as a deadly combustible that may at any moment set the world aflame."

"But is he skilled in the use of arms?"

Abdullah laughed.

"Modern rulers fight only by proxy, theoretically they win or lose battles, though actually they are many miles removed from the scene of combat."

They left Corfu the next morning, and all day Rames sat alternately dreaming and studying the English books Abdullah had been teaching him to read. The sea was like satin, and toward evening the shadowy cliffs of Sicily appeared a purple blur on the horizon, growing lovelier as they came nearer.

The sun was setting in flaming glory behind them, and the water rippled like molten gold under the keel of the ship. The breeze carried out to them the scent of orange blossoms. As they drew nearer they could see the delicate pink and blue of the stucco houses against the dark green of the slopes. Some graceful white yachts lay idly swinging at anchor, and a big, dark-sailed fishing-boat swept silently by, blotting out for a moment the wakening harbor lights. Above it all, majestic, stately, crowned with its summit of eternal snow from which a delicate plume of smoke drifted across the darkening sky, towered Etna.

Rames watched the red glow above the smoke cloud.

"Abdullah," he said, "is that a beacon fire burning on the summit of yonder white mountain?"

The little Egyptian stared at this strange man to whom not only the works of human hands were unknown, but who was unfamiliar with the wonders of Nature.

"That is Mt. Etna," he said. "It is a volcano, a fire mountain. There is always snow on the summit and always fire in the crater!"

The new words made Rames knit his black brows.

"The white that I see is—what?"

"Snow," answered Abdullah, "it is frozen rain," and he explained carefully. "Etna is one of the highest volcanoes in the world, it is very cold at the top. But the flames come from the center of the earth where everything is still fire."

"The center of the earth!" repeated Rames to himself. "The underworld where is the hall of the gods! So men say that also is destroyed!"

The steamer put in at Messina, but it was too late for passengers to go ashore. Through the gathering darkness, Abdullah pointed out the pitiful ruins.

"What conquerer leveled this city?" asked Rames.

"The greatest conquerer of all," answered Abdullah, "the forces of Nature," and he explained the swift, mighty shock of an earthquake.

Rames listened with eager interest. To him it was the manifested wrath of the gods. Despite the desecration of their altars, they were still mighty!

As they sailed through the Straits of Messina, Abdullah pointed out Scylla and Charybdis, and the patronizing smile with which he recounted these legends of a bygone faith, made Rames sigh. A faith that had scarcely been born when he had lived in Thebes, was now, it seemed, mere tales to amuse school boys. Of what good to sigh for the vanished glories of man when even the gods could be forgotten!

He looked up at the brilliant beauty of the stars in the deep purple sky, shining down on this new world as they had shone on Thebes.

They alone were unchanging!

He stayed in his deck-chair all night, and Abdullah, unwilling to leave him alone, dozed by his side.

But Rames' eyes were wide and sleepless. Ages

between what had been and what was! He and the
stars alone remained the same!

As they neared Naples, the dawn was breaking
in a red streak back of Vesuvius which lifted its
dark cone against an opalescent sky. From its
crater, a thin line of smoke rose straight into the
still air. The sky brightened in a blaze of gold
and orange, and the sweeping crescent of the most
beautiful bay in the world lay sparkling before
their eyes.

The sun was well up when they drew near the great
wharf. Many small boats had come out to meet them,
their crews of ragged, unkempt men shouting and
gesticulating wildly. A violin wailed above the
raucous voices, a guitar twanged, a welcoming song
rippled out in a high tenor. Other voices joined as
a flat boat filled with musicians came alongside.
Baskets of fruits, orange, crimson, vivid green;
trays of roses, violets, many-colored flowers were
held aloft temptingly. Brown-skinned boys swam
about the ship or poised on the gunwales of grimy
row-boats, ready to dive for the coins thrown by the
passengers grouped along the rail. In defiance of the
oaths and buckets of water flung at them, agile men
clambered up the sides of the vessel, eager touts,
each striving to be the first aboard, to enlist as many
passengers as possible for the cheap hotel he represented.

The great ship glided alongside the pier, and
amid a rattling and clattering of chains, and shouting of orders, the gangplank was lowered.

Beggars, cripples, ragged women holding aloft
naked babies, implored the *soldi* of the rich stran-

gers. Porters and ragamuffins pushed, jostled, shouting, swearing, laughing!

Before Rames' interested eyes, the noisy, teeming, swarming life that is Naples, lay bathed in the warm gold of the morning sun, a riot of color, a pandemonium of sound!

As they stepped ashore, Abdullah fought a way for Rames through a swarm of howling, yelling humanity, each one intent on seizing their luggage, acting as guide, or conducting them to a cab.

"This is Naples," he laughed, "don't mind them, but follow closely."

Rames was inclined to demur at the officious little men who insisted on the opening of their luggage, but Abdullah touched his arm reassuringly, and convinced now that whatever Abdullah said was right, he watched the process of searching the bags and strapping them up again as indifferently as he could.

"This is the *doggana,* the custom-house," explained the secretary. "Trade is protected by making visitors pay extra for certain things which they bring into the country with them. Ancient Carthage might still be standing if the Romans had had a law like that."

"You mean?"

"That if the figs of Carthage had not been sold so cheaply in the Imperial City, Rome would not have feared a rival whose swift galleys could bring perishable goods into her market and undersell her merchants."

"Are there then no trade rivalries between countries today?" asked Rames, interested, but before

Abdullah could answer, their cab started through the bedlam and began threading its way along the crowded streets, and Rames' attention was distracted by the color and dirt and medley about them.

Ragged children, *carabiniere* with rakish feather-trimmed helmets, filthy beggars asking alms, soldiers in trim uniforms, and sauntering pedestrians filled the narrow, steep streets. The brightly-colored ragged garments flapping from lines stretched between the windows, the carol of a gay song, the cracking of whips and the hoarse profanity of their own *cocchiere* shouting to his horses, all this was new and wonderful to Rames, accustomed to the poise of the east, fresh from the calm of Athens.

At one doorway they saw a herd of goats, huddled patiently, while their owner milked one of them into a pail a woman had lowered from an upper window from which she leaned her frowzy, unkempt head as she watched the process.

In the shadow of a narrow alleyway whose steep steps were cluttered with dirty children and gossiping women, hung rows of long yellow strings.

"That is the food dearest to the Neapolitan's heart," said Abdullah pointing, "that is what they call *spaghetti*."

Everywhere they looked was dirt, color, poverty and sunshine.

They left their cab at the entrance to a lift, and as they ascended to the heights above, where was located their hotel, Rames' eyes sparkled. It was all so wonderful, the charm and sunshine were like a heady wine.

Later, as they sat in the garden over their luncheon, Abdullah leaned back with a sigh of content and looked about him.

"Naples is—well, Naples," he said, "nowhere else are the people so poor, yet so happy. Shall I order some spaghetti?"

Rames looked up quickly. He remembered the filthy alley between whose houses had hung the yellow strings, the dirty children playing about.

"No thank you," he said emphatically. "None, please!" and Abdullah, understanding, smiled.

"Naples is really the link between Greece and Rome," he said after awhile. "The early Greeks built it on the site of an older town and called it Neopolis. Do you hear them ——?"

They listened to the plaintive melody of some singers far below them in the street.

"Addio, mia bella Napoli!"

"Napoli," said Rames, "is it so they say Neopolis? You cannot quite obliterate the ancient, can you?"

"You will find traces of the Greeks and Romans everywhere," said Abdullah, "all the languages of Europe are founded on theirs."

"And the Egyptians?" asked Rames with a trace of wistfulness in his voice.

"Ancient Egypt is too ancient," smiled Abdullah.

They roamed about the city through the lovely sunny afternoon. The great Galleria Humberto Primo proved particularly interesting to Rames with its huge arched glass roof and its flanking rows of shops displaying coral, carved lava, cameos, gayly colored silk scarfs, bronze and marble statues and curios of all description.

"You say the Romans had their palaces near Naples?" he asked. "Where are they now? Is there no trace of them remaining?"

For answer Abdullah pointed to the great mountain that brooded over the city.

"Behold their destroyer," he said. "In the days when the Roman villas gave Baia, over yonder, the name of the Golden Shore, Vesuvius wasn't the smoking torch it is now. Its crater was a grassy ring where games were held, its slopes were covered with vineyards and planted fields."

Rames looked across the blue stretch of bay to where a plume of smoke rose in the air.

"What changed it all?" he asked, and Abdullah told him of the mountain's awakening, of the terrible destruction and havoc it had wrought.

"Tomorrow, if you wish, we shall go out to see the ruins of Pompeii!" he said.

"First," answered Rames, "I wish to go nearer to the monster that brought about its destruction."

They started up the mountain early the next morning. A little railway carried them nearly to the top, but there was still quite a distance to go through the slippery ashes.

Abdullah availed himself of the help of two stalwart guides who offered their shoulders, but Rames, remembering his climb up the Great Pyramid, declined and made his own difficult way to the top.

He stood at the edge of the huge crater looking down into its fiery depths. Crimson, orange, iridescent blue, boiled and seethed the molten mass between the clouds of steam. Beneath his feet the ashes were hot and slippery. The sulphur fumes that rose intermittently, turned him slightly dizzy.

"What if the mountain were to awaken now?" he said softly. The guide, a stalwart, black-haired Neopolitan, shrank away. Rames saw his hand clinch in a peculiar gesture as he folded the two middle fingers in his palm and raised the others.

When at last they were safely down the slippery sides and once more on the road back to Naples, he asked Abdullah what the frightened gesture had meant.

"That," said the all-knowing one, "is to ward off the evil eye. These people are very superstitious. They think that speaking of misfortune invokes it!"

Rames smiled. He thought of the amulets his own people wore to guard against wicked spirits, the gestures they used to avert their evil power. Though the wisdom of his fathers had perished, their superstitions survived!

On the way out to Pompeii, Abdullah discoursed glibly about its story in history and art, so that when Rames stepped from the motor-car, he was eager to see everything that his secretary had described.

It was a wonderful, clear day such as the spring loves to bestow upon Italy, and the mass of Vesuvius rose against the deep blue vault of the sky like a sleeping monster, the vapor of whose poisonous breath alone gave warning that it lived.

Abdullah was in his element. He led the way from one point of interest to another, giving picturesque details of its history.

In one of the narrow streets they were jostled by a party of people whose costumes, together with the little red book they carried, proclaimed them to be of that same caste which had been so numerous in Cairo.

As they passed, a tall, angular girl was exclaiming to her companions:

"What a terrible waste of ground! Chicago wouldn't let ruins clutter up a place for so many years, without pulling them down and building apartment houses or something!"

Abdullah laughed, but Rames looked puzzled. Her English was different, somehow, to that which he had been so carefully studying. He had missed her meaning.

The little Egyptian led the way about the Great Theatre, explaining the opening in the ground for the rising and falling of the curtain, the stone rings which had supported the poles for the awnings, the pool whose water was sent over the audience in a refreshing cloud of spray.

"Isn't it marvelous how much those old chaps built like the people of today? We haven't advanced much, have we?"

Rames looked about him at the ruined tiers of seats, grass-grown and splotched with lichen. A goat was grazing contentedly where a great noble might once have rested, and on the long, narrow stage, gay little field flowers nodded and bowed in the faint breeze as though they were the actors responding to applause.

The theatre had not been born, nor dreamed of when he had gone out of Thebes, and now his eyes looked upon these sculptured stones whose age was youth compared to his.

Sometimes he felt himself the embodiment of the unchanging universe. Those were the times when Nature faced him as eternally young as he. Sometimes he felt old beyond the idea of time, and those were moments like this, when he gazed at the ancient ruins of a city that was as yet unborn when he had come into being.

Abdullah interrupted his reverie.

"Look at those ruts worn in the cobblestones. Heavy wagons they must have had, eh?" he said, as they made their way across the high stepping-stones that led from one side of the street to the other. "And over on those walls you can still see the scribblings of idle boys, or men who held a certain political candidate in higher esteem than another!"

Rames stared at the faded letters painted in red.

"Can men read those?" he asked.

"Of course, I can myself," and Abdullah translated freely some of the scrawled lines.

The scribblings of idle boys, accidentally preserved these centuries were read easily and as carefully guarded as those carved and painted inscriptions of his own people that told of deeds of valor and triumph. What was the standard set as worthy of perpetuity?

He became conscious of the secretary's voice, how much he had missed, he did not know.

"—worshipped the gods of Rome," Abdullah was saying, "but they seem to have been broadminded as to the religions of others. For instance, here among these temples to Jupiter, Juno, and the rest, is a little temple to Isis."

"Isis!" Rames pulse quickened. In all these days

of new and strange adventure, here was the first hint of his own gods. "Isis!" he repeated, "do the people in Rome worship the holy Mother today?"

"Indeed they do," said Abdullah, looking at him in astonishment, "but I had no idea that you were Catholic!"

"Catholic?" Rames knit his brows, "I do not understand," and he followed Abdullah into the little museum. Here were stored cases of articles found in the ruins; jewelry, vases, ornaments of bronze and terra-cotta. How eloquent these things were of the busy daily life that had been cut short in one awful moment of devastation. Here were things whose original shape and use he could have explained to Abdullah. In Thebes he had seen almost the same, but Abdullah as usual was busy explaining to him.

"Look at these casts," he was saying, "the ashes made a perfect mould of what they covered and some ingenious man hit upon the idea of filling them with plaster of Paris, thus preserving the original form. See the ring on this young girl's finger? That dog certainly died in agony, didn't he?"

"And those others," added Rames, "perhaps thought that by making the same sign as the guide on Vesuvius, they might ward away the evil that was upon them!"

Abdullah looked closely at the figures lying in the cases. Some of the fingers were bent down into the palms with the familiar gesture of the Italian peasant.

"I never noticed that," he said in surprise, "but

I probably should have if I had looked again. I don't miss much, you know!"

And although the idiom was new to Rames' ears, if he had· understood, he would have agreed. Abdullah was omniscient.

Later, as they wandered about the deserted streets, the empty echoing houses, the ruined temples and Forum, Abdullah, his straw hat set a shade rakishly on his sleek black hair, launched into a history of the development of the Roman state, its use, growth, and power.

"Why," he said, grandiloquently declaiming for the benefit of some straggling tourists who had become separated from their party, "Persia conquered Greece! Greece conquered Persia! Rome conquered the world! Egypt gave us our wisdom, Greece our art, and Rome our civic guidance, we——" but Rames touched his arm.

"Come," he said, "these people—they stare—you are telling me, not the world! Save some for when we are in Rome!"

They had just entered their motor-car to drive back to Naples, when from the direction of the bay there came a loud sound that speedily rose to a staccato roar.

The people about him craned their necks in its direction.

The noise came nearer, its volume increased. Even Abdullah was excited, the expression on his eager little face seemed to say:

"All the wonders you have been seeing are but mere dross compared to what you are about to behold!"

Rames heard sharp exclamations all about him. His gaze followed the pointing fingers and his heart leaped with a feeling that was half awe, half amazement, for above them, clearly outlined against the deep blue of the sky, soared a bird of a size and form he had never dreamed could exist in nature.

Its mighty wings poised in a span that would have overshadowed the terrace of his house in Thebes, the roar of its voice was like a tempest sweeping through a forest. Yet no one about him showed the least sign of fear or apprehension, their faces reflected only the most eager interest.

"Look, *effendi*," cried Abdullah excitedly, his finger pointing upward, "an aeroplane!"

"A bird?"

"Yes, but one made by man!" and his face shone with a complacent grin as though, in some intangible way, he were responsible for the marvel above their heads. "It is faster and a thousand times more powerful than any bird in Nature!"

"It lives!" breathed Rames in wonder.

"It's a machine," explained Abdullah, "guided by a man and driven by a motor very similar to the one in this car.

Rames stared at the monster above them. It was climbing higher, circling in graceful spirals, the roar of the motor growing fainter and fainter until it became inaudible and his eye alone could follow the diminishing speck that was the acme of human inventiveness.

Man had at last become one with the birds! Earth, like a jealous mistress, no longer chained him to her bosom!

CHAPTER XIII

THE human mind is so constituted that any amazing or wonderful thing is only miraculous the first time it is witnessed. After that, it is accepted as a matter of course.

Each marvel was carefully stored away in Rames' memory against the day when he must redeem his oath to Hotep.

But astounding as were all the wonders of this new world, his presence in it was more amazing still, and it was the contemplation of this that enabled him to accept them with composure. And so, as the train steamed along through the Campania, he leaned back calmly against the velvet cushions of the private compartment the little Egyptian had engaged so that they might be alone.

The air was filled with the perfume of spring and awakening life, and Abdullah leaned out of the window and filled his lungs with great breaths of it, but Rames' thoughts were far away in a distant land and a still more distant age.

His eyes held no vision of the fertile Campania that flew past the train windows. The velvet-cushioned railway carriage and Abdullah's alert, dark-skinned face had faded away.

Instead, he was in a temple garden in a far country, sitting beside a limpid pool on whose surface floated delicately scented lotus blossoms, shadowed by the branches of tamarisk trees. At his side, so near he could feel the warm lure of her, sat a girl with liquid, scintillating eyes and hair like burnished bronze.

Instead of the monotonous pounding of a flat wheel on one of the coaches and the creaking of the swaying carriage, he could hear her voice.

"Through all the ages thy soul and mine shall be side by side!"

His memories of her were all that life held for him. He almost cried her name aloud with the anguish of his longing.

He was startled from his reverie by a touch on the arm.

"Look," said his companion, "we are nearing Rome. There lie the Sabine and the Alban mountains. The little town you see at the foot is Frascati. There are the tombs along the Appian Way, and yonder, the arches of the ancient Aqueduct!"

Rome was to Abdullah, like the well-thumbed leaves of a beloved book, and it was with a joyous eagerness that he led his pupil about the Eternal City.

They wandered over the Forum, and through the magic of his description, the crumbling ruins took shape.

Rames saw again the glitter and pomp of Rome under the Emperors, beheld the splendor of a Cæsar's triumph, heard the eloquence of Cicero and Antony, the ravings of Caligula, and shuddered at the cruelties of a Nero.

Emperors, statesmen and heroes passed in magnificent procession, climbed to dizzy heights, and went down into the destruction that had left but these broken stones to mock their glory!

They watched the tawny flood of the Tiber moving sluggishly under its bridges, and as Abdullah pointed to the massive arches that had withstood the turbid waters for so many centuries, Rames realized why the men who built them had conquered the world. His own people had erected mighty temples to their gods, lasting monuments to the dead, but here had been reared structures that were of use to living men, who therefore served their own interests by perpetuating them.

Late in the afternoon they leaned over the parapet of the Pincio hill, looking down on the wide Piazza below them. In the center, tall, slender, the gilded cross on its top catching the rays of the setting sun, rose an obelisk, with the black of the tall cypress trees behind it.

"What does that token of Egypt do here in Rome?" asked Rames.

"It commemorates its subjugation," was the answer. "Augustus Cæsar brought eleven of them here in memory of his conquest."

"If these Romans think their city is ancient," said Rames half to himself, "let them look on that!" and then he added aloud, "What is the meaning of the symbol at its top? I see it everywhere here in Rome!"

Abdullah glanced at him quickly. He could not fathom the mystery of this strange man. His progress in the ways of a civilization seemingly unknown to him, had been so rapid that it was only by a question such as this that his mentor was brought back to the realization that there were many of the most obvious facts of the modern world of which he was still in ignorance.

"That is the Cross," he said, "the symbol of Christianity!"

"Christianity?"

"The religion that banished the gods of Greece and Rome, the religion of Europe. Curious, isn't it? Ancient Egypt's symbol of the sun, brought to Pagan Rome to commemorate a victory, topped and pedestaled by a mediæval pope! Why, that old shaft of granite undoubtedly looked on a great civilization when Rome's walls were still only a dream in the mind of Romulus! It stood on this spot when these gardens belonged to Lucullus, the Sybarite! It survived the ravages of Alaric and his hordes! It watched the building of yonder great cathedral and it will probably look down on the ruins of the world!"

St. Peter's, with its vast, echoing spaces, its marbles and mosaics, was a never-failing source of interest to Rames.

This was a temple where a living God was worshipped. The beautiful ruins of those others built in honor of his own deities and those of the Greeks and Romans were roofless and shattered, like empty sockets staring pitifully at the sky. But here was a temple, nearly as vast as those to Amen-Ra, almost as magnificent. He came day after day to hear the priests celebrate the mass.

The clouds of incense rising up into the dim reaches of the vaulted roof carried him back to his own age. The tinkling bells that punctuated the service were like the sound of the silver sistra, the chanting voices of the priests and even parts of the impressive service recalled vividly scenes in the great temples on the Nile. The very form of the structure was not unlike those of Thebes.

When Abdullah had first brought him here, he had been startled by the sonorous voices of the priests as they chanted the "Amen."

"To what god do they pray?" he asked, "surely not to the gods of ancient Egypt; you told me they were no longer worshipped!"

Abdullah frowned. Sometimes he wondered if this man were really sane.

"Why do you ask that?" he said, "we are in a Christian church and Christian churches are built in honor of Christ."

"But they sing 'Amen!' and Amen-Ra is—was the greatest, mightiest god of Egypt."

"Amen is the end of prayer," said Abdullah. "Christians, Mohammedans and Jews all use it. It means 'truth!' "

" 'Truth!' " echoed Rames. "What is truth?" and Abdullah might have launched into a lengthy dissertation on the antiquity of that question, but they had planned to go to the Vatican galleries, and the afternoon was waning.

At Athens, Rames had first been able to compare the sculpture of his own people with the art of Greece. The graceful figures, with their beautifully moulded draperies that so cunningly emphasized the forms they covered, the arrested motion of the athlete, each muscle ready to spring into action, how

different they were from the granite figures of his
own gods and Pharaohs stiffly erect or stolidly
seated, hands on knees, wide eyes staring inscrutably.

And the pictures so much more modern, but still
centuries old, how soft and warm the colors, how
delicate the blending, how sure the rhythm of line
and contour.

In Thebes the reds, blues and gold of the
paintings had been vivid, blazing, wonderful, but
there had been none of the delicate tints of flesh,
none of the half-imagined transparencies of light
and shade as there were here. And most wonderful of all was the art which could depict Nature
as she was!

He thought of the decorations at Thebes, with
their flat, profile figures, unnaturally placed arms
and feet, and the indiscriminate disposition of various objects irrespective of position or size. Here all
things seemed to take their places in relation to the
central figures, each line vanishing into distance as
the eye saw it in Nature.

In answer to his questioning, Abdullah told him
something of the science of perspective.

If one of these masters could but have painted
the face that always floated before his vision! Here
would be colors worthy of the greatest brush, in
the elusive glint of the iridescent eyes, the bronze
gleam of the dark hair!

"O, Teta! Teta!" he cried in the depths of his
aching heart, "How alone I am in a world that
knows thee not!"

In going about among the churches of Rome,

Abdullah spoke of the blood that had drenched the early days of Christianity, of the persecutions and martyrdoms.

"The new religion was forbidden," he said, "and so these Christians took refuge in underground hiding-places, where many of them were found and executed. Today these places are a Mecca for those of the Christian faith. Shall we visit one of them?"

When they stepped from their cab at the Catacombs of St. Calixtus, a bearded monk came forward, and giving them each a long taper, led the way down into a darkness so dense that the feeble light they carried but served to intensify the shadows. A cold, damp smell assailed the nostrils, there was an air of mouldy decay, and even if Abdullah had not told him of the heaps of human bones that were stored there, he would have felt himself in a charnel house.

As they followed the silent-footed guide, voices suddenly echoed against the rocky walls, and a laugh, light, girlish, and extremely musical, rippled out.

"Another party is just ahead of us," said Abdullah, "Rome is always full of tourists, and this is one of the places every one sees."

As he spoke a faint glow shone around a corner, quite a long way down the corridor, shadows wavered across it, and presently a number of twinkling lights came into view.

There were perhaps four or five in the party, as that many tiny flames sent tall grotesque shadows dancing on the walls and low ceilings.

About thirty feet from where Abdullah and Rames stood with their guide was a bend in the intricate labyrinth that wound off into inky blackness. The other party turned into this, and as the last member was following, the little taper was lifted and out of the surrounding blackness suddenly sprang into sharp relief the face of a girl.

It was only for an instant, then the light disappeared and the corridor was once more utter darkness.

But that one fleeting glimpse left Rames white and shaken, leaning against the wall for support.

For the face that had appeared out of the blackness was Teta's! Unmistakable were the limpid, translucent eyes, the delicate arch of the brow, the tender curve of cheek and lip, unmistakable the bronze light on the heavy bands of hair.

Suddenly regaining his senses, he rushed in the direction where the lights had disappeared, Abdullah and the monk hurrying after, but when he reached the corner, Teta had vanished into the darkness out of which her face had shone for one brief moment.

Was this a vision he had seen, a phantasy conjured up by his longing for her, or was Teta, the embodiment of light, whose delicate beauty was as the bloom of the lotus flower, wandering in the foul blackness of this vast sepulchre!

"Let us go out," he said, "I—I am suffocated here——"

As they hurried through the winding passages parties of tourists met and passed them. Rames stared almost rudely into each face by the light of the flickering taper, but the one he sought was not among them.

As they emerged into the sunlight again, a motor-car was just pulling away from the gate, and something in the carriage of a graceful head swathed in a dull green motor veil made his heart pound again wildly. But before they could find their own cab and follow, the motor was lost in the distance.

Through the next day and the next he was filled with a feverish unrest, an unsatisfied longing.

In vain Abdullah pointed out ancient monuments and recounted their history in his best manner. He strove unsuccessfully to amuse and interest his master with new books, new words to learn.

But marvelous as it was, the color and life of this new world had faded. The vision he had seen outlined against the darkness of the Catacombs had brought back a flood of memories that precluded all other thoughts.

Anxiously he scanned each graceful girl who passed, for he had told himself that what he had seen might have been only a resemblance, and he longed to see again the face that looked so like the one he loved.

Abdullah was worried. Was the Roman fever, of which strangers were warned, stirring in his master's blood? Perhaps they had better leave Rome.

"North of here is a wonderful city," he tempted, "a city that is unlike any in the world. In the middle ages it——"

"O pray, don't teach me things tonight," sighed Rames, "I am weary!"

Abdullah shook his head.

"Shall we not go to Venice," he urged. "Rome is noisy. Venice is quiet, peaceful, soothing!"

And reluctantly Rames decided to go on with the pilgrimage as chance dictated.

CHAPTER XIV

IT was twilight when they stepped from the train at the railroad station in Venice. The city rose from the golden water in purple mystery. Here and there lights began to flash out, and as Rames stood waiting while his secretary selected a gondola from the mass of black-painted boats, he looked about him curiously.

Abdullah had told him something of the city where all the streets were canals and where were neither horses nor motor-cars, only graceful, swift-moving water-craft. He had chattered all the way from Rome about the Byzantine splendor, the wealth of art, the beauty of Venice, but Rames had listened only half-heartedly. His thoughts had been with the vision he had seen in the Catacombs. Once, when the train had stopped at a station, he had been on the point of leaving it and returning to Rome to resume his search. Nothing could shake his conviction that, impossible as it seemed, it had been Teta herself whose face had suddenly emerged from the darkness.

He took his place in the gondola and as they glided noiselessly out from among the others, Abdullah leaned toward him eagerly.

"Are you disappointed? Did I not promise you should see something unique?" But Rames was too filled with the beauty of the scene to answer.

By the time they were comfortably settled at the hotel, the moon had risen and the canal beneath their windows shone silver in its light, with long dancing ribbons of reflections from colored lanterns rippling into its depths.

Abdullah brought chairs out onto the balcony and Rames rested his elbows on the railing, his chin in his hands. The quiet peace of the night was soothing after the stir of Rome, the bustle and noise of Naples. He could almost fancy himself back in one of the silver Egyptian nights, with the Nile at his feet, and Teta——

From somewhere across the water rippled a tenor voice, clear, sweet, full of the pathos that the Italians express so well.

Below them, like moving shadows, drifted boats, colored lights at their bows, and now and then came the echo of soft laughter and whispered words. Against the sky rose a slender tower and once a bell sounded, deep-toned and solemn.

The peace, the carefree happiness that seemed to pervade the place, the gentle lapping of the water under the silent oars of the gondoliers, the musical call that prefaced the turning of corners, the mystic beauty of the palaces that rose, moon-silvered from the canal, the moon itself, it was all perfect, and yet——.

Abdullah came out onto the balcony.

"What a night," he sighed ecstatically, "who could not feel young and in love, here in Venice under such a moon!"

Rames smiled.

"Is love a matter of moons?" he asked.

"I've heard it said the moon is responsible for a great deal of nonsense," was the answer, "of course, I don't know, but——"

Before them, across the wide space of the water, was a cluster of lights, trembling, swaying like masses of brilliant flowers. From their midst came the voice of the singer, and now as they listened, a clear, sweet soprano took up the refrain:

"Sul mare luccica,
L'astro d'argento—"

Another voice joined, deeper, more resonant, that made a rich background for the silver notes that rang so clearly through the night.

"What do all those lights signify," asked Rames, "is there a festival perhaps?"

"No," answered Abdullah, "the gondolas bring their passengers here every evening to listen to the music. Shall we go among them?" He was indefatigable, but Rames shook his head.

"Not tonight," he said. "I want to be alone and think. Tomorrow I shall be rested. We will go then!"

"Good, then I can finish what I have to do, and, perhaps, if you do not need me, I shall take a little jaunt myself," and Abdullah rose energetically, his bright eyes shining. The moon and Venice were stirring in his blood.

After he had left, Rames sat for long hours on the balcony, dreaming. The mystery of the night, the silver enchantment that lay like a veil over the old palaces, the soft ripple below him, the music floating across the water, filled him with a longing that was bitter pain. His arms ached to hold again the tender form he so loved, his lips yearned for her kisses, the touch of her delicate fingers.

"Teta," he whispered, "Teta, the days are long and my love but grows the stronger!"

Through the moonlight, he seemed to see again the face that had looked out from the blackness of the Catacombs, but even as he gazed it faded away. His arms dropped at his sides hopelessly. Abdullah had been right, the moon was responsible for much. He must have imagined he had seen her face in Rome. Out of his longing had been born the precious vision.

The lights were disappearing. One by one they drifted away. The singing died off in the distance.

Venice slept under the moon.

Early the next morning Abdullah opened wide the shutters and let the brilliant Venetian sunlight flood the great chamber where Rames lay. His sleep had been the heavy one of utter exhaustion, and now he stirred restlessly under the light.

"Hotep," he murmured, in his own tongue, "Hotep, let me awaken!"

"It is Abdullah!" said the secretary. "You have been sleeping all these wonderful hours away. Venice is so beautiful, I am impatient to show it to you!"

They breakfasted out on the balcony, and in the pitiless light of day, Rames was surprised to see that much of the fairy splendor had vanished.

Abdullah saw the look of surprise.

"Queer, isn't it," he said, "how different Venice

looks in the sunlight? It always makes me think of Cinderella. The moon is the fairy godmother and dresses her up in gold and silver lace, and the gondola lanterns are her jewels, but in the morning she has to return once more to her rags."

But even in the sunlight, the scene was one of beauty, and Rames let his eyes wander over it tenderly.

"We do not cease to care for what we have once loved, because its beauty has faded," he said. "Love is of the soul, not of the eyes!"

Abdullah had engaged a gondola for their stay, and when they descended later it was waiting for them at the marble steps of the hotel. The gondolier ("the best in Venice, Signore," he had assured the secretary), stood tall and picturesque at his oar, his white shirt open at the throat, a brilliant red sash twisted about his waist.

"*Buon giorno, signor!*" he said in a soft drawl, "*Ecco una bella mattina!*"

Abdullah gave him directions in his own tongue. His secretary's ability to answer whatever was said to him in no matter what language, was a never-ceasing marvel to Rames, but he had been content to concentrate on one, the sibilant, difficult English.

They floated silently along the Grand Canal, Rames leaning back among the cushions under the hood of the gondola, dreaming. In his garden in Thebes a small canal had wound among the tamarisk and palm trees. Its surface had been dappled with pale lotus blooms and along its banks the delicate, feathery papyrus had risen. Here, in a small gilded boat, drawn by Amrou, the slave, who walked along the bank, he and Teta had sometimes floated together in the hush of the silver nights. The gondola, save that it was painted black, was not unlike the little boat on the Theban lagoon. Even the musical call of the gondolier as he approached the turning of corners, stirred a faint echo in his heart, for so had the voice of the Egyptian slave called across the silence of the garden.

But for Abdullah there were no inward visions. Venice and today filled his eyes, and eagerly he pointed out the beauty about them.

"Some day you will read of this wonderful city in the works of the greatest poet of the world," he said. "There is the Rialto. For centuries that was the only bridge across the canal, and if its own beauty had not made it immortal, Shakespeare's words would have.

"Shakespeare?"

"The English poet who made his characters walk about here. Shylock and Othello, Desdemona and Portia. You will read of them all some day."

"Do the English love this city?" asked Rames.

"The whole world loves it," was Abdullah's answer. "In one of those palaces lived Byron; in another, George Sand; over there, Robert Browning, who wrote—

"Open my heart and you will see
Graved inside of it 'Italy.' "

The stillness, the calm wrapped them close. The gondola glided against the landing steps at the

Rialto and reluctantly, Rames followed Abdullah ashore.

"Let us walk back," said the secretary. "You will find all these little twisting lanes and numerous bridges very interesting."

He was full of bits of information, interesting anecdotes, opinions and explanations, and here in this lovely dream city, Rames was content to wander at his side and listen. But when they came out into the Piazza San Marco, his eyes widened.

The gold and blue of the mosaics, the glittering splendor of the glided domes, the delicate tracery of the marble balconies, all bathed in the warm Venetian sunlight against a turquoise sky, the pigeons that fluttered or poised about them, here was beauty satisfying even to his Eastern eye.

"The king lives here?" he asked.

"No, it is a cathedral, a temple, one of the most beautiful in the world. Venice never had a king until she united with the rest of Italy. She had always been a republic!"

"Republic?" here was another new word.

"A country where the people rule;" explained Abdullah.

Rames remembered a quiet hour in the Temple garden and Hotep's deep voice.

"There will come a day when the priests will no longer be able to keep knowledge from the people. When that times comes, kings will pass away!"

"Are there many republics?" he asked.

"Oh, yes, very great ones, France is one, and America."

"France, America!" What a wonderful store

of knowledge this new world held, and how pitifully inadequate the time allotted him.

The Doge's Palace was before them now, and
Abdullah watched Rames' deep eyes glow over its
beauties.

They stood at the edge of the Piazetta looking
back at the lovely scene; the stately Palace, beyond
it, the glittering façade of San Marco with its
bronze horses, and against the sky, tall, graceful,
the point catching the golden sunlight, the Cam-
panile.

Near the edge of the water stood two tall granite
shafts, on one a statue, on the other a winged lion.

"That is the famous lion of St. Mark," said
Abdullah pointing, "and between the columns a
scaffold used to be erected where criminals were
executed. The Venetians had imbibed much of the
Eastern symbolism, for this was once the gateway
to the Orient. The condemned were placed with
their faces to the water, for the land rejected them
and the sea meant eternity!"

Eternity, mused Rames, these people whose poor
little lives covered the sorry space of threescore
years and ten, what could they know of Eternity?
While he——

But Abdullah's energetic voice broke in on his
reverie.

"Queer, isn't it, the difference between the East
and the West? The Oriental is full of dreams, of
symbolism, of leaving things to Kismet. The Occidental is practical, energetic, active. He believes
himself master of his Fate. The schools of England knocked a lot of my Orientalism out of me.

That's why I never stay in the East long."

"You tell me the English do not dream," said Rames, "and yet you say the greatest poet of the world was English!"

"Exceptions, of course, but generally speaking the West stands for energy, and yet in this very city that holds so much of the East, some of the biggest movements of the world have begun."

"What, for instance?" Rames was interested, Abdullah's exhaustless flood of information was a never-failing source of wonder.

"The first bank in Europe was founded here, the first newspaper printed in the world was sold over there in the square for a small piece of money called a 'gazetta,' and even today newspapers are called gazettes! Now come and see the Bridge of Sighs! How many hopeless footsteps have passed over its marble arch, prisoners led to torture or condemned for life to horrible, slimy dungeons, and those going to execution whose bodies were afterwards rowed out to sea, to be thrown into the water in a spot where it was forbidden to cast a net on pain of death!"

At the steps of the Piazetta they entered a gondola and rowed out onto the lagoon.

"Every year on a certain feast day," said Abdullah pointing back to the quay from which they had just embarked, "the Doge stepped down from there and into his waiting gondola. It wasn't a plain black one like this, but ebony and mother-of-pearl, with rich canopies of cloth-of-gold and velvet. There were eighty men at the gilded oars, and to the sound of music they floated out to the sea. Here the cortege stopped, the Doge, magnificently dressed, stood in the prow of the boat and threw a golden ring into the water, saying:

"We wed thee, oh Sea, emblem of our rightful and perpetual dominion!"

Abdullah's voice was full and resonant as he proclaimed the words and threw his hand out with a gesture that a Doge himself might have envied.

Rames looked before him at the sparkling blue of the Adriatic and back at the fairy city rising from its waves.

"Ancient Egypt had such ceremonies," he said, "even more beautiful, more picturesque."

Abdullah was nettled.

"Whenever I tell you of the wonders and beauties of the world," he said, "you always say there was something more beautiful in ancient Egypt. What a pity, *effendi,* you did not live in those days!" And turning to the gondolier with some instructions, he failed to notice the startled look in his master's eyes.

That evening, slightly weary and appreciating the calm of his surroundings, Rames rested, musing, on his balcony. Twilight was slipping away like a shimmering veil and a clear beautiful star had just swung out over the tower of San Georgio.

"Tonight we shall go on the water," said Abdullah, coming through the long window. "Pietro is waiting for us, are you ready?"

Back of the towers, the moon was rising, a warm golden moon that paled as it rose higher, bathing the façades of the palaces in its silver sheen, and unrolling a glittering path across the water.

Presently out of the stillness floated a woman's voice, clear, softly sustained, another joined, then a tenor, and deeper, fuller, like the shadows that accentuated the silver moonlight, a rich baritone threaded its notes through the others.

Rames was thrilled. The music of the new world more than all its other wonders stirred him. He lay back among the cushions with his eyes half closed, his heart full of longing brought into being by the appealing sweetness of the singing.

The gondolas, their colored lanterns like trembling jewels, collected about the musicians, and Pietro, with the ingenuity of his class, dextrously edged into the inner circle.

The moon sailed higher, a gleaming silver shield, the crowds of gondolas about the musicians grew denser, Abdullah touched his arm.

"Shall we go now?" he asked, and Rames was just about to nod, when a gondola which was backing out from among the others, glided almost by the side of theirs.

As it passed, the light from one of the other boats fell full upon the face of a girl who was sitting back among the cushions.

She was so close, he could almost have put out his hand and touched her. He leaned forward, every nerve tense. His eyes looked full into hers. Amazement, awe, and a stupendous wonder swept over him, for it was the same face he had seen in the Catacombs.

Then he had not dreamed! His longing mind had not conjured up a vision!

There was no doubt. It was the face of Teta!

But before he could speak, the gondola had vanished in the darkness.

"Abdullah," he cried hoarsely,'' tell the man to turn and follow!"

The secretary put a remonstrating hand on his arm.

"My master," he said, "it is not well to pursue every pretty face. There is enough trouble in the world."

But Rames shook off his hand impatiently.

"Give him gold, much gold," he said pointing to the gondolier, "give him all he asks, if he will only find her!"

Abdullah shrugged.

Men were the same the world over, he reasoned. In one thing they did not differ. Resignedly, he gave Pietro his orders, and although the man scarcely knew of what he was in search, the size of the reward would have made him try to find the most impossible thing. He turned his boat and rowed madly in the direction Abdullah indicated.

"Find her!" urged Rames. "You must find her! She must not be lost to me!" But into what one of the many small canals the gondola they sought had disappeared, they could not tell.

Discouraged and heartsick, Rames at last consented to return to the hotel, but all night long he paced his room. His emotions were conflicting, disturbing, undefinable. Was this vision sent only to torture him? Was this one of the trials of which Hotep had warned?

Abdullah watched him curiously. His whole manner was changed. The poise, the calm, seemed to have left him. His eyes were over-brilliant, his hands clutched and unclutched nervously as he swung up and down the great room. What was the trouble that had come to this man of mystery? Surely he was not the type the mere sight of a pretty face would so disturb. But long after Abdullah had retired to his own room, he heard the steady tread of the restless feet going back and forth.

The next morning Rames was ready and waiting for him on the balcony with every appearance of having been up for hours.

There were fine lines drawn about his deep eyes, unmistakable signs of a long vigil.

"What shall we do today?" asked the secretary.

"Take me into the streets where people gather," was the answer.

There was that in his manner that precluded further questioning, and in silence they walked through the Piazzetta, across the Piazza San Marco, and into the Merceria.

Rames stared into the face of every woman who passed, eagerly, expectantly, his whole attention so given to his search that at last Abdullah, who had been trotting along at his side, summoned up courage to ask:

"Tell me, *effendi*, is there someone whom you desire to find? Someone in particular?"

"Yes," he said earnestly, "I am seeking someone, someone whom I must find! Last night and once before in Rome, I saw a vision, I am following that! The nobles, those of the highest caste, where do they spend the different hours of the day?"

Abdullah hid a smirk behind his hand. Truly men were alike the world over. A pretty face, a graceful ankle, and empires could fall!

"From four to five in the afternoon," he said, "the fashionable people gather at the Lido and have tea."

"Is that a hotel?"

"No, it is a beach, a bathing-place not far away."

"Order the gondola, we go at once!"

Abdullah bit his lip at the peremptory tone, but he hurried back to the Piazetta and seated himself in the gondola beside his impatient master.

All the way out to the Lido, they spoke no word. Once or twice the secretary opened his lips, but the expression on the proud face beside him discouraged any attempt at conversation, and so at last with a sigh, for it was difficult for Abdullah to keep quiet long, he leaned back and studied his companion.

They went directly to the Pavilion and, finding a table that commanded a view of the large room, settled themselves to watch the gay parties which came and went.

The tea and toast that had been ordered perfunctorily, remained untasted. Rames' eyes roved about the room, and presently Abdullah saw him stiffen in his chair, a dark flush creeping under the clear bronze of his cheek. He turned to follow his gaze and saw a group of five people coming in at the door.

They made their way through the labyrinth of

tables to one quite close, and as they took their seats, the secretary saw the skin whiten across the knuckles of the hand with which Rames clutched the side of the table.

In the party were two young men, an elderly lady, and two younger ones, one of whom, a slender girl with curious, shadowy eyes and heavy bronze hair that showed beneath a wide-brimmed hat, sat almost directly facing them.

Rames uttered a low exclamation.

It was Teta! Teta in the flesh, dressed in these clumsy English clothes that concealed the beauty of her slender body and round arms, the curious head-dress hiding the wonder of her hair, but nevertheless Teta, the girl he had loved and lost in that far distant yesterday!

With every nerve straining for the moment when she would look at him, Rames waited. It was beyond his understanding, but the fact remained and he did not question. Was his presence not equally strange? She was here, near him, that was all he cared to know.

The little party was a merry one, and laughed and talked gayly among themselves, but at last the girl, impelled perhaps by his magnetic gaze, turned and looked at him.

His face was burning, eager, his eyes ablaze. For a moment she met his gaze full, and then slowly turned her head and smiled at some sally from the youth at her side.

The color faded from Rames' face, his mouth set in a bitter line, the light in his eyes died.

The tragedy of it! She did not know him!

His hands trembled where they gripped the edge of the little table. He had a curious sense of being in a mad dream from which he was struggling to awaken.

Abdullah's approving eye had taken in the grace and charm of the girl and he leaned toward his companion, smiling.

"Is this the young lady you are seeking?" he asked in a low voice, and without taking his eyes from the girl opposite, Rames nodded. He sat as one who beholds a vision which he fears will fade. Once again the girl looked at him, impelled by his eyes, but immediately turned away, flushing. These glances which saw, yet did not see him, which held no faintest recognition, were like knife-thrusts in his heart.

At last the elderly lady, leaning toward one of the young men, said something in an undertone, and presently the party prepared to go.

As they passed his table Rames half rose from his chair, but Abdullah put a restraining hand on his arm.

"Don't," he whispered, "it isn't done! You will not only bring trouble to yourself, but annoyance to her. Be patient, there will be some way to meet the young lady. Wait!"

In a sort of daze Rames saw her leave. The sunlight seemed to fade, the air grew suffocating.

"Let us go," he muttered, and rising, hurried between the rows of tables and out to where the Adriatic lay shining and calm as satin, under the sapphire arch of the sky. Gay shouts and laughter came up to them from the beach where bright spots of color bobbed up and down in the waves, but in all the throng about them there was no sign of the girl or her party. Once more she had slipped away, vanished like a dream. But this time the dream was more real, more tangible. In spite of the mystery of it, inconceivable as it seemed, she had followed him out of that past which lay buried with the ruins of ancient Kampt.

Abdullah, seeing his evident desire to be alone, wandered off, and Rames stood staring out to sea, lost in his own thoughts.

The last message that Amrou had brought echoed in his mind.

"Tell him I will come again!"

She had kept her promise, but the veil of those many centuries had obscured her vision. Her eyes could not penetrate it. She had come again, but she did not know him.

The sun was setting in a blaze of glory. A transparent golden haze hung over the water. Great banks of crimson and mauve, of orange and delicate amber barred the horizon. The blue of the water had turned ruddy gold. The dark sail of a fishing boat hovered like a great bird in the distance.

Rames turned and beckoned Abdullah, who stood in lively conversation with a pretty French actress, whose small dog had brought about the acquaintance, and silent, wrapped in sorrowful reverie, he returned to Venice.

Later, Abdullah at his side, he drifted about among the gondolas hoping for a glimpse of her face again. But although many lovely eyes smiled into his, the ones he sought were nowhere to be found.

That night he dreamed that he had crossed a great ocean, whose vastness was beyond the imagination of man. Hopelessly, sorrowfully, he stood and gazed back on the distant shore where he had left Teta. He saw her standing wrapped in a mysterious light that touched to living gold the bronze of her hair, and shone translucently in her deep eyes. She held out her arms to him, the measureless waste vanished, and with a wonderful joy, he drew her to him and knew peace again!

CHAPTER XV

WHEN Abdullah entered the next morning, he found his master fully dressed and almost cheerful.

"Use the morning to do as you desire," he said. "I shall spend the time in reading the papers that tell the news of the world."

In the writing-room of the hotel were the usual tables for the convenience of guests, and also, at one side, a rack in which were laid a number of magazines and newspapers.

Rames had learned to read with some degree of ease, and picking up a magazine whose cover bore the gayly colored picture of a beautiful girl and a handsome youth, locked in each other's embrace, he turned the pages curiously. These little black marks so neat and well ordered, covering the white sheets in long columns, how strange that they could convey the tenderest or the most lofty thoughts of man, and the pictures that were so cunningly devised to fit them, how they accentuated the printed words. The ingenuity that could invent so comprehensive a form of inscription as to cause the reader to know every emotion that man is capable of feeling, excited his admiration.

He thought of Thebes and the crowds that gathered in the market-place to hear the wandering men who entertained them with stories; of the jesters in the houses of the nobles, and the tales they told to amuse the guests. Here in this new world, each man could be his own scribe, his own tale-teller. Of course there had been great libraries in Thebes, rolls upon rolls of papyrus. There was the great Book of the Dead which was buried with the mummies, the Book of Thoth, that told of magic spells, books of wisdom and learning. But these were for the priests and were written in a language which they alone could understand. Here everyone could read, and not only the thoughts of the wise and learned were considered worthy of recording, but jests and witty anecdotes. Even the most insignificant happenings were flashed from one far country to another and put in a form that all might understand.

With a sense of pleasure he realized that he was beginning to comprehend these symbols which were so much more complete than those of his own country. His vocabulary was growing, and he found that the words illustrative of the subject discussed, came readily to his mind. The slight accent which was little more than a lingering of the tongue over certain words, was still apparent, but it was vague, difficult to place, and although his phrases were sometimes stilted, Abdullah's Oxford training showed in his pupil's careful English.

The writing-room had been quite empty when he came in and the quiet and peace soothed his troubled spirit. The soft April breeze swayed the long curtains at the windows and stirred the pages before him.

He bent over a particularly difficult passage, his black brows drawn together. Some of the English idioms were tantalizingly elusive. He laid the magazine back on the rack, and turning in his chair, looked straight into a pair of eyes that sent the blood leaping through his veins.

The girl had evidently come into the room while he was absorbed in his reading, for he had heard no sound, and now she sat facing him at one of the small desks close by.

For a long moment his eyes held hers with something in their depths, so intense, so filled with a sort of reverence, that against her will she stared back at him, her heart fluttering curiously. Slowly the warm color mantled her cheeks, and she bent once more over her writing, but his gaze was so magnetic, so impelling, that involuntarily she raised her head again. The look she met was full of tender yearning, a pleading wistfulness, that seemed to implore recognition. With an effort she lowered her eyes and gathering her letters, rose and started toward the door.

He followed hurriedly, his hands held out to her. "Teta——!".

She turned, the vibrant voice holding her more strongly than had the strange look in his dark eyes.

"Teta," he repeated in his own tongue, "it is I! Rames! Do you not know me?"

The girl shook her head.

"I do not understand the language you speak," she said, smiling faintly, "you evidently mistake me for someone else."

She spoke English, but the voice with its every

modulation was Teta's. He put out his hand as though to touch her, but she drew back startled.

There could be no mistaking that he sincerely believed her to be someone else. What a curious language he spoke and how strangely he looked at her. A feeling of vague unrest seized her as though some dim emotion which had lain dormant for countless ages was suddenly stirring, waking into life.

"Do you not speak English?" she asked, and added in spite of herself. "Is there someone in the world so like me that you mistake me for her?"

"But you are Teta!" he repeated. "Teta, I am Rames!"

His manner was so strange that the girl was frightened. Perhaps he was a little mad. She looked about her startled, and then bowing slightly, turned and hurried from the room.

He stood gazing after her with his soul in his eyes.

He had seen and spoken to a living Teta and she did not know him.

As he stared at the door through which she had vanished, Abdullah came hastily in.

"I have news for you," he said, "the young lady whom you so much admired yesterday is staying here at this very hotel!"

Rames turned away with a sigh.

"Yes," he said dully, "I have seen her."

Abdullah was disappointed.

"I thought you would be pleased to know," he said. "I've even discovered her name!"

"What is it?"

"Miss Iris Waverly of New York City. The lady with the gray hair is her mother."

Never for a moment did Rames doubt that this girl whose face had twice shone out from the surrounding shadows was Teta, the same Teta that he had known and loved. Yet her name was different, a name that was difficult for his unaccustomed tongue to pronounce. Her dress was that of the women of this new world, her language was theirs, and strangest of all, she had a mother, a tall, stately gray-haired mother.

The Teta of Thebes had been an orphan from early childhood, ward of Hotep, the High Priest, lady of an ancient line. She had sworn that her heart would wait through all the ages, and yet she had forgotten him!

He rose wearily.

"Come, Abdullah," he said, "let us go out on the water. Let us sail to the very edge of the sea!"

Meantime Miss Iris Waverly, of New York City, sat resting her pretty chin in the palms of her hands, looking out over the canal from her window.

Who was this strange man, she wondered. He was different from anyone she had ever seen. From what country did he come? He might be a high-caste Hindu, she thought, with his clear olive skin, and delicately marked features, or he might be a Spaniard, but she knew a little Spanish and the language in which he had addressed her was certainly not that. His dark eyes, the beautiful lines of his supple figure, the proud lift of his chin, were before her eyes now as she gazed out over the water. Who was he? Who was the girl for whom he had mistaken her? Teta! What an odd name! Teta!

"Iris," called her mother, "we are waiting, dear."

Later, as they went through the hotel lobby, Abdullah passed her. Making an excuse, she turned back for a moment, while the others waited at the steps for their gondola.

The *concièrge,* a large, gold-laced individual, came toward her, bowing.

"Can you tell me?" she asked hurriedly, as she slipped a coin into his ready hand, "Who is that dark, foreign-looking gentleman?" and she nodded toward the little Egyptian who was just entering the lift.

"He is secretary to Prince Rames," answered the man pompously, "the Signorina may have noticed him. He is very handsome and very rich. The secretary speaks many languages. More than even I!"

Iris glanced around nervously. She felt a sort of wonder at herself that she should be asking questions like this of a servant, but something impelled her to find out all she could.

"From, what country are they?" she asked.

The man raised his shoulders expressively.

" I do not know, Signorina, I only know he is a prince, he is very rich, very distinguished, he occupies the royal suite. Even I can discover no more about him!"

The girl flushed under his knowing smile, and

slipping another coin into his hand, hurried out onto the terrace.

She was half inclined to tell her mother of her experience, but the thought that perhaps Mrs. Waverly would judge as impertinence what she felt certain was a genuine mistake, made her decide not to mention it, but all morning as they floated along the Grand Canal, or wandered through the shops in the Merceria, the dark face with its compelling eyes and mysterious charm, drifted before her vision.

Abdullah had also been busy with questions and in consequence had discovered that the Waverlys and their party usually lunched at the hotel. He arranged for a table as near theirs as possible and later, when Iris and her mother entered the dining-room, the girl flushed as she took her place, for again she looked straight into the dark eyes of which she had been thinking.

Abdullah leaned toward his companion.

"Do not stare so," he admonished, "you are making the young lady uncomfortable. Listen; I have a plan. Tonight there is to be an entertainment here in the hotel. The money will go to charity. One of the young men with whom you saw her at the Lido is very prominent in the affair. He will undoubtedly come to me for a donation and when he does I will refer him to you. You must be generous, so generous that you will win his gratitude. This will lead to an acquaintance, and then perhaps he will introduce you to the young lady."

Rames frowned.

"Why all this form?" he asked. "I do not want to speak with him, it is she, only she in whom I am interested."

"All very well," agreed Abdullah. "She certainly is a very pretty girl, but these people are particular. You must meet her in the conventional way of Europe, and that is to be introduced· by someone who knows you both."

Abdullah's quick intelligence and cosmopolitan training made it a simple matter for him to form acquaintances, and it was not long after the unfolding of his plan that Rames, who was sitting in the little writing-room studying ·over the magazines, saw him approaching accompanied by the blond young man who he remembered seeing at the Lido.

"Prince," said the little Egyptian as Rames rose, "this gentleman wishes to speak to you," and, bowing, he left them.

"Your secretary tells me," began the American, as he seated himself, "that you might contribute something to our enterprise tonight."

"I shall be honored," answered Rames. "Would a thousand *lire* be of any assistance to you?"

"You are very generous," said the American. "May I know whom I am to thank?"

"I am Prince Rames."

"And I am John Reading of New York City. Have you ever been there?"

"Not yet," was the answer; "but some day I hope to go. Is it very wonderful?"

"Don't get me started on America," laughed Reading. "Of course I think it's the greatest place in the world!"

"So?" Rames was interested. "More wonderful than Rome, Athens, Cairo?"

"Than every other place put together; but Cairo is great, isn't it?" And soon they were deep in a discussion of the city of the Arabian Nights. When at last Reading rose to go, it was with a sense of intense interest in this distinguished stranger whose nationality puzzled him.

That night Rames saw very little of the performance. His eyes were filled with a vision of Iris as she sat with her friends on the far side of the great ball-room.

She looked very lovely in a dark-green evening gown, her shoulders and arms white against the shimmer of the satin, her bronze hair framing the delicate oval of her face.

Reading, sitting beside her, bowed across to Rames, who knew from the flush on the girl's cheeks that he was being discussed.

"My plan is working," whispered Abdullah, "soon you will be introduced to the young lady and things will go as you wish." But, although they sat patiently all through the performance, at its conclusion they saw Iris and her mother leave and the rest of her party were swallowed up in the crowd.

"Have patience," encouraged Abdullah, "tomorrow is another day!"

CHAPTER XVI

READING greeted Rames cordially the next day when they met in the lobby.

"This is a great place, isn't it?" he smiled: "Such air, such sunshine! We're all going out to the Lido to have a swim."

"I go, also," said Rames—the Lido had suddenly become a place of engrossing interest—"the water, it is delightful!"

"Good," was the cordial answer, "I hope I shall see you there."

"Indeed, yes," Rames' eyes blazed eagerly, "that will charm me," and they parted with the curious gesture of these Europeans, a clasp of the hand.

From his balcony he watched Iris and her mother step into the gondola, and, as they glided away, he turned to Abdullah.

"I go to the Lido," he said. "I will return later," and although the secretary's anxious inquiries as to whether he felt able to cope with gondoliers and bath-house attendants disquieted him somewhat, he held to his purpose and set out alone.

The sunny beach with its joyous crowds of bathers, the blue of the sparkling water rippling away to the horizon, made no impression upon his mind. He sat apart watching the gay throngs, his eager eyes carefully scanning each group in search of one face, one slender graceful form.

Then he saw her!

She and her friends were gathered about a huge, gayly striped sunshade. They were all in bathing dress except Mrs. Waverly. Beside her sat Iris, her long slender legs encased in black silk stockings, a smart black costume following the lines of her supple body. Her bronze hair was hidden under a brilliant red silk handkerchief, and her rounded arms gleamed bare to the shoulders.

How he longed to be one of the merry party that surrounded her, but for him there was no place. A feeling of utter loneliness filled his heart as he realized how completely isolated he was from the rest of the world.

As though in response to his intent gaze, Reading turned his head and, observing him, waved a friendly greeting. He saw him bend toward Mrs. Waverly and Iris and divined that he was the subject of their remarks. Presently, the young American rose and came toward him and, after the usual exchange of conventionalities, invited him to meet his friends.

In a daze Rames went through the introductions, bowed over the hand of Mrs. Waverly, and at last seated himself on the warm sand at Iris' side.

The wonder of it! He had found her!

For a moment it was impossible for him to recall one of the new words he had been at such pains to learn. He could only look at her, his eyes filled with the longing for recognition.

Surely this was the same girl who had leaned from a latticed window in Thebes, and said:

"Until my lips shall rest again on thine, I shall know neither happiness nor peace!"

And now she looked at him with eyes that expressed only polite interest, and he must converse with her in the casual manner of two people meeting for the first time, when he was longing to tell her what an agony of loneliness life had been without her, how he needed her, how he loved her!

The other girl in the party, a pretty little blonde, leaned forward with a friendly smile, and he forced himself to answer her questions, although his eyes, filled with a sort of reverent awe, were centered on Iris, whose face, whose manner, whose very voice belonged to the Teta of Thebes, lovelier than ever, even in this curious costume.

"Yes, Venice is very charming," he heard himself saying, and they were all soon launched in a conversation about the places they had seen, the things they had done, after the manner of travelers whose paths cross.

Mrs. Waverly studied him closely; what an unusual type he was. The trim, blue bathing costume which Abdullah's foresight had provided, displayed the beautiful lines of his figure to advantage, and the bronze limbs with the delicate curve of muscle and satin smoothness of skin, the fine, well-formed arms and shoulders, compelled her admiration. She was sure he was not an Italian, but from what country he came, she could not guess.

She observed that the laughing sallies and quick American phrases puzzled him, and that in spite of his careful, perfectly pronounced English, there were many words in common use with which he was unfamiliar.

At last Reading suggested they have their swim.

Rames had never before bathed in the sea. The Nile, with its palm-fringed banks and the deep pool in his garden had been his only experience. The buoyancy of this cool salt water was delightfully exhilarating. He felt as though his body were a feather, a thing without weight.

But he was filled with amazement as he watched the grace and daring of Iris. The Teta of Thebes had never learned the art of swimming, nor indeed was it commonly practiced by women of her class, but this girl swam as though the water were her native element.

On the way back to Venice it was suggested that he be one of their party that evening to hear the music on the Grand Canal, and long before the hour appointed, he was waiting for them on the terrace.

Adroitly he managed to have Iris step into his own gondola, and although the boats drifted side by side, under the hood of the little craft he had the girl to himself.

She leaned back against the cushions, the moonlight touching with a silver pencil the delicate lines of her profile.

"How curious," she said, "that you should have mistaken me for someone else."

"I am not mistaken, you have forgotten, that is all!"

The gondolas were gathering about the clustered lights. The palaces which in the sunlight showed pitifully stained and old, were fairy-like and wonderful under the magic of the moon. A tender love song throbbed across the water.

"Tell me," she said softly, "where have we met before?"

There was something in the dark eyes looking so intently into hers, that thrilled her. She was vitally conscious of his presence, of an intangible emotion that half pleased, half frightened her.

She heard his voice, low, vibrant.

"Have you ever drifted, through the hush of the evening, in a golden boat on a still pool with lotus flowers swaying against your hands, and the sound of a lute coming plaintively from the shadows of the tamarisks?"

"How wonderful that would be," she said softly. "I wish I had—I should love to—but I never have!"

"Have you ever wandered through a scented garden in the cool of the day, and listened to some one telling of wonderful journeys you and he were to make together? Have you ever knelt by his side and looked at your two faces in crystal water? Oh, Teta, Teta, have you forgotten!"

He leaned toward her, but she drew away breathlessly.

"Are you a poet?" she asked.

He straightened his shoulders and stared ahead of him.

"No poet," he said, "only a man with a memory!"

She leaned back in the shadows where her eyes could rest on the fine profile unobserved.

"You called me Teta," she said half timidly, "may I not know more of her? It seems so strange that there should be someone in the world who so exactly resembles me!"

He looked at her earnestly.

"Have you no memory of the desert under a pitiless sun, with desolate hills against a burnished sky? A ring of savage, fierce-eyed men—the clash of arms —shrieks of terror and a wild ride into a trackless waste?"

"How strangely you talk," she said, laughing nervously. "I have never seen a desert!"

With a sigh he turned away.

Was this all a dream from which he would presently awaken?

Who was this man, she wondered, what was he?

She tried tactfully to make him speak of himself, but he evaded the subject, and yet she was sure that his reticence was not because he wished to surround himself with the interest of mystery. She felt instinctively that he had suffered greatly, and for this reason she readily forgave questions concerning herself which from another man would have been regarded as impertinent.

The curious ring he wore attracted her attention. The wonderfully carved figures were unlike anything she had ever seen and the gem fascinated her with its strange, pulsating fire:

"It is a talisman," he said in response to her questions, "some day I shall tell you its history."

Later as they stepped ashore at the hotel, Rames held the girl's hand a moment in his.

"Venice is wonderful!" he said softly. "This evening shall hold its place among those others I have spoken of, dearer even than they!"

CHAPTER XVII

THE days that followed were wonderful halcyon days. Venice with all its treasures lay before them like a lovely volume of fairy tales. The Lido with its golden sands, and the clear blue waters of the Adriatic, beckoned. The canals, twisting and turning between the marble palaces, invited their exploration. The silver calm of the nights with the water whispering under the keel of their gondola, the lights trailing into the shadows like shimmering banners hung from invisible balconies, the tender appeal of distant music, all cast their enchantment about them.

To Rames it was only finding again the golden thread of a romance that had been lost for centuries, but for Iris life was just beginning, opening radiant vistas of which she had never dreamed. Iris was falling in love.

Only one shadow marred their happiness. Rames felt instinctively her sorrow because of his reticence concerning himself. Things that should have been spoken of quite casually, which in themselves were of no moment, took gigantic shape because of his evident wish not to discuss them. The look in her eyes went to his heart when he was forced to evade some of her innocent questions. But to tell his secret meant that she would either look upon him as a mad man or a thing with which no other creature could hold communion.

"You are like Lohengrin," she said to him one day. "I have a feeling that if I were to ask you certain questions you would look at me with those mysterious eyes and step out of my life forever!"

"I shall not go until you send me," he answered, "but some day I must obey a summons. Until then, keep me by your side!"

"You will persist in calling me Teta," she said half resentfully. "My name is Iris! It means the rainbow, you know."

He looked at her for a moment, startled, and then a great light came into his eyes.

"The rainbow!" he repeated softly. "The bridge that reaches from one horizon to the other! Iris, I have crossed that bridge and found you at its end!"

That night in the quiet of her room, the girl repeated his words, and thought her name had never sounded so sweet as when he had said it. But Mrs. Waverly, although intensely interested in this fascinating stranger, watched with practical eyes the trend of affairs.

She was one of those representative women of America, the type that embodies great charm with intellect, and had no conventions that were not founded on sane principles.

"You are from the East, Prince?" she asked one day.

Rames' answer had been vague, evasive, and although her questions were as direct as good breeding would permit, he managed to elude them adroitly and change the subject. But the knowledge that his reticence might prove unsatisfactory to the elder lady troubled him. He must find some way to avert her suspicions.

Abdullah watched with interest the growing intimacy between his master and Iris, and suggested many things that would please the girl and her mother. It was he who selected interesting books, flowers, and candy for them.

"These must be your only gifts," he assured Rames, "else her mother will not allow her to accept them. That is the custom." And Rames had to be content.

Mrs. Waverly was fond of jewels, not for adornment, as were so many of her country women, but simply for their beauty, and in going about on their shopping expeditions, Rames had manifested his knowledge of gems.

"I wish I knew as much about precious stones as you do, Prince," she said one day. "Gems, to me, are like visible souls; I love them!"

"I have some very fine ones," he said simply, "may I show them to you?"

Mrs. Waverly thanked him and it was arranged that he bring them to her apartment that afternoon.

Iris and her mother were in ecstasies over the beauty of the gems that he spread before them. Rubies, glowing like sparks of living fire; emeralds, whose clear depths mocked the translucent waters of the Adriatic; black opals burning, shimmering, pulsating; only a few in all, but these few would have ransomed a king.

"How beautiful!" exclaimed Mrs. Waverly. "I have never seen such wonderful stones!" And seeing an opportunity for information, added, "They are heirlooms, I presume?"

"They have passed through many generations," replied Rames with a faint smile.

Certain leading questions crowded to Mrs. Waverly's lips, but the manner of asking them eluded her and she bent over the splendid jewels admiringly, appreciating their great value At least this man was no fortune hunter, she thought, and for the time she dismissed the slight distrust which his reticence and the mystery surrounding him had caused.

As the days slipped by, they wandered about the lovely dream city, Abdullah always discreetly in the background as both chaperone and guide.

Then Iris, her voice shaking a little, came to him with the information that her mother had decided to leave for Paris the next day, and within a week they were to sail for America.

Rames was stunned, Teta was leaving him again! That last horrible journey came back to him with crushing force. But Mrs. Waverly laughed when he begged them to stay.

"My dear Prince," she said, "America is our home, we have been away for ages. Some day perhaps you will be coming there, then we shall see each other again."

Resolving in his secret mind that America should be the next stage of his pilgrimage, he begged to be allowed to spend this last evening with Iris on the Grand Canal.

"My dear child," Mrs. Waverly admonished as Iris threw an evening cape over her shoulders, "he is very fascinating, very charming, and evidently very much impressed with you, but I rely on your good sense to remember that after all we know nothing of him, who he is, what he is, nor even from where he comes. Your father would be very much annoyed if I should allow any entanglements, so be careful, dear, and be as nice to him as you can be without—you understand!"

In her heart, the girl knew her mother was right, but she also knew that it did not matter who he was, nor what he was, and although he had not put into words what she had seen in his eyes, yet she understood and was happy.

They stepped into a gondola, and glided out into the moonlight. The shadow of the black hood hid them close. Pietro, the gondolier, poised gracefully on the edge of the stern behind them. They were as alone as though the world held only they two.

For a time they drifted silently; Iris sensing the words trembling on his lips, waited.

At last he reached out his hand and covered hers. Her warm, slender fingers closed on his.

"Teta," he murmured, "how can I let you go again? How can I bear separation a second time?"

"That first time must have been ages ago, I can't even remember it," her voice was bravely gay. "New York isn't far, you will come there?"

"I mean to follow you to the end of the world," he said, and then, turning suddenly, he crushed her in his arms.

"Teta, Teta," he whispered against her lips, "I love you, my love will outlast these very waters,

will survive even the stars reflected in them—
Teta!"

Swept before the storm of his passion, she could
only cling to him murmuring over and over:

"I love you! I love you!"

Pietro's oar dipped rhythmically into the luminous
water that whispered against the side of the gondola, telling of other lovers who had drifted here
and plighted vows everlasting.

"You will come soon to New York?" she said.
"Otherwise I shall think all this was only a wonderful dream!"

He held her close to him.

"No dream could be half so enchanting," he
said.

From his pocket he drew a ring. The stone
flashed back the moonlight in a ruby gleam. She
saw that it was one of the most exquisite of the
gems he had shown her mother and herself and that
it had been set in a curiously wrought band.

"This is my heart," he said. "I am giving it into
your keeping!"

"It shall fill the place where mine has been,"
she said softly.

He lifted her face to his.

"Beloved," he said earnestly, "this hour was foretold centuries ago. You have forgotten, but the gods
have decreed that we shall be one!"

Their good-byes were said out under the moon
and when Iris slept that night, the ruby ring lay
against her heart.

"I shall wear it there until he comes for me," she
thought, "his heart against mine!"

The next morning Rames was in the lobby to bid them good-bye. He bowed over the hand of Mrs. Waverly and thanked her for her polite hopes of seeing him in New York, and to Iris, the look in his eyes told her all he wished to say, although his words were conventional.

As she stepped into the waiting gondola, his heart cried to take her once more in his arms, to feel her warm lips again on his, but he only lifted his hat as Abdullah had taught him and watched until they were out of sight. Then he turned away, all the glory and romance of Venice faded and dead.

CHAPTER XVIII

THE first few days after Iris had gone were empty ones for Rames. He lived over again the time in Thebes when Amrou had returned with his dreadful message. His longing became almost anguish.

In vain Abdullah tried to lift him from the melancholy into which the girl's departure had thrown him. He held out all the tempting baits he could devise. Germany, France, England were suggested, artfully garnished with information such as had been, in his experience, of eager interest to his master. But Rames refused them all.

"Tell me of this great ocean she is to cross," he said, "tell me of her country!"

Abdullah spent hours patiently describing every detail of the journey that was to carry Iris into New York. He had lived some time in America and so was able to paint a vivid picture for his earnest listener.

"They will probably land two weeks from to-day," he said one morning. "I can almost see the Goddess of Liberty now. New York Harbor is a great sight. I love it myself!"

Rames sat suddenly straight in his chair.

"Abdullah," he said, "can we reach New York before she does?"

The secretary by now had grown used to his patron's sudden whims.

"A ship leaves from Genoa the day after tomorrow," he said quietly. "It will reach New York within twelve days!"

Rames rose to his feet, an eager light in his eyes. To be in that far country when she should come! To meet her as she set foot on land! What wonderful happiness that would be! And how strange that he, the most alien of all the people in her country, should be the first to welcome her home!

"Abdullah," he said, "we will go to New York!"

Rames no longer questioned his secretary's ability to accomplish no matter what difficult task he proposed. He felt almost like that great king of the Jews at whose word genii came to do his bidding.

So it was arranged that they leave the next day for Genoa.

The steamer they boarded brought forth no wondering remark from Rames as had the one at Alexandria. The marvel of modern transportation was becoming a matter of course. He stood at the rail as they slowly steamed out of the harbor. The breeze carried the long ribbon of smoke pouring from her great funnels far astern and spread wide the folds of the flag she flew.

Out into the color, light and sunshine of the Mediterranean, the great ship ploughed her stately way.

Although Rames was no longer amazed at many of the usages of this new world, his mind, trained by Theban priests, still clung to his belief in magic.

Abdullah had tried to convince him that magic, in these days, meant taking rabbits out of silk hats or coins from the ears of innocent bystanders. But Rames, whose very presence here was magic, smiled and shook his head. To be sure, much of what had seemed marvelous in his own age, had perished by contrast with this.

"Modern science has explained most of what was magic to the ancients," said Abdullah one day. "The worship of animals in Egypt for instance, the sanctity of the Nile, the so-called miracles of those wise old priests!"

Rames regarded him curiously.

"Just what do the men of today say of those things?" he asked.

Abdullah puffed out his narrow chest.

"The ancient Egyptians made certain animals sacred because they were so necessary to them," he said, "also it was forbidden to pollute the Nile for fear of pestilence. The priests played upon the credulity of the people with seeming miracles so as to inspire their awe, and so serve their selfish ends. Today every one knows their pretended magic was mere trickery!"

So that was how the wisdom of his fathers had died! The marvelous plant nurtured through so many centuries and culminating in the brain of Ho-tep, had withered beneath the breath of ridicule.

What would these people, who mocked at the knowledge of ancient Kampt, say if they could know the means by which he had entered their world?

Musing, wrapped in thought, he paced the deck

alone, or gazed out to where the rugged mountains of Sardinia rose above the horizon.

They passed Gibraltar on a clear, beautiful morning. The great rock lifted its impregnable mass against a cloudless sky.

"This was once supposed to be the end of the world," said Abdullah, "the pillars of Hercules were as far as the ancients dared to go."

The next day he pointed a slender brown finger to where, far on the horizon, deep purple against the sky, shadowy and vague, rose the irregular line of Fayal and Pico.

"There are the Azores," he said, "where Columbus put in to repair his ships," and Rames listened with eager interest to the story of the man whose watchword in the face of the greatest discouragement had been, "Sail on!"

His pilgrimage, also, was toward the setting sun; he, too, must hold before him that courageous motto, no matter what the end would be.

They passed quite close to the islands and the pink, white and buff-colored houses could be plainly seen. Back of them shone the clear blue of the sky through the lacy pyramids of occasional pine trees, and above, ringed by fleecy clouds, rose sharp peaks of the mountains. It was very lovely, and Rames stood at the rail watching the fairy islands until they faded away in the distance.

The days that followed with nothing but sea and sky about them, with the wind that blows from the ends of the world whipping in their faces and the sharp salt spray stinging their cheeks, filled Rames with a torturing longing.

Somewhere out on this boundless waste her ship tossed too, so Abdullah had told him, and Abdullah was omniscient; but his straining eyes searched in vain for even a thread of smoke that would tell him of another steamer. The circle of the horizon was empty; tossing waves, flying clouds, smooth seas or wonderful purple and golden sunsets, but no living thing between the sea and sky as far as his eyes could reach. And yet proudly, steadily, in response to the hand that guided her great steel engines, the stately ship went on, nearer and nearer the goal of his heart, the day of his dreams.

At last one morning Abdullah came hurrying into the stateroom.

"Land is in sight," he said, "come up on deck and see New York!"

Rames followed him up the wide stair and out into the clear bright sunshine.

The sky was a deep, soft blue and the water sparkled around them iridescently. Hundreds of great grey gulls swooped about the ship, and along the rail the passengers were grouped, their steamer clothes discarded for smart-looking costumes that made them appear quite different from the veiled and plaid-capped creatures who had filled the long rows of chairs or paced the smooth white decks.

As the ship swung slowly on, flat green meadows came into view, then an irregular line of wheels and the towers of tawdry looking buildings.

"Good old Coney Island," laughed someone at his side, "I'm glad to see even that again!"

Rames watched the eager faces about him.

"How they love their country!" he said.   "It must be wonderful!"

"There's the Goddess of Liberty," said Abdullah. "At night the torch in her hand lights up the harbor.   The Americans like to say it illuminates the whole world!"

Up the bay a great statue was swinging into sight, majestic, dignified and graceful, despite its gigantic size.

"Liberty, all hail!" cried an enthusiastic youngster, whipping off his cap and waving it about.

"That is the symbol of this vast country," explained Abdullah, "its constitution reads, 'all men are created free and equal,' every man has a chance here."

The great buildings of lower Manhattan were looming into view.   Marvelous structures of a people who had revolutionized architecture to meet abnormal conditions.   Golden domes flashed in the sunlight, magnificent reaches of perpendicular line towered hundreds of feet into the air, the streets between them like deep canyons cut in the living rock. One superb creation rose in lofty grandeur above all the others, its gleaming white surface covered with a delicate fretwork that resembled the filmiest veil of lace.

Rames was filled with amazement.

"There are no kings here, you tell me," he said at last, "yet who but a Pharaoh could command enough slaves to rear such stupendous palaces and temples?"

"These people once fought a great war that abolished kings, and another that set free thousands of slaves," answered Abdullah. "Those buildings are neither temples nor palaces, they are simply great beehives where the work of the city is done. Why, these Americans can put up a skyscraper like one of those, in less time almost than it has taken you and me to come from Cairo here!"

As the inimitable sky-line of New York drifted nearer, Rames thought of the years that had gone to the building of the colossal monuments of his own country, of the thousands of slaves whose backs had chafed under the lash and the hauling ropes, of the burdens of taxes that had ground the people under their weight so that a Pharaoh might be exalted; and here was a mighty city whose proud head rose nearer to the sky than even the Pyramids, and there was neither a Pharaoh nor a king to lash the people on, for in this land, all "men were created equal!"

As the ship came alongside the dock, he watched curiously the crowds of eager people awaiting the arrival of loved ones. On board stewards were bustling to and fro, luggage was being wheeled out into the corridors, the atmosphere of quiet and calm that had filled the ship in mid-ocean was gone. The hurry and nervous excitement of land ran throbingly through her iron veins.

Rames followed Abdullah and their room-steward to the far end of the pier, where his luggage was stacked under a huge letter *R*, and as they waited for the custom officer to go through their belongings, the little Egyptian looked about him complacently.

"I'm glad to be back again," he said, "there is

only one New York in the world. Here you will see life really. The city throbs with it. Americans don't know what the word 'rest' means."

On the way up to the hotel in a comfortable little motor-car, Rames peered out at the crowded streets that flew past.

"How can the sun ever shine down between these high walls?" he asked. "The streets seem like some great crevice cut between giant cliffs. Do people actually live up there so near the sky?" and he craned his neck to see the top of the tall buildings.

"Up there," said Abdullah, "great business schemes are devised, laws are read, merchandise is manufactured."

The clanging surface cars, the scurrying automobiles with their warning sirens, the great trucks pausing at the raised hand of a stalwart, blue-clad figure who stood sentinel at the crossing, the hurrying throngs of busy, preoccupied men and women who jostled each other or threaded their way amongst the traffic, the great bridges of iron over which trains thundered above their heads, the noise, the clamor, the shifting, seething, hurrying scene, made Rames stare through the taxi windows in excited wonder.

Cairo had been entrancing, with the slow languor of the East. Athens in her beautiful blue and marble calm, had soothed him. Naples, with her sunshine, squalor and flowers was fascinating, as was Rome, modern mistress of ancient ruin, and in Venice, beautiful, silent, fairy-like Venice, had been redeemed the promise that had endured through all the ages. But this was different.

They alighted at one of the great hotels on a splendid avenue that seemed to run miles away into the distance. Rames could see its converging lines narrow into a point almost on the horizon.

"Fifth Avenue," explained Abdullah, with a wave of his hand, "famous everywhere, very fine!"

The wide, palm-fringed corridors of the hotel were filled with a shifting throng of richly dressed women, jewel-hung, silken-clad, with slender, well-shod feet, alert-eyed men and hurrying, smartly uniformed attendants. From somewhere in the distance came music, and as they passed a doorway, they saw a great room filled with many tables at which people were lunching.

"You call this a new country?" Rames asked as they started to explore the city the next day. "Surely all this magnificence and splendor must be the result of centuries of development."

"America is an infant among the nations of the world," replied Abdullah, "when Venice was in her glory, these streets were primeval forests."

When Venice was in her glory! mused Rames, and when he had walked the streets of Thebes, Venice herself had been a trackless swamp.

They walked briskly along what Abdullah called Broadway. Presently the little Egyptian turned and descended a covered stairway above which hung a sign,

"Subway,
        Downtown."

"Most of the great army of workers in New York," he said, "live many miles from their places of employment, and this is the means by which they may travel quickly to and fro."

He placed a coin before a tiny opening in a small window and two blue tickets were pushed out to him, which he dropped into a glass case, and they stepped out onto a long, concrete platform.

"What are these tracks?" asked Rames, peering into the long, black tunnel. "Are they for trains such as I have seen on the iron lattice-work over our heads?"

"The city is honeycombed with these subterranean passages," answered Abdullah. "A train runs under nearly every street, even beneath the beds of the rivers!"

A city in three tiers! Overhead, on the surface, underneath, were highways for the hurrying populace!

With a rumble and roar the train rolled along the platform on which they stood, and as they stepped aboard, Rames looked about him at the faces filling the cars. How indifferent they seemed. How unconscious of the wonders among which they lived.

"Do you feel a buzzing in your ears?" asked Abdullah. "We are under the bed of the river now, over our heads float monster ships. Strange, isn't it?"

New York grew more astounding every hour to this visitor from another age, and when, that night, Abdullah suggested that they go to a picture show, Rames eagerly consented, feeling sure that whatever he should see in this new world, would be wonderful.

The theater was one of the modern, almost palatial ones erected for the film dramas, and the cleverly manipulated lights and soft, well-chosen decorations were pleasing as well as beautiful.

They seated themselves in the comfortable velvet chairs to which a pretty grey-clad girl directed them. Presently the splendid orchestra burst into a flood of melody, the lights faded slowly, leaving everything in darkness except a brilliantly illuminated square on whose surface words suddenly appeared. Rames watched in astonishment as the letters vanished and were instantly replaced by men and women dressed in picturesque clothes, who began a sequence of most extraordinary adventures. They rode wild horses, swung dizzily from perpendicular cliffs, leaped chasms, fought enemies, narrowly escaping death in a dozen dreadful and complicated forms. From all of which, two lovers emerged triumphant, and the last scene, which faded slowly from view, showed them locked in each other's embrace.

Rames sank back in his seat.

"Is this real," he gasped, "or am I dreaming?"

"It is only a picture," Abdullah assured him, "but real people acted for it!"

"Pictures do not move! This is life except that it has no color."

"Moving pictures, one of the inventions of this wonderful people!" and then Abdullah went into a long explanation of the mechanism of the camera.

"They have even learned to photograph the skeletons of living men," he continued, as a series of X-ray pictures were flashed on the screen, jaw bones in action, knee sockets slipping smoothly as their owners walked up stairs.   Fingers that in one picture tapered delicately about the long stem of a rose, in the next instant, by the magic of the X-ray, showed only gruesome bones clutching a shadow.

"Here, indeed, is the skeleton at the feast," said Rames.   "Do not such scenes make people stop and think how soon their own flesh will wither and be as these?"

Abdullah laughed.

"You are so serious," he said, "I'm afraid it only makes them think that they may as well enjoy youth and life while it lasts.   Look about you.   These people come here to be entertained.   Their only thought is will the villain be punished and the hero receive his reward!   Philosophy is above the heads of an American 'movie' audience!"

"In ancient Egypt," began Rames, but Abdullah cut him short.

"In ancient Egypt indeed!   For all its knowledge, where is ancient Egypt today?"

And Rames was forced to echo his query, "Where indeed?"

CHAPTER XIX

EACH morning they eagerly scanned the newspapers for the arrival of the ship which was
to bring Iris, and at last Abdullah pointed out
the small line of print which spelled happiness for
Rames. The insignificant little item, hidden away
on the back page, stared out at him as though it
had been printed in huge headlines. Her ship was
sighted, would dock the next morning. Once more
he could look into those clear eyes that were his
world.

Abdullah had gained admission to the pier, and
at, an early hour they alighted from their motor
among the huge drays, express wagons, and taxi-
cabs that crowded the wide cobble-paved street on
the river front.

They made their way along the huge dock where
a crowd was already gathered, awaiting the incoming voyagers.

Rames glanced at the eager faces about him.
For the first time since he had come into the new
world, he had a sympathy in common with those
who surrounded him. They also awaited loved
ones!

The crowd began to stir and rustle and move
eagerly toward the end of the dock.

"There she comes," cried Abdullah, and majestically, gracefully, despite the two puffing little tugs

which escorted her, the great vessel swung into the slip.

Rames anxiously searched the faces that lined the rail. There were so many that at first he failed to see her, but at last Abdullah's quick eye singled out Mrs. Waverly and at her side, cheeks aglow with the excitement of home-coming, Rames saw Iris.

He drew back a little, a curious diffidence tugging at his heart, but as the ship was made fast and the gang-plank put into place by the hurrying, blue-jacketed sailors, he stepped close to the rope that railed off the waiting throng; but it was not until the first passengers began to disembark that the girl saw him.

At first she stared incredulously, then a wonderful glow lighted her face that made his heart beat wildly. With a little cry that only reached him faintly, she held out her hands to him across the space between.

His emotion almost choked him, whipped a mist across his eyes. His hands tightened on the rope.

"Look," whispered Abdullah, "do you see her? She is waving to you!"

Mrs. Waverly's cordiality was a trifle strained. It was one thing to meet a fascinating stranger in romantic Venice, but quite another thing to find that he had turned up in New York. Iris' shining eyes and flushed cheeks told their own story and her mother wondered with some misgiving what the girl's father would say.

As they stood a moment over their greetings, a tall, gray-haired man rushed up hurriedly.

"Lora, my dear!" he cried. Mrs. Waverly turned to him smiling happily, and Iris flung her arms about his neck.

"Daddy, dear old daddy!" she cried between kisses.

For a few moments mother and daughter were engrossed by the newcomer, and Rames stood sulkily by, wondering.

" 'Daddy' " he said to Abdullah at his elbow. "What did she mean by that?"

"He is her father," was the answer. "What are your plans now?"

At that moment the girl turned and smiled at him shyly.

"I want you to meet Prince Rames, father," she said softly, and Rames found himself being politely scrutinized by a pair of very keen gray eyes.

"My wife and daughter have informed me of your kindness to them in Venice," was the greeting as he held out his hand, "I want to thank you and hope that we may have the pleasure of seeing you at our home."

Mrs. Waverly was relieved. This interesting acquaintance had won her husband's approval. Now she was free to extend her hospitality.

"Perhaps you will dine with us this evening," she said cordially, and Rames, looking into Iris' glowing face, joyfully accepted.

The Waverly residence was one of those substantial brownstone houses that have sedately withstood the march of encroaching apartment palaces which have swallowed up so many of their fellows. While not situated directly on New York's most aristocratic avenue, it was near enough to bask in the halo of its proximity.

That evening, as Rames waited in the tastefully furnished, softly lighted drawing-room, he looked about him curiously. It was the first time in this new world that he had been in a private house excepting that of the wealthy Arab in Cairo. How different this was. A grave, dignified-looking man in livery had shown him in. The room was quiet, restful. Here and there were things he had seen in museums—tapestries, a painting or two, some bronzes, a slender vase of delicate white narcissus, a bowl of roses, deeply, lustrously red, and over all, the soft glow of shaded lamps.

Quick footsteps sounded in the hall. He rose to his feet as the door opened and Iris came in. For a moment she stood poised on the threshold, her slender shoulders and arms white against the dull green of her gown, her face radiant with its welcome for him.

"Teta," he whispered, "Teta!" but as he made a step toward her, Mr. and Mrs. Waverly entered. The girl's arms dropped at her sides, but her eyes smouldered with a fire that filled him with ecstasy.

At dinner Iris sat across from him, her white lids veiling that wonderful light. In his carefully correct English, he discussed many things with her parents, while his heart sang over and over in the language of an ancient people, his love for this girl who had been true to a promise made in a once fair garden that now lay buried in the desert sands, and when his black eyes rested for a moment on hers, she was conscious of a vague fluttering as though memory,

like an imprisoned bird, were trying to free itself
and wing its way into the open.

This elusive something that stirred in her with
every thought of Rames, filled her with emotions
difficult to analyze. Every day since they had parted
she had dreamed of this man who had crossed her
path. About her neck, suspended by a slender plati-
num chain, was the ruby ring he had given her in
Venice. She had told no one of it, and often,
alone in her own room, as she had gazed into its
smouldering depths, strange visions of unfamiliar
things and places seemed to rise mistily before her,
like the half-forgotten memory of a dream. And
now as she sat at her father's table, surrounded by
the objects which were a part of her every-day life,
the low voice of the guest, with its baffling accent,
wove again with gossamer threads those haunting
fantasies.

Instead of the irreproachable evening clothes, she
seemed to see the lithe, graceful figure with its dark,
clear-cut face, clothed in barbaric color, banded with
splendid jewels! It was ridiculous, she knew, to
give way to such foolish visionings. She gave herself a little mental shake.

Her father was talking in his slightly pompous
way of Wall Street and politics.

"My dear Prince," he was saying, "all of the
big moneyed interests in this country are intimately
connected with the Government, we———"

She heard her mother give a whispered order to
Poole, the English butler, and then she was dreaming again.

Venice, a golden moon, the thrilling echo of a

song, the slow pressure of strong fingers on hers, and that moment of ecstasy when———.

But her mother had risen, and with a quick intake of the breath she followed her.

During the remainder of the evening, her father managed politely, but none the less firmly, to see that there were no moments alone, and Rames, chafing under the restraint, was obliged to listen to never-ending remarks on Wall Street and politics.

To Mrs. Waverly he seemed even more interesting than in Venice, and since her husband had invited him to their home, she felt she could indulge the feeling of admiration which he inspired in her.

Her eyes wandered from the handsome dark face to her daughter. How well these two looked together, she mused, with the first thought of a woman. And yet what was it about this man, who, although he interested her so deeply, still left her conscious that behind the smiling, gracious surface was a man she could never know. As she studied the clear-cut aquiline profile, the deep sadness in the brilliant dark eyes, she felt a keen desire to say:

"Let me be your friend! Let me really know who you are!" and although Iris' father talked interestedly and listened to his guest's comments on his country with polite deference, when at last Rames rose to go, Mr. Waverly was aware of an impassable gulf between himself and this man that irritated and antagonized him, and he made up his mind that what he had read in his guest's eyes when they rested on his daughter, would not be encouraged.

The family were to leave town shortly for the

summer, and his secret decision was that the sooner they left the better.

Rames bowed over Mrs. Waverly's hand.

"It has been very nice to have you with us, Prince," she said graciously. "It seems almost like Venice; I hope you will come again very soon!"

Iris smiled into his eyes.

"Perhaps you will go motoring with me tomorrow," she said.

"Tomorrow!" his voice was eager, "when shall I come?"

"Shall we say three?"

Her father frowned slightly, but made no comment as he bade him good-night.

During the drive down the Avenue, Rames leaned back in the taxicab, his mind filled with a picture of the glint of soft lights on bronze hair and a pair of deep eyes which had looked tenderly into his.

"Tomorrow at three!" he said half aloud. "Ah, Teta, it is hard to wait even that much longer."

CHAPTER XX

THE next morning when Rames went to his window, the strip of sky that he could see between the tall buildings, shone blue and cloudless. It made him wish for a cool, green vista upon which to rest his eyes.

"Why is it these people have no gardens or trees in whose shade they may rest?" he asked Abdullah. "Here the only plants and flowers which I have seen are behind the glass windows of some few shops."

Abdullah came to his side and looked out over the gray stretch of Avenue that lay basking in the sunshine.

"Land is so valuable here," he said, "that the individual cannot afford to use any of his property for the purpose of a garden. But the people love trees and flowers and green fields, therefore they have all contributed toward the cultivation of a great community garden which is for the enjoyment and recreation of everyone. It is called Central Park!"

"Let us go there, my Abdullah," said Rames, "I long for the sight of growing things!"

The foliage was still the fresh sweet green of early summer before the city's dust covers it. Westward, above the tree tops, rose the tall masses of apartment houses, and in the east a great copper dome glimmered through the lacy branches. As they crossed the Mall, laughing children circled about its paved surface with little wheels on their feet, or sat astride queer vehicles which Abdullah called "bicycles."

The toys of the Theban children had been crude dolls, colored balls and wooden animals that jerked their limbs when a string was pulled, but these wheeled shoes and unsteady vehicles were unknown. Rames stood and watched the merry youngsters and their staid nurses. Some small boys near him were tossing a ball backward and forward. It flew past one of them and rolled to his feet. He picked it up and stood staring at the little leather sphere in his hand. It was stitched and put together exactly as the ball with which he had played in his own Theban garden those many centuries ago. He gave it into the hands of the boy and turned away, a wistful smile in his eyes. Thebes and her glory was almost forgotten, but the simple toy of a child had come unchanged through the ages.

"Abdullah," he said, "you and I, the supreme work of the gods, will go back into the dust out of which we sprung, but some small thought of man, like yonder plaything, lives on. Who are the greater, the gods or their creations?"

Abdullah eyed him sidewise.

"The gods," he said, "who are the gods? Allah or Jehovah, Brahma or Christ?"

"Call the Supreme Force by whatever name you will," answered Rames, "symbolize its creations and make lesser gods of them, or raise your supplicating hands to the One Only. Even let man set his own Ego on an altar before which he burns incense or dances the sacred dance, the great cycles wheel back to the one center, the Principle that governs all things."

"I thought you were an unbeliever," said Abdullah, "a pagan!"

"Pagan or Christian, Moslem or Jew, or heathen of ancient Nubia and the desert lands, what difference is there, so long as man sets something above himself up to which he looks with awe?"

The breeze was cool and sweet against their faces. Overhead the young leaves rustled gently, equestrians cantered along the bridle-path, their horses' sleek sides shining in the sunlight. Motors rolled by in a steady stream, and now and then a decrepit, slow-pacing cab horse driven by an ancient coachman crawled along near the curb. The shadows of the lacy trees lay in quivering, blue, transparent patches over the gravel walks, the scent of wistaria hung faintly on the air. On a bench nearby two lovers sat engrossed in one another. The girl's face glowing happily, the boy, sturdy, young, of the working-class, bending over her with the light in his eyes that is the same in prince or peasant. Not far away a wheeled chair stood in the sunshine, a white-faced man lay propped among its pillows, a woman with sad eyes and shabby clothes sat next him reading aloud in a soft, throaty voice. Children romped past, rolling great hoops or dragging clanking, gaudily colored wooden toys. Nursemaids in caps and aprons, or long gray veils, propelled small-hooded carriages containing rosy-faced babies.

Everywhere was the breath of summer, the stir of growing things.

They returned to their hotel on the top of an awkward-looking vehicle which Abdullah called a "bus," and from their lofty seat he pointed out to Rames objects and places of interest.

When three o'clock came, he found Iris ready and waiting. Her clear skin was set off by the smart green motor coat she wore, and a small, close-fitting hat was drawn over her hair.

As they stepped into the machine, the girl leaned forward with a word of instruction to the chauffeur and with a purr, the car drew away from the curb and swung into the park.

Love is progressive, and Rames' adoration had grown until it swept him before it like a mighty flood. His eyes burned into hers. With an effort he restrained the impulse to take her in his arms. The longing to feel the touch of her hands made him dizzy.

"My loved one," he said huskily, "how I have missed you! Venice was black and dead when you had gone! I could not wait! I could not live without seeing you! Hours were years, days eternity—and so I came!"

She smiled happily.

"How wonderful you are," she said. "When I saw you standing on the pier, I thought my heart would burst with joy!" and then she added softly, "I, too, have been lonely!"

Iris was joyously, unrestrainedly happy, like a bird that had found its mate. She loved this man.

She had given him her whole heart and was not ashamed to show it.

He leaned toward her quickly, his black eyes alight, but she drew back.

"Rames, we are not in Venice," she said hastily, "people will see and wonder."

He straightened against the cushions.

"Pardon," he said. "I forget all but you!"

They had crossed the city through the cool shadows of the park and were now speeding along the river front.

Through a golden haze, shimmered the towering masses of the Palisades, and far below them on the breast of the water, drifted small boats and dingy barges. Out from the other shore they could see a squat red ferry-boat sweeping across, trailing a feathery wake behind it. Gray gulls swooped and floated over the water, and down along the river bank, a puffing train steamed on its way into the busy city.

In Rames' mind all this gave place to the golden sunlight of the Nile country, the swaying fronds of palms, the glittering pageants of the Pharaohs, the splendid masses of giant temples and the hush of a scented garden where a maid and a man, kneeling by each other's side, gazed deep into a lotus pool.

Iris broke in on his reverie half resentfully.

"Rames," she said, "how far away you are!"

He looked at her tenderly, his eyes filled with the baffling expression which had so often puzzled her.

"Very far away," he said, "but still with you!"

"Venice?" she asked shyly.

"My Princess," he said, "I cannot forget one single moment I have ever spent with you, but you —does Venice begin all things for you?"

"There is nothing worth remembering before that," she said simply.

For the girl, the book of life was opening at its most wonderful pages. For the man, it was the continuation of a story that had been interrupted ages before.

He saw her again in the familiar dress of Thebes. Her round, white arms, the jeweled band holding back the thick, bronze tresses! How different she was in this strange costume with its enveloping folds. But she was lovely either way!

The car had turned east again, and now was swinging back down the Avenue.

"Must I leave you so soon?" he asked as he observed their direction.

Iris smiled.

"You are coming home to tea with me," she said.

The recollection of Mr. Waverly's remarks on Wall Street were fresh in his mind, and he was rather dubious about exchanging the present situation for the polite obligations of the Waverly drawing-room. He rejoiced, therefore, to find when they arrived, that Iris' father was at his club, and her mother had not yet come in.

She led the way into the library. Through the long windows the afternoon sun came in a rosy glow. The staid butler followed them with the tea things, which he set carefully on a small table and quietly withdrew.

Rames' eyes were filled with the girl before him. She had laid aside her motor coat and hat, and her slim loveliness was clothed in a soft blue gown with white lace about her throat and wrists.

He watched her slender hands stirring among the tea things. The pink-tipped, tapering fingers suggested the petals of a flower. He stooped suddenly and crushed them to his lips.

"Teta, mine now and always," he murmured brokenly, "nothing must ever part us again!"

Her heart was overflowing.

"Tell me I am foolish, dear," she said; "but I have a vague fear, a dread of something strange, menacing. I love you so much, it frightens me!"

He drew her close.

"Nothing must ever part us again," he repeated, his lips on hers.

"Rames," she said at last, "let us tell dad and mother of our happiness. I—I want them to know!"

"Loved one," he answered, "tell them what you will. All the world must know that we have found each other!"

The girl hesitated.

"Father will ask you questions, dear," she said at last, "he—he will want to know—things—I——"

"What things?"

"About yourself—your family—your country—Oh, my dearest," she added hastily, as she saw his brows contract, "it doesn't matter to me one bit who you are, whether you are rich or poor. To me you are the man I love! That is all I care to know!"

Her arms were about his neck, her heart beating against his own, his whole being quivered with ecstasy, when across his memory like a hot stab flashed a picture of the secret room in the Theban hills. A menacing shadow, the figure of the High Priest, seemed to tower above him, the words of the oath he had uttered echoed thunderingly across his consciousness.

"Above all there must be no woman! Swear it!"

He had sworn by all things sacred, by the *Ka* of his father, by his mother's mummy, he had sworn by his very love for Teta, and now——

His manner startled the girl. She loosened her arms and drew away from him.

"Rames," she cried. "Tell me. What is it? You look so strange!"

His eyes were filled with an unutterable sadness, a tragedy of sorrow that tore at his·heart.

"Rames, Rames, tell me!"

He turned away, his face white and drawn.

"I must go," he said, "I must be alone—to-morrow——"

The girl, watching, felt a cold fear clutch at her throat.

At the door he turned.

"Beloved," he said softly, "I cannot answer the questions your father would ask. We must wait. Trust me! It is all I can say now!" and then, he was gone.

CHAPTER XXI

ALONE in his room, Rames sat staring into space.

Separation between him and Teta was written in the stars.

The oath he had sworn was the most solemn and binding man could make. When he had made it, he had looked ahead to a weary year's pilgrimage from which he should return gladly. He had thought Teta lost to him forever. How could he have dreamed that he was to find her in this new world? He had laughed bitterly at the thought of another woman coming into his life.

But Iris was no other woman, she was Teta, lovely as on that day when their kiss had been mirrored in the little pool of Isis.

Would even Hotep's rigid code exclude this love that had been his always?

Was there no hope for him? Must he turn away from the very threshold of Paradise, now that he had reached it?

He rose to his feet and paced restlessly up and down the apartment. Under his window rumbled the sounds of twentieth century New York, honking motor-horns, raucous voices of news venders crying the evening papers, and the continuous roar of traffic.

This knowledge which he had been sent to gather, what good would it do Hotep and Egypt?

Would his going back again into that distant past avert the tragedy of his country?

If he fulfilled his mission would his prophecies be the means of enshrining those broken stones, those shattered monuments that now were Thebes, in even greater glory than he had known? Would they heed his warnings, they who had builded against the only enemy they feared, Time? Would he be able to teach them a way to fortify themselves against the vandal hand of man's arch enemy, Man?

He remembered the insolent pride with which he had rejected the tidings that the Assyrian horde had invaded Kampt. How much more so then would his warning be unheeded! Would Thebes, in the full glory of her strength, believe that she would one day be brought low, utterly pass away and be no more, as a story that is told? Was he to sacrifice himself and this woman the gods had given him, only to be reviled as a false prophet, a dreamer of dreams?

Hotep had warned that he might have need of superhuman courage, that he must be prepared for fiery trials.

The gods perhaps had planned this greatest test, so that through it he might attain their heights, but with memory of warm lips on his, of gentle arms about his neck, he knew that he would require almost the strength of a god to become so much more a man.

"Teta, Teta," he cried aloud in his anguish, "must I go back into a world that holds thee not?

Must I plod slowly through the passing ages until I shall come to thee again?"

An unlucky star had risen at his birth, whose decree dashed the cup of happiness from his hand each time he held it to his lips.

Born in an age that questioned not the workings of Fate, that followed blindly the destiny of the stars, there was no thought of rebelling against what had been ordained for him, there was only the mighty struggle between a human soul, and his heart.

Hotep's teachings had been that man does not live for himself alone, but only that he might serve the creative force that had brought him into being, and while he knew that he would not forswear the oath that bound him, love was a thing over which man had no volition.

Abdullah had knocked at his door, and been instructed not to disturb him until morning. Battling with himself, Rames struggled through the long hours, and when at last he went to his window, he looked out over a sleeping city.

The long, silent stretch of the Avenue cut straight away into the distance, the globes of the street lights merging into a golden streak.

Iris' face as he had bade her good-bye, came before his vision. The sweet eyes filled with tears, the droop of the tender mouth. And he had not been able to explain, he would never be able to explain!

Bitter as was his pain, there was the added sorrow that she must suffer also.

For a long time he stood looking out over a world that held his happiness, but like Moses gazing from the hills of Moab, he could only view it from afar.

The darkness faded and the faint light that precedes the dawn came shimmering over the city.

He had discarded the irksome twentieth century clothes, and the fine muscles gleamed smooth and supple under the bare, polished skin. He stood motionless, rigid, until the first rays of the rising sun bathed his body in a red glow, then he raised his arms above his head, the palms of his hands outward, the fingers closely held together.

"Horus, son of the morning! Amen-Ra, lord of the universe! Isis, holiest of mothers! Hear me renew my oath! I swear again to fulfill my mission, nor let desire nor longing, nay, love itself, tempt me from my purpose!"

Beneath him, the city like an awakening giant was beginning to stir with life. A cart rattled noisily along. An early trolley-car hummed its rising crescendo, and gradually, the murmur of traffic merged into the continuous roar of day. Into every thoroughfare poured throngs of people, a mighty river of humanity hurrying to the day's occupation, and the spectator from another age looked down and watched it as it passed!

CHAPTER XXII

THERE had been a consultation in the Waverly household after Rames' visit. Mr. Waverly was for taking Iris to the country at once.

"Lora," he said, emphatically, "fascination and charm are all very well, but what about the real things that count? What do you know about this man, anyway?"

"Well," began Mrs. Waverly, "I only know that his manner exactly corresponds with his title, and he seems to have unlimited means."

"My dear, money buys anything, even a title, but money or a title cannot buy our little girl. Take her to the country tomorrow."

"But Lemuel," pleaded his wife, "I've only just returned, and I have many things that must be attended to before I can leave again. The Prince has done nothing that we should refuse him the house, and I promise to be ready within ten days!

With a shake of his head Mr. Waverly agreed, and so it was arranged that for the time the family remained in town, Rames would be received.

The Waverlys' place in society was such as to open many doors for anyone they were pleased to sponsor. It has been said "that nowhere is a prince so beloved as in a republic," and Rames soon found that he was included in many delightful invitations which came to him through Iris.

They were together almost constantly and Abdullah saw with a sort of envious resentment his office of mentor slipping from him, but with a clear remembrance of a time when he had not only been ears but tongue as well for this man whom he had come to love, he determined to be as near as possible, and see that no harm came to him.

At his suggestion, Rames had bought a powerful touring car, and much of the time that hung upon his hands, Abdullah had employed in learning to drive it, and with a pleasant sense of having them in his charge, he took them for many delightful rides through the surrounding country. It pleased him to see passers-by turn and look at the huge olive car with the bronze-haired girl and his handsome master.

The theater was a source of never-ending interest to Rames, and Iris, watching him enjoy the comedy or suffer with the tragedy, wondered where his youth had been spent that all this seemed so new to him.

One evening Mrs. Waverly chaperoned a party to a restaurant where an elaborate cabaret was in progress.

"Have you seen this sort of thing before, Prince?" she asked, and to her surprise, he answered:

"Yes, many times I have been at feasts where acrobats and dancers entertained the guests. It is a custom in my country."

On Mrs. Waverly's tongue was the question:

"Where is your country?" but an interruption occurred and the opportunity was lost.

John Reading, who had introduced them in Venice, was one of Iris' best friends. They had been companions since childhood and in the hearts of both families was a wish that these two might some day marry.

"John," said Mrs. Waverly one day, "I am so worried about the way things are going. You can see how much Iris is interested in the Prince, and he seems to have eyes only for her. But you know her father's ideas. What are we going to do?"

Reading shook his head.

"I suppose it is my fault," he said, a little bitterly, "I wonder why I was ever such an idiot as to introduce them in Venice."

"Can't you find out something about him? He doesn't exactly invite questions, and—well—do find out what you can, dear boy! Thank goodness we leave for the country next week."

But in spite of Reading's adroit detective work, Rames remained as much a mystery as ever.

Iris never tired of answering his naïve questions. Things she supposed familiar to everyone, he found new and startling. Some of the appurtenances with which modern life is made easy were absolutely unknown to him.

He loved music, although he made it plain he knew nothing of it. One day when he was trying to recall a melody they had heard together in Venice, Iris left the room for a moment and suddenly a clear, sweet tenor voice floated in through the open door.

Rames listened entranced.

"Who is it that sings so beautifully?" he asked, when the song was finished, "a friend?"

"No, I have never met him," said Iris smiling.

"You do not know him, yet he sings in your house?"

"He sings in many houses where he is a stranger," said Iris; "come, I will show you," she led the way into the music room and paused before an elaborately carved mahogany case.

"This is the singer, have you never heard a phonograph before?" and to Rames' astonishment, at a touch of her hand, the silvery voice repeated the song he had heard.

What stupendous magic was here! The ability to imprison a glorious voice that could be liberated at will and delight the ear with its thrilling cadence!

His bewilderment in the mazes of the great shops puzzled her.

"Surely," she said as they went about one day, "you, who have seen so much are not surprised at these!"

"But these are not shops," he said, "they are museums! They are housed like kings and furnished beyond the dreams of princes. What vast armies it must take to supply them!"

Iris wrinkled her pretty brows.

"I never thought of that," she said; "you see, all this luxury has come to be such a matter of course with us, that I am afraid we forget the millions of workers who have created it."

Rames thought of the bazaars of Thebes, of his own vague wish to become a great merchant. All the riches of the East seemed gathered here under one roof; stuffs whose very weave he did not know, linens, fine as those that wrapped a Pharaoh's mummy, jewels, gold and ornaments, and hundreds of young and comely women to serve those who wished to buy! The *Muski* at Cairo had been of a form familiar to him, the Galleria in Naples and the shops in Rome had seemed wonderful, but here in this new land, the display of wealth seemed without limitation.

"How strange," she said on another occasion, "you speak English so well, and yet mispronounce some of the simplest words."

"I have had to learn your language as a child does," he answered, "help me when you can, correct me always!" and although she longed to ask of his native tongue, she refrained, because intuition told her he preferred not to speak of it.

Others, however, were not so delicate. The air of mystery that surrounded him was so profound that there were those, more curious than tactful, who could not refrain from questions, to all of which his answers were politely evasive and noncommittal. There were many heads shaken over this fascinating stranger, many speculations as to what the usually careful Lemuel Waverly was thinking of to allow his pretty daughter to go about with a man of whom no one knew anything. To those of her friends who remonstrated with her, Iris was sweetly final.

"The Prince and I are very dear friends," she said, "and I do not discuss my friends."

Those hours which Iris could not give him, he

spent in exploring the city with Abdullah, who was happy again to be at his side.

"Where are the poor?" he asked one day as they motored along Riverside Drive, "one seems to see only opulence and splendor here. Have these people no beggars?"

Abdullah dextrously swerved ahead of a crawling hansom cab.

"There are laws which make it a crime to beg on the streets," he said, "but there are many poor. Would you care to see how they live?"

The next day they took the surface car down to the city's crowded East Side.

The streets, like narrow canyons between the nondescript houses, were crowded with push-carts and peddlers, about which gathered women bargaining loudly in a strange language. Dirty children tumbled and played under the very feet of the slow-moving horses and the wheels of the motor-trucks which blew their horns continuously as they made their way through the throngs. Unkempt, long-bearded Jews sold their wares at the little carts; gayly colored bandanas, cheap, worn-looking furs, hats, and shoes.

Other carts were piled with vegetables around which the crowds jostled and shoved as the swarthy, black-eyed venders weighed out their purchases.

Women gossiped in dirty doorways with sickly-looking babies in their arms and ragged, smear-faced children clinging to their skirts.

From the windows bedding was piled for a needed airing, and over it, as from a parapet, leaned tousled heads.

The noise and confusion was incessant, the warning clang of trolley-cars, the shouts of hucksters, the shrill wail of a child, quarrelling voices of women, the rumble of the elevated trains, and through it all the jerking notes of a street organ.

"Here is the city of the poor," said Abdullah.

"But I still see no beggars," wondered Rames. Even on the most magnificent of the Theban avenues had been men and women in filthy rags who pleaded for the mercy of the passer-by.

"Can we go into the houses?" he asked.

Abdullah considered. He knew how resentful were the city's poor against the intrusion of the well-meaning investigator. But he prided himself on supplying everything his master wished.

"Yes, we can say we come from the Charities," he replied, and led the way down a short flight of steps into a small shop below the level of the street.

It was dingy and piled with pots and pans, candlesticks and samovars. A sputtering gas jet lit up a small circle in the middle, but the corners remained in gloom, out of which glowed a flash of ancient copper, and the yellow gleam of brass.

An old man, bent and long-bearded, came forward rubbing his hands in the unmistakable Eastern fashion.

"What can I do for the gentlemen?" he asked in a gutteral voice.

"We are from the Charities," explained Abdullah, "can you tell us who are the most deserving poor near here?"

The old creature grunted.

"How should I know? My business is brasses," he said ungraciously.

Abdullah put a coin in his hand.

And thus encouraged, the brass dealer led them to the ramshackle entrance at the side of his shop.

"Three flights," he said, waving a dirty claw-like hand into the gloom. "Ida Kransky. Next floor, Isaac Abramovitch, he got six children!" and grumbling to himself, he turned and reentered his shop.

"Shall we go up?" asked Abdullah.

"I must see," was the answer, "why in a country of such plenty, there is not a more even distribution!"

They climbed the rickety stair, which was cluttered with garbage cans, empty coal scuttles, and dirty milk bottles. Bits of newspaper, ground under countless muddy heels, strewed the way, an emaciated cat slunk from behind the rubbish. The air was foul with the smell of unclean humanity mingled with cooking vegetables.

On the third landing Rames knocked at a door from behind which came a fitful wailing. A feeble voice bade them enter. They saw a bare room, swept clear of everything except one chair.

On this a woman sat with a bundle at her meagre breast.

She raised a pair of great, hollow eyes as they entered and clutched tighter the wailing baby in her arms.

"You ain't going to have him," she cried, "you get out and let me alone!"

"We have come to help you, Ida Kransky," said Abdullah.

"That's what they all say!" the woman's voice was fiercely high-pitched. "They say it'll help me and the kid if I let 'em have him. But I won't! He's all I got!"

Rames signed to Abdullah.

"Take this, Ida Kransky," said the secretary, "we want you to keep your child," and he handed her some money.

The woman stared at the crisp yellow notes unbelievingly.

"You're fooling me!" she said at last. "I—I can't stand being fooled," her voice broke pitifully.

"It's yours, take it, keep your baby, buy something to eat!" And as they climbed the dirty stair they heard her sobbing brokenly.

The door of the Abramovitch room was open and a fat, unwholesome-looking woman rose heavily from a dilapidated rocking-chair as they entered.

"Tilly," she called, "dust a place for the gentlemen. You are from the Charities, yes?" she began to whine, thick tears gushing from her bleary eyes.

"We are very poor, my man—Tilly, tell your father he should come—he's got a cough—we got six children!"

Rames looked about at the filth and squalor of the room. It was piled with dirty rags, bits of kindling, broken crockery. Despite the warmth of the day, the one small window was tightly shut, and the air was almost unbearable.

Abdullah made a wry face.

"Is there no water to clean this place?" he asked.

The woman sniveled.

"We are so poor," she repeated, scenting money.

Tilly, an ungainly, pale-eyed child of twelve, came in panting, three other children of varying years younger, stood behind her short skirts, staring.

"Here's father," she announced, as a thin, stoop-shouldered man with the unmistakable flush of tuberculosis came into the room.

"How d'do," he smirked, and coughed nervously.

Rames eyed the group of children.

"How many are there?" he asked.

"Six," promptly answered the mother, "Mosy, he works, he's fourteen—no, sixteen"—Abramovitch had jostled his wife's elbow. Sixteen had been sworn to in the boy's working papers.

"Here's the baby," she said, throwing open the door of a dark closet. "Come, Myra," and a feeble child tottered out, absolutely naked, its little round stomach bloated with insufficient food, its thin legs scarcely able to carry it.

"We keep her there when we all go out," said the mother, "she can't get hurt then!"

For these wretched creatures, this one filthy room was home!

Rames shuddered.

How much poorer is the penniless wretch, forced to live in a garret in the congested centers of civilization, than the beggar, who though he has but a tree to shelter him, still has the sun to warm him by day, the stars for company at night, and a habitation that reaches to the edge of the horizon.

"Give them money," he said. "Come, I must get into the sunlight!"

As they stepped again from the subway into Broadway, Rames drew a sharp breath.

Poverty had disappeared, no trace of it remained. Here was nothing but the display of wealth, and so near, so very near, was all that filth and squalor and misery.

This new world which lay so far ahead of his own times had still failed to solve the problem of the poor!

In Thebes there was the magnificence of the temples, the glory of the Pharaoh and the wealth of his nobles, and to keep this splendor bright the people writhed under taxes that stripped them to their hides.

Here there were no nobles, no Pharaohs, and yet there were the poor!

Hotep's wisdom had foretold a time when all men should be equal. America's constitution declared that all men *were* equal, and yet there was Broadway, Fifth Avenue, Riverside Drive—and Allen Street!

How easy it was to speak wonderful words! How difficult to do as wonderful deeds!

CHAPTER XXIII

IRIS' sweet loveliness, each hour he spent with her, tore at his heart with the longing to crush her in his arms, to tell her how he loved her, that life was meaningless without her. But when the words trembled on his lips, the tall form of Hotep, the High Priest, rose before his eyes, and with a mighty effort he was silent.

Never since that one day when he had held her in his arms and felt the thrill of her answering kiss, had he spoken of his love, but however tightly one may seal the lips, the eyes will have their say, and Iris, seeing the unquenchable fire that burned in his, knew that he loved her.

But a woman craves the spoken word, she longs to hear over and over the assurances of devotion.

The male, accustomed through generations to feel that his emotions, his passions, are the stronger, given the right through the ages to cry them from the housetops if he will, forgets that the feminine nature has the same longings, the same desires, the same capability of loving deeply as he, but that through the ages she has been taught suppression, taught to hide as immodest the natural craving for her mate. Woman, with her more sensitive organization, has a deeper power for a more lasting affection. Nature has given her the same rights as man, but man himself has taken them away, and with a strength beyond his, she submerges herself and bows to his decree, and for this the reward she asks is "tell me again and yet again, that you love me!"

And Iris, thrilling with the memory of Venice, and that hour here in her father's house, wondered wistfully at Rames' silence. A thousand reasons suggested themselves to her. In that far country of his, perhaps there was some tie that bound him. Who was Teta, for whom he had mistaken her that first day in Venice? Teta! She felt a vague jealousy for this girl who had filled his heart before he had come from that distant land of his, about which he had told her nothing. The sorrow in his face made her heart ache. It was so seldom he smiled that she fell into little ways of trying to amuse him. Often when they returned from a walk in the park, Iris would seat herself at the piano, and soft melodies would drift out into the quiet room.

Once she had turned to him quickly, her hands dropping with a little crash on the keys.

"Won't you tell me what is troubling you?" she asked. "Forgive me the question, but I cannot help seeing that you are sad. Please, tell me!"

His eyes glowed as he looked at her.

"It is the music that draws at my heart," he said.

One evening, shortly before the family were to leave for their country place, Mrs. Waverly came into Iris' room.

"Your father asks me to tell you, dear," she said,

"that he does not wish you to see so much of the Prince this summer!"

The girl's face whitened. She looked at her mother, startled.

Mrs. Waverly put her arm tenderly about the slender shoulders. There had always been a close comradeship between her and this idolized only child.

"Of course, dear," she half whispered, "if he should care to come to the Inn for a week-end, we could say nothing——"

Iris smiled happily and kissed her mother affectionately as she discerned the thought in her heart. And so it came to pass that when she bade good-bye to Rames, it was with the understanding that he was to come to the shore within a few days.

With the departure of Iris, New York, like Venice, lost its charm, the glamour disappeared. He only lived for the hour when they could be together once more.

In vain Abdullah tried to dispel his melancholy. He drove the new car to Coney Island, and to other watering-places about the city, hoping that the sight of this side of life would awaken a new interest. But Rames sat sullen and quiet, wrapped impenetrably in his own thoughts.

Then one morning came a letter from Iris!

Abdullah had explained the methods of the modern post, but this was the first communication that had ever been addressed to him. He opened it eagerly and read its contents.

Here was a glorious compensation for his labors

in learning to read the inscriptions of this new world.

She missed him! She was lonely without him! She desired that he come to her at once!

He read it over and over, fearful that he might lose the meaning of one word.

As he held the letter to his lips, his surroundings faded away, and he stood again in a moonlit garden, with that last missive in his hand.

The characters by which the Teta of long ago had told of her journey into the Libyan hills would have been meaningless to Iris. One letter had come by the medium of a slave, slow and feeble with age, the other had been borne on the swift wings of this modern messenger of iron and steam. But the love which both expressed was the same!

The next day he and Abdullah, in the olive car, left the city on their way to Iris.

The early summer landscape spread before them in gracious lines, rolling hills, shadowy woods, broad fields, with here and there a red barn and the long, low lines of a farmhouse. They sped through village after village, down the main street, with its row of small shops, past the church, and then the residence section, cool and shady, its neat houses set well back from the road, the lawns edged with masses of flowers, and so out into the country again.

Rames studied the foliage intently as they passed.

"Why is it I do not see the palm and the tamerisk among these trees?" he asked.

Abdullah turned and looked wonderingly into the dark face beside him.

"We are in a different climate," he said, "for six months of the year it is very cold here; the palm would not live."

Rames frowned, puzzled.

"I do not understand," he said, and the marveling Abdullah explained the changes of the seasons.

The Waverlys' summer home was in one of those charming colonies that cluster along the Sound, and as the car swung into the village, Rames glanced about him at the quaint winding streets with their overhanging trees. It was all so quiet and peaceful that involuntarily he drew a deep breath.

"I like this country," he said. "It rests me!"

They drove to the comfortable Inn where they were to stay, and as soon as it was possible, he called Iris on the telephone. The magic of the little instrument that could bring to him instantly the sweet voice he was longing to hear, had ceased to fill him with wonder. As he waited to be connected with the Waverly home he thought how he would have fallen down in worship before such a seeming manifestation of the gods, had he still been in ancient Thebes. But daily use had dispelled his awe, and there was simply a sense of impatience at the delay of Central.

In the book from which the little Egyptian had taught him to read, was a sentence, "Familiarity breeds contempt!"

At the time, he had only half understood Abdullah's explanation of it, but now he smiled as he remembered his exaggerated wonder at many things which had become commonplace.

Presently, across the wire came Iris' voice.

No familiarity could lessen his joy in that sound.

As soon as he had dined, Abdullah drove him over through the twilight to the Waverlys'.

The house lay some distance from the village, down a long country road with the waters of the Sound showing through the trees. Its two wings spread broad and low, like a pair of hospitable arms held out to welcome the coming guest, and from the windows, lights twinkled through the gathering dusk. Great stone pillars guarded the gateway and between them the drive wound in a wide sweep up to the door. As the headlights of the machine turned in at the gate, a white-robed figure came to the edge of the verandah and waited.

The car drew up with a jerk and almost before it stopped, Rames was out and up the steps.

"Teta!" he said softly, "Teta!"

"Welcome to 'Loralea,' " she said smiling; "but it is Iris, not Teta, who is happy because you are here!"

CHAPTER XXIV

H E sat for a long while that night at the window in his room looking over the water.
Through the still darkness came the hushed whisper of the waves. What was life without Teta? He had found the end of the rainbow, but could only stand and gaze longingly on the treasure.

The wonderful love that had sent her soul wandering untiring through the ages to redeem her promise, had brought them to the haven of each other's arms, and now he must leave her!

How wistful she had looked when she bade him good-night. Her questioning eyes cut into his heart.

"I know you love me," they seemed to say, "and I am all yours! I am not ashamed to have you know! I am proud to give you all the love my heart can hold! Why are you silent? Why do you let me come so near only to shut the doors of your soul upon me, when I want so much to be all things to you?"

He lifted his eyes to the stars.

"Is there no offering I can make to turn you from your inexorable decree?" he cried in his own tongue. "Must my heart and hers be crushed in the grinding of your mills?"

Through the trees in the direction of her home, a light that had shown from a distant window, died away.

He threw himself on his bed, but sleep would not come. . Every moment of this wonderful pilgrimage passed before his eyes, and like a man condemned to death, he measured the days that remained to him.

With the first faint flush of dawn, he rose and crept softly down the stairs and out of the house. A bird twittered, warbled a snatch of song, and was silent. A fresh breeze played among the leaves, the crimson streaks on the horizon widened, bars of gold and little flecks of purple dappled the brightening sky.

For a moment he stood at the door looking out at the wakening world, breathing deeply the wine of the morning air, then he made his way over the dew-wet grass to the flight of steps that led down the bank to the shore.

The sun was rising in a golden haze as he stepped onto the white crescent of the beach. Little waves crept with reaching foam-fingers to where the sea-weed lay, a shining, irregular brown line. A curlew picked its dainty way among the shells, and swooping, floating, with a broad sweep of gray wings, a solitary gull circled above the water.

He sat down on an overturned boat drawn up beyond the reach of the tide.

Abdullah had said there were no more slaves, yet the shackles that bound him were stronger than any the Pharaohs had welded about the Israelites. He must retrace his way across the Bridge of Time. He must leave Teta as far beyond his reach as were the stars which had decreed his fate.

The waves at his feet murmured a refrain to his bitter thoughts, a monotonous, insistent song whose words he could not understand. They had been purling up toward the high mark of the shining brown weeds, each new wave, as it broke, further away, each ripple as it receded left a larger margin of glistening shells and pebbles.

The tide was ebbing, slowly, irresistibly, beyond the holding of man.

The sun was well up by now and the long curve of the beach lay glistening and white. In the distance an old clam-digger, bag on shoulder, splashed along the edge of the water in great rubber boots, but otherwise no one was in sight.

His eyes swept the brilliant horizon, and returned to the foaming scallops of the receding waves. The tide of his own brief visit into this dream century was also turning, his days were ebbing, nothing could stay the approaching time when his year would be over, when he must leave this girl who was Teta and go alone again into an age from which she had vanished.

Insistent, pounding, monotonous, the waves broke on the sand, each one further away from the line of weeds, each one vainly striving to reach where it had touched before. Then they seemed to pause, to sway backward and forward as though irresolute, and as he watched, slowly but surely, they came creeping back again up the glistening sands.

He studied the incoming water, half dreaming. The sound of each tiny wave as it reached higher, seemed to speak to him in a familiar language. It penetrated his consciousness, and in a blinding flash he understood!

With a cry he leaped to his feet, his arms held out to the rising sun.

"I will come again!" he cried. "The tide ebbs! The tide flows! I will come again!"

He would keep his oath. He would carry back with him into the secret chamber of the Theban hills the wonders of this new world. But his mission accomplished, his promise fulfilled, he would be free to again dare the perilous passage, to return once more through the ages to Iris who was Teta. When the time came for him to leave her, it would be with the promise that the separation would be as brief as he could make it. Surely Hotep must grant him this, once he had fulfilled his oath.

The thought of a time when he could come again with no binding promise to keep him from the arms he loved, filled him with a wonderful ecstasy. For the first time since Amrou had brought his tragic tidings, Rames saw happiness.

"O Tide!" he said in his own tongue, "so surely as thou comest again to bring thy offerings to this shore who is thy bride, so will I return to her who is the breath of life to me!"

He slipped out of his clothes and swam far out, his clean, powerful strokes cutting the water rhythmically. It was as though all the sorrow and longing of the past months were being washed away by the fresh salt water. At last he turned and came ashore, and as he emerged, a dripping, bronze figure, he turned and faced the sun again.

"Amen-Ra, mighty among the gods, take thou the thanks of thy grateful son!"

Abdullah was waiting for him on the verandah,

a trace of anxiety on his dark face. Observing his master's expression of exaltation, he eyed him quizzically.

"Yesterday was very wonderful?" he questioned.

Rames nodded.

"And the days that shall come will be more wonderful still!" he said.

Iris, also, had spent a sleepless night. She had hoped that when he came to her again, the veil of sadness that had fallen over him would be lifted, but the lines of sorrow in his face had only grown deeper with the passing days, and although he looked at her with eyes that burned with passionate adoration, she waited in vain for the words she longed to hear.

So that now when the big car drew up before her door, and she saw his radiant face, her heart leaped with joy.

"What good wind has blown away the clouds?" she asked as she held out her hand.

He looked at her with shining eyes.

"I have been wandering in the darkness," he said, "but at last I have found the light!"

She smiled happily.

"Never let the shadows come again," she said; "your sadness is mine, too, you know, and we have the best reason in the world for being perfectly happy!"

She looked very sweet and wholesome in her fresh white dress as she led the way toward a shady bower beneath some tall elms.

Here the shadows of the overhanging trees softened the light in her hair and eyes. On the wide stretch of lawn and the hills beyond, the sunlight blazed in warm gold.

"Tell me," she said, "what good genie I have to thank for the wonderful change since yesterday?"

He leaned toward her and gathered her hands in his.

"Iris," he whispered, "look at me!"

She raised her eyes filled with deep, trusting love.

"Dearest one," he said, "I know there are many questions concerning myself which, because they are unanswered, have caused you pain!"

The girl flushed.

"Rames, dear," she cried, "I do not ask—I——"

"I know you do not," his voice was very tender, "but others do, others very near and dear to you, and it is because I have not been able to explain to them that I have been sad! There are many things which I had thought I could never be able to tell even you, but the gods have decreed that we are to be happy, and today the way has been made plain to me!"

She listened, her whole soul engrossed in what he was saying.

"I have a mission to perform," he continued, "which I am sworn to by the most binding oath that man can make. When it is accomplished I must leave you for awhile——"

The girl started involuntarily. Her hand tightened in his.

"I must go on a pilgrimage, but I will return before a year has passed; and when I come again,

I shall tell you the story of the most wonderful journey man has ever made!"

Her lip quivered.

"A year, a whole long year!" she said. "That is eternity for one who waits!"

"We still have many happy days before I must go," he said tenderly, "hours that I shall part with as reluctantly as a miser does his gold, moments that shall be strung as pearls upon the silken thread of memory!"

She clung to his hands, trembling.

"I believe that what I am trying to remember is that I have always loved you!"

He drew her close in his arms.

"Dearest in all the world," he murmured, "love me still, and we shall know such happiness as was never given to mortals!"

CHAPTER XXV

A S the summer advanced, the Inn filled with guests, and Rames spent those hours when he was not with Iris in a secluded corner of the verandah, Abdullah at his side, watching with intense interest the elaborate system of amusements that seemed necessary to the existence of the people of this new world.

Apparently it was the serious business of half the populace to amuse and entertain the other half. Diversion was purchased as one bought goods from a merchant, the quality depending upon the price paid.

Apart from theaters and other paid entertainments, there was an endless variety of games in which everyone, even the most unskillful, could participate. And how hard they seemed to work at their play! This energy, otherwise directed, would rear structures to overshadow the Pyramids.

"To what land do these men belong?" he asked Abdullah one morning as a party went down the steps and into a waiting motor. "Their costume is different from all these others and they carry weapons I have never seen before."

The little Egyptian smiled.

"They are Americans like the others," he said, "but they are dressed to amuse themselves. They are going to play a game called 'golf.' Those are not weapons they carry, but clubs to knock a little ball about a huge field."

"How many games they play with a ball in this country," wondered Rames. "I had thought it only to amuse children, but I find it is the favorite toy of everyone. Mr. Waverly walks for hours around a green-topped table pushing about a small ivory sphere; these staid-looking men carrying bags of heavy clubs are going, perhaps, miles to knock about another little ball. The young men and girls spend hours hitting one back and forth across a net, and as we drove out of New York I remember passing a great open space bordered with crowds of cheering people, while a few men knocked a ball from one to the other with heavy sticks. It is very curious!"

Abdullah puffed at his cigarette as he let his eyes rest a moment on his master's face.

Constant association with this strange man who had so accidentally come into his life, had only increased his wonder and affection. The treasure chamber from which he was sure Rames drew the jewels he gave him to dispose of whenever their funds were running low, still remained a mystery, but he no longer dreamed of attempting to discover its hiding-place. His only incentive was to please and serve his master to the utmost of his ability.

The other guests at the Inn speculated curiously as to the identity and nationality of this unusual-looking man who held himself so aloof.

He was always courteous to the advances made him, but aside from Iris, these people crossing the screen of his days, meant nothing but pictures. He watched them with the same interest he had given the film plays Abdullah had taken him to see in New York.

He was always being asked to join boating parties, tennis, golf or swimming. His excuses were couched in such politely regretful terms that no one took offense, but hoped for another time when he would be at leisure.

"These people live to amuse themselves, is it not so, my Abdullah?" said Rames. "I see no serious face among them."

"It is the play season," was the answer, "and besides, these are the rich, not those who live on Allen Street."

A pompous matron came bustling up to them, her ample form swathed in a youthful costume, a pearl necklace snuggled comfortably beneath her plural chins.

"Good morning, Prince," she smiled as Rames rose. "I'm so glad to find you. Now please don't say you have something else to do, we want you to make a fourth at bridge."

Rames looked at her helplessly.

"Bridge?" he said, "I'm afraid I don't——"

"Now that is too bad, you really must learn! One is so out of it if one doesn't play bridge!" and with a smile she sailed away to find someone who did.

"What did she mean, Abdullah?" Rames turned perplexedly to his mentor, "you say 'bridge' is something to cross, but she——"

"Another game," said the little Egyptian laconically. "Shall we look on?"

Rames followed Abdullah into the card room of the Inn, a dim, drapery-hung place, with many nooks and corners piled with Oriental cushions in a manner wholly foreign to Oriental custom.

At a small table sat four people. The stout matron who had accosted him was one. She chuckled with a throaty little gurgle:

"We'll make a bridge player of you yet, Prince; you'll simply adore it when you once learn!"

Rames watched them sort the bits of cardboard. They seemed to love the colored pictures, the spots of black and red, and parted with them reluctantly. Each in turn threw one upon the table and the four were then gathered in by a player who arranged them in neat little piles. The phrases they used were curious. There were references to precious stones, implements for digging, weapons, and even to hearts, and yet he saw no evidence of any of these things, and stranger still, the pleasant smiles gave place to frowns, dark looks, sarcasm, and even veiled insults.

Not wishing to be present at what threatened to be a quarrel, Rames rose and left the room with Abdullah.

"You are right," he said when they were outside, "they certainly take their amusements seriously. I am afraid they will not be friends long."

The gambling spirit common to all Orientals was very strong in the little Egyptian.

"These fifty-two pieces of card-board are very

interesting," he said, "very entertaining. You can win and lose much money."

Rames remembered how the nobles and the wealthy youth of Thebes had staked gold pieces on the toss of cubes of marked bone, had bet upon the winners at draughts, and had made wagers as to how far the inundations of the rising Nile would reach or when the Pharaoh's fleet would return.

He must study the amusements of the people of this new world, for it was their recreations as well as their wisdom he must carry back with him.

Iris loved to listen while Rames told her what she called "stories." With his growing knowledge of English came a surprising eloquence. What seemed to the girl wonderful romances of a distant past, were to him vivid memories. He told her of glittering festivals in honor of ancient gods, triumphal processions of mighty kings, of journeys across desert wastes beneath a tropical sun, and the shock of battle against fierce, barbaric foes.

"There was a garden," he began one day when they were alone, "whose perfumed shadows now lie buried under desert sand. You and I once rested in that garden, over us the tamarisks drooped their grey-green plumes, a crested hoopoo called and at our feet the pink-tipped lotus swayed above a quiet pool." He leaned toward her, his dark eyes filled with longing. "Teta, have you forgotten?"

The girl sighed.

"Do you know, I believe I can see that very pool!" she said. "How wonderful, how real are some of the pictures that exist only in one's imagination!"

He sighed. Imagination!

"Dear heart," he said softly, "these are not things I only imagine, these are things that I *remember!*"

She smiled.

"May it not be possible, Rames, since we are taught that our souls never die, that what we call imagination is really that soul's remembering?"

"You are beginning to understand," he said. "How wonderful it will be when you really do!"

For a moment they sat silent, the man's thoughts bridging the space between his world and hers, the girl's busy with a tender hope for the future.

When Mrs. Waverly came into Iris' room that night, she found the girl sitting at the window. She turned quickly as her mother entered and drew her down beside her on the wide seat.

A full moon sailed high in the heavens. Against its light the trees made a pattern like rich black lace through which shone the silvered waters of the Sound.

"How beautiful the world is!" she said. Her mother smiled with perfect understanding.

"More beautiful than it has been?" she asked. Iris gazed dreamily out into the moonlight.

"Much more beautiful," she said softly, "love has come into it!"

It was late when her mother left, and when Iris kissed her good-night, she knew that here was a staunch ally to help meet any opposition which might arise from her father, who, preoccupied man that he was, had not been too busy to notice her radiant face, the evident joy she expressed in Rames' presence, and that strange psychological blossoming that takes place in every woman when love finds her.

The growing romance had been the subject of more than one conversation between the girl's parents. Mr. Waverly was of a rather severe nature, accustomed to having his own way. He was for bringing matters to a climax by asking Rames his intentions, but Mrs. Waverly dissuaded him.

"Do let them alone, Lemuel," she begged. "He will come and talk to you in good time.' In the meanwhile give them their happy summer!"

And he had consented to wait, although Rames' delay in seeking an interview disappointed him.

A few days later Abdullah brought his master a large, square envelope which contained an invitation to a costume ball to be given at the home of one of Iris' friends.

He knit his black brows over the embossed script.

"Just what does this mean?" he asked the little Egyptian.

Abdullah read it carefully.

"A costume ball," he said presently, "is an occasion where people are given the opportunity of appearing for a brief period as the characters or personages whom they have always secretly fancied themselves to resemble.

"You will see emperors whose reign is but for a few hours, bandits and pirates who in private life are law-abiding citizens, unwarlike crusaders, queens in tinsel and paste-board crowns, heroines of all ages, both in years and historical periods. Gentlemen of good figure embrace this opportunity to advertise it; gentlemen of no figure reveal their ignorance of the fact.

"It is very picturesque and amusing, a riot of color, comedy, and conceit!"

Rames studied the invitation in his hand. At this festival, where every one would endeavor to be other than they were, why could he not go clothed in the familiar manner of his own age?

The fancy pleased him. In a pageant of make-believe, he alone would be genuine!

They motored down to New York, where a famous theatrical costumer was consulted. He described, down to the most minute detail, the garments he had worn at a great feast at the palace of the Pharaoh. He also decided to wear some of the jewels which he had brought from the secret chamber, and which he had ordered set in the fashion of his own day.

New York was hot and sultry. He found the heat more trying than the fierce glare of his own cloudless skies. The city seemed to stir with a vague unrest. There was more than the usual number of newspaper extras. Everywhere people scanned them with eager interest. Their faces suggested the expressions of the men of Thebes when had come the first rumors of the approach of the Assyrians.

"What is it, my Abdullah?" he asked, "is there something unusual taking place?"

Abdullah spread a newspaper before him, the huge black letters of the headlines filling half the page.

"It means war!" he said. "A great noble has

been assassinated and for his life, of little account, millions of useful ones may be sacrificed."

The subject was on the lips of every one. In the streets, drawing-rooms and in the tenements! All the nations of the earth were girding on their armor for a herculean combat.

"How will they fight?" asked Rames. "The emperor whom we saw at Corfu, he seemed neither fierce nor strong enough to enforce his will in defiance of the whole world!"

"For forty years," said Abdullah, "he has devoted the energies of his subjects to the forging of arms, and cannot forbear putting them to the test."

"What are their weapons?" asked Rames.

Abdullah looked at him in astonishment.

"Guns that can fire hundreds of shots a minute!" he said. "Others of monstrous size that can throw a ton of metal many miles, where it will burst and scatter death and destruction! Aeroplanes such as we saw at Naples, will view the manœuvers of their foes from lofty altitudes or rain devastation upon them from the clouds! Gigantic ships of steel, armed for combat, will sweep the seas, while others, smaller but no less deadly, will lurk beneath the surface in wait for prey!"

"But the spearmen—the archers——," began Rames.

Abdullah smiled sarcastically.

"The last archer died centuries ago," he said. "In these enlightened days, warriors stand several miles apart and kill each other with more civilized and efficient weapons!"

Rames studied his paper.

Germany, France, England, Russia—all the great nations of the earth! Civilization or the progress of the ages had not, then, done away with the need of arms. Man must still resort to brute force.

When he had swallowed the magic draught, the mailed fist of the Assyrian was hammering at his own gates, the invader's heel was already on the breast of Memphis. When he had emerged into this new world, the utter devastation and ruin of his country had loudly proclaimed that which can come to man in his pride.

Thebes in all her glory and grandeur was gone, her mightiest monuments only a jumble of stupendous stones to excite the passing wonder of idle travelers, her philosophy and learning forever lost to posterity.

Were these people, also, about to enact the same tragic drama that would bring about the destruction of all that was beautiful in this wonderful age? He longed to cry aloud in a voice that would reach to the furthermost edge of the horizon:

"Think! wait! Waste not the fruits of your labors in quarreling among yourselves. Have mercy on generations yet unborn!"

CHAPTER XXVI

RAMES stood before his mirror on the night of the ball, and as he confronted his image in the familiar costume of his own country, a curious sense of unreality, of being a figure in a dream, assailed him. How brief seemed the time since he had stepped from his litter into the vast magnificence of the Pharaoh's hall, and now he was going among a people to whom his dress would be only mimicry, his story, had he told it, only the ravings of a mad man.

A sleeveless white tunic, fastened at the shoulder by jeweled clasps, followed the straight, firm lines of his figure to just below the hips, about which was a broad, flexible girdle richly encrusted with gems, which gave with the movements of his body. His arms were encircled by cunningly wrought bands of gold, thick-set with flashing stones, and about his brows was bound the golden badge of princes, its heavy fringe falling to his shoulder.

Wrapping himself in the white folds of a great mantle, he stepped into the olive car where Abdullah waited.

When he had gone to the banquet of the Pharaoh, clad as he now was, he had sat among the rich cushions of a carved and painted litter, borne upon the shoulders of four stalwart slaves.

Before him had run Amrou, a golden-tipped ivory staff in his hand, making way for him along the narrow, crowded streets. Now he was being carried swiftly along a quiet country road in a great car which was guided by a descendant of a people who would have thought it a chariot of the gods.

As he made his way through the gay crowd to where his hostess was greeting her guests, a murmur of admiration and comment followed him.

The great ballroom was brilliant with light and color, the air heavy with the perfume of flowers, the strains of soft, alluring music floated from some hidden place.

To the other guests his costume was daring in the extreme, they marveled at its scantiness as well as its splendor, but he seemed wholly unconscious of his bare limbs. Any other man would have been looked at askance, but his perfect poise, together with the great beauty of his figure, excited only admiration.

At one end of the room was a great bay window with a seat running below it. From here Rames could study the animated picture which wove before him a gorgeous fabric of many colors.

There were richly embroidered coats, satin knee breeches, snowy wigs tied with black ribbons, brocaded tunics and long silken hose, diaphanous, nymph-like draperies, short, bell-shaped skirts of many folds and hues, long trains of velvet and glittering jeweled bodices, fringed leather trousers, spurs and broad-brimmed hats, many-hued feathers and strings of colored beads, shawls of black lace which spread their web-like patterns over skirts of scarlet and yellow, loose white coats and pantaloons, huge black pompons and peaked caps, and costumes that were brilliantly red, like moving flame.

Courtiers, bandits, dairy maids and queens, mendicants and emperors passed before him, the laughter, light and color all mingling in dazzling phantasmagoria.

As he watched the vivid scene, suddenly its unreal mimicry, its color and light merged into one amazing reality, for through the shifting throng came Teta herself as she had been in the garden of the Temple of Ra!

A narrow slip of some sparking material was girded about her delicate hips by a broad belt, whose jeweled ends fell to her slender, sandaled feet. Her arms were bare save for the glittering gems that encircled them. The lustrous, bronze hair fell on either side of her face in innumerable little plaits, each tipped with a golden ornament, and encircling it, two birds of beautifully wrought and colored enamel held in their beaks against her white forehead, a jeweled ornament of rubies and emeralds. A thin veil floated about her, filmy, mysterious, like the scented cloud that rises from burning incense.

He sprang to his feet.

"Teta," he whispered hoarsely. The brilliant scene that had so engrossed him faded away, leaving only this girl and memory!

Iris flushed; she felt instinctively the attention they were attracting. Her companion, a thin, stoop-shouldered man, adjusted a pair of thick glasses and scrutinized Rames through them.

"My word," he said admiringly, "you certainly have been careful of detail. My compliments on the accuracy of your costume!"

His words came as a relief to Iris, who though pleased at the effect of her appearance, still, was keenly aware of the many eyes which were centered on them.

"This is Professor Dodge," she said, glad of the diversion, "he is one of our foremost Egyptologists, and was kind enough to help me with all this!" and her slender hands touched the folds of her dress.

Rames looked at the man's ungainly figure. He wore a pair of garnet trunks slashed with yellow, his long, thin legs were encased in ill-fitting garnet hose, making him look like some sort of attenuated bird. His doublet, smart perhaps on some more gallant figure, seemed somehow to emphasize his awkwardness. The ruff about his neck had wilted and hung limp, leaving his large-featured face unsoftened under a peaked hat and feather.

"Tell me, my dear Prince," he said, "where did you get your authority? I had no idea there was a costumer in New York who could turn out anything so perfect. As a rule they don't know the difference between an Egyptian Prince and a knight of the Round Table! Allow me," and he stooped to examine some of the details closer through his glasses.

"My authority is unquestioned," said Rames stiffly. He resented the inquisitiveness of this stranger.

"My dear Prince," the learned bore insisted,

"do let us go somewhere where we can discuss what is evidently your hobby as well as mine!"

"I must beg you to excuse me—another time—" said Rames, and turned again to Iris. He wanted to get away, to be alone with her, to ask what had impelled her to dress as she did tonight, why she had flown back into the past as he had emerged from it, but before he could speak Reading joined them.

The American was a very manly figure in a dull green brocaded doublet and well-fitting silk hose, a jeweled dagger in his girdle, a small green cap with a long heron feather on his blonde hair.

The two men bowed rather coldly, and Iris noticed with a feeling of resentment that Reading did not offer his hand.

"Will you dance this with me?" he said, as the appealing strains of a waltz drifted out across the room.

"I'm sorry, John," she said gently, "but I have promised this to Rames."

Reading flushed slightly. He was conscious of a sudden stab of hatred for this man. He resented bitterly Iris' familiar use of his name and that he must give place to him. He forced a smile, however, and with a bow turned away.

"Shall we walk in the garden?" Rames asked when the other had disappeared. "It is very beautiful there!"

They crossed the lawn to where little paths wound among the shrubbery. Here, the mystery of night surrounded them with enchantment. Strings of many colored lights hung festooned from the branches, where they gleamed like brilliant flowers. Vast, unexplored avenues of shadow stretched away into limitless space, huge trees towered whispering above them through whose foliage the moonlight fell in little silver patches that caressed Iris' hair and dappled the tissue of her gown. They wandered in a dream world in which the only thing real was the scent of honeysuckle and roses.

"Rames," she said a little sadly, "who is Teta? You have called me by her name so often, but tonight when you saw me in this costume you said it as though it came from your very soul!"

"Dearest one," he said, "my heart strains with longing to tell you things I may not, things I dare not! My life, my place in the world is so strange, that sometimes I wonder if it is not all a dream from which I will awaken! Sometimes I think that if I were to tell you my story, it would kill your love and cause you to shrink from me in terror!"

"Rames," she cried, her voice trembling, "don't talk like that, you frighten me! Nothing can make me cease to love you!"

"Forgive me," he said tenderly. "Some day you will know everything and understand why I must now be silent!"

For awhile they walked slowly through the soft shadows, her hand close-held in his.

"Rames," she said at last, wistfully, "was Teta more to you than I am?"

"Tonight and always you are Teta!" he said. "So long ago that you have lost the memory of it, your soul and mine were pledged to one another! It is only you who fill all my dreams!"

As they emerged from the shadows of the trees, a tall figure came toward them.

"Is that you, Iris?" he said. "I've been looking for you everywhere.'

"I'm sorry to have kept you waiting, John," she said contritely, "will an extra dance make amends?"

Reading nodded curtly to Rames, and offering the girl his arm, led her away.

"Do you mind if we stay out here, instead of dancing?" he asked. "It's warm inside and—I have something I want to tell you!"

His manner was strained, unlike the usual boyish comradeship to which she was accustomed. It agitated her a little.

"I hope you are not going to scold me," she said.

"No," he answered quietly, "it's something more serious than that." He paused and stared out over the moonlit waters of the Sound.

Iris watched him nervously.

"Tell me, John," she said at last, "why do you dislike Ra—the Prince?"

"Does it matter?" he asked.

"Very much. I had hoped that you would be good friends. I know he admires you."

"I regret that is so," he said coldly, "for my part I hate him "

"Why?"

"I don't know. It's one of those intangible things that cannot be explained From the beginning I've resented the mystery with which he surrounds himself, and lately I've been told that—that—well, I can't believe it!"

"Believe what, John?" she said quietly.

"That you're in love with the fellow!"

She drew her arm from his and stopped.

"John," she began, "you presume too much on friendship. It scarcely gives you the right to say these things to me."

"Forgive me, Iris," he said, "we've known each other since we were children, but what I'm saying is not prompted by friendship. Don't you know? Can't you understand what I mean?"

He took her hand gently in his.

"No," she said weakly, "I——"

"Iris, I love you! I want you to be my wife!"

With a sigh that was half a sob, she closed her fingers over his.

"Oh, John," she whispered, "I'm so sorry!"

"I had taken it for granted that you would care a little," he went on huskily. "I've always loved you so much. I never admitted to myself the possibility of losing you!"

"I never knew," she said miserably. "It grieves me more than I can tell you to cause you pain, but —it can never be!"

There was a moment of silence.

"Then it's true, what I've heard," he said bitterly. "This stranger about whom no one knows anything! A man with no friends, no connections of any sort! Iris, you can't mean it!"

She drew away from him, her face white in the moonlight.

"John," she said quietly, "I value your friendship

very much and I hope nothing will ever jeopardize it. Love goes where it pleases, not where it is sent. I never dreamed that you thought of me other than as a friend. Let us forget what you have said and continue to be always what we were!"

He sighed deeply.

"Iris, may I ask you one question? Do you love this man?"

She wanted to tell him, to tell the whole world, but Rames had said that for the present they must be silent.

"I cannot answer your question, John," she said at last.

"You have," he said sadly; "but Iris, you have no brothers. If you ever need me, no matter what service it is you desire, remember I shall always be ready!"

She held out her hand to him.

"John," she said softly, "the knowledge that you care for me is very precious. If I ever need a friend I shall not forget."

When she had locked the door of her room that night, Iris stood poised before the long mirror. Her hair hung dark and golden-tipped about her face, and from under the cloud of it her eyes gazed back at her, scintillating with a strange, unfamiliar light.

As she looked at the image, it seemed to her as though the walls of her room and the familiar things about her vanished. This was the dress she should always wear. The other was the masquerade. She seemed to see Rames again at her side. How wonderful he had looked in the short linen slip, his handsome limbs bare, his fine head banded with the jeweled badge. She realized, with a sense of wonder, that she had not been surprised to see that he had chosen this dress that matched hers. It had seemed his rightful garb.

She held out her arms to her image.

"Teta," she whispered, calling the girl in the mirror by the name Rames used, "Teta, you curious, half-real woman of another country, another age, tell me something about us both. Who are you, and what am I? Is it Iris he loves, or is it only the shadowy remembrance that exists in his mind, as you live in the mirror?"

CHAPTER XXVII

SUMMER waned. The sultry days of August gave place to the cool of September. There appeared the first tint that heralded the blaze of color which was to overspread the foliage, the breath of autumn was in the air and the tang of burning leaves.

Rames spent every moment he could at Iris' side. There were long rides through the shadowy lanes, delightful excursions in her little green canoe, and rambles through the woods that lay cool and fragrant beyond Loralea.

Each day he discovered a trait of character that had been Teta's. Like the translation of a beautiful poem into another language, he found that Iris not only had Teta's face, but her mind and heart as well.

But as the time passed, Mr. Waverly's impatience increased. Iris' mother had loyally hoped and persuaded him to wait, although she was secretly disappointed at Rames' continued silence. She dreaded lest her husband's displeasure would mar the happiness she saw shining in the girl's eyes, and resolved to avoid it, if possible, by speaking to the Prince herself.

One afternoon when Iris was busy pouring tea for some guests, Mrs. Waverly beckoned him to her side.

He admired this woman with her fine, aristocratic features. The calm dignity of her bearing pleased him.

"Have you enjoyed your summer in our country, Prince?" she asked.

"It has been very wonderful. My only regret is that it cannot last!"

She sighed.

"Isn't that the shadow that falls on all wonderful things?"

"I believe," he said, "that whatever is really beautiful can never die! There is a selective affinity in all things, which is progressive. An idea born in the mind of a philosopher ten centuries ago, blossoms into a noble deed in this!"

"But after all," she mused, "we must not overlook the needs of today in gazing toward a distant horizon!"

Rames leaned back where he could see Iris among her guests.

"Dear lady," he said, "the happiness of today can be perpetuated, but we must make the journey to the goal of our heart's desire step by step. The eagerness for haste is natural, but the fruit should not be gathered until it is ripe!"

She realized that he understood her thoughts and that she must accept this as an answer.

When she had a moment alone with Iris again, she told her of her father's determination.

"We feel, dear," she said gently, "that we must know a little of the Prince's intentions. You are together so much, people are beginning to wonder!"

Her mother's words filled Iris with foreboding.

Never in her life had she been denied anything that her parents could give her. Surely her father would not prevent her from realizing the supreme happiness of her life.

That afternoon as they cantered through the cool shadows of the woods, she drew her horse to a walk.

"Rames," she said, "I'm sorry, but father intends to speak to you when he sees you next, about —me! Won't you—can't you make it easier for me by speaking first? Can't we tell him how happy we are?"

They rode along in silence for awhile, his dark face troubled, his eyes staring ahead into space. He knew that he could no longer evade the inevitable. He must face this hour and pray his gods to help him. He looked at her graceful figure in its well-fitting habit. Her cheeks were flushed, her eyes shone. How lovely she was!

"I shall speak to your father tomorrow," he said at last. "I can tell him little of myself, but this he shall know, that I love you as no man ever loved a woman before!"

The next morning Iris stood at her window looking out toward the hills against the eastern sky. How beautiful the world looked, bathed in the warm sunshine.

She ran lightly down the stair and out onto the verandah where her father sat reading his morning paper, the day's mail lying at his side on a small table.

"Good morning, dad," she said, and kissing him

affectionately, perched herself on the arm of his chair.

"I hope I'm not interrupting you," her eyes on the piles of important looking letters at his elbow. "May I stay a few minutes? I—I want to talk to you!"

He laid down his paper and smiling whimsically, slipped his hand into his pocket.

"How much do you want?" he teased.

But Iris shook her head gravely.

"It's something more serious than money," she said. "It's about—about other things."

Her father leaned back in his chair and studied her shrewdly.

"It's about—about Rames. I want you to know that to me he is the most wonderful man in the world!"

She was silent for a moment.

"You love him, daughter?" he asked a little sadly.

Her eyes, those strange iridescent eyes that were like neither his nor her mother's, were gazing in a sort of rapturous dream toward a horizon far beyond the one that met the clear autumn sky.

"I love him," she said softly, "and it seems to me that I have loved him since the world began."

Her father put his arm about her shoulders and drew her to him.

"Daughter," he said, "you know that both your mother and I have always tried to do everything we could to insure your happiness. If Rames can prove to me that he will do as much, I think we can arrange the rest."

She threw her arm around his neck and kissed him happily.

"Dear dad," she cried, "I want you to love him too, he is so very wonderful, and you are an angel!"

As she spoke the olive car turned in at the gates.

"Speaking of angels——" said Mr. Waverly, and Iris, flushing rosily, sprang to her feet.

Rames, in immaculate, twentieth century flannels, seemed to personify the fire and vigor of eternal youth, although the shadows in his dark eyes had grown deeper, more baffling. He took the girl's hand in his in a warm, quick pressure and nodded to Abdullah, who swung the car about the loop of the drive and out on the road.

Mr. Waverly came forward.

"Good morning, Prince," he said pleasantly, "you evidently believe in early rising."

Rames smiled.

"I have been up for hours," he said. "Abdullah and I have our swim almost at sunrise every morning."

"Indeed?" Mr. Waverly was politely interested. "That is perhaps why you always look so fit. I had hoped you would call this morning. If Iris will excuse you, I should like to have a few minutes of your time," and he motioned Rames to a chair.

The girl's face flushed. Surely her father was not going to speak first!

"Father dear," she began hastily, "we have planned——"

But Rames interrupted her with a smile.

"What we have planned can wait," he said with

quiet dignity, "I am at your father's service!" and Iris, after one appealing look, turned and went into the house.

"My dear Prince," began Mr. Waverly, nervously clearing his throat when they were seated, "perhaps you can guess why I have asked to speak to you alone. Iris is the dearest treasure of her mother's heart and mine; she tells me that between you there is some sort of an understanding." He waited expectantly, but Rames was silent, his dark eyes looking at him steadily. "Of course, he went on after a moment, "we old chaps haven't forgotten the romance of our youthful days, but I think you will agree with me that there are other things that must be considered." He paused again, and Rames nodded gravely.

"You can, of course," went on Mr. Waverly, "give me such little—er—customary details and credentials. You were born in——?" he waited.

Rames shook off the silence that had bound him.

"Mr. Waverly," he said, "I quite understand your desire to know more of one whose dearest wish is to become the custodian of your daughter's happiness. You desire to know my nationality, my right to my title, the source of my income——"

The older man leaned back in his chair with a nod of satisfaction. His daughter's suitor knew the required customs, evidently the matter was to be adjusted more easily than he had anticipated. He smiled almost genially.

Rames paused a moment, his face slightly pale and set.

"Mr. Waverly," he said quietly, "it grieves me deeply, but—I can answer none of your questions!"

The other sat up straight, his face flushed a dark red, his thick brows pulled down over his sharp eyes, angrily.

"And do you imagine," he said, "that I can be satisfied with that answer?"

"I am sorry," said Rames, "but the only thing I can say is that I love your daughter as no man ever loved a woman before. I believe—I know she cares for me as I care for her. Surely you cannot mean to let convention stand between her happiness and mine?"

Mr. Waverly sprang to his feet.

"You are presuming to point out to me the course of my actions? To tell me what to do to insure my daughter's happiness?"

Rames rose and stood before him.

"I beg of you," he pleaded, "bear with me. If I were to answer your questions, you would not believe me, you would brand me as a mad man or an impostor. Is it not enough to swear to you my deep, my undying love for Iris, my sacred intention of serving her in all honor and loyalty?"

Mr. Waverly's face was purple.

"You have given yourself names I should have hesitated to utter," he fumed, "but since you have, I can only repeat them. I will never consent to my daughter's marriage to a man who may not even mention his birthplace, who calls himself an impostor!"

Rames drew himself up proudly.

"Mr. Waverly——" he began, but the older man broke in furiously.

"Not a word more, sir, and further, I must ask you to cease your visits here! In the future you will please remember that as far as my daughter is concerned, you do not exist. I bid you good morning!" and turning, his gray head held stiffly erect, he entered the house.

Rames stood gazing after him sadly for a moment. A barrier had suddenly risen between Iris and himself, a barrier seemingly as insurmountable as when the desert men had borne Teta away.

With a groan he went down the steps. He could not wait for Abdullah and the car since he had been turned from the house. He squared his shoulders, his mouth set in a determined line.

When he came again, he could lay his story before Mr. Waverly to believe or not as he chose, but nothing could take Iris from him. She was Teta whom he had found again at the end of the prismatic arch that had spanned his age with this. Nothing could ever part them again!

As he swung along the lovely country road, he seemed to hear the words of Hotep, ringing in his ears.

"Above all, no woman must come into your life, for that could only mean misery to yourself and her!"

Misery! What a weak, inadequate word for the anguish he was enduring. And Iris, what of her? What would this separation mean to her?

Back at Loralea, Mr. Waverly was pacing up and down the library. Mrs. Waverly was crying softly behind her handkerchief, and Iris stood white-faced and silent at the window from where she could see Rames' tall figure swinging down the road.

"The scoundrel, to presume upon our hospitality!" fumed Mr. Waverly. "The cad! The damned impostor!"

"Please, Lemuel!" begged Mrs. Waverly as Iris winced under his words.

Mr. Waverly's hands beat themselves against each other behind his back.

"He said if he were to tell me who he was or from where he came he would be branded as a mad man, or liar! How do I know we haven't been letting Iris go about with an escaped criminal? That's what comes of your taking people for granted, Lora. By Gad, I'll never let you travel alone again!"

Iris took a step forward. Her face was very pale. Her iridescent eyes shone brilliant and almost black, a little pulse fluttered visibly in her throat.

"Father," she said, "I am sorry if I have caused you and mother a moment's worry; you both have spent your lives trying to give me all the happiness you could. I want you to know how grateful I am, and I think I have always tried to do everything as you wished me to. But this is different! For me there is only one happiness, one life possible, and that is with Rames! What does it matter to me who he is? He is the man I love! And he loves me. That is all I care to know! No power on earth can ever separate us!"

Her father looked at her in astonishment.

"Are you defying me, Iris?"

The girl lifted her head, her clear eyes looking straight into his.

"This house is yours, father," she said quietly, "it must be ordered as you dispose. But I am a free agent. I shall do exactly as I see fit, and nothing short of Rames' own will can separate him and me!"

This was a new phase of the daughter who to him was still a child. It seemed only yesterday that she had come to him with her broken toys, her school-girl troubles, and now she faced him a woman roused in defense of her mate.

He sank into a chair, suddenly old and worn-looking.

"Iris," he said sadly, "would you leave your mother and me who love you so, for this man whom we scarcely know?"

The girl threw herself on her knees beside him, her arms about his neck.

"Father, father," she sobbed, "I love you both so much, but oh, you can't know what Rames means to me. If he doesn't answer your questions, I'm sure he must have some very good reason. Can't you trust him as I do?"

Mr. Waverly put her arms aside.

"Iris," he said firmly, "you will never marry this man with my consent! I forbid you to see him! What possible reasons could there be for his refusing to answer my very natural questions, the questions that any parent would insist upon asking before he entrusted his daughter into a man's keeping. It is because I love you that I want to safeguard you. Believe me, the reason he does not answer is because he dare not, because some disgraceful chapter in his life will come to light!"

Iris rose and faced him.

"Father," she said quietly, "I understand how reasonable what you say is, and how difficult it is for you to believe otherwise, but how poor a thing my love would be if I doubted him! No matter what may appear to the contrary, my faith shall remain unshaken!" And as she turned and left the room, there was a light in her eyes that her parents had never seen before.

CHAPTER XXVIII

ABDULLAH showed no surprise when he was told of the decision to go back to town at once. What his master ordained must be accomplished, and immediately he set about packing their bags and boxes.

"I shall return when everything is ready," Rames had said. He wanted to see Iris for a few minutes before he left. Her voice on the telephone was breathless, trembling, but she had said she would see him at once.

There was a little path through the woods where they had often walked and here he went to meet her. The newly fallen leaves rustled under his feet. Above his head the maples flamed scarlet and gold, an inquisitive little squirrel peered at him with friendly interest, a crow cawed hoarsely as it settled high in a dead tree-top, and everywhere was the appeal of the autumn woods. With an aching heart he watched the girl as she came toward him. How bitter the thought that these beautiful days together must end even for a time.

She held out her hands to him, and he drew her to his breast. For a moment they stood silent, his eyes deep and tragic, as they looked out over her trembling shoulders.

"My loved one," he said, "all this is because of my selfishness. I should never have come into your life. I should have been content to worship you at a distance. Your father asks me questions which if I were to answer would make him think me mad, or worse. Some day I shall come to you and tell you everything and you will understand. Until then perhaps it is wiser for us both that I obey his wishes and not see you."

She clung to him.

"Rames," she sobbed, "you can't go! I can't let you! I need you! My father will change his mind, if he does not it will not matter, I——"

But he shook his head.

"Listen," he said, "look at me, I want you to hear and understand every word I say, then we can decide what is best to do."

She raised her eyes, deep pools of affection, as he remembered them in Thebes.

"My hope, my determination," he said at last, "is to make you my wife, to bind you to me forever, but before I may do that, there is a long and perilous journey which must be made by the end of this year, a journey filled with dangers which may keep me away from you a long time, but by everything that you and I hold sacred, by the same oath which has led us together now, I swear that I will come back to you! And when I do, you will know everything! Are you content to wait?"

"Look into my eyes," she said, "you will see your image reflected there. So shall it be mirrored in my heart every moment that you are absent from me!"

He kissed her hands, her hair, her eyes, her lips, and then was gone.

She watched him until he was out of sight and then retraced her steps to Loralea, the warm colors of the foliage blurred through her tears.

On the way back to the city, Rames sat absorbed in his own thoughts. Without Iris this new world was black and empty. Some of the grief he had known when he had lost her in Thebes surged over him again, and with it came a feeling of rage against the Fate that deferred his happiness now that it was within his reach.

He cursed the oath that must bring him so much sorrow in order that a people far away in another age might see their errors and profit by them.

The city looked gray and dusty after the cool spaces of the country. The streets teemed and seethed with humanity battling for an existence. The swarming automobiles, clanging trolleys, shouting newsboys, and general pandemonium that makes up the symphony of New York, struck on his ear discordantly, deafeningly.

Amazing and efficient as were the appliances of this new world, they were had at the sacrifice of many things most desirable to man. He wondered if these people were happier than had been those of his own age, whether this striving after super-comfort and speed had not after all defeated its own ends?

Might not the knowledge Hotep sought bring evil upon his country? But the responsibility was the priest's, not his.

To Abdullah's delight they renewed their walks about the city. Once more he became the mentor, the all-knowing one.

They visited the mills, laboratories, and work-shops where all the marvels of this wonderful age were fabricated, and much of the mystery, with which the priests of Thebes had awed Rames, vanished with his increasing understanding.

Electricity, the marvelous force that turned the wheels of this new world and seemed to be the means by which all its wonders were accomplished, could this be the same power the priests had harnessed for their mystic uses? He remembered their foreknowledge of victory or defeat for the Pharaoh's hosts, the instant transmission of messages from one temple to another, the tales of the magic lighting of certain places within the sanctuaries. Had the sages of ancient Kampt understood many of the wonders of this age and kept them secret, so as to strengthen their hold on the people?

But he had failed to find among these strangers one thing of which Hotep had often spoken to his eager pupil.

"Hidden within the bosom of the earth," he had said, "is the warm energy that is life itself. Some day man will find it, and when he does, the last link that binds him to the brute will be severed. Sickness, pestilence, and all the evils that assail his physical and mental state will pass away, and it may be that even death will be conquered!"

Had these people, to whom all nature seemed to have opened up her store of treasures, found this most wonderful of them all? He put the question in a guarded form to Abdullah, but for once the little Egyptian was at a loss.

"You are speaking of a dream, I am afraid," he

said. "In the Middle Ages there were men who called themselves philosophers who spent their lives searching for the elixir of life, and for the touch-stone that was to turn all things to gold, but they never found it. The scientists of today laugh at them and say that what they sought did not exist."

"Is it not the philosophy of all ages to laugh at what they do not understand?" asked Rames.

"True," and Abdullah nodded his head wisely, "it has been the fashion to speak half-pityingly of those old alchemists who believed in the theory of the transmutation of metals, but now Madam Curie announces that she has discovered a new element, and when our modern sages examine it, they are obliged to admit that there may have been something in those laughed-at ideas, after all!"

"A new element? Tell me of it!"

Abdullah shook his head ruefully.

"There's very little that I or anyone else can tell about Radium," he said. "It is extremely valuable and only a very small quantity exists. The chemists give it as a symbol the word '*Ra.*' I've heard it called 'the soul of heat and light'!"

The soul of heat and light, mused Rames, Ra was indeed that! Could this be the substance of which Hotep had dreamed?

"Take me where I can learn something of it," he said, and with Abdullah's assistance, they secured all the information possible on the subject. Their quest carried them to one of the large hospitals where Radium was used to exterminate disease.

Inside the cool, white halls, where the sounds of the street did not penetrate, men and women in white clothes hurried to and fro noiselessly. The air was filled with a peculiar odor that was clean and refreshing, yet somehow disturbing. In a small room at one side sat pallid, wretched-looking people who seemed to be fearfully waiting for something.

"Who are these?" asked Rames.

"The city's poor, who are ill," said Abdullah. "They come here to be cared for."

"I am glad to see your interest in our work," said the young doctor who was showing them about. "Of course, we're just beginning to understand our bodies, but when you think how awful it must have been to live in those dim ages when surgery was unknown, it makes you mighty proud to be even hanging onto the skirts of science!"

"Was there a time when surgery was unknown?" Rames was politely curious. "The ancient Egyptians——"

Abdullah sighed. His master was about to launch forth on his favorite topic again, but their guide interrupted.

"Oh, yes," he said, "those old chaps had some sort of an idea, but it was very crude. For instance, they performed all their operations without anæsthetics, and as for antiseptic arrangements, they were absolutely unknown."

As they drove away, Abdullah explained his meaning.

"Cleanliness is one of the gods these people worship," he said, "and a good thing, too. Think of the filth and dirt of Egypt today!"

"The ancient Egyptians——" began Rames, but Abdullah became suddenly engrossed in the intrica-

cies of the traffic, and the comparison remained un-
finished.

One morning a letter came from Iris, saying:

"We are motoring down to Virginia. They insist
on my going, but I shall be in New York again
before you sail. Wait for me!"

A little package had accompanied the note. It
contained her miniature, painted on ivory, and set
in a plain gold locket with her monogram engraved
on the back.

It had been done in Italy and was beautifully
executed. Out of the creamy surface, warm and
softly tinted, shone the delicate oval of her face.
There was a dreamy, half-wistful look in the translucent eyes that smiled at him as though recalling
some tender memory.

"My Princess," he murmured in his own tongue,
"how can I live until that day when thou shalt be
all mine own!"

*   *   *   *   *   *

As the conflagration across the water continued
to spread, and the armies of the nations, locked in
deadly combat, surged back and forth across the face
of Europe, Rames grew anxious as to America's
being drawn into the maelstrom and the difficulty
which might ensue for him to get back to the secret
chamber in the Theban hills. With conditions such
as they were, he knew he must allow himself ample
time to return to Egypt before his year of pilgrimage should end.

He eagerly questioned those men whom he knew
and insisted on Abdullah's gleaning information and
opinions from wherever he happened to be. Often

he would sit far into the night listening as the little
Egyptian recounted a street speech he had heard, or
an argument in some café.

Rames of all men who walked the earth, could most
clearly visualize this great struggle. It was as
though he were the sole spectator viewing a mighty
drama on the world's stage and without bias, saw it
as it was. He had come to have a feeling almost
of affection for these people who were Iris', and as
the menacing shadow reached out from those distant
shores, he foresaw the hour of destiny. He longed
passionately to silence every voice that spoke
against the need of preparation, remembering how
his countrymen had been lulled into a false sense
of security because of their wealth and distance
from the enemy. If Egypt had given more thought
to her defenses and less to the awing of her neigh-
bors by a parade of riches, the Assyrian would not
have dared set foot upon her soil.

One night he stood at his window looking down
on the sleeping city.

"Is there no power that will make you conscious
of what lies ahead?" he murmured under his breath.
"Awake! Arise! Gird on your shields and battle-
axes! Bid your archers stand with drawn bows
along your ramparts! Keep your beacon fires burning! For only so can you avert the fate that has
befallen ancient Kampt!"

The days were growing shorter and colder.
Abdullah was no lover of snow and the piercing
winds of winter. "Shall we not go where it is
warmer?" he asked one day. "Miss Waverly's
family has gone South, why do we not——" But

Rames shook his head. She had promised to come, he could only wait.

The bleakness of December filled the air, the street lights were already glowing at four in the afternoon, some of New York were swathed in furs and great coats, and some shivered blue-lipped and ragged.

The shops had taken on a new splendor. The windows were hung with holly and crimson bells, and blazed with tempting displays.

Abdullah had told him that soon was to be celebrated the greatest feast of the Occidental world.

"It is an occasion when everyone is obliged to make gifts," he explained.

"Why are they obliged to make them?" asked Rames.

"It is a mutual exchange," said Abdullah smiling, "and when the day arrives they are divided between rage at having been forgotten by the people they remembered, and mortification at having been remembered by the people they forgot!"

Late one afternoon, wrapped in a handsome fur coat, Rames walked among the holiday throngs. The snow swirled about him in eddies, and beat against his face with each sharp gust of wind. His skin and eyes, unused to the cold, smarted and ached, and he dug his hands deep into the pockets of his coat, his chin buried in the collar.

The streets were filled with people hurrying from one shop to another making their purchases. The lights were reflected in long waving yellow streamers on the wet asphalt, the lamps of the motor-cars making their slow progress along the crush of the

avenue, blinked through the swirling snow whose
fleecy whiteness was instantly converted into a black
muddy slush by the hundreds of trampling feet.

How different were the turquoise skies and golden
sunshine of Thebes, and the joyousness and mirth
that marked her feast days!

When he returned to the hotel, he found a message.

"Beloved, I am home again. Mother has consented to my seeing you once more. When shall
it be?"

The pilgrimage was ended. The time had come
for him to retrace his steps, to leave this world of
wonder. Tomorrow he would sail away toward the
sunrise, to that land where had been sown the seed
from which had sprung the mighty works of this
age. There was a vague, though deadly unrest at
his heart, a cold foreboding that, try as he would,
he could not shake off.

Every preparation had been made for the journey. Abdullah had gone about his task joyfully;
he was longing for the warmth and sunshine of his
own country, but Rames looked at every familiar
object with the wish to print its image indelibly
upon his memory.

That evening, waiting for Iris in the dimly lit
library of her father's house, he stared into the logs
blazing on the wide hearth. Pictures, wild, fantastic, sombre and tragic ascended with the smoke.

The room was very quiet, and in the glow of the
logs, his clear, finely marked profile looked unreal.
It seemed to emerge from the surrounding shadows
like a vision from another world, and Iris, watching

him from the doorway, felt a curious tightening at her throat. She longed to throw her arms about him and hold him back from that darkness from which he had come and which threatened again to engulf him.

She moved nearer, and, impelled by the magic of her gaze, he turned and rose to his feet. For a long moment they looked into each other's eyes, and then she was in his arms.

"The days have been so empty without you!" he murmured against her lips. "It has been an eternity of waiting!"

He drew her beside him on the couch before the fire. Her white arms and shoulders were touched with a soft glow and her eyes shone deeply tender as they rested on his.

"Iris," he said, and his voice sounded hoarse and unreal, "the time is come when I must leave you!"

She turned to him, her lips quivering.

"And I may not even know your destination!"

He was staring into the heart of the glowing logs.

"Will it mean anything to you to know that I am going toward the rising sun?" he said at last. "That my way lies back to where our love had its beginning?"

Iris had always felt that Rames' birthplace lay somewhere in that mysterious region called the "East."

"I have never been to your country," she said, "but I feel that were I to go, I would find that it was all familiar to me. It must be only fancy, but sometimes I seem to remember things that I am sure have never happened to me!"

"It is not fancy," he said, "we are but the continued life of our ancestors and therefore must have some recollection of their experiences. Certain events and emotions stamp themselves so indelibly that what seems to be only a figment of the mind is simply a lifting of the veil of memory. I have a vision of a girl with bronze hair and eyes like limpid pools. The moonlight softly caresses her rounded arms as she leans from a latticed window. The air is perfumed with the scent of lotus and jasmine, and I can hear her voice, like silver music, murmuring words of love that you have echoed."

"And she was Teta," she asked half-timidly, "whom some ancestor of yours so loved that her memory has never been forgotten?"

"You are Teta," he said, "who has come to me again as you promised you would!"

"But I do not understand. It all seems so like a dream. I feel there never was a time when I did not love you, but my life before we met seems so apart from the possibility of what you have just said, and my ancestors came from Europe—England and France!"

He smiled into her eyes.

"And where did their ancestors come from?"

"I—I do not quite know. Was it as long ago as that?"

"It was in an age so remote from this as to seem lost in the mists of Time, but to the gods who ordained that we should meet again, it is but a fleeting moment!"

"But tomorrow———" her voice was full of tears.

"Tomorrow I start on my journey. Where I go I may not say, but when you look toward the rising sun each morning, your heart will whisper, 'he is there!' "

"Wherever you are going," she said softly, "remember that with each new morning I shall be saying, 'he is one day nearer his destination and to me,' for every hour that passes hastens the time when we shall be together again!"

He drew a dull leather case from his pocket.

"This is the season of gifts," he said, and as he lifted the lid, Iris uttered an exclamation of astonished delight. Against the creamy satin cushion lay the remainder of his store of gems which were set in ornaments such as had been worn by a princess of Thebes.

"I have brought you these," he said, "so that their fire and light may speak to you of me and remind you that all this has not been a dream!"

"A dream!" she repeated. "Life was never real to me before!"

Her cheeks were flushed, her eyes rivaled the luster of the jewels, as she bent over them.

"But these would excite the envy of a queen!" she said.

"And are you not that?" he asked gently.

For a long while they sat silent, the precious stones glittering against the satin of her gown. Half in a dream she watched their glowing hearts as, her hand held close in his, he spoke of the happiness that was to be theirs when he should return.

The fire had died down, the logs fell apart with a soft little crash and a sudden lighting of the dim room. Somewhere in the distance Christmas chimes were ringing out on the frosty air, and once or twice the silver jingle of sleigh-bells danced out of the silence and back into it again. The great carved clock on the stair-landing chimed eleven. He raised her hands and pressed the soft palms against his lips, his eyes, his forehead and then drew her close, passionately, yearningly.

She lifted her eyes to his, the love that had outlived the centuries glowing in their depths.

"Kiss me," she said, "and know that until my lips shall rest again on yours, until my arms shall once more hold you close, I shall know neither happiness nor peace!"

"Teta," he breathed, his lips against hers, "when you said those words to me last, you kept your faith. I know I shall find you waiting when I come again!"

Then he was gone, and Iris threw herself, weeping, on the couch, the jewels he had given her held close against her heart.

CHAPTER XXIX

THE great ship slipped away in a heavy fog early the next morning, Rames and Abdullah standing at the rail. The clear brightness of yesterday had vanished; the damp air was bitterly cold, and the giant buildings were shrouded in the heavy gray folds of mist. The vague form of another ship emerged from the pall, drifted past, and was lost to view, the hoarse voice of her siren cutting the thick air. Now and then a solitary gull swooped out of the fog and back again. The water looked black and filthy with floating refuse and bits of ice that swirled against the ship's sides. There were few passengers aboard and these had deserted the decks, leaving only the two lonely figures, muffled in great coats, staring back through the heavy veil that jealous Nature had hung between the present and the future.

The last vague outline vanished; contact with the shore was gone. The great ship seemed a mere speck lost in measureless space. Rames, staring into the grayness, shuddered. This was like the enveloping mantle that he had torn away, to find the sunlight beyond.

Had Nature and the awful forces of the gods some hideous punishment in store for his defiance? Or did they feel that he had suffered enough?

Against the pearl gray of the mist, he seemed to

see the beloved face again, her eyes filled with the sadness of parting.

Impatiently he paced the deck. If the long journey were over, if this vast monotony of water only lay behind him!

Abdullah, bursting with the gossip of the sailors, tried to regale him with tales of submarines, of dangers threatened by the Enemy of Europe. But even though the ship steamed ahead, all lights extinguished and life-boats swung out and ready, it failed to rouse his interest. He lived now only for the time when, his vow fulfilled, Hotep should open once more the portal that led back to Iris.

With the sunshine and warmth that came as they ploughed into the southern waters, Abdullah's spirits rose. The veneer of his Western training had never quite submerged the Oriental love of warmth and light, and he had shivered and cursed the bitter winter of New York which pierced his clothing, no matter how heavy. Once more he could have his beloved master to himself, to wander with him through the languor of the Orient.

When they touched at Gibraltar the first indication of the great war became apparent. Soldiers were everywhere, bronze cheeked, alert, who forbade the landing of those passengers booked for other ports.

At Naples they found little change, except a spirit of curiosity and unrest, such as had been in New York. Here they waited for the ship that was to take them to Egypt. It was small and overcrowded with soldiers of many nationalities.

When they arrived at Alexandria they found the

streets and public places of the city filled with troops.   Among the khaki-clad English and Australians were many Soudanese and East Indians, in their picturesque uniforms, and others in gray-blue who, Abdullah told him, were French.

The nations of the earth were girded for war. He wondered if the world that he was leaving might not be utterly consumed by the fires of hate that were devouring it.   Would another generation see but the blackened ashes of the glories upon which he had looked?   Was it to a dying world that he was bidding adieu?

At Cairo they found the change most apparent. Gone were the crowds of carefree tourists, of beautifully gowned and jeweled women, and the merry parties that were wont to take tea on the hotel terraces.   In their place were French and English officers, who hurried to and fro, deeply engrossed in the business of war.

Even Abdullah, with all his ingenuity, was unable to secure immediate transportation to Luxor. and the greater part of the day was consumed in going about from one official to another to gain the required permission to continue their journey.   But obstacles were as meat and drink to the little Egyptian.   He revelled in accomplishing the seemingly impossible, and late in the afternoon he returned to his master, a smile cutting an ivory crescent across his brown face.

"I have here our tickets," he announced triumphantly, "we leave at eight tonight!"

"And the sleeping accommodations?" asked Rames.

Abdullah's face fell.

"That was not within the power of man!" he said. "The trains are mostly given over to the troops and there are no sleeping-cars attached."

Rames shrugged.

"Ah. well, my Abdullah, good company shortens the road; perhaps we shall not mind a little inconvenience!"

The journey to Luxor was hot and dusty and consisted of many jerking starts and long stops where shouting Arabs ran past their window swinging lanterns, and more soldiers kept piling into the already crowded train. A score of times Abdullah was obliged to show their tickets and explain the object of their journey; several times they were on the point of being refused further transportation on the ground of insufficient reasons for traveling at all, but Rames' inexhaustible gold, and Abdullah's glib tongue smoothed the way. The train was many hours late and the afternoon sun was already low in the West when they arrived at Luxor.

As they drove toward the hotel, Rames looked about him curiously. Here his eyes had first beheld this new world. How wonderful it had seemed! Just a year had elapsed, yet it had all grown familiar to him, almost a matter of course. He looked down at his correct European clothes and thought of how he had crawled, a naked, wondering creature, out of the secret chamber in those hills which he could see mistily blue against the glowing Western sky.

Abdullah also was thinking.

"You have grown in knowledge since our first meeting, my master," he said.

Rames shook his head.

"Great wisdom is but the realization of how little one knows!"

He smiled as the obsequious attendants came forward to serve him, remembering how he had once lurked outside in the shadows, famished and in rags, and had at last crept away to seek what shelter he might among the ruins of the temple.

While Abdullah was arranging for rooms and the other necessities of a stay, Rames wrote his last letter to Iris. He spoke of their love that was to endure forever, which grew with each day of separation and increased his longing for her.

"Beloved of my heart," he said, "as I write I can see the sun sinking below the hills in a blaze of glory to make his course through the nether world. Just such a journey is before me, and as surely as he shall rise again in the eastern sky, so shall I return to you! Let nothing daunt your courage or faith, for when our day dawns, the gods themselves will envy our happiness!"

After he had finished, he called Abdullah from his task of unpacking the luggage.

"When does the next train return to Cairo?" he asked.

"There is an express about midnight; shall I see that your letter is put aboard?"

"You are to return to Cairo *with* my letter," said Rames quietly.

The little Egyptian stared at his master in astonishment.

"Cairo," he stammered. "We're not going back there already!"

"No," replied Rames, "not *we*, but you!"

Abdullah's face flushed.

"You mean that I may no longer serve you? Have I displeased you in some way?"

Rames laid his hand kindly on the little man's shoulder.

"You have served me well and faithfully since that first day when Fate or the will of the gods brought us together. Now that I am about to ask you for one last proof of your loyalty, do not fail me!"

Abdullah fell on his knees, his forehead against his master's hand.

"What you will of me is my wish to do!" he said. "Only so that I may continue to serve you!"

Rames raised him to his feet.

"Come," he said. "If you are faithful we need not be separated for long. There is a journey that I must make, to a far country, and I must go alone. Carry this letter back to Alexandria, see that it starts for America on the first ship, then return here and await my coming."

"Master," pleaded Abdullah, "take me with you into this unknown land that calls you!"

"That may not be," said Rames kindly. "Within six months I shall join you, after that we shall never be separated so long as we both live!"

Abdullah took the letter and placed it carefully in his breast pocket.

"I shall guard it with my life," he said.

The belt that had so long been wound about his

body, Rames had unfastened. This he put into Abdullah's hands.

"What remains here is yours," he said. "It will keep you in comfort until I return again."

Abdullah knelt and kissed his master's hand.

"Farewell," he said; "may Allah keep thee safe until we meet again!"

When the door had closed on the faithful companion of his pilgrimage, Rames drew the miniature of Iris from his pocket, and sat staring sadly into the sweet, pictured face.

"Dear love that was taken from me in Thebes, whom I have left to await my coming in this new and more wonderful world, may the gods have thee in their keeping until I return to claim thee for mine own!"

Following his master's directions, Abdullah had settled their account and arranged to have the hotel store the luggage, and now the Arab porters entered to carry the trunks and bags to a safe place.

When the men had left, Rames walked to the window. The moon had risen and the outside world was bathed in its clear silver. The hotel gardens lay black in the shadow of the acacias, the pathways dappled with the moonlight, and beyond wound the Nile, the same unchanging, mysterious, sacred river.

The last knot was loosened, the last link that bound him to this age of wonder was severed. Nothing remained but to follow the path back across the desert into the Theban hills.

He left the hotel and made his way to the river. An Arab boatman ferried him to the deserted strip of shore from where he had crossed a year before. Here he sprang out and emptied what money still remained in his pockets into the hands of the eager native. ·

"Go back," he said. "I shall stay here tonight!"

The astonished man put off again and Rames stood watching the silver wake of his craft until it reached the other shore, then he turned his face toward the hills where lay his destination.

The road was heavy with sand and cut by the deep black shadows· of the overhanging cliffs, but he made good progress and presently came to the great slab of rock on the surface of which was rudely carved the symbol of the Key of Life. With all his strength he pressed against the stone at the intersection of the cross and circle, and the heavy door swung silently open.

Before him lay the black passage that was to lead back across the ages, behind him, the moonlit world of today.

The lights of the hotel on the other side of the river gleamed like pin pricks in a card held before a lamp. The moon turned the calm surface of the Nile into a burnished ribbon. Over the edge of a distant sand dune, sharply outlined against the sky, crawled a long line of men mounted on camels, their shadows black and' clearly defined. They might have been figures in a dream, so silently they wound their slow way over the sands.

They, too, were probably going to throw their might into that Maelstrom of Hatred whose mad whirl threatened to engulf the world.

He let his gaze sweep slowly along the wide

horizon. White in the moonlight as the blanched bones of men, lay the ruins that had been Thebes, and breaking over them, covering what had been their splendor, swept the waves of the desert. The moon, low in the heavens, had turned to a dull red, under it the sand lay darkly crimson, as though blood had been spilt and dried as it sank into its depths. From far away on the still air came the plaintive note of a bugle, sounding taps..

He held out his arms to the West where Iris waited, and with a last gesture, as one who waves farewell to someone at a distance, he turned and plunged into the blackness of the Theban hills.

CHAPTER XXX

INSIDE the secret chamber, he held the lamp above his head and looked about him. Everything was as he had left it. The giant heads of the gods, vaguely seen in the shadows, stared immutable.

He replenished the powder in the metal brazier as Hotep had done, then extinguishing his lamp, set it carefully away where he could find it again. As the weird blue light from the burning incense flared up, it was caught and flashed back by the gems and heaps of precious things. Here was wealth that surpassed the greatest fortune of this new world, and when he came again, it would be his to use as he pleased!

He had observed the power of gold both for good and evil among these people. He would make this treasure an instrument to help banish poverty and suffering! The wisdom contained in these rolls of papyrus and blocks of sculptured stone would be given to man so that his comfort and happiness might be increased. No princess would be more royally housed than Iris. With love and the means to supply her every wish, their world would be a paradise. She would be a spur to his ambition! With this store of knowledge and material things, to what heights might he not climb when he came again to take his place among her people!

The flickering light fell upon the faces of the

images of his gods. Was it only fancy or did their eyes follow him? There was something portentous in their brooding calm, as though they awaited an hour that was to come. Thus would they gaze down upon him during that long period when he should again be wrapped in oblivion. Might they not approach his silent couch and bend their stony faces close to his, smiling in mockery upon this mortal who had dared defy their laws?

A shudder passed over him and cold drops stood upon his brow. Summoning all his courage, he crossed to the figure of Anubis and took from the recess in its breast the tall jar of carved alabaster and the remaining phial, whose contents palpitated with living ruby-colored flame.

He placed his precious burden on a small carved table near the couch, then took from his pocket the little miniature of Iris. Once more he looked into the sweet face and held it to his lips.

"Farewell," he whispered, "I love thee!"

His words, echoing against the rocky walls, returned to him as though the voice of Iris herself repeated softly:

"I love thee!"

He hung the miniature about his neck by its golden chain, and divesting himself of his clothing, proceeded to rub and knead his body with the precious oil in the alabaster jar, as Hotep had done.

Immediately, he felt the same sense of relaxation that had come to him before, all weight and substance seemed to leave him, fear and apprehension vanished. He sank on the couch and poured the liquid into the golden goblet. For an instant, he watched the lambent, living, scintillating flame, then threw back his head and drank.

An overwhelming force seemed to crush him, as though the hills beneath which he lay were piled upon his chest. His ear-drums seemed to burst. All the might and energy of nature were concentrated on the mere atom of his being, every fiber was telescoped into itself with irresistible power, as though two worlds, rushing through space, had collided and caught his body between them. His soul receded to a distance, vast beyond the power of imagination, and then—oblivion!

* * * * * *

Within the velvet darkness of the secret chamber, Time marked no division of days and nights, nor of months or years. There was only a space, a void that was part of Eternity.

In the black silence, the brooding, inscrutable images of the gods kept their vigil, until at last the still form lying on the ebony couch came, shuddering convulsively, back to consciousness. Sick and giddy, he staggered to his feet, and gasping in the heavy air, groped his way with shaking, outstretched hands to the lamp, and with difficulty succeeded in lighting it.

The flame stirred into life a thousand points of dazzling color where it fell on the gold and jewels in the treasure coffers. The stone faces of the gods stared dimly from the shadows. There seemed to be an expression of triumph on their inexorable faces as though the hour for which they waited had come.

He was conscious of strange, vague memories

which he tried vainly to recall, as one awaking from sleep endeavors to weave again the raveled fabric of a dream.

He drew his hand across his eyes. Hotep had brought him to this hidden chamber. He had sworn an oath, but what it was eluded him. He had been asleep and dreamed a wonderful dream. That it was wonderful, he knew, but it was all so illusive, so baffling.

On the floor near the couch was a little mound of fine gray dust, and near it, a small ivory disk framed in dull gold. He picked it up and looked at it curiously. On its smooth surface lay a dim shadow, misty and uncertain of outline. He held it close to his eyes and studied it intently, and as he did so, it seemed to take form and a pair of wistful eyes smiled back into his.

For a moment he stared, his brain throbbing with a confusion of emotions, then, like the rending of a veil, memory came flooding back. He had indeed journeyed into unborn ages where he had found Teta, whom he had thought lost to him forever.

On the little porphyry table lay the two small phials that had contained the magic elixir. They were dry and empty, but Hotep would fill them again, Hotep, who was to hear his story and then give him as his reward this key that should unlock the door to that far-off time where Teta waited.

He glanced down at his naked body and then at the heap of gray dust on the floor. So this was all that remained of the garments of that strange world!

The atmosphere was suffocating, he felt an intense longing to breathe the free air again, and throwing his weight against the door, scarcely waited for it to swing wide, before he squeezed through the opening. The passage was stifling and he almost ran along its narrow way. As the outer door gave slowly, a cool breeze filled his panting lungs. He rejoiced to see a shaft of moonlight cut the darkness. The night would hide his nakedness. He drew a deep breath of the sweet air and stepped forth into the world, the great door swinging to behind him.

His eye swept the horizon anxiously. Across the Nile a dull glow reddened the sky, as though in the distance the last embers of a vast conflagration still smouldered.

Stumbling through the clinging sand, he hastened toward the river. Presently he heard the faint murmur of voices and paused a moment irresolute, then, picking his way cautiously through the darkness in the direction of the sound, he came upon a huddled group of people.

A tall shaven figure in a tattered white robe that hung about his lean body, rose to meet him.

"Thou also, to judge by thy nakedness, art fleeing the invader," he said, in the deep, sonorous tones of ancient Kampt. "Come among us, and, miserable though we are, we will help thee from our pitiful store."

The familiar tones of his own tongue thrilled Rames. These were his people! He had come back, but to what?

Silently he let them wrap his body in some filthy

rags, and bent his head in gratitude when a woman brought a bowl of lentils and set it before him.

"Eat," said the old man who had greeted him first, "there may be days coming when even this will be denied thee!"

As Rames devoured the coarse food, he looked at the wretched creatures about him. Some were lying exhausted on the sand, others rocked and swayed in silent grief, frightened children clung to weeping mothers, a number of men bore ghastly wounds which were being dressed with crude bandages.

The tall patriarch who had accosted him stood staring tragically back where the fires smouldered.

"Gods of my fathers," he prayed aloud, "visit thy vengeance on the foul heel that crushes thy children! Deliver us from the oppressor and spare those who are still within his grasp!"

There came a long-drawn, bitter wail from the huddled figures about him.

"Holy Isis," pleaded a woman's voice, "give me back my son! He was so strong and beautiful, the staff of my declining years; and the Assyrians have nailed him to a door!"

"May Ra visit his fury upon those who dragged my infants from my arms and murdered them," cried another.

All about him from the darkness came the groans of men, the suppressed sobs of women, the wailing of children, and curses of bitter hatred against the invader who had destroyed their homes and driven them forth to wander hopelessly in the desert.

Rames listened, amazement, rage, and agony filling his heart.

The unheeded warning of the approach of the barbarian had resulted in disaster for his unhappy people. Thebes the glorious, was conquered! Her proud head was bowed beneath the heel of the Assyrian!

He rose and went to the side of the tall, gaunt figure of the priest, who stood looking grimly in the direction of his desecrated temple.

"Tell me," he asked, "is Thebes vanquished? Is the mighty Pharoah no longer secure upon his throne?"

The old man looked at him in bewilderment.

"My son," he said, "hath suffering turned thy brain so that thou hast forgotten the affliction that has come upon us?"

Rames passed his hand before his eyes with a weary, uncertain gesture.

"My mind wanders in darkness, oh my father," he said. "Reveal unto me that which hath befallen the city chosen of the gods!"

The aged one raised his hands in astonishment.

"Knowest thou not, my son, that Thebes is fallen? The Pharaoh's power is broken, the gods are hiding their faces from their children, the Sanctuary is defiled, and the waters of the Holy River are polluted with the bodies of the slain!"

A dreadful fear clutched at Rames' heart.

"And Hotep, High Priest of Amen-Ra, what of him?"

The other shook his head.

"I know not," he said, "all who could, have fled

before the sword of the Assyrian and are scattered like chaff before the wind!"

Rames' eyes were fixed on the lurid glow in the distance. He must reach Hotep before it should be too late.

"Yet must I enter the city," he said at last; "I seek one on whom my very life depends!"

"Not life, but death awaits thee there," warned the old man, "rest thou here, in the darkness we are safe!"

But Rames put aside the detaining hand, and with the prayers of the old man ringing in his ears, hastened away.

At the river bank he paused and girding his rags about him, plunged in and struck out strongly for the opposite shore.

The swift current carried him down stream and when at last he reached the other side, it was at the great quay before the citadel. He clung a moment to one of the huge stone rings fastened to the step and then cautiously drew himself from the water. It was very dark in the shadow and he thought the quay deserted, but suddenly something touched his arm, and a rough hand slid over his mouth stifling the cry that almost escaped him.

"Not a sound or thou art a dead man," whispered a voice hoarsely.

He wrenched himself free, and with a swift movement threw his assailant to the ground, and set one knee upon his chest.

"Mercy!" gasped the man, "I did but seek freedom from this place of torment! Mercy!"

Something in the sound of his voice made Rames bend and stare into the upturned face.

"Amrou," he cried, "thou!"

The man struggled to his knees.

"Praise to the might and glory of Ra!" he whispered. "Thou art come again! Oh, master, where hast thou hidden thyself since these unhappy days have come upon the city of thy fathers?"

Rames helped the trembling wretch to his feet and drew him from the shadow of the wall.

"Let me look at thee," he said, "thou hast come through some sore trial!" and indeed the slave bore the marks of brutal usage. There were great welts across his back and shoulders, and the skin of his wrists and ankles was torn and bleeding. He drew Rames back into the shadow, terrified.

"Stay not here, master," he implored. "My guard slept, drunk on the sacred wine. With my teeth I gnawed the cords that bound me and made my way hither! Hark!" on the still air came the sound of shrieks, the brazen clatter of shields and the sound of brutal laughter.

Amrou fell on his knees again.

"Master," he cried, "go not into the city, nothing is left but death and ruin!"

But Rames shook his head.

"I must seek Hotep. Knowest thou aught of him?"

"Mine eyes have not beheld him, master. There be those who say he has fled Kampt."

Rames smiled. Hotep leave his country in a crisis? The mere thought was impossible! To him the glory of Kampt was only second to that of Ra!

"I shall find him, Amrou," he said quietly, "have no fear for me. Go thou into the Libyan hills where safety waits thee! Some day we shall meet again!"

The slave clung to his hand touching it with his forehead, and as he raised his face, Rames stared into the pinched features with wonder and amazement, for far away, in another age, he had beheld this same face and called it, "Abdullah." The vaguely familiar something that he had always observed in the appearance of the companion of his pilgrimage, and the fate that had bound up the little Egyptian's fortunes with his, was explained. He pressed Amrou's hand warmly.

"Verily," he said, "thou and I shall meet again!" and as the slave plunged into the water and struck out for the far shore, Rames turned his face once more toward the city.

CHAPTER XXXI

WHEN he came out into the great sphinx-lined Avenue, the first banners of the new day unfurled across the eastern sky and the brazen note of a horn cut the stillness.

There followed hoarse shouts of command, the clatter of shields and weapons, the murmur of voices, tramping of many feet, the beat of hoofs, the rumble of chariot wheels, and through it all, like the shrill scream of a Fury urging to carnage, the sound of trumpets. A company of soldiers came in sight, the rising sun blazing on their helmets and the polished surface of their shields. He slipped behind one of the great stone figures and watched them pass. They were stalwart, fierce-eyed men, with curly black beards and brutal, lustful faces.

To Rames, who had seen the highest development of the finer sensibilities of man, they seemed as savage and merciless as beasts of prey, and yet were there not men in that other age equally pitiless to those who had fallen into their power?

When they had disappeared, he stole from behind the sphinx and made his way along the Avenue. A sentry challenged him, but seeing his rags, judged him of no importance and permitted him to pass.

Everywhere havoc and devastation met his eye. Some of the beautiful villas had been burned and

340

among the blackened ruins, the fires still smouldered. The bodies of the slain polluted the air. Unspeakable horror was on every side. A group of captives passed, guarded and in chains. They were nobles of the Pharaoh's household, men whom Rames had known, and he shuddered to think of the fate that awaited them. In an open space he beheld a ghastly heap of severed heads, gruesome toll of barbarous war!

For hours he wandered like one in some horrible dream, seeking one face he knew, one familiar spot left inviolate. Sick at heart and filled with a blind rage against this monster of destruction, he came at last to the great temple. Its halls were silent and empty, the mighty columns, despoiled of the golden inlay that had flashed back the sunlight, and over the floor were strewn the broken and battered remains of the sacred barque from whose sides had been stripped the gems and ornaments. Everywhere were the marks of ruthless hands, of savage, wanton spoliation.

This was infinitely more tragic than the ruins which he had found in that far-off age. They were but the bleached skeleton of a splendor that was then only a memory! But this ravage still bore the hue of life, like the beautiful body of a slain woman from which the breath has just fled.

The silence within the vast temple lay like a pall. It was not the solemn quiet known of old. There was something ominous in its velvet depths that portended evil, and a dark foreboding lay heavy at his heart as he moved slowly toward the Sanctuary.

The rich curtains were torn from their rods and

trailed, rent and smeared with dark stains, on the tesselated floor; the holy vessels of precious metal which had been used in the services were gone. The face of the god had been mutilated, and at his feet lay the body of a young priest. The tightly clenched hands and strong teeth sunk into the lower lip gave mute testimony of secrets guarded unto death, the eyes staring in ghastly, unseeing wonder on the image of the deity who had permitted this desecration of his shrine.

He looked once more at the defiled splendor that a reverent people had erected to an impotent god. The desolation was absolute, save for himself and this silent form, the vast temple was empty. He must seek Hotep elsewhere.

Slowly, and with much difficulty, he made his way at last to the house of the Acacia where the High Priest had dwelt with Teta. The heavy gate was wrenched from its hinges, the walks of the garden trampled and strewn with broken pottery and furniture. The little lake was filled with floating rubbish. The windows of the house were shutterless and staring wide.

Filled with a dread he dared not put into words, Rames hurried up the path and into the open doorway. The hall was deserted, ransacked of all its treasures and littered with objects deemed too worthless to carry away.

He clapped his hands loudly but there was no response. Once he thought he heard a furtive, shuffling footstep, then everything was silent again.

"A friend calls," he cried, "is there no one within?"

After what seemed an interminable time, the faint sound was repeated, and presently the bleareyed, disheveled head of a man peered cautiously around a corner.

"Is it indeed a friend?" he whined, "there is naught here of value, oh mighty, conquering stranger, naught but four bare walls; canst not leave Ostanes this?"

"Knowest me not, Ostanes?" asked Rames. "I am thy master's friend."

The man lifted his head and stared with redrimmed eyes as though he beheld a vision from another world. Then suddenly he collapsed into a crumpled heap at Rames' feet.

"Master, master," he wailed, "everything is lost, and thou art come again in the midst of ruin!"

Rames looked with pity at the grovelling wretch.

"Ostanes," he sighed, "all seems indeed lost. Where is Hotep, thy master?"

The steward crouched at his feet, trembling. He was lean and filthy, the skin hung in loose folds about his jaws, his hands shook as with palsy.

"Everything is lost," he repeated, "the end of the world has come!"

"Tell me of thy master," cried Rames. "Hotep, the Hight Priest of Amen-Ra! Where is he?"

Something in his words seemed to recall the man's wandering senses.

"The High Priest of Ra," he repeated, and then suddenly staggered to his feet, his lean hands clenched and shaking above his head.

"They shall not find him!" he shrieked. "They shall never find him, not the Assyrians nor the

Ethiopians, nor the people of Kampt who flee before the enemy! No man shall seek him out!"

Rames seized him roughly by the shoulder.

"Speak!" he cried, "Loosen thy palsied tongue and tell me, Rames, the beloved disciple of the Priest of Ra. I must find him! Dost hear? Lead me to his side! Or by the gods, I'll tear thy limbs asunder!"

The poor wretch collapsed again, at his feet.

"Master, master," he whimpered, "have pity! Have mercy! Thou, nor any mortal man shall ever look upon his face again! Hotep, the High Priest of Ra, is dead!"

For a moment the words beat meaninglessly on Rames' ears. Then their full significance sank into his consciousness.

Hotep the High Priest of Ra was dead!

He had kept his oath for no purpose, and in the secret chamber, deep in the Theban hills, lay the two tiny phials that had held the magic elixir. They were dry and empty!

He turned from the trembling slave, his arms stretched above his head in agony. Hotep was dead and the way back to Iris was closed forever.

"O most noble Rames," Ostanes was muttering, "the vile conqueror stripped my master, who dwelleth in the halls of Osiris, of his honors, took away his life, but the priests stole his body, embalmed it in the holy custom, laid it in the priceless sarcophagus reserved for Ra's most faithful servant, and hid it safely even from the Assyrian plunderer! It was laid in a secret tomb. No man shall find it until the world ends! Only Ra, the all-seeing, and the High Priest's own *Ka,* know where he lies! The Assyrians have tortured and killed the priests of the temple, but they would not reveal the secret of his hiding-place!"

Rames, staring bitterly out into the ruined garden, thought of the museum in Cairo and the richly decorated sarcophagus whose inscription read:

"I am Osiris-Hotep, High Priest of Amen-Ra, Lord of the world and the universe, now and forever!"

And the priests of Ra had died to guard the secret of his tomb! Verily, Time, alone, is the only conqueror!

He went out again into the devastated streets, more lonely in this ruined world of his own, than he had been even in that distant age wherein he had no place.

His own house had lain at the outskirts of the city. His heart torn with agony, he made his way thither, unchallenged by the invaders who, as the day waned, grew drunk on the temple wines.

As he reached his own gate, the sun was setting, its great copper disk hung poised on the edge of the purple hills in a ruddy haze, as though the blood of the plundered city had splashed the heavens. The house was bare, pillaged of everything of value, the garden uprooted and despoiled. The little golden boat in which he and Teta had drifted under the moon was dragged upon the bank and lay overturned and broken.

As the sun disappeared behind the hills, Rames climbed wearily to the roof. The velvet dusk fell quickly, like a tender hand drawing a veil on what had once been so beautiful.   One by one the stars pierced through the darkness.   The ruin and devastation of Thebes lay mercifully shrouded in the mantle of night.

The door into that world where Teta waited was closed to him forever.   He must take the long way down through the centuries if he would keep faith with his love who had gone before.

His eyes swept the vast arch of the heavens.

"Yesterday, today, tomorrow, are one in Eternity," he mused.   "We and our works are the only things that pass away, but whichever star in all this wide firmament looks down on me, its creature, knows that not even thy inexorable decree can keep me from my beloved!"

He drew the little golden locket from his rags and stared into the faintly pictured face.

The soft Egyptian night wrapped him close, the stars gleamed and sparkled as they would on ages to come.

Turning to where, black against a purple sky, rose the line of the Libyan hills, he looked beyond the ruin and devastation of the Assyrians, beyond the trackless desert, to a far, fair country in a distant age.

Slowly he lifted his arms toward the Western heaven.

"My Princess," he said, "keep thou thy faith in me! I set my foot on the long path that joins my world with thine!   Love's beacon shall light my way and though ages pass, I will come to thee!"

CHAPTER XXXII

DEATH is but a bridge by which we pass to new life.

Time destroys, and renders again to dust and mould, so that from decay life may be reborn. The falling leaves of autumn live again in summer's fairest flowers; the rotting carcass of the Nemæan lion might have nourished the herb that fed a lamb, and out of the ashes of the lowly may spring the seed of kings.

Revenge, greed, ambition's cruelty, sorrow's tears, and the triumph of the conqueror are swallowed up in the maw of passing ages. The rage and hate of Today vanish before the breath of fleeting Time, but Hope lives always and Love is eternal.

In New York, where Iris waited, February had come with its consorts of ice and snow and bitter cold. She spent long hours before her fire, gazing into the heart of the burning logs, half-dreaming, half-longing to know where lay that unknown country to which Rames had journeyed. She seemed to see him surrounded by a strange people clad in rich costumes and jewels that glittered in the hot sunlight; there were splendid pageants of pomp and color which she had never seen, and yet it was all curiously familiar, and stirred her memory like the wordless voice of the shell that murmurs of the sea.

The savage breath of winter vanished before the

magic of her thoughts; visions of tropical gardens through whose cool green glowed gorgeous flowers of many hues and swift flashes of brilliant wings; of a silent, smoothly flowing river winding its shimmering way out of the unknown into the golden haze of the far horizon, a river on whose tranquil bosom floated painted sails trailing their reflections deep into the still waters; beyond, vast reaches of burning sand, desolate, wild, trackless, and over all, a sky whose arch was like the burnished surface of a turquoise. Her dreams were vague, formless, like the first outlines of a beautiful picture whose finished perfection still lives only in the artist's mind; but there was always this strange, palm-bordered, mystic river.

And then his letter came.

She scanned the postmark eagerly.

"Alexandria."

Was this his destination, she wondered, or merely a mile-stone on his way further east?

Breaking the seal she unfolded the thin sheets covered with his large, flowing characters. Across the top of the pages was engraved, "The Winter Palace, Luxor."

With flushed cheeks and glowing eyes, she devoured the letter, clinging to each word, sensing with tenderest sympathy his desire to make these inadequate pages bridge the distance between them. It was as though she heard his voice speaking the words her eyes beheld, as though he whispered to her across that vast gulf.

"I love you! The sun is sinking, night enfolds the earth in darkness which shall not be dispelled until I hold you in my arms again, for love is the light of the world!"

She read it over and over, each time finding more happiness.

Written at Luxor and mailed at Alexandria! Why was this, she wondered, as she once more carefully studied the postmark. The letter gave her no clue, but she knew that when he returned, he would make everything clear to her.

Then followed weary months of expectation, of empty, colorless days filled with that bitterest and most difficult of tasks, waiting, when the hours crawl by with the slow crunch of centuries, the heart feeds on hope, and the staff of faith bends beneath the weight of longing!

Summer came and touched the fields and woods with magic fingers, filling them with swift-winged visitors from southern lands and butterflies which like animated flowers, poised above the blossoms whose colors they rivaled.

Here Iris walked and lived on memories!

The tactless questions of her friends and acquaintances caused her endless torture, the growing doubt in her mother's eyes filled her with pain, but despite his continued silence, her belief in Rames was unshaken. The letter that had come from Luxor she carried with her always and when her loneliness and longing grew almost unbearable, she would read it again, each time seeming to hear his voice asking her to keep her faith and wait for the wonderful day that was so surely to dawn for them.

The ruby ring excited many of the remarks and questions that wounded her feelings, but he had said

it was his heart that he was giving into her keeping
and she wore it proudly.   Often at night, alone in
her room, she would spread beneath the lamp on
her dressing-table, those other splendid jewels which
had been his parting gift.

As light seen through the windows of some distant fairy castle, the gems glowed and sparkled with
alluring, mystic fire; orange, ruby, deepest azure
and lambent emerald, and again those vague, formless pictures half-fancy, half-memory, struggled for
expression.   The room about her seemed to fade
away and she saw once more those enchanting vistas
of palm-shaded gardens and the gleam of that
majestic river.

As the months passed, her mother watched with
anxiety the girl's eyes grow larger and larger in the
thinning oval of her face.   Several times she tried to
speak of Rames' silence.

"We shall hear, mother dear," Iris would say.
"He is detained by some power over which he has
no control."

"But why does he not write?" asked Mrs. Waverly.

"He will explain when he returns," replied Iris.

Her mother shook her head dubiously, but said
no more.

*   *   *   *   *   *

The mighty struggle going on in Erope was assuming titanic proportions and here in America men
advocated preparation against the day when their
country might be drawn into the maelstrom.   The
United States had given her heart to the cause of
the Allies though she still withheld her hand, and

as a benevolent neutral was sending supplies to sustain the fighters and feed those helpless ones whose misfortune it had been to have stood in the path of the invader. Adventurous youths, hearkening to the voice of romance and their crusading progenitors, gallantly masquerading as Canadians, sailed away to take their place in the struggle for the freedom of humanity, their sisters assuming the no less heroic task of ministering to the wounded.

Of these, Iris determined to be one, and having made the necessary arrangements, threw herself into the required training. Her father objected at first, fearing that the close application and the ensuing hardships would endanger her health, but her mother, wiser in the ways of women, realized that what the girl needed was outside interests, something to keep her busy and to occupy her mind, and in this way lessen the pain of separation and uncertainty.

So Iris worked early and late and went from the preliminary stages of bandage rolling and packing, through the regular course that would fit her to become a qualified nurse. From under the white kerchief that bound her brows, the deep, wistful eyes looked out with an appealing sadness. She gave no time to social affairs, and saw only her oldest and dearest friends.

John Reading came often to see her, and Iris felt a sense of comfort in his understanding companionship. They never spoke of Rames, although Reading fully realized that even in the face of this utter silence, the girl's heart would never turn from the man she loved, and so resigned himself to the friendship which seemed to have grown in her loneliness.

But the longer a great emotion is held in check, the more vehement will be its expression when it can no longer be restrained.

"Iris," he said one day, "this man who means so much to you has been gone now for more than a year and no word has come from him. I don't want to shake your faith; he may be everything you believe, but you must know that there is no place on earth from where he could not send you a letter if he wished to do so. Has not a reasonable time elapsed? Under the circumstances could any honorable man expect you to wait longer? Are you to deny yourself all possible happiness and contentment? I love you; I know you do not love me now, but you have known me all your life, we have been friends since we were children; won't you marry me and let me try and teach you to care? All that a man can do, I will, to make you happy!"

"John, John," she sighed. "How good you are. Why can't you give all this beautiful, generous love to someone who has—who will have everything to give in return? I realize why you and other people may not understand my faith in the man I love, but I know he will keep his promise to me!"

With a sigh of resignation, Reading bowed his head.

"Some of us are born to see but one star," he said. "I must be content if I can but gaze on mine!"

But the months dragged by and no word came. Iris drew more and more within herself, living on the memory of their wonderful hours together and in those visions of another world in which she seemed so strangely to have a part.

The terrible days of the second year of the war had passed into history, and the monotony of her waiting was still unbroken. Her parents, watching the thinning cheeks, the growing wistfulness in her eyes, were divided between rage at Rames and fear of accentuating her sorrow if they made their doubts plain.

"Daughter," Mr. Waverly said one day, "your happiness is all your mother and I live for, and we want to do everything possible to bring it about. If this prince of yours comes back——"

Iris smiled into his eyes.

"Dear dad," she said, "*when* he comes back, not *if!*"

Her father patted her cheek affectionately.

"Very well, then," he said cheerfully, "*when* he comes back, let us hope he will show himself worthy of the splendid faith you have in him."

Her face brightened. Here at least was one great obstacle removed.

Then one day came a letter from Abdullah postmarked "Somewhere in France."

She read the precise, carefully worded phrases eagerly. How he had waited at Luxor as the Prince had commanded, but the months passed and no message came. Allah alone knew what kept him, but he was sure they were to meet again. His heart heavy with loneliness, he watched the sad change that had come over the face of Egypt, due to the great war, the despair of the dragomans and

merchants because the tourists came no more. Then
the British recruiting office had taken him into the
army where, owing to his knowledge of languages,
he had become an interpreter. If it were not too
much for one so humble as himself to ask, would
she acquaint him with any information regarding
his beloved master, for Abdullah lived but for the
day when he might be privileged once more to serve
him and become her humble servant.

She replied at once, telling him that she still
waited for word from Rames and that she was
planning to become a nurse. The letter had come
like a ray of sunshine; she rejoiced that there was
one other in the world who still had faith that the
man she loved would return. She wanted to see
Abdullah, who would be the one person with whom
she could discuss the subject nearest her heart, and
it was this incentive that hastened her decision to
apply for service in France at once.

Her mother wept when the orders came to sail
and her father's voice was husky as he held her
close in his arms.

"If you were a boy," he said, "I would want you
to go and fight for this just cause. Since a son has
been denied me I rejoice that you are to minister to
the sons of other men!"

How different was this silent slipping away of the
huge gray ship with its darkened portholes and extinguished lights, to the life and gayety of the great
trans-Atlantic steamers so familiar to her. How
different the rigid adherence to rules, from those
joyous, carefree days when she had crossed that
last time, which was to bring Rames and love into

her life. She found she had to go about night and day with a clumsy life-preserver strapped over her uniform, that, waking or sleeping, it must be always with her for fear of the danger which threatened every moment. There were drills to be gone through and hours of study, but when she lay down in her narrow little berth at night, it was with the utmost faith that just as this great ship, despite the dangers that beset it, would come safely into port, so the man into whose keeping she had placed her life's happiness would one day return to her.

CHAPTER XXXIII

THE first few weeks among the pitifully wounded and maimed men, shattered wrecks of heroic manhood, were like a dreadful nightmare to Iris. She had nerved herself for the ordeal, but the mind can only prepare for that which is limited by the imagination, and she could not picture the terrible mutilation to which the human body can be subjected and yet live. And they were all so young, their very youth and virility adding to their suffering.

At first it did not seem possible that she could bear the sights and sounds about her, but if reason is unshaken, humanity can adjust itself to undreamed-of circumstances, and as the days went by, certain sensibilities became blunted, the shuddering horror that hampered her skill and usefulness passed, leaving only a great pity.

For the first time in many months she knew peace. Her own sorrow was buried deep in her heart, but because of it, her patience and tenderness with those who suffered were the greater. With deft, cool fingers she soothed fevered heads, hoping that some gentle hand might be ministering to him if he needed it, eased pain, and patiently wrote half-delirious or rambling messages dictated by dying lips, longing that someone might send such a message to her if there were one to send. Cheerfully,

356

untiringly, she went about her duties, with a deftness and ability that won the admiration and love of all about her.

In a ghastly, never-ending stream, war's grim harvest passed before her. Some stayed but a little while, then closed their eyes forever in quiet, profound peace; others lay inert for many weeks, and then went forth to grope their way through a world of perpetual darkness, or drag what had been youth's manly grace on counterfeit limbs that mocked at Nature; but most pitiful were those doomed to walk among their fellow men with faces blasted from all human semblance.

Iris was interested in the variety of types she nursed. They had come from every walk of life, but no matter what their status in society had been, here in this vast Armageddon that knew no class distinction, in the fullest meaning of the word, they were men.

On rare occasions a face she had known during happier days would emerge from the encrusting dirt and blood and bring a more intimate relation to the task of relieving pain and suffering. The maternal spirit was strong in her and she came to know a certain sense of happiness in ministering to these men who never complained.

One day in the midst of her duties, as she hurried from one sufferer to another, her attention was attracted to a man who had just been brought from the firing-line. He lay on a narrow cot, swathed in bandages through some of which blood had oozed. His head and face were entirely covered, leaving only the tip of his chin visible, but as her eyes fell on the slender hand lying on the blanket, her heart stopped beating, the blood pounded in her ears deafeningly, the room seemed to sway and whirl about her, for on the little finger shone the ancient ring that had belonged to Rames.

She caught at the foot of the bed dizzily for support and the doctor who had been bending over the man looked up quickly.

"Are you ill, Miss Waverly?" he asked.

With a great effort, Iris regained her composure; nothing must take her from this room, now. As from a great distance, she heard the surgeon's voice.

"I want these bandages removed and fresh ones applied. He won't feel anything, but be careful, I don't know yet just what the damage is!"

With the concentrated instinct of motherhood, and hands that had never been so steady, or more gentle, she set about her task, and as the last stained strip of gauze was drawn carefully away, a wave of marveling happiness, mingled with a great compassion, passed over her, for bloody and scarred though it was, the face of the senseless man that lay so still and ghastly against the pillow, was that of Rames!

Unconsciously, she breathed his name aloud as she knelt at his side, and took his hand.

"You know him?" the surgeon asked in astonishment. Her eyes never left the inert form.

"He is the man. I—he is my fiance," she whispered.

The surgeon looked at her rather dubiously.

"In that case, Miss Waverly," he said, "I don't believe that I should permit you to nurse him. He

has been wounded badly about the head with shrapnel and is suffering from shell shock. He'll need
the most careful attention possible to pull him
through."

She smiled at him. There was a wonderful light
in her eyes, as one long blind restored to sight.

"And do you suppose, doctor, that I would do
anything to impede his recovery?"

The surgeon laid his hand kindly on her shoulder.

"What I fear is that you will give him too much
attention, too much sympathy, in other words, that
you will kill him with kindness." But Iris only
smiled at him again and turned once more to the
wounded man, her whole manner gentle yet so
firmly resolved, that the doctor, after readjusting
the bandages, left her in charge.

When he had gone, she fell on her knees beside
the cot.

"Rames," she whispered, "out of pain, yours and
mine, this meeting was born." She pressed her
warm lips against the slim, brown hand, murmuring
over and over her thankfulness, but the man lay
silent and motionless, wrapped in the oblivion in
which the shock of battle had left him.

She studied the card that gave the history of his
case, her brows contracting, her lips curving in a
half-wistful smile over the name she read:

> Captain Richard Lackland,
> Foreign Legion—
> French Army."

Then followed, "Shell shock," shrapnel wounds
about the head, left arm broken, etc.," and the

name of the place and action in which he had been wounded.

"Richard Lackland!" She looked from the card to the man lying on the cot. So this was the mysterious journey he had to make that was so fraught with dangers! But he had told her he must leave her before the war had come. How could he have known? How was his and her fate bound up in this great struggle, and why had he taken this different name? It was all so strange, a puzzle too deep for her to solve; she must bring him back to health and strength again, so that he might tell her everything!

Summoning all her skill, she worked and watched untiringly through the long hours of waiting, while the forces of the body struggled to knit again the frayed thread of life that hung so feebly by a single strand, and at last the dark eyes, which the new bandages had left uncovered, opened and looked into hers.

"Rames," she whispered softly.

The man closed his eyes again. The terrific shock caused by the bursting shell had scattered his sensibilities which memory was endeavoring painfully to re-establish. He had a vision of a radiant face bending over him, and heard a murmured name, "Rames!" The face was lovely, and the name tenderly spoken, but neither had a place in his recollection.

Then came long days and nights when he hovered on the edge of the Great Beyond and Iris, with the measureless endurance which love calls into being, fought Death to his very lair and pushed the cold grim hands back by the sheer force of her indomitable spirit each time they stretched out to seize the man she believed to be Rames.

At last the veil began to lift and, slowly, consciousness returned. The fever abated, leaving him pitifully weak, though safely embarked on the road to recovery, but with returning strength came no recognition of herself. It caused her unutterable anguish to have him look at her with eyes that beheld only the nurse and not the girl who trembled with hopeful expectancy that his mind would awaken to recollections that were so dear to her. But though each day brought added strength, his memory regarding those happy hours remained a blank.

With tender patience, she tried to recall to him their days together, his promise to return to her, the letter from Luxor, gently chiding him the while for not having written her about his entering the army. But although he began to remember things that had happened before he received his wounds, and to speak of the events of the war, to all her questions, her wistful reminders, he could only shake his head hopelessly.

Somehow it suggested that never-to-be-forgotten moment in Venice, when Rames had first spoken to her, calling her by the name of Teta, and she understood how he must have felt when she had not recognized him.

The chief surgeon had watched the girl's tireless devotion with the interest of a father, and after each disappointment would encourage her to further effort.

"They are often like this after shell shock," he would say. "It's only a question of time and he will remember everything."

As the days went by and Lackland grew stronger, he came to realize that she had vested him in a personality other than his own. At first he had accepted the name she called him as a corruption of his own name, Richard; her many questions merely puzzled him, and when she asked him to try and remember, he smiled and said that he would try, hard, and as he grew better, he wanted to remember, but reason told him that he was seeing this radiant face and hearing this gentle voice for the first time, and a great wave of self-pity surged up in his heart. He felt inexpressibly sorry for himself, he knew he would gladly undergo again all the suffering through which he had just passed to know that the love he saw shining in her eyes was really for him, and not for the man she supposed him to be. He would lie for hours staring at the ceiling trying to work out the meaning of it all. Could it be possible that there was someone in the world so like himself?

When he was strong enough, he was transferred to a hospital further in the rear, and through the intercessions of the chief surgeon, Iris was sent with him. The building, a magnificent château, had been donated by its owner to the wounded soldiers of France. Here, far from the sound of the muttering guns, he improved rapidly.

One day when Iris had wheeled his chair close to the window, from which could be seen the vine-clad hills that border the Loire, he retained her warm hand in both his feeble ones.

"Little nurse," he said, "come and sit close by me for awhile. Let's dream the world is really as beautiful as it looks out there!"

Iris slipped to her knees beside him.

"Rames," she whispered, "everything would be so wonderful if you could only remember."

"Tell me again some of the things I have forgotten," his voice was very gentle.

"Venice," she said, her eyes shining, "Venice and the moon on the Grand Canal—the night of the masquerade, you in your wonderful Egyptian costume, I, as a Princess of the Nile—and that last night by the glow of the fire—O, Rames, have you forgotten everything?"

He held her fingers against his lips.

"Dear little nurse," he murmured, "tell me more. For many days you have been everything that has made it possible for me to live, can you not now be memory, too?"

She looked at him shyly for a moment, then bending close, whispered:

"Rames, have you forgotten that I have promised to be your wife?"

A spot of color came into the man's pale cheeks and his voice trembled.

"Iris," he said, "I want to forget all else and remember only that!"

One day when he had been able to walk about a little and was resting later in the sun, he asked her how she had known him that first day while his face was still swathed in bandages.

"By your ring," she answered.

He looked at her in astonishment.

"But that would not be possible—there is no other like it in the world, it has never been from my finger—how could you——" he broke off suddenly, flushing to the ears.

She laughed nervously.

"But Rames, I *do* know there is no other like it, and that you have worn it always!"

She turned the ring on his thin finger and studied it closely.

"Do you know," she continued, "it may be only fancy, but I imagine it looks different than when I saw it last."

"How?" He was observing her with the most engrossing attention.

"Well, it seems much more worn for one thing; those beautiful little figures that I thought were so clear now appear to be almost rubbed smooth. What is its history, have you forgotten that you promised to tell me?"

"Bear with my lack of memory," he said, "and let us go over first from the very beginning just how we met, and everything that happened up to the day we parted."

And filled with the hope that holding before him the mirror of their past experiences would wake to life his sleeping memory, patiently, tenderly, she told him everything.

He listened with rapt attention, weighing every word. When she had finished, he sat for a long time in profound thought.

"Let us send for Abdullah," he said at last.

CHAPTER XXXIV

HOPING that he might be the means of reviving the lost memory, Iris wrote to Abdullah to come as soon as he could get leave, and a few days later the little Egyptian walked into the hospital. His slight form looked unfamiliar in the trim khaki, but his smile was as broad as ever and his round black eyes shone eagerly with the expectation of seeing his beloved master again. Iris carefully explained the patient's condition and warned him that he might not be recognized. He listened respectfully, but in his mind he scoffed at the idea that the man who had been his daily companion for so many months and to whom he had explained the ways of the modern world, could fail to know him.

After one look into the pale, scarred face, the little Egyptian forgot his Occidental veneer and fell on his knees, pressing the feeble hand to his forehead in the gesture of the East. There were tears in his eyes and his voice trembled.

"Master," he said, "Abdullah waited patiently for the day of your return. Why could he not have known that the battlefield was the far country to which you had been called. Abdullah shared with you the pleasant things of life, could he not have accompanied you through the dangers of war?"

Lackland looked curiously into the eager little

face. There was a dog-like devotion in the dark eyes that left no doubt that he firmly believed him to be the same mysterious man who was enshrined in Iris' memory.

The girl stood beside them, waiting hopefully for the spark of recognition, but to all appearances Lackland was seeing Abdullah for the first time. She sighed resignedly. Perhaps if she were to leave them alone, the little Egyptian's reminiscences might dispel the shadows which darkened his memory.

When she had left them, Abdullah wheeled the invalid's chair into the sunshine of the garden. Here he launched into a flood of recollections of places and events he believed they had seen together, his mind apparently unable to accept the fact that it was all unfamiliar to his hearer.

Lackland listened attentively, while the Egyptian, at his request, patiently went over every incident of their supposed companionship. He followed the eager voice earnestly, as Abdullah told of days together and wanderings in countries where he knew he had never been.

"I would give all I possess," he said, when the other had finished, "if I could remember the things of which you speak. Perhaps some day we will live them all over again. Miss Waverly has helped me over many of the rough places, but there is much which still seems strange to me."

"I have been with you more than Miss Waverly," said Abdullah a little jealously. "We had those months together before you met her. I can recall to you much that she has never known."

"You say you taught me English?" said Lackland, smiling at the memory of his years at Rugby and Oxford, and his difficulty with any language other than his mother tongue.

Abdullah nodded.

"When I met you first, *effendi,* we spoke by signs, have you forgotten?"

"And we met in——"

"In Luxor, in the market-place, two years ago."

Luxor! He had never been in Egypt, but it was from there Iris had told him that last letter had been sent. From what country had this stranger come, and into what mysterious land had he vanished?

Abdullah, watching the dark eyes, shook his head in pity.

"Is it all lost, *effendi?*" he said. "Try to remember—you in the flowing robes of a Bedouin sheik, I in the costume of a European, save for my red *tarbûsh*—your wonder at all things, the train, the telephone, the automobile—how you laid aside your Eastern robes at Cairo and donned the clothes of the English—the ship at Alexandria—the day in the Catacombs at Rome—and Venice—have you forgotten our search in Venice and the finding of Miss Waverly?"

Lackland leaned his head against the pillow and closed his eyes. What land claimed this man whom he so strangely resembled? A man who had begun by speaking in signs, and whose English in so short a time had become as flawless as his own, for neither Iris nor Abdullah had wondered at his pronunciation. And strangest of all, this man had worn an ancient ring exactly like the one upon his own finger, which had been the property of his family for countless generations.

He had heard somewhere that each man embodied in himself all of his progenitors. There was a miniature of his grandfather among his treasures, which, but for the difference in dress, might have been his own portrait. Was there anything in all this that might explain this strange enigma?

But the ring! He turned it on his finger as he mused.

Abdullah's eyes followed the action.

"Your ring seems older than when I saw it first," he said. "What a pity that wonderful carving is nearly worn smooth!"

Lackland smiled incredulously.

"I have never seen it different than it is. This ring has belonged to my family for so many centuries that its origin is forgotten. There is no other like it in the world. Whoever you saw wearing it must have been——"

"Yourself, *effendi*." Abdullah spoke gently, but with the unanswerable finality with which one answers a child.

"My friend," said Lackland, "whoever I am, or however my life is bound up with this man whom you call your beloved master, will you be to me what you were to him?" and with the winning smile that Abdullah knew and loved, he held out his unbandaged hand.

The little Egyptian pressed it against his forehead.

"Abdullah is your slave," he said, "yours and the beautiful lady's whom you love!"

A light came into the wounded man's eyes.

The lady whom he loved!

Out of all this fabric of dreams this alone was real. But did the lady love him, who was but the effigy of that other who had come from no one knew where and vanished again into oblivion? Could he hope to take the place in her heart this unknown had filled?

But no matter what the consequence, it must be made clear to her that he was not the man she thought him. He must win her as Richard Lackland, not as the shadow of another man.

He straightened himself in the chair, and his mouth set in a firm line as he turned to Abdullah.

"Would you mind asking Miss Waverly to come to me?" he said, and as the little Egyptian hurried on his errand, he sighed. What would Iris say when she knew the truth? What would be her verdict? Would she go on with her search for that other or would she still feel that she had found him?

Then he saw her coming along the path, her dress white against the dark background of the trees, the veil with its tiny red cross framing the delicate oval of her face.

"Has Abdullah succeeded in helping you recall things you have forgotten?" she asked as she came toward him.

Lackland held out his hand.

"He can never do that," he said seriously, "because they have no place in my experiences." A shadow crossed her face.

"Don't let it make you unhappy," he pleaded;

"your smile is the fountain of all the joy in the world.   Come, sit beside me, I do not want to remember what Rames told you, I want you to listen to what Richard Lackland has to say!"

The corner of the garden where they sat was quiet and secluded.   Great lilac bushes screened it from the house, and from a trellis near, some late roses faintly scented the air with their perfume.

For a long moment they were silent, the girl's eyes fixed dreamily on a huge bumble-bee which with noisy abandon was dining from a half-opened rose.

Lackland studied the sweet profile tenderly.   Happiness is the greatest beautifier, and since that day when Fate had discovered this man to her, the bloom had returned to her cheeks, the lustre to her eyes.

At last he spoke.

"When you remind me of stories I am supposed to have told you in those other days of which my mind holds no remembrance, stories of temple gardens and pools afloat with lotus blossoms; of desert wastes and fierce men; of wonderful pageants and splendors of a vanished time, even when you speak the name of Teta, something within me seems to stir as though with the faint and blurred recollection of a dream.   But my reason tells me none of these things ever happened to me.   Do you suppose it would be possible for me to forget having met you?   Memory never held a recollection half so sweet!"

She looked at him half startled, half wonderingly, the warm color mantling her cheeks.

"I could not have met you in Venice," he continued, "because I have never been there, nor to any of the other places you mentioned. Most of my life has been spent in England, where I was born. My parents died when I was quite young. I had been living in Paris for some years when the war began and my affection for the French people induced me to enlist under their flag."

"But I do not understand," she said, "it all seems so like a dream—and the ring, how do you account for that?"

"This ring," he explained, "has been handed down through my family for countless generations, even from that remote day when they made their way (so the tradition goes), out of Egypt. It is supposed to mirror the future."

He drew it from his finger and they bent over it, studying the ancient carving and looking deep into the smouldering heart of the jewel.

"What do you see?" she asked softly.

"I see a long road that stretches back into regions remote beyond the power of imagination, and a man who has journeyed all its weary length to where at the end, a girl is waiting!"

"And the man is Rames?" she began.

"No, not Rames," his voice was very tender, very wistful, "only Richard Lackland, who has loved you always, for Love never began and never ends, and those of us to whom it comes in its greatest and most wonderful sense, are conscious of other meetings."

She raised her eyes to his. The light he feared to see die, shone steadily in their iridescent depths.

"You are Rames to me," she said earnestly, "just as I was Teta to him!"

"He may have been the soul of my ancient self, blazing the way to you."

"Who knows?" she said softly. "Perhaps the shadowy figures which form our past and which are to us but vague, uncertain dreams, may never take tangible shape; only one thing is clear——"

"And that is——?" he asked gently.

The rich color flooded her cheeks again and he had to draw her very close to hear her whispered, "I love you!"

THE END

www.ingramcontent.com/pod-product-compliance
Lightning Source LLC
Chambersburg PA
CBHW022142010726
47493CB00002B/301